Two classic romances from
NEW YORK TIMES BESTSELLING AUTHOR

BARBARA DELINSKY

Forbidden Love

D0047753

"Delinsky combines her understanding of
human nature with absorbing, unpredictable
storytelling—a winning combination."
—*Publishers Weekly*

Two timeless love stories from *New York Times* and *USA TODAY* bestselling author

BARBARA DELINSKY

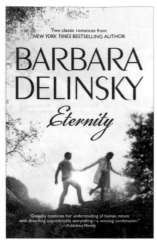

"Delinsky combines her understanding of human nature with absorbing, unpredictable storytelling—a winning combination."
—*Publishers Weekly*

Available now!

ISBN-13: 978-0-373-77817-1

50799

HARLEQUIN® HQN™
www.Harlequin.com

PHBD1113IFC

Praise for the novels of
BARBARA DELINSKY

"There's no bigger name in women's fiction
than Barbara Delinsky."
—*Rocky Mountain News* (Denver)

"Delinsky is one of those authors who knows how to
introduce characters to her readers in such a way that
they become more like old friends than works of fiction."
—*Flint Journal*

"Barbara Delinsky knows the human heart
and its capacity to love and believe."
—*Observer-Reporter* (Washington, Pennsylvania)

"With brilliant precision and compassionate insight,
Ms. Delinsky explores the innermost depths of her
beautifully realized characters, creating a powerful,
ultimately uplifting novel of love and redemption."
—*Rave Reviews* on *More Than Friends*

"Ms. Delinsky is a master storyteller!
Her talent to create living characters is remarkable.
Her writing and plotting are first-rate."
— *Rendezvous*

"When you care enough to read the very best, the name
of Barbara Delinsky should come immediately to mind."
—*Rave Reviews* on *A Woman Betrayed*

"Definitely one of today's quintessential writers
of women's fiction, Barbara Delinsky
pulls out all the stops in this perceptive novel."
—*RT Book Reviews* on *The Passions of Chelsea Kane*

"Women's fiction at its finest."
—*RT Book Reviews*

BARBARA DELINSKY

Forbidden Love

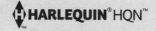

HARLEQUIN® HQN™

If you purchased this book without a cover you should be aware that this book is stolen property. It was reported as "unsold and destroyed" to the publisher, and neither the author nor the publisher has received any payment for this "stripped book."

ISBN-13: 978-0-373-77817-1

FORBIDDEN LOVE

Copyright © 2013 by Harlequin Books S.A.

The publisher acknowledges the copyright holder of the individual works as follows:

FIRST, BEST AND ONLY
Copyright © 1986 by Barbara Delinsky

A SINGLE ROSE
Copyright © 1987 by Barbara Delinsky

Recycling programs for this product may not exist in your area.

All rights reserved. Except for use in any review, the reproduction or utilization of this work in whole or in part in any form by any electronic, mechanical or other means, now known or hereafter invented, including xerography, photocopying and recording, or in any information storage or retrieval system, is forbidden without the written permission of the publisher, Harlequin HQN, 225 Duncan Mill Road, Don Mills, Ontario M3B 3K9, Canada.

This is a work of fiction. Names, characters, places and incidents are either the product of the author's imagination or are used fictitiously, and any resemblance to actual persons, living or dead, business establishments, events or locales is entirely coincidental.

This edition published by arrangement with Harlequin Books S.A.

For questions and comments about the quality of this book, please contact us at CustomerService@Harlequin.com.

® and TM are trademarks of Harlequin Enterprises Limited or its corporate affiliates. Trademarks indicated with ® are registered in the United States Patent and Trademark Office, the Canadian Trade Marks Office and in other countries.

Printed in U.S.A.

HARLEQUIN®
www.Harlequin.com

CONTENTS

FIRST, BEST AND ONLY

CHAPTER ONE

INSTINCT TOLD MARNIE LANGE that it was wrong, but she'd long ago learned not to blindly trust her instincts. For that very reason she'd surrounded herself with the best, the brightest, the most capable vice presidents, directors and miscellaneous other personnel to manage those ventures in which she'd invested. Now her staff was telling her something, and though she disagreed, she had to listen.

"It's a spectacular idea, Marni," Edgar Welles was saying, sitting forward with his arms on the leather conference table and his fingers interlaced. His bald head gleamed under the Tiffany lamps. "There's no doubt about it. The exposure will be marvelous."

"As vice president of public relations, you'd be expected to say that," Marni returned dryly.

"But I agree," chimed in Anne Underwood, "and I'm the editor in chief of this new baby. I think you'd be perfect for the premier cover of *Class*. You've got the looks and the status. If we're aiming at the successful woman over thirty, you epitomize her."

"I'm barely thirty-one, and I'm not a model," Marni argued.

Cynthia Cummings, Anne's art director, joined the fray. "You may not be a model, but you do have the looks."

"I'm too short. I'm only five-five."

"And this will be a waist-up shot, so your height is irrelevant," Cynthia went on, undaunted. "You've got classic features, a flawless complexion, thick auburn hair. You're a natural for something like this. We wouldn't be suggesting you do it if that weren't true."

Anne shifted in her seat to more fully face Marni, who had opted to sit among her staff rather than in the high-backed chair at the head of the long table. "Cynthia's right. We have pretty high stakes in this, too. You may be putting up the money, but those of us at the magazine have our reputations on the line. We've already poured thousands of hours into the conception and realization of *Class*. Do you think we'd risk everything with a cover we didn't think was absolutely outstanding?"

"I'm sure you wouldn't," Marni answered quietly, then looked at Edgar. "But won't it be awfully…presumptuous…my appearing in vivid color on every newsstand in the country?"

Edgar smiled affectionately. He'd been working with Marni since she'd taken over the presidency of the Lange Corporation three years before. Personally, he'd been glad when her father had stepped down, retaining the more titular position of chairman of the board. Marni was easier to work with any day. "You've always worked hard and avoided the limelight. It's about time you sampled it."

"I don't like the limelight, Edgar. You know that."

"I know you prefer being in the background, yes. But this is something else, something new. Lange may not be a novice at publishing, but we've never dealt with fashion before. *Class* is an adventure for the publications division. It's an adventure for *all* of us. You want it to be a success, don't you?" It was a rhetorical question, needing no answer. "It's not as though you're going to give speech after speech in front of crowds of stockholders or face the harsh floodlights of the media."

"I'd almost prefer that. This seems somehow arrogant."

"You have a right to arrogance," broke in Steve O'Brien. Steve headed the publications division of the corporation, and he'd been a staunch supporter both of Marni and of *Class* from the start. "In three years you've nearly doubled our annual profit margin. *Three years*. It's remarkable."

Marni shrugged. She couldn't dispute the figures, yet she was modest about flaunting them. "It's really been more than three years, Steve. I've been working under Dad since I graduated from business school. That adds another four years to the total. He gave me a pretty free hand to do what I wanted."

"Doesn't matter," Steve said with a dismissive wave of his hand. "Three, five, seven years—you've done wonders. You've got every right to have your picture on the cover of *Class*."

"One session in a photographer's studio," Edgar coaxed before Marni could argue further. "That's all we ask. One session. Simple and painless."

She grimaced. "Painless? I *hate* being photographed."

"But you're photogenic," came the argument from Dan Sobel, *Class*'s creative director. He was a good-looking man, no doubt photogenic himself, Marni mused, though she felt no more physical attraction for him than she did for either Edgar or Steve. "You've got so much more going for you than some of the people who've been on magazine covers. Hell, look what Scavullo did with Martha Mitchell!"

Marni rolled her eyes. "Thanks."

"You know what I mean. And don't tell me *she* had any more right to be on a cover than you do."

Marni couldn't answer that one. "Okay," she said, waving her hand. "Aside from my other arguments, we're not talking Scavullo or Avedon here. We're talking Webster." She eyed Anne. "You're still convinced he's the right one?"

"Absolutely," Anne answered with a determined nod.

"I've shown you his covers. We've pored over them our-selves—" her gaze swept momentarily toward Cynthia and Dan "—and compared them to other cover work. As far as I'm concerned, even if Scavullo or Avedon had been available I'd have picked Webster. He brings a freshness, a vitality to his covers. This is a man who loves women, loves working with them, loves making them look great. He has a definite way with models, and with his camera."

Marni's "Hmmph" went unnoticed as Dan spoke up in support of Anne's claim.

"We're lucky to get him, Marni. He hasn't been will-ing to work on a regular basis for one magazine before."

"Then why is he now?"

"Because he likes the concept of the magazine, for one thing. He's forty himself. He can identify with it."

"Just because a man reaches the age of forty doesn't mean that he tires of nubile young girls," Marni pointed out. "We all have friends whose husbands grab for their *Vogue*s and *Bazaar*s as soon as they arrive."

Dan agreed. "Yes, and I'm not saying that Webster's given up on nineteen-year-old models. But I think he un-derstands the need for a publication like ours. From what he said, he often deals with celebrities who are totally in-secure about the issue of age. They want him to make them look twenty-one. He wants to make them look damned good at whatever age they are. He claims that some of the most beautiful women he's photographed in the last few years have been in their mid-forties."

"Wonderful man," Anne said, beaming brightly.

Marni sent an amused smile in her direction. Anne was in her mid-forties and extremely attractive.

Dan continued. "I think there's more, though, at least as to why Webster is willing to work with us. When a man reaches the age of forty, he tends to take stock of his life and think about where's he's going. Brian Webster has been phenomenally successful in the past ten years, but he's done it the hard way. He didn't have a mentor, so to speak, or a sponsor. He didn't have an 'in' at any one magazine or another. He's built his reputation purely on merit, by showing his stuff and relying on its quality to draw in work. And it has. He calls his own shots, and even aside from his fashion work gets more than enough commissions for portraits of celebrities to keep him busy. But he may just be ready to consolidate his interests. Theoretically, through *Class*, his name could become as much a household word as Scavullo or Avedon. If we're successful, and *he*'s successful, he could work less and do better financially than before. Besides, his first book of photographs is due out next summer. The work for it is done and that particular pressure's off. I think we lucked out and hit him at exactly the right time."

"And he's agreed to stick with us for a while?" Marni asked, then glanced from one face to another. "It was the general consensus that we have a consistent look from one issue to the next."

"We're preparing a contract," Steve put in. "Twelve issues, with options to expand on that. He says he'll sign."

Marni pressed her lips together and nodded. Her argument wasn't really with the choice of Webster as a photographer; it was with the choice of that first cover face. "Okay. So Webster's our man." Her eyes narrowed as she looked around the group again. "And since I have faith in you all and trust that you're a little more objective on the matter of this cover than I am, it looks like I'll be your guinea pig. What's the schedule?" She gave a crooked grin. "Do I have time for plastic surgery first? I could take off five pounds while I'm recuperating."

"Don't you dare!" Anne chided. "On either score." She

sat back. "Once Webster's signed the contract, we'll set up an appointment. It should be within the next two weeks."

Marni took in a loud breath and studied the ceiling. "Take your time. Please."

IT WAS ACTUALLY closer to three weeks before the photographer's contract had been signed and delivered and Marni was due to be photographed. She wasn't looking forward to it. That same tiny voice in the back of her mind kept screaming in protest, but the wheels were in motion. And she did trust that Edgar, Anne and company knew what they were doing.

That didn't keep her from breaking two fingernails within days of the session, or feeling that her almost shoulder-length hair had been cut a fraction of an inch too short, or watching in dire frustration while a tiny pimple worked its way to the surface of her "flawless" skin at one temple.

Mercifully, she didn't have to worry about what to wear. Marjorie Semple, the fashion director for *Class*, was taking care of that. All Marni had to do was to show up bright and early on the prescribed morning and put herself into the hands of the hairstylist, the makeup artist, the dresser, numerous other assistants and, of course, Brian Webster. Unfortunately, Edgar, Steve, Anne, Dan, Cynthia, Marjorie and a handful of others from the magazine were also planning to attend the session.

"Do you *all* have to be there?" Marni asked nervously when she spoke with Anne the day before the scheduled shoot.

"Most of us do. At least the first time. Webster knows what kind of feeling we want in this picture, but I think our presence will be a reminder to him of the investment we have in this."

"He's a professional. He knows what he's being paid for. I thought you had faith in him."

"I do," Anne responded with confidence. "Maybe what I'm trying to say is that it's good PR for us to be there."

"It may be good PR, but it's not doing anything for my peace of mind. It'll be bad enough with all of Webster's people there. With all of *you* there, I'll feel like I'm a public spectacle. My God," she muttered under her breath, "I don't know how I let myself be talked into this."

"You let yourself be talked into it because you know it's going to be a smashing success. The session itself will be a piece of cake after all the agonizing you've done about it. You've been photographed before, Marni. I've seen those shots. They were marvelous."

"A standard black-and-white publicity photo is one thing. This is different."

"It's easier. All you have to do is *be* there. Everything else will be taken care of."

They'd been through this all before, and Marni had too many other things that needed her attention to rehash old arguments. "Okay, Anne. But please. Keep the *Class* staff presence at a minimum. Edgar was going to take me to the studio, but I think I'll tell him to stay here. Steve can take me—*Class* is his special project. The last thing I need is a corporative audience."

As it happened, Steve couldn't take her, since he was flying in from meetings in Atlanta and would have to join the session when it was already underway. So Edgar swung by in the company limousine and picked her up at her Fifth Avenue co-op that Tuesday morning. She was wearing a silk blouse of a pale lavender that coordinated with the deeper lavender shade of her pencil-slim wool skirt and its matching long, oversized jacket. Over the lot she wore

a chic wool topcoat that reached mid-calf and was suitably
protective against the cold February air.

In a moment's impulsiveness, she'd considered showing
up at the session in jeans, a sweatshirt and sneakers, with
her hair unwashed and her face perfectly naked. After all,
she'd never been "made over" before. But she hadn't been
able to do it. For one thing, she had every intention of going
to the office directly from the shoot, hence her choice of
clothes. For another, she believed she had an image to up-
hold. Wearing jeans and a sweatshirt, as she so often did
at home alone on weekends, she looked young and vulnerable. But she was thirty-one and the president of her family's corporation. Confidence had to radiate from her, as
well as sophistication and maturity. True, Webster's hairstylist would probably rewash her hair and then do his own
thing with it. The makeup artist would remove even those
faint traces of makeup she'd applied that morning. But at
least she'd walk into the studio and meet those artists for
the first time looking like the successful, over-thirty businesswoman she was supposed to be.

The crosstown traffic was heavy, and the drive to the
studio took longer than she'd expected. Edgar, God bless
him, had his briefcase open and was reviewing spread
sheets aloud. Not that it was necessary. She'd already been
over the figures in question, and even if she hadn't, she
was a staunch believer in the delegation of authority, as
Edgar well knew. But she sensed he was trying to get her
mind off the upcoming session, and though his ploy did
little to salve her unease, she was grateful for the effort.

The limousine pulled to the curb outside a large, seem-
ingly abandoned warehouse by the river on the west side of
Manhattan. Dubious, Marni studied the building through
the darkened window of the car.

"This is it," Edgar said. He tucked his papers inside his

briefcase, then snapped it shut. "It doesn't look like much, but Brian Webster's been producing great things inside it for years." He climbed from the limousine, then put out a hand to help her.

Moments later they were walking past piles of packing crates toward a large freight elevator, which carried them up. Marni didn't waste time wondering what was on the second, third and fourth floors. She was too busy trying to imagine the scene on the fifth, which, according to the button Edgar had pressed, was where they were headed.

The door slid open. A brightly lit reception area spread before them, its white walls decorated with a modest, if well-chosen, sampling of the photographer's work. The receptionist, an exquisite young woman with raven-black hair, amber eyes and a surprisingly shy smile, immediately came forward from behind her desk and extended her hand.

"Ms. Lange? I'm Angie. I hope you found us all right."

Marni shook her hand, but simply nodded, slightly awed by the young woman's raw beauty. Because of it, she was that little bit more unsettled than she might have been if Webster's receptionist had been middle-aged and frumpy. Not only was Angie tall, but she wore a black wool mini-dress with a high-collared, long-sleeved fuchsia blouse layered underneath, fuchsia tights and a matching belt double-looped around her slender waist. She was a model, or a would-be model, Marni realized, and it seemed far more fitting that she should be there than Marni herself.

Angie didn't seem at all disturbed by the silence. "I think just about everyone else is here. If you'll come this way…"

Marni and Edgar followed her to a door, then through it into what was very obviously the studio. It was a huge room, as brightly lit as the reception area had been. Its central focus was a seamless expanse of white wall, curving from the ceiling to the floor without a break. Numerous lights, reflecting panels and other paraphernalia were scattered around the area, and at the center was a tripod and camera.

Marni absorbed all of this in a moment, for that was all the time she was given. Anne was quickly at her side, introducing her to Webster's chief assistant and to the others who'd be aiding in one way or another. Marni was beginning to feel very much like a fish in a bowl when Anne said, "Brian will be back in a minute. Angie's gone to call him down."

"Down?"

"He lives upstairs. When he saw that everything was set up here, he went back to make a few phone calls." Her gaze skipped past Marni, and she smiled. "There he is now. Come. I'll introduce you."

Marni turned obediently, but at the sight of the tall, dark-haired man approaching, her pulse tripped. A face from the past...yet vaguely different; she had to be imagining. But she was frozen to the spot, staring in disbelief as he drew nearer. Webster was a common name...it wouldn't be him, not *him*. But he was looking at her, too, and his eyes said she wasn't mistaken. Those blue eyes... she could never mistake those eyes!

Her breath was caught in her throat, and her heart began to hammer at her chest as though it were caught, trapped, locked in a place it didn't want to be. Which was exactly the way she felt herself. "Oh, no," she whispered in dismay.

Anne felt both her momentary paralysis and the ensuing trembling. "It's okay," she murmured soothingly by Marni's ear. "He may be gorgeous, but he's a nice guy to boot."

Marni barely heard her. She stared, stunned and shaken, as Brian Webster approached. His eyes were on her, as they'd been from the moment she'd turned and caught sight of him, but they held none of the shock Marni's did. He'd known, she realized. Of course. He'd known. There was only one Lange Corporation, and only one Marni Lange to go with it. But Webster? It was a common name, as was Brian. Not that it would have made a difference. Around her house he'd been referred to as "that wild kid" or simply "him." As for Marni, she'd never even known his first name. He'd been "Web" to her.

"Brian," Anne was saying brightly, "this is Marni."

He'd stopped two feet away, taking in the look in Marni's eyes, the ashen hue of her skin, her frozen stance. "I know," he said softly, his voice barely carrying over the animated chatter of the others in the room. "We've met before."

"You've met...but I don't understand." Anne turned confused eyes on Marni. "You didn't say..." Her words trailed off. She'd never seen a human being turn into a shadow before, but that was exactly what seemed to be happening. "Marni?" she asked worriedly. "Are you all right?"

It was Web who answered, his eyes still glued to Marni's. "I think she needs a minute alone." He took her arm gently, adding to Anne, "We'll be back soon. Coffee and doughnuts are on the way, so that should keep everyone satisfied until we're ready." His fingers tightened fractionally, and he led Marni back across the floor. She wasn't sure if he was afraid she'd make a scene and resist, or if he simply sensed she needed the support. As it was, she could do nothing but go along with him. Her mind was in too great a turmoil to allow for any other action.

The din of the studio died the minute Web closed the door behind them. They were in a bright hall off which no less than half a dozen doors led, but it was to the open spiral staircase that he guided her, then up through another door and into the large living room that was obviously his own. Natural light poured through skylights to give the simply but elegantly furnished room an aura of cheer, but none of that cheer seeped into Marni, who was encased in a crowding prison of memory.

He led her to a chrome-framed, cushioned chair, eased her down, then turned and headed for the bar.

Marni watched him go. He moved with the same fluidity, the same stealthy grace he'd possessed years before when she'd known him. He seemed taller, though perhaps he'd just filled out in maturity. His legs were lean and long as they'd been then, though they were sheathed in clean, stylishly stitched, button-fly jeans rather than the faded, worn denim he had once sported. The muscle-hugging T-shirt had been replaced with a more reputable chambray shirt, rolled to the elbows and open at the neck. His shoulders seemed broader, his hair definitely shorter and darker.

He'd aged well.

"I know it's a little early in the day to imbibe," he said, giving a brittle smile as he returned to her, "but I think you ought to drink this." He placed a wineglass in her shaky fingers, then watched while she took a healthy swallow of the pale amber liquid. Her eyes didn't leave his, not while she drank, nor when he crossed to the nearby sofa and sat down.

He propped his elbows on his outspread thighs and dangled his hands between his knees. "You didn't know," he stated in a very quiet voice.

Marni took another swallow of wine, then slowly shook her head.

He was grateful to see that she'd stopped shaking, and could only hope that a little more wine would restore the color to her cheeks. He sympathized with her, could understand what she was feeling. He'd been living with the same feelings for the past three months, ever since he'd first been approached by *Class*. And those feelings had only intensified when he'd learned that the editorial staff had decided to use the chief executive officer on its first cover.

He'd had the advantage that Marni hadn't, and still he was stunned seeing her, being with her after all that had happened fourteen years before.

"I'm sorry," he said, meaning it. "I thought for sure that you'd have been involved on some level when the decision was made to hire me."

"I was," Marni heard herself say. Her voice was distant, weak, and it didn't sound at all like her own. She took a deep, unsteady breath and went on, trying to sound more like the executive she was. "I've been involved with every major decision involving *Class*, including the one to hire you. But I never knew your name was Brian, and even if I had I probably would never have guessed *the* Brian Webster to be you."

His half smile was chilly. "I've come a ways since we knew each other."

"That's two of us," she murmured somberly. She looked down at her glass, looked back at Web, then finally took another swallow. Afterward she clutched the stem of the wineglass with both hands and frowned at her whitened knuckles. "I had bad vibes about this from the start. Right from the start."

"About hiring me?"

"About posing for the cover. I argued with my people for a good long time, but I've always been one to delegate authority. In the end I told myself that they were specialists and had to know what they were doing. I couldn't possibly have known who you were, but I was *still* reluctant to do it. I shouldn't have agreed." She punctuated her words with one harsh nod, then another. "I should have stuck to my guns."

There was a lengthy silence in the room. As long as Marni was thinking of business, as long as she wasn't looking at Web, she felt better. Maybe the wine had helped. Tipping her head back, she drained the glass.

"I think they're right," Web said softly.

Her head shot up and, in that instant, the fact of his identity hit her squarely in the face again. The bright blotches that had risen on her cheeks faded quickly. "You can't be serious," she whispered tremulously.

"I am." He leaned back and threw one long arm across the back of the sofa. His forearm was tanned, corded, lightly furred with hair. "You're right for the cover, Marni. I've spent a lot of time going over the concept of the magazine with your staff, and you're right for the cover. You've got the looks. You've always had the looks, only they're better now. More mature. And God knows you've got the position to back them up."

His voice took on a harder edge at the end. Marni thought she heard sarcasm in it, and she bolted to her feet.

It was a mistake. She swayed, whether from the wine or the lingering shock of seeing Web after all these years, she didn't know. But that was irrelevant; before she could utter a protest, she found herself back in the chair with her head pressed between her knees.

Web was on his haunches before her. "Deep breaths. Just relax." His large hand chafed her neck, urging the flow of blood back to her head. But the flood that came to Marni was of memories—memories of a gentler touch, of ecstasy, then of grief, utter and total. Seared by pain she hadn't known in years, she threw his hand off and pressed herself back in the chair, clutching its arms with strained fingers.

"Don't touch me," she seethed, eyes wide and wild.

Web felt as though she'd struck him, yet she looked as though she'd been struck herself. As he watched, she seemed to crumble. Her chest caved in, her shoulders hunched, and she curled her arms protectively around her stomach. She was shaking again, and it looked like she might cry. She blinked once, twice, took a slow breath, then forcibly straightened her body. Only then did she look at him again.

"You knew. I didn't, but you did. Why did you agree to this?"

"To work for *Class*? Because I think it's an idea whose time has come."

"But you had to have learned pretty quickly who the publisher was. Why did you go ahead?"

"If your father had still been at the helm, I might not have. I wouldn't have worked for him. I knew he'd been kicked upstairs, and I'd been told you ran everything, but I wasn't sure how involved he still was. For a while there I waited to get that thank-you-but-no-thank-you call, and if it had been from him I would have said the words before he did."

"He only comes in for quarterly meetings," she said, defending her father against the bitterness in Web's tone. "He isn't interested in the details of the business anymore. And even if he'd heard your name, I doubt he'd have said anything."

Web gave a harsh laugh. "Don't tell me he's forgiven and forgotten."

"Not by a long shot," she muttered, then added pointedly, "None of us has. But he wouldn't have associated that...that Web we once knew with Brian Webster the photographer any more than I did." Her renewed disbelief mixed with confusion. "But *you* knew, and still you went ahead. Why?"

He shrugged, but it was a studied act. "I told you, the idea was good. I felt it might be the right move for my career."

"I don't recall your being ambitious."

A muscle in his jaw flexed. "I've changed."

He'd spoken in a deep voice that held cynicism, yes, but a certain sadness, even regret as well. All of it worked its painful way through Marni's system. When she spoke, her voice was little more than a whisper. "But when you found out you'd be photographing me, didn't you have second thoughts?"

"Oh, yes."

"And still you agreed to it. *Why?*"

It took him longer to answer, because he wanted to give her the truth. He felt he owed her that much. "Curiosity," he said at last.

She shook her head, unable to believe him. If he'd said "revenge" or "arrogance" or "sadism," she might have bought it, but he wouldn't have said any of those. He'd always been a charmer.

She couldn't take her eyes from his, and the longer she looked the more mired in memory she became. "This isn't going to work," she finally said in a low, shaky voice.

Web stood, feeling nearly as stiff as she looked. One part of him agreed with her, that part swamped with pain and guilt. The other part was the one that had grown over the years, that had come to accept things that couldn't be changed. He was a professional now. He had a name, a reputation and a contract. "You can't back out, Marni," he forced himself to say. "There's an entire crew out there waiting to go to work."

She eyed him defensively. "I don't care about the crew.

I'll pay for the services they would have given today, and for yours. We can find another model for this cover."

"On such short notice? Not likely. And you've got a production deadline to meet."

"We're way ahead, and if necessary we'll change the schedule. I can't do this."

His eyes hardened. He wasn't sure why—yes, he'd had personal reservations when the idea had first been presented to him—but he was determined to photograph her. Oh, he'd been curious all right, curious as to what she'd be like, what she'd look like fourteen years later. He hadn't expected to feel something for her, and those feelings were so confused that he couldn't quickly sort them out. But they were there. And he *was* going to photograph her.

He wondered if it was the challenge of it, or sheer pride on his part, or even the desire for a small measure of vengeance. Marni Lange's family had treated him like scum once upon a time. He was damned if one of them, least of all Marni, would ever do it again.

"Why can't you do it?" he asked coolly.

She stared at him, amazed that he'd even have to ask. "I didn't know you'd be the photographer."

"That shouldn't bother you. You smiled plenty for me once upon a time."

She flinched, then caught herself. "That was a world away, Web."

"Brian. I'm called Brian now...or Mr. Webster."

"I look at you and I see Web. That's why I can't go through with this."

"Funny," he said, scratching the back of his head, another studied act, "I thought you'd be above emotionalism at this point in your life." His hand dropped to his side. "You're a powerful woman, Marni. A powerful businesswoman. You must be used to pressure, to acting under it. I'd have thought you'd be able to rise to the occasion."

He was goading her, and she knew it. "I'm a human being."

He mouthed an exaggerated "ahhhhh."

"What do you want from me?" she cried, and something in her voice tore at him quite against his will.

His gaze dropped from her drained face to her neck, her breasts, her waist, her hips. He remembered. Oh, yes, he remembered. Sweet memories made bitter by a senseless accident and the vicious indictment of a family in mourning.

But that was in the past. The present was a studio, a production crew and equipment waiting, and a magazine cover to be shot.

"I want to take your picture," he said very quietly. "I want you to pull yourself together, walk out into that studio and act like the publisher of this magazine we're trying to get off the ground. I want you to put yourself into the hands of my staff, then sit in front of my camera and work with me." His voice had grown harder again, though he barely noticed. Despite his mental preparation for this day, he was as raw, emotionally, as Marni was.

He dragged in a breath, and his jaw was tight. "I want to see if this time you'll have the guts to stand on your own two feet and see something through."

Marni's head snapped back, and her eyes widened, then grew moist. As she'd done before, though, she blinked once, then again, and the tears were gone. "You are a bastard," she whispered as she pushed herself to her feet.

"From birth," he said without pride. "But I never told you that, did I?"

"You never told me much. I don't think I realized it until now. What we had was…was…" Unable to find the right words when her thoughts were whirling, she simply closed her mouth, turned and left the room. She walked very slowly down the winding staircase, taking one step at a time, gathering her composure. He'd issued a challenge, and she was determined to meet it. He wanted a picture; he'd get a picture. She *was* the publisher of this magazine, and, yes, she was a powerful businesswoman. Web had decimated her once before. She was not going to let it happen again.

By the time she reentered the studio, she was concentrating on business, her sole source of salvation. Anne rushed to her side and studied her closely. "Are you okay?"

"I'm fine," she said.

"God, I'm sorry, Marni. I didn't realize that you knew him."

"Neither did I."

"Are you over the shock?"

"The shock, yes."

"But he's not your favorite person. You don't know how *awful* I feel. Here we've been shoving him at you—"

"But you were right, Anne. He's a superb photographer, and he's the right man for *Class*. My personal feelings are irrelevant. This is pure business." Her chin was tipped up, but Anne couldn't miss the pinched look around her mouth.

"But you didn't want to be on the cover to begin with, and now you've got to cope with Brian."

"Brian won't bother me." It was Web who would...if she let him. She simply wouldn't allow it. That was that! "I think we'd better get going. I've got piles of things waiting for me at the office."

Anne gave her a last skeptical once-over before turning and gesturing to Webster's assistant.

In the hour that followed, Marni was shuttled from side room to side room. She submitted to having her hair completely done, all the while concentrating on the meeting she would set up the next day with the management of her computer division. She watched her face as it was cleaned, then skillfully made up, but her thoughts were on a newly risen distribution problem in the medical supplies section. She let herself be stripped, then dressed, but her mind was on the possibility of luring one particularly brilliant competitor to head Lange's market research department. As a result, she was as oblivious to the vividly patterned silk skirt and blouse, to the onyx necklace, bracelet and earrings put on her as she was to the fact that the finished product was positively breathtaking.

The audience in the main room was oblivious to no such thing. The minute she stepped from the dressing room she was met by a series of "ooohs" and "ahhhs," immediately followed by a cacophony of chatter.

But she was insulated. In the time it had taken for Webster's people to make her camera-ready, she'd built a wall around herself. She was barely aware of being led to a high, backless stool set in the center of the seamless expanse of curving white wall. She was barely aware of the man who continued to poke at her hair, or the one who lightly brushed powder on her neck, throat and the narrow V between her breasts, or the woman who smoothed her skirt into gentle folds around her legs and adjusted the neckline of her blouse.

She was aware of Web, though, the minute he came to stand before her with his legs planted apart and his eyes scrutinizing what she'd become. She felt her heart beat faster, so she conjured the image of that particularly brilliant competitor she wanted to head the market research division. She'd met the man several times, yet now his image kept fading. She blinked, swallowed and tried again, this time thinking of the upcoming stockholders' meeting and the issues to be dealt with. But the issues slipped from mind. Something about rewriting bylaws…hostile takeover attempts…

Web turned to issue orders to his assistants, and she let out the breath she hadn't realized she'd been holding. A quartz floodlight was set here, another there. Reflectors were placed appropriately. A smaller spotlight was put farther to one side, another to the back, several more brought down from overhead. Web moved around her, studying her from every angle, consulting his light meter at each one.

She felt like a yo-yo, spinning to the end of its rope when he looked at her, recoiling in relief when he looked away. She didn't want to think ahead to when he'd be behind his camera focusing solely on her, for it filled her with dread. So she closed her eyes and thought yoga thoughts, blank mind, deep steady breaths, relaxation.

She'd never been all that good at yoga.

She put herself into a field of wildflowers glowing in the springtime sun. But the sun was too hot, and the wildflowers began doing something to her sinuses, not to mention her stomach. And there was a noise that should have been appropriate but somehow was grating. The chirping of birds, the trickle of a nearby stream… No, the sounds of a gentle piano…a lilting love song…

Her eyes riveted to Web, who approached her barehanded. "That music," she breathed. "Is it necessary?"

He spoke as softly as she had. "I thought it might relax you, put you in the mood."

"You've got to be kidding."

"Actually, I wasn't. If it bothers you—"

"It does. I don't like it."

"Would you like something else?"

"Silence would be fine."

"I need to be put in the mood, too."

"Then put on something else," she whispered plaintively, and breathed a sigh of relief when he walked to the side to talk with one of his assistants, who promptly headed off in the other direction. Marni barely had time to register the spectators gathered in haphazard clusters beyond camera range, sipping coffee, munching doughnuts and talking among themselves as they observed the proceedings, when Web returned. He stood very close and regarded her gently. She felt the muscles around her heart constrict.

He put his hands on her shoulders and tightened his fingers when she would have leaned back out of his grasp. "I want you to relax," he ordered very softly, his face inches above hers. He began to slowly knead the tension from her shoulders. "If we're going to get anything out of this, you've got to relax."

The background music stopped abruptly. "I can't relax when you're touching me," she whispered.

"You'll have to get used to that. I'll have to touch you, to turn you here or there where I want you."

"You can tell me what to do. You don't have to do it for me."

His hands kept up their kneading, though her muscles refused to respond. "I enjoy touching you. You're a very beautiful woman."

She closed her eyes. "Please, no. Don't play your games with me."

"I'm not playing games. I'm very serious."

"I can't take it." Just then the music began again, this time to a more popular, faster beat. Her eyes flew open. "Oh, God, you're not going to have me *move,* are you?"

He had to smile at the sheer terror in her eyes. "Would it be so awful?"

Her expression was mutinous. "I won't do that, Web. I'm not a model, or a dancer, or an exhibitionist, and I *refuse* to make an utter fool out of myself in front of all these people."

He was still smiling. At the age of thirty-one, she was more beautiful than he'd ever imagined she'd be. Though he had no right to, he felt a certain pride in her. "Take it easy, Marni. I won't make you dance. Or move. We'll just both flow with the music. How does that sound?"

It sounded awful, and his smile was upsetting her all the more. "I'm not really up for flowing."

"What are you up for?"

Her eyes widened on his face in search of smugness, but there was none. Nor had there been suggestiveness in his tone, which maintained the same soft and gentle lilt. He was trying to be understanding of her and of the situation they'd found themselves in, she realized. She also realized that there were tiny crow's-feet at either corner of his eyes and smile lines by his mouth, and that his skin had the rougher texture maturity gave a man. A thicker beard, though recently shaven, left a virile shadow around his mouth and along his jaw.

His hands on her shoulders had stopped moving. She averted her gaze to the floor. "I'm not up for much right about now, but I guess we'd better get on with this."

"A bit of pain...a blaze of glory?"

She jerked her eyes back to his, and quite helplessly they flooded. "How *could* you?" she whispered brokenly.

He leaned forward and pressed his lips to her damp brow, then murmured against her skin, for her ears alone, "I want you to remember, Marni. I want you to think about what we had. That first time on the shore, the other times in the woods and on my narrow little cot."

Too weak to pull away from him, and further hamstrung by the people watching, she simply closed her eyes and struggled to regain her self-control. Web drew back and brushed a tear from the corner of her eye.

"Remember it, Marni," he whispered gently. "Remember how good it was, how soft and warm and exciting. Pretend we're back there now, that we're lovers stealing away from the real world, keeping secrets only the two of us share. Pretend that there's danger, that what we're doing is slightly illicit, but that we're very, very sure of ourselves."

"But the rest—"

"Remember the good part, babe. Remember it when you look at me now. I want confidence from you. I want defiance and promise and success, and that special kind of feminine spirit that captivated me from the start. You've got it in you. Let me see it."

He stepped back then and, without another word, went to his camera.

Stunned and more confused than ever, Marni stared after him. Brushes dabbed at her cheeks and glossed her lips; fingers plucked at her hair. She wanted to push them away, because they intruded on her thoughts. But she had no more power to lift a hand than she had to get up and walk from the room as that tiny voice of instinct told her to do.

It began then. With his legs braced apart and his eyes alternating between the camera lens and her, Web gave soft commands to the lighting crew. Then, "Let's get a few straightforward shots first. Look here, Marni."

She'd been looking at him all along, watching as he peered through the lens, then stepped to the side holding the remote cord to the shutter. She felt wooden. "I don't know what to do. Am I supposed to...smile?"

"Just relax. Do whatever you want. Tip your head up...a little to the left...atta girl." Click.

Marni made no attempt to smile. She didn't want to

smile. What she wanted to do was cry, but she couldn't do that.

"Run your tongue over your lips." Click. "Good. Again." Click. Click. "Shake your head...that's the way...like the ocean breeze...warm summer's night..."

Marni stared at the camera in agony, wanting to remember as he was urging but simultaneously fighting the pain.

He left the camera and came to her, shifting her on the stool, repositioning her legs, her arms, her shoulders, her head, all the time murmuring soft words of encouragement that backfired in her mind. He returned to the camera, tripped the lens twice, then lifted the tripod and moved the entire apparatus forward.

"Okay, Marni," he said, his voice modulated so that it just reached her, "now I want you to turn your face away from me. That's it. Just your head. Now close your eyes and remember what I told you. Think sand and stars and a beautiful full moon. Let the music help you." The words of a trendy pop ballad were shimmering through the room. "That's it. Now, very slowly, turn back toward me...open your eyes...a smug little smile..."

Marni struggled. She turned her head as he'd said. She thought of sand—she and Web lying on it—and stars and a beautiful full moon—she and Web lying beneath them— and she very slowly turned back toward him. But when she opened her eyes, they were filled with tears, and she couldn't muster even the smallest smile.

Web didn't take a shot. Patiently, he straightened, then put out a hand when Anne started toward Marni. She retreated, and Web moved forward. "Not exactly what I was looking for," he said on a wistfully teasing note.

"I'm sorry." She blinked once, twice, then she was in control again. The music had picked up, and she caught sight of feet tapping, knees bending, bodies rocking rhyth-mically on the sidelines. "I feel awkward."

"It's okay. We'll try again." He gestured for his aides to touch her up, then returned to stand by his camera with the remote cord in his hand. "Okay, Marni. Let your head fall back. That's it. Now concentrate on relaxing your shoulders. Riiiiight. Now bring your head back up real quick and look the camera in the eye. Good. That's my girl! Better." He advanced the film once, then again, and a third time. What he was capturing was better than what had come before, he knew, but it was nowhere near the look, the feeling he wanted.

He could have her hair fixed, or her clothes, or her makeup. He could shift her this way or that, could put her in any number of poses. But he couldn't take the pain from her eyes.

He'd told her to remember the good and the beautiful, because that was what he wanted to do himself. But she couldn't separate the good from all that had come after and, with sorrow on her face and pain in her eyes, he couldn't either.

So he took a different tack, a more businesslike one he felt would be more palatable to her. He talked to her, still softly, but of the magazine now, of the image they all wanted for it, of the success it was going to be. He posed her, coaxed her, took several shots, then frowned. He took the stool away, replaced one lens with another his assis-tant handed him and exposed nearly a roll of film with her standing—straight, then with her weight balanced on one hip, with her hands folded before her, one hand on her hip, one hand on each, the two clasped behind her head. When her legs began to visibly tremble, he set her back on the stool.

He changed lights, bathing the background in green,

then yellow, then pale blue. He switched to a handheld camera so that he could more freely move around, changing lenses and the angle of his shots, building a momentum in the hopes of distracting Marni from the thoughts that brought tears to her eyes every time he was on the verge of getting something good.

For Marni it was trial by fire, and she knew she was failing miserably. When Web, infuriatingly solicitous, approached her between a series of shots, she put the blame on the self-consciousness she felt, then on the heat of the lights, then on the crick in her neck. One hour became two, then three. When she began to wilt, she was whisked off for a change of clothes and a glass of orange juice, but the remedial treatment was akin to a finger in the dike. She ached from the inside out, and it was all she could do to keep from crumbling.

The coffee grew cold, the doughnuts stale. The bystanders watched with growing restlessness, no longer tapping their feet to the music but looking more somber with each passing minute. There were conferences—between Edgar, Anne, Marni and Web, between Dan, Edgar and Web, between Cynthia, Anne and Marni.

Nothing helped.

As a final resort, when they were well into the fourth hour of the shot, Web turned on a small fan to stir Marni's hair from behind. He showed her how to stand, showed her how to slowly sway her body and gently swing her arms, told her to lower her chin and look directly at him.

She followed his instructions to the letter, in truth so exhausted that she was dipping into a reserve of sheer grit. She couldn't take much more, she knew. She *wouldn't* take much more. Wasn't she the one in command here? Wasn't she the employer of every last person in the room?

While she ran the gamut of indignant thought, Web

stood back and studied her, and for the first time in hours he felt he might have something special. Moving that way, with her hair billowing softly, she was the girl he remembered from that summer in Maine. She was direct and honest, serious but free, and she exuded the aura of power that came from success.

He caught his breath, then quickly raised his camera and prepared to shoot. "That's it. Oh, sunshine, that's it...."

Her movement stopped abruptly. *Sunshine.* It was what he'd always called her at the height of passion, when she would whisper that she loved him and would have to settle for an endearment in place of a returned vow.

It was the final straw. No longer able to stem the tears she'd fought so valiantly, she covered her face with her hands and, heedless of all around her, began to weep softly.

CHAPTER TWO

MARNI LANGE WAS on top of the world. Seventeen and eager to live life to its fullest, she'd just graduated from high school and would be entering Wellesley College in the fall. As they did every June, her parents, brother and sister and herself had come to their summer home in Camden, Maine, to sun and sail, barbecue and party to their hearts' content.

Ethan, her older brother by eight years, had looked forward to this particular summer as the first he'd be spending as a working man on vacation. Having graduated from business school, he'd spent the past eight months as a vice president of the Lange Corporation, which had been formed by their father, Jonathan, some thirty years before. Privileged by being the son of the founder, president and chairman of the board of the corporation, Ethan was, like his father, conducting what work he had to do during the summer months from Camden.

Tanya, Marni's older sister by two years, had looked forward to the summer as a well-earned vacation from college, which she was attending only because her parents had insisted on it. If she'd had her way she'd be traveling the world, dallying with every good-looking man in sight. College men bored her nearly as much as her classes did, she'd discovered quickly. She needed an older man, she bluntly claimed, a man with experience and savvy and style.

Marni felt light-years away from her sister, and always

had. They were as different as night and day in looks, personality and aspirations. While Tanya was intent on having a good time until the day she reeled in the oil baron who would free her from her parents and assure her of the good life forever, Marni was quieter, serious about commitment yet fun-loving. She wanted to get an education, then perhaps go out to work for a while, and the major requirement she had for a husband was that he adore her.

A husband was the last thing on her mind that summer, though. She was young. She'd dated aplenty, partying gaily within society's elite circles, but she'd never formed a relationship she would have called deep. Too many of the young men she'd known seemed shallow, unable to discuss world news or the stock market or the latest nonfiction bestseller. She wanted to grow, to meet interesting people, to broaden her existence before she thought of settling down.

The summer began as it always did, with reunion parties among the families whose sumptuous homes, closed all winter, were now buzzing with life. Marni enjoyed seeing friends she hadn't seen since the summer before, and she felt that much more buoyant with both her high school degree and her college acceptance letter lying on the desk in her room back at the Langes' Long Island estate.

After the reunions came the real fun—days of yachting along the Maine coast, hours sunning on the beach or hanging out on the town green or cruising the narrow roads in late-model cars whose almost obscene luxury was fully taken for granted by the young people in question.

Marni had her own group of friends, as did Tanya, but for very obvious reasons both groups tagged along with Ethan and his friends whenever possible. Ethan never put up much of a fight...for equally obvious reasons. Though his own tastes ran toward shapely brunettes a year or two

older than Tanya, he knew that several of his group preferred the even younger blood of Marni's friends.

It was because of the latter, or perhaps because Ethan
was feeling restless about something he couldn't understand, that this particular summer he made a new friend.
His last name was Webster, but the world knew him simply as Web—at least, the world that came into contact with
the Camden Inn and Resort where he was employed alternately as lifeguard, bellboy and handyman.

Ethan had been using the pool when he struck up that
first conversation with Web, whom he discovered to be
far more interesting than any of the friends he was with.
Web was twenty-six, footloose and fancy-free, something
which, for all his social and material status, Ethan had
never been. While Ethan had jetted from high-class hotel
to high-class hotel abroad, Web had traveled the world on
freighters, passenger liners or any other vehicle on which
he could find employment. While Ethan, under his father's
vigilant eye, had met and hobnobbed with the luminar-
ies of the world, Web had read about them in the quiet of
whatever small room he was renting at the time.

Web was as educated as he and perhaps even brighter,
Ethan decided early on in their friendship, and the luxury
of Web's life was that he was beholden to no one. Ethan
envied and admired it to the extent that he found himself
spending more and more time with Web.

It was inevitable that Marni should meet him, nearly as
inevitable that she should be taken with him from the first.
He was mature. He was good-looking. He was carefree
and adventurous, yet soft-spoken and thoughtful. Given
the diverse and oftentimes risky things he'd experienced
in life, there was an excitement about him that Marni had
never found in another human being. He was free. He was
his own man.

He was also a roamer. She knew that well before she fell in love with him, but that didn't stop it from happening. Puppy love, Ethan had called it, infatuation. But Marni knew differently.

After her introduction to Web, she was forever on Ethan's tail. At first she tried to be subtle. She'd just come for a swim, she told Web minutes before she dived into the resort pool, leaving the two men behind to talk. But she wore her best bikini and made sure that the lounge chair she stretched out on in the sun was well within Web's range of vision.

She tagged along with Ethan when he and Web went out boating, claiming that she had nothing to do at home and was bored. She sandwiched herself into the back of Ethan's two-seater sports car when he and Web drove to Bar Harbor on Web's day off, professing that she needed a day off too from the monotony of Camden. She sat intently, with her chin in her palm, while the two played chess in Web's small room at the rear of the Inn, insisting that she'd never learn the game unless she could observe two masters at it.

Ethan and Web did other things, wilder things—racing the wind on the beach at two in the morning on the back of Web's motorcycle, playing pool and drinking themselves silly at a local tavern, diving by moonlight to steal lobsters from traps not far from shore, then boiling them in a pot over a fire on the sand. Marni wasn't allowed to join them at such times, but she knew where they went and what they did, and it added to her fascination for Web... as did the fact that Jonathan and Adele Lange thoroughly disapproved of him.

Marni had never been perverse or rebellious where her parents were concerned. She'd enjoyed her share of mischief when she'd been younger, and still took delight in the occasional scheme that drew arched brows and pursed lips from her parents. But Web drew far more than that.

"Who *is* he?" her mother would ask when Ethan announced that he was meeting with Web yet again. "Where does he come from?"

"Lots of places," Ethan would answer, indulging in his own adult prerogative for independence.

Jonathan Lange agreed wholeheartedly with his wife. "But you don't know anything about the man, Ethan. For all you know, he's been on the wrong side of the law at some point in his, uh, illustrious career."

"Maybe," Ethan would say with a grin. "But he happens to know a hell of a lot about a hell of a lot. He's an extension of my education…like night school. Look at it that way."

The elder Langes never did, and Web's existence continued to be viewed as something distasteful. He was never invited to the Lange home, and he became the scapegoat for any and all differences of opinion the Langes had with their son. Starry-eyed, Marni didn't believe a word her parents said in their attempts to discredit Web. If anything, their dislike of him added an element of danger, of challenge, to her own attempts to catch his eye.

She liked looking at him—at his deeply tanned face, which sported the bluest of eyes; his brown hair, which had been kissed golden by the sun; his knowing and experienced hands. His body was solid and muscular, and his fluid, lean-hipped walk spoke of self-assurance. She knew he liked looking at her, too, for she'd find him staring at her from time to time, those blue eyes alight with desire. At least she thought it was desire. She never really knew, because he didn't follow up on it. Oh, he touched her—held her hand to help her from the car, bodily lifted her from the boat to the dock, stopped in his rounds of the pool to add a smidgen of suntan lotion to a spot she'd missed on her back—but he never let his touch wander, as increasingly she wished he would.

Frustration became a mainstay in her existence. She dressed her prettiest when she knew she'd see Web, made sure her long auburn hair was clean and shiny, painted her toenails and fingernails in hopes of looking older. But, for whatever his reasons, Web kept his distance, and short of physically attacking the man, Marni didn't know what more she could do.

Then came a day when Ethan was ill. Web was off duty, and the two had planned to go mountain climbing, but Ethan had been sick to his stomach all night and could barely lift his head come morning. Marni, who'd spent the previous two days pestering Ethan to take her along, was sitting on his bed at seven o'clock.

"I'll go in your place," she announced, leaning conspiratorially close. Her parents were still in bed at the other end of the house.

"You will not," Ethan managed to say through dry lips. He closed his eyes and moaned. "God, do I feel awful."

"I'm going, Ethan. Web has been looking forward to this—I heard him talking. There's no reason in the world why he has to either cancel or go alone."

"For Pete's sake, Marni, don't be absurd."

"There's nothing absurd about my going mountain climbing."

"With Web there is. You'll slow him down."

"I won't. I've got more energy than you do even when you're well. I've got youth on my side."

"Exactly. And you think Web's going to *want* you along? You're seventeen and absolutely drooling for him. Come on, sweetheart. Be realistic. We both know why you want to go, and it's got nothing to do with the clean, fresh air." He rolled to his side, tucked his knees up and moaned again.

Marni knew he was indulgent when it came to her attraction for Web. He humored her, never quite taking her seriously. So, she mused, fair was fair... "Okay, then. I'll go over to his place and explain that you can't go."

"Call him."

She was already on her feet. "I'll go over. *He* can be the one to make the decision." And she left.

Web was more than surprised to find Marni on his doorstep at the very moment Ethan should have been. He was also slightly wary. "You're trying to trick me into something, Marni Lange," he accused, with only a half smile to take the edge off his voice.

"I'm not, Web. I like the outdoors, and I've climbed mountains before."

"When?" he shot back.

"When I was at camp."

"How long ago?"

"Four...five years."

"Ahhh. Those must have been quite some mountains you twelve-year-old girls climbed."

"They were mountains, no less than the one you and Ethan were planning to climb."

"Hmmph.... Do your parents know you're here?"

"What's that got to do with anything?"

"Do they know?"

"They know I won't be home till late." She paused, then at Web's arched brow added more sheepishly, "I told them I was driving with a couple of friends down to Old Orchard. They won't worry. I'm a big girl."

"That's right," he said, very slowly dropping his gaze along the lines of her body. It was the first time he'd looked at her that way, and Marni felt a ripple of excitement surge through her because there was a special spark that was never in his eyes when Ethan was around. It was the spark that kept her spirits up when he went on to drawl, "You're a big girl, all right. Seventeen years old."

When she would have argued—like the seventeen-year-old she was—she controlled herself. "My age doesn't have anything to do with my coming today or not," she said with what she hoped was quiet reserve. "I'd really like to go mountain climbing, and since you'd planned to do it anyway, I didn't see any harm in asking to join you. Ethan would have been here if he hadn't been sick." She turned and took a step away from his door. "Then again, maybe you'd rather wait till he's better."

She was halfway down the hall when he called her back, and she was careful to look properly subdued when he grabbed his things from just inside the door, shut it behind him, then collared her with his hand and propelled them both off.

It was the most beautiful day Marni had ever spent. Web drove her car—he smilingly claimed that he didn't trust her experience, or lack of it, at the wheel—and they reached the appointed mountain by ten. It wasn't a huge mountain, though it was indeed higher and steeper than any Marni had ever climbed. She held her own, though, taking Web's offered hand over tough spots for the sake of the delicious contact more than physical necessity.

The day had started out chilly but warmed as they went, and they slowly peeled off layers of clothing and stuffed them in their backpacks. By the time they stopped for lunch, Marni was grateful for the rest. She'd brought along the food Cook had packed for Ethan and had made one addition of her own—a bottle of wine pilfered quite remorselessly from the huge stock in the Langes' cellar.

"Nice touch," Web mused, skillfully uncorking the wine

and pouring them each a paper cup full. "Maybe not too wise, though. A little of this and we're apt to have a tough time of it on the way back down."

"There's beer if you prefer," Marni pointed out gently. "Ethan had it already chilled, so evidently he wasn't worried about its effects."

"No, no. Wine's fine." He sipped it, then cocked his head. "It suits you. I can't imagine your drinking beer."

"Why not?"

He propped himself on an elbow and crossed his legs at the ankle. Then he looked at her, studying her intently. Finally, he reached for a thick ham sandwich. "You're more delicate than beer," he said, his eyes focusing nowhere in particular.

"If that's a compliment, I thank you," she said, making great efforts—and succeeding overall—to hide her glee. She helped herself to a sandwich and leaned back against a tree. "This is nice. Very quiet. Peaceful."

"You like peaceful places?"

"Not all the time," she mused softly, staring off into the woods. "I like activity, things happening, but this is the best kind of break." And the best kind of company, she might have added if she'd dared. She didn't dare.

"Are you looking forward to going to Wellesley?"

Her bright eyes found his. "Oh, yes. It was my first choice. I was deferred for early admission—I guess my board scores weren't as high as they might have been—and if I hadn't gotten in I suppose I would have gone somewhere else and been perfectly happy. But I'm glad it never came down to that."

Web asked her what she wanted to study, and she told him. He asked what schools her friends were going to, and she told him. He asked what she wanted to do with her future, and she told him—up to a point. She didn't say that she wanted a husband and kids and a house in Connecticut because she'd simply taken that all for granted, and it somehow seemed inappropriate to say to Web. He wasn't the house-in-Connecticut type. At this precise moment, being with him as she'd dreamed of being so often, she wasn't either.

They talked more as they ate. Web was curious about her life, and she eagerly answered his questions. She asked some of her own about the jobs he'd had and their accompanying adventures, and with minor coaxing he regaled her with tales, some tall, some not. They worked steadily through the bottle of wine, and by the time it was done and every bit of their lunch had been demolished, they were both feeling rather lazy.

"See? What did I tell you?" Web teased. He lay on his back with his head pillowed on his arms. Marni was in a similar position not far from him. He tipped his head and warmed her with his blue eyes. "We might never get down from this place."

Her heart was fluttering. "We haven't reached the top yet."

"We will. It's just a little way more, and the trip down is faster and easier. Only thing is—" he paused to bend one knee up "—I'm not sure I want to move."

"There's no rush," she said softly.

"No," he mused thoughtfully. His eyes held hers for a long time before he spoke in a deep, very quiet, subtly warning voice. "Don't look at me that way, Marni."

"What way?" she breathed.

"*That* way. I'm only human."

She didn't know if he was pleased or angry. "I'm sorry. I didn't mean—"

"Of course you didn't mean. You're seventeen. How

are you supposed to know what happens when you look at a man that way?"

"What way?"

"With your heart on your sleeve."

"Oh." She looked away. She hadn't realized she'd been so transparent, and she was sure she'd made Web uncomfortable. "I'm sorry," she murmured.

Neither of them said anything for a minute, and Marni stared blindly at a nearby bush.

"Ah, hell," Web growled suddenly, and grabbed her arm. "Come over here. I want you smiling, not all misty-eyed."

"I wasn't misty-eyed," she argued, but she made no argument when he pulled her head to the crook of his shoulder. "It's just that…maybe Ethan was right. I am a pest. You didn't want me along today. I'm only seventeen."

"You were the one who pointed out that your age was irrelevant to your going mountain climbing."

"It is. But…" Her cheeks grew red, and she couldn't finish. It seemed she was only making things worse.

He brushed a lock of hair from her hot cheek and tucked it behind her ear. The action brought his forearm close to her face. Marni closed her eyes, breathed in the warm male scent of his skin, knew she was halfway to heaven and was about to be tossed back down.

"I think it's about time we talk about this, Marni," he said, continuing to gently stroke her hair. "You're seventeen and I'm twenty-six. We have a definite problem here."

"I'm the one with the problem," she began, but Web was suddenly on his elbow leaning over her.

"Is that what you think…that you're the only one?"

Her gaze was unsteady, faintly hopeful. "Am I wrong?"

"Very."

She held her breath.

"You're a beautiful woman," he murmured as his eyes moved from one of her features to the next.

"I'm a girl," she whispered.

"That's what I keep trying to tell myself, but my body doesn't seem to want to believe it. I've tried, Marni. For the past month I've tried to keep my hands off. It was dangerous to come here today."

Marni reached heaven by leaps and bounds. Her body began to relax against his, and she grew aware of his firm lines, his strength. "You didn't do it single-handedly."

"But I'm older. I should know better."

"Are there rules that come with age?"

"There's common sense. And my common sense tells me that I shouldn't be lying here with you curled against me this way."

"You were the one who pulled me over," she pointed out.

"And you're not protesting."

She couldn't possibly protest when she was floating on a cloud of bliss. "Would you like me to?"

"Damn right I would. One of us should show some measure of sanity."

"There's nothing insane about this," she murmured, distracted because she'd let her hand glide over his chest. She could feel every muscle, every crinkling hair beneath his T-shirt, even the small dot of his nipple beneath her palm.

"No?" he asked. Abruptly he flipped over and was on top of her. His blue eyes grilled hers heatedly, and his voice was hoarse. "Y'know, Marni, I'm not one of your little high school friends, or even one of the college guys I'm sure you've dated." He took both of her hands and anchored them by her shoulders. Though his forearms took some of his weight, the boldness of his body imprinted itself on hers. "I've had women. Lots of them. If one of them were here instead of you, we wouldn't be playing around. We'd be stark naked and we'd be making love already."

Marni didn't know where she found the strength to speak. His words—the experience and maturity and adventure they embodied—set her on fire. Her blood was boiling, and her bones were melting. "Is that what we're doing...playing?"

He shifted his lower body in apt answer to her question, then arched a brow at the flare of color in her cheeks. "You don't want to play, do you? You want it all."

She was breathing faster. "I just want you to kiss me," she managed to whisper. The blatancy of his masculinity was reducing her to mush.

"Just a kiss?" he murmured throatily. "Okay, Marni Lange, let's see how you kiss."

She held her breath as he lowered his head, then felt the touch of his mouth on hers for the first time. His lips were hot, and she drew back, scalded, only to find that his heat was tempting, incendiary where the rest of her body was concerned. So she didn't pull back when he touched her a second time, and her lips quickly parted beneath the urging of his.

He tasted and caressed, then drank with unslaked thirst. Marni responded on instinct, kissing him back, feeding on his hunger, willingly offering the inside of her mouth and her tongue when he sought them out.

His breathing was as unsteady as hers when he drew back and looked at her again. "You don't kiss like a seventeen-year-old."

She gave a timid smile. She'd never before received or responded to a kiss like that, but she didn't want Web to know how inexperienced she really was. "I run in fast circles."

"Is that so?" His mouth devoured her smile in a second

mind-bending kiss, and he released one of her hands and framed her throat, slowly drawing his palm down until the fullness of her breast throbbed beneath it. "God, Marni, you're lovely," he rasped. "Lovely and strong and fresh..."

Her hands were in his hair, sifting through its thickness as she held him close. "Kiss me again," she pleaded.

"I may be damned for this," he murmured under his breath, "but I want it, too." So he kissed her many, many more times, and he touched her breasts and her belly and her thighs. When his hand closed over the spot where he wanted most to be, she arched convulsively.

"Tell me, Marni," he panted next to her ear, "I need to know. Have you done this before?"

She knew he'd stop if she told him the truth, and one part of her ached so badly she was tempted to lie. But she wasn't irresponsible. Nor could she play the role of the conniving female. He'd know, one way or the other. "No," she finally whispered, but with obvious regret.

Web held himself still, suspended above her for a moment, then gave a loud groan and rolled away.

She was up on her elbow in an instant. "Web? It doesn't matter. I want to. Most of my friends—"

"I don't give a damn about most of your friends," he growled, throwing an arm over his eyes. "You're seventeen, the kid sister of a man who's become my good friend. I can't do it."

"Don't you want to?"

He lifted his arm and stared at her, then grabbed her hand and drew it down to cover the faded fly of his jeans. The fabric was strained. He pressed her hand against his fullness, then groaned again and rolled abruptly to his side away from her.

Her question had been answered quite eloquently. Marni felt the knot of frustration in her belly, but she'd also felt his. "Can I...can I do something?" she whispered, wanting to satisfy him almost as much as she wanted to be satisfied herself.

"Oh, you can do something," was his muffled reply, "but it'd only shock you and I don't think you're ready for that."

She leaned over him. "I'm ready, Web. I want to do it."

Glaring, he rolled back to face her, but his glare faded when he saw the sincerity of her expression. His eyes grew soft, his features compassionate. He raised a hand to gently stroke the side of her face. "If you really want to do something," he murmured, "you can help me clean up here, then race me to the top of this hill and down. By the time we're back at the bottom, we should both be in control. Either that," he added with a wry smile, "or too tired to do anything about it."

It was his smile and the ensuing swelling of her heart that first told Marni she was in love. Over the next week she pined, because Web made sure that they weren't alone again. He looked at her though, and she could see that he wasn't immune to her. He went out of his way not to touch her and, much as she craved those knowing hands on her again, she didn't push him for fear she'd come across as being exactly what she was—a seventeen-year-old girl with hots that were nearly out of control. She knew that in time she could get through to Web. He felt something for her, something strong. But time was her enemy. The summer was half over, and though she wanted it to last forever, it wouldn't.

She was right on the button when it came to Web and his feelings for her. He wasn't immune, not by a long shot. He told himself it was crazy, that he'd never before craved untried flesh, but there was something more that attracted him to her, something that the women he'd had, the women he continued to have, didn't possess.

So when a group of Ethan's friends and their dates gathered for a party at someone's boathouse, Web quite helplessly dragged Marni to a hidden spot and kissed her willing lips until they were swollen.

"What was that for?" she asked. Her arms were around his neck, and she was on tiptoe, her back pressed to the weathered board of the house.

"Are you protesting?" he teased, knowing she'd returned the kiss with a fever.

"No way. Just curious. You've gone out of your way to avoid me." She didn't quite pout, but her accusation was clear.

He insinuated his body more snugly against hers. "I've tried. Again…still. It's not working." He framed her face with his hands, burying his fingers in her hair. "I want you, Marni. I lie in bed at night remembering that day on the mountain and how good you felt under me, and I tell myself that it's nonsense, but the chemistry's there, damn it."

"I know," she agreed in an awed whisper.

"So what are we going to do about it?"

She shrugged, then drew her hands from his shoulders to lightly caress the strong cords of his neck. "You can make love to me if you want."

"Is it what you want?" His soberness compelled her to meet his gaze.

She blinked, her only show of timidity. "I've wanted it for days now. I feel so…empty when I think of you. I get this ache…way down low…"

"Your parents would kill you. And me."

"There are different kinds of killing. Right now I'm dying because I want you, and I'm afraid you still think of me as a little kid who's playing with fire. I may only be seventeen, but I've been with enough men to know when I find one who's different."

He could have substituted his own age for hers and repeated the statement. He didn't understand it, but it was the truth, and it went beyond raw chemistry. Marni had a kind of depth he'd never found in a woman before. He'd watched her participate in conversations with Ethan and his friends, holding her own both intellectually and emotionally. She was sophisticated beyond her years, perhaps not physically, but he felt that urgency in her now.

"I'm serious about your parents," he finally said. "They dislike me as it is. If I up and seduce their little girl—"

"You're not seducing me. It's a mutual thing." Made bold by the emotions she felt when she was in this man's arms, she slid her hand between their bodies and gently caressed the hard evidence of his sex. "I've never done this to another man, never touched another man this way," she whispered. "And I'm not afraid, because when I do this to you—" she rotated her palm and felt him shudder and arch into it "—I feel it inside me, too. Please, Web. Make love to me."

Her nearness, the untutored but instinctively perfect motion of her hand, was making it hard for him to breathe. "Can you get out later?" he managed in a choked whisper.

"Tonight? I think so."

He set her back, leaving his fingers digging into her shoulders. "Think about it until then, and if you still feel the same way, come to me. I'll be on the beach behind the Wayward Pines at two o'clock. You know the one."

She nodded, unable to say a word as the weight of what she was about to agree to settled on her shoulders. He left her then to return to the group. She went straight home and sat in the darkness of her room, giving herself every reason why she should undress and go to sleep for the night but knowing that she'd never sleep, that her body tingled all over, that her craving was becoming obsessive, and that she loved Web.

It didn't seem to matter that he was a roamer, that he'd be gone at the end of the summer, that he couldn't offer her any kind of future. The fact was that she loved him and that she wanted him to be the first man to know, to teach her the secrets of her body.

Wearing nothing but a T-shirt, cutoffs and sandals, she stole out of the house at one-forty-five and ran all the way to the beach. It was an isolated strip just beyond an aging house whose owner visited rarely. As its name suggested, tall pines loomed uncharacteristically close to the shore, giving it a sheltered feeling, a precious one.

Web was propped against the tallest of the pines, and her heart began to thud when he straightened. Out of breath, and now breathless for other reasons, she stopped, then advanced more slowly.

"I wasn't sure you'd come," he said softly, his eyes never leaving hers as he held out his hand.

"I had to," was all she said, ignoring his hand and throwing her arms around his neck. His own circled her, lifting her clear off her feet, and he held her tightly as he buried his face in her hair.

Then he set her down and loosened his grip. "Are you sure? Are you sure this is what you want?"

In answer, she reached for the hem of her T-shirt and drew it over her head. She hadn't worn a bra. Her pert breasts gleamed in the pale moonlight. Less confidently, she reached for one of his hands and put it on her swelling flesh. "Please, Web. Touch me. Teach me."

He didn't need any further encouragement. He dipped his head and took her lips while his hands explored the curves of her breasts, palms kneading in circles, fingers moving inexorably toward the tight nubs that puckered for him.

She cried out at the sweet torment he created, and reached for him, needing to touch him, to know him as he was coming to know her. He held her off only long enough for him to whip his own T-shirt over his head, then he hauled her against him and embraced her with arms that trembled.

"Oh, Web!" she gasped when their flesh came together.

"Feels nice, doesn't it?" His voice held no smugness, only the same awe hers had held. She was running her hands over his back, pressing small kisses to his throat. "Easy, Marni," he whispered hoarsely. "Let's just take it slow this first time."

"I don't think I can," she cried. "I feel...I feel..."

He smiled. His own hands had already covered her back and were dipping into the meager space at the back of her shorts. "I know." He dragged in a shuddering breath, then said more thickly, "Let's get these off." He was on his knees then, unsnapping and unzipping her shorts, tugging them down. She hadn't worn panties. He sucked in his breath. "Marni!"

Her legs were visibly shaking, and she was clutching his sinewed shoulders for support. "Please don't think I'm awful, Web. I just want you so badly!"

He pressed his face to her naked stomach, then spread kisses even lower. "Not any more so than I want you," he whispered. Then he was on his feet, tugging at the snaps of his jeans, pushing the denim and his briefs down and off.

Seconds later they were tumbling onto the sand, their greedy bodies straining to feel more of the other's, hands equally as rapacious. Marni was inflamed by his size, his strength, the manly scent that mixed with that of the pines and the salty sea air to make her drunk. She felt more open than she'd ever been in her life, but more protected.

And more loved. Web didn't say the words, but his hands gave her a message as they touched her. They were hungry and restless, but ever gentle as they stimulated her, leaving no inch of her body untouched. Her breasts, her back, her belly, thighs and bottom—nothing escaped him, nor did she want it to. If she'd ever thought she'd feel shy at exposing herself this way to a man, the desire, the love she felt ruled that out. There was a rightness to Web's liberty, a rightness to the feel of his lips on her body, to the feel of his weight settling between her thighs.

Her fingers dug into the lean flesh of his hips, urging him down, crying wordlessly for him to make her his. She felt his fingers between her legs, and she arched against him as he stroked her.

"Marni…Marni," he whispered as one finger ventured even deeper. "Oh, sunshine, you're so ready for me…how did I ever deserve this…"

"Please…now…I need you…" When he pulled back, she whimpered, "Web?"

"It's okay." He was reaching behind him. "I need to protect you." He took a small foil packet from the pocket of his jeans and within minutes was back, looming over her, finding that hot, enfolding place between her splayed thighs.

He poised himself, then stroked her cheeks with his thumbs. "Kiss me, sunshine," he commanded deeply.

She did, and she felt him begin to enter her. It was the most wonderful, most frustrating experience yet. She thrust her hips upward, not quite realizing that it was her own inner body that resisted him.

He was breathing heavily, his lips against hers. "Sweet… so sweet. A bit of pain…a blaze of glory…" Then he surged forward, forcefully rupturing the membrane that gave proof of her virginity but was no more.

She cried out at the sharp pain, but it eased almost immediately.

"Okay?" he asked, panting as she was, holding himself still inside her while her torn flesh accommodated itself to him. It was all he could do not to climax there and then. She was so tight, so sleek, so hot and new and all his.

"Okay," she whispered tightly.

"Just relax," he crooned. He ducked his head and teased the tip of her nipple with his tongue. "I'm inside you now," he breathed, warm against that knotted bud. "Let's go for the glory."

She couldn't say a word then, for he withdrew partway, gently returned, withdrew a little more, returned with growing ardor, withdrew nearly completely, returned with a slam, and the feel of him inside her, stroking that dark, hidden part was so astonishing, so electric that she could only clutch his shoulders and hang on.

Nothing else mattered at that moment but Web. Marni wasn't thinking of her parents and how furious they'd be, of her brother and how shocked he'd be, of her friends and how envious they'd be. She wasn't thinking of the past or the future, simply the present.

"I love you," she cried over and over again. His presence had become part and parcel of her being. Without fear, she raised her hips to his rhythm, and rather than discomfort she felt an excitement that grew and grew until she was sure she'd simply explode.

"Ahhh, sunshine…so good…that's it…oh, God!"

His body was slick above hers, their flesh slapping together in time with the waves on the shore. Then that sound too fell aside, and all awareness was suspended as first

Marni, then Web, strained and cried out, one body, then the next, breaking into fierce orgasmic shudders.

It was a long time before either of them spoke, a long time before the spasms slowed and their gasps quieted to a more controlled breathing. Web slid to her side and drew her tightly into his arms. "You are something, Marni Lange," he whispered against her damp forehead.

"Web...Web...unbelievable!"

He gave a deep, satisfied, purely male laugh. "I think I'd have to agree with you."

She nestled her head more snugly against his breast. "Then I...I did okay?"

"You did more than okay. You did *super*."

She smiled. "Thank you." She raised her head so that she could see those blue, blue eyes she adored. At night, in the moonlight, they were a beacon. "Thank you, Web," she said more softly. "I wanted you to be the first. It was very special...very, very special." She wanted to say again that she loved him, but he hadn't returned the words, and she didn't want to put him on the spot. She was grateful for what she felt, for what he'd made her feel, for what he'd given her. For the time being it was more than enough.

They rested in each other's arms for a while, listening to the sounds of the sea until those became too tempting to resist. So they raced into the water, laughing, playing, finally making love again there in the waves, wrapped up enough in each other not to care whether the rest of the world saw or heard or knew.

In the two weeks that followed, they were slightly more cautious. Unable to stay away from each other, they timed their rendezvous with care, meeting at odd hours and in odd places where they could forget the rest of the world existed and could live those brief times solely for each other and themselves. Marni was wildly happy and pas-

sionately in love; that justified her actions. She found Web
to be intelligent and worldly, exquisitely sensitive and tender when she was in his arms. Web only knew that there
was something special about her, something bright and
luminous. She was a free spirit, forthright and fresh. She
was a ray of sunshine in his life.

Marni's parents suspected that something was going on,
but Marni always had a ready excuse to give them when
they asked where she was going or where she'd been, and
she was careful never to mention Web's name. Ethan knew
what was happening and, though he worried, he adored
Marni and was fond enough of Web to trust that he was in
control of things. Tanya was jealous, plainly and simply.
She'd been stringing along another of Ethan's friends for
most of the summer, but when—inevitably, through one
of Marni's friends—she got wind of Marni's involvement
with Web, she suddenly realized what she'd overlooked
and sought to remedy the situation. Web wasn't interested,
which only irked her all the more, and at the time Marni
made no attempt to reason with her sister.

It was shortsighted on her part, but then none of them
ever dreamed that the summer would end prematurely
and tragically.

With a week left before Labor Day, Web and Ethan set
out in search of an evening's adventure in the university
town of Orono. Marni had wanted to come along, but Ethan
had been adamant. He claimed that their parents had been
questioning him about her relationship with Web, and that
the best way to mollify them would be for him to take off
with Web while she spent the evening home for a change.
She'd still protested, whereupon Ethan had conned Web
into taking the motorcycle. It only sat two; there was no
room for her.

For months and months after that, Marni would go over

the what-ifs again and again. What if she hadn't pestered and the two had taken Ethan's car as they'd originally planned? What if she'd made noise enough to make them cancel the trip? What if her parents hadn't been suspicious of her relationship with Web? What if there hadn't been anything to be suspicious of? But all the what-ifs in the world—and there were even more she grappled with— couldn't change the facts.

It had begun to rain shortly after eleven. The road had been dark. Two cars had collided at a blind intersection. The motorcycle had skidded wildly in their wake. Ethan had been thrown, had hit a tree and had been killed instantly.

CHAPTER THREE

"OKAY," WEB SIGHED, straightening. "That's it for today."

Anne rushed to him, her eyes on Marni's hunched form. "But you haven't got what you want," she argued in quiet concern.

"I know that and you know that, but Marni's in no shape to give us anything else right now." He handed his camera to an assistant, then raked a hand through his hair. "I'm not sure I am either," he said. In truth he was disgusted with himself. Sunshine. How could he have slipped that way? He hadn't planned to do it; the endearment had just come out. But then, it appeared he'd handled Marni wrong from the start.

Dismayed murmurs filtered through the room, but Web ignored them to approach the stool where Marni sat. He put an arm around her shoulder and bent his head close, using his body as a shield between her and any onlookers. "I'm sorry, Marni. That was my fault. It wasn't intentional, believe me."

She was crying silently, whitened fingers pressed to her downcast face.

"Why don't you go on in and change. We'll make a stab at this another day."

She shook her head, but said nothing. Web crooked his finger at Anne, then, when she neared, tossed his head in the direction of the dressing room and left the two women alone.

"Come on, Marni," Anne said softly. It was her arm around Marni's shoulders now, and she was gently urging her to her feet.

"I've spoiled everything," Marni whispered, "and made a fool of myself in the process."

"You certainly have not," Anne insisted as they started slowly toward the dressing room. "We all knew you weren't wild about doing this. So you've shown us that you're human, and that there are some kinds of pressure you just can't take."

"We'll have to get someone else for the cover."

"Let's talk about that when you've calmed down."

Anne stayed with her while she changed into her own clothes. She was blotting at the moistness below her eyes when a knock came at the door. Anne answered it, then stepped outside, and Web came in, closing the door behind him.

"Are you okay?" he asked, leaning against the door. Though he barred her escape, he made no move to come closer.

She nodded.

"Maybe you were right," he said. "Maybe there are too many people around. You felt awkward. I should have insisted they leave."

She stared at him for a minute. "That was only part of the problem."

He returned her stare with one of his own. "I know."

"I told you I couldn't do this."

"We'll give it another try."

"No. I'm not going through it again."

He blinked. "It'll be easier next time. Fewer people. And I'll know what not to do."

Marni shook her head. "I'm not going through it again."

"Because it brought back memories?"

"Exactly."

"Memories you don't want."

"Memories that bring pain."

"But if you don't face them, they'll haunt you forever."

"They haven't haunted me before today."

He didn't believe her. She probably didn't dwell on those memories any more than he did, but he knew there were moments, fleeting moments when memory clawed at his gut. He couldn't believe she was callous enough not to have similar experiences. "Maybe you've repressed them."

"Maybe so. But I can't change the past."

"Neither can I. But there are still things that gnaw at me from time to time."

Marni held up a hand. "I don't want to get into this. I can't. Not now. Besides, I have to get into the office. I've already wasted enough time on this fiasco."

Web took a step closer. His voice was calm, too calm, his expression hard. "This is what I do for a living, Marni. I'm successful at it, and I'm respected. Don't you ever, ever call it a fiasco."

Too late she realized that she'd hit a sore spot. Her voice softened. "I'm sorry. I didn't mean it that way. I respect what you are and what you do, too, or else we'd never be paying you the kind of money we are. The fiasco was in using me for a model, particularly given what you and I had…what we had once." She looked away to find her purse, then, head bent, moved toward the door.

"I'm taking you to dinner tonight," Web announced quietly.

Her head shot up. "Oh, no. That would be rubbing salt in the wound."

"Maybe it would be cleansing it, getting the infection out. It's been festering, Marni. For fourteen years it's been festering. Maybe neither of us was aware of it. Maybe we never would have been if we hadn't run into each other today. But it's there, and I don't know about you, but I won't be able to put it out of my mind until we've talked. If we're going to work together—"

"We're not! That's what I keep trying to tell you! We tried today and failed, so it's done. Over. We'll get another model for the cover, and I can go back to what I do best."

"Burying your head in the sand?"

"I do *not* bury my head in the sand." Her eyes were flashing, but his were no less so, and the set of his jaw spoke of freshly stirred emotion.

"No? Fourteen years ago you said you loved me. Then I lay there after the accident, and you didn't visit me once, not once, Marni!" His teeth were gritted. "Two months I was in that hospital. *Two months,* and not a call, not a card, nothing."

Marni felt her eyes well anew with tears. "I can't talk about this," she whispered. "I can't handle it now."

"Tonight then."

She passed him and reached for the door, but he pressed a firm hand against it. "Please," she begged. "I have to go."

"Eight-thirty tonight. I'll pick you up at your place."

"No."

"I'll be there, Marni." He let his hand drop, and she opened the door. "Eight-thirty."

She shook her head, but said nothing more as she made good her escape. Unfortunately, Edgar and Steve, Anne, Cynthia, Dan and Marjorie were waiting for her. When they all started talking at once, she held up a hand.

"I'm going to the office." She looked at the crew from *Class.* "Go through your files, put your heads together and come up with several other suggestions for a cover face. Not necessarily a model, maybe someone in the business world. We'll meet about it tomorrow morning." She turned her attention to Edgar and Steve, but she was already moving away. "I'm taking the limousine. Are you coming?"

Without argument, they both hurried after her.

Web watched them go, a small smile on his lips. She could command when she wanted to, he mused, and she was quite a sight to behold. Five feet five inches of auburn-haired beauty, all fired up and decisive. She'd change her mind, of course, at least about doing the cover shot. He'd *make* her change her mind...if for no other reason than to prove to himself that, at last, he had what it took.

EIGHT-THIRTY THAT NIGHT found Marni sitting stiffly in her living room, her hands clenched in her lap. She jumped when the phone rang, wondering if Web had changed his mind. But it was the security guard calling from downstairs to announce that Brian Webster had indeed arrived.

She'd debated how to handle him and had known somehow that the proper way would *not* be to refuse to see him. She had more dignity than that, and more respect for Web professionally. Besides, he'd thrown an accusation at her earlier that day, and she simply had to answer it.

With a deep breath, she instructed the guard to send him up.

By the time the doorbell rang, her palms were damp. She rubbed them together, then blotted them on her skirt. It was the same skirt she'd worn that morning, the same jacket, the same blouse. She wanted Web to know that this was nothing more than an extension of her business day. Perhaps she wanted to remind herself of it. The prospect of having dinner with him was a little less painful that way.

What she hadn't expected was to open the door and find him wearing a stylish navy topcoat, between whose open lapels his dark suit, crisp white shirt and tie were clearly visible. He looked every bit as businesslike as she wanted to feel, but he threw her off-balance.

"May I come in?" he asked when she'd been unable to find her tongue.

"Uh, yes." She stood back dumbly. "Please do." She closed the door behind him.

"You seem surprised." Amused, he glanced down at himself. "Am I that shocking?"

"I, uh, I just didn't expect…I've never seen you in…"

"You didn't expect me to show up in a T-shirt and jeans, did you?"

"No, I…it's just…"

"Fourteen years, Marni. We all grow up at one point or another."

She didn't want to *touch* that one. "Can I…can I take your coat? Would you like a drink?" She hadn't planned to offer him any such thing, but then she didn't know quite *what* she'd planned. She couldn't just launch into an argument, not with him looking so…so urbane.

He shrugged out of the topcoat and set it on a nearby chair. "That would be nice. Bourbon and water, if you've got it," he said quietly, then watched her approach the bar at the far end of the room. She was still a little shaky, but he'd expected that. Hell, he was shaky, too, though he tried his best to hide it. "This is a beautiful place you've got." He admired the white French provincial decor, the original artwork on the walls. Everything was spotless and bright. "Have you been here long?"

"Three years," she said without turning. She was trying to pour the bourbon without splashing it all over the place. Her hands weren't terribly steady.

"Where were you before that?" he asked conversationally.

"I had another place. It was smaller. When I took over

from...took over the presidency of the corporation, I realized I'd need a larger place for entertaining."

"Do you do much?"

She returned with his drink, her full concentration on keeping the glass steady. "Much?"

"Entertaining." He accepted the drink and sat back.

"Enough."

"Do you enjoy it?"

She took a seat across from him, half wishing she'd fixed a hefty something for herself but loath to trust her legs a second time. "Sometimes."

He eyed her over the rim of his glass. "You must be very skilled at it...upbringing and all." He took a drink.

"I suppose you could say that. My family's always done its share of entertaining."

He nodded, threw his arm over the back of the sofa and looked around the room again. It was a diversionary measure. He wasn't quite sure what to say. Marni was uncomfortable. He wanted her to relax, but he wasn't sure how to achieve that. In the end, he realized that his best shot was with the truth.

"I wasn't sure you'd be here tonight. I was half worried that you'd find something else to do—a late meeting or a business dinner or a date."

She looked at her hands, tautly entwined in her lap, and spoke softly, honestly. "I haven't been good for much today, business or otherwise."

"But you went back to the office after you left the studio."

"For all the good it did me." She hadn't accomplished a thing, at least nothing that wouldn't have to be reexamined tomorrow. She'd been thoroughly distracted. She'd read contracts, talked on the phone, sat through a meeting, but for the life of her she couldn't remember what any of it had been about. She raised her eyes quickly, unable to hide the urgency she felt. "I want you to know something, Web. That time you were in the hospital…it wasn't that I wasn't thinking about you. I just…couldn't get away. I called the hospital to find out how you were, but I…I couldn't get there." Her eyes were growing misty again. It was the last thing Web wanted.

"I didn't come here to talk about that, Marni. I'm sorry I exploded that way this morning—"

"But you meant it. You're still angry—"

"Not this minute. And I really *didn't* come here to talk about it."

"You said we had to talk things out."

"We will. In time."

In time? In *future time?* "But we haven't got any time." She looked away, and her voice dropped. "We never really did. It seemed to run out barely before it had begun."

"We've got time. I spoke with Anne this afternoon. She agrees with me that you're still the best one for this cover. You said yourself that we're well ahead of the production schedule."

A spurt of anger brought Marni's gaze back to his. "I told you, it's done. I will not pose for that cover. You and Anne can conspire all you want, but I'm still the publisher of this magazine, and as such I have the final say. I'm not a child anymore, Web. I'm thirty-one now, not seventeen."

He sat forward and spoke gently. "I know that, Marni."

"I won't be told what's good for me and what isn't."

"Seems to me you could *never* be told that. In your own quiet way, you were headstrong even back then."

She caught her breath and bowed her head. "Not really."

"I don't believe you," was his quiet rejoinder. When she simply shrugged, he realized that she wasn't ready to go into that. In many respects, he wasn't either. He took another drink, then turned the glass slowly in his hands. "Look, Marni. I don't think either of us wants to rehash the past just yet. What I'd like—the real reason I'm here now—is for us to get to know each other. We've both changed in fourteen years. In addition to other things, we were friends once upon a time. I don't know about you, but I'm curious to know what my friend's been doing, what her life is like now."

"To what end?" There was a thread of desperation in her voice.

"To make it easier for us to shoot this picture, for one thing." When she opened her mouth to protest, he held up a hand and spoke more quickly. "I know. You're not doing it. But the reason you're not is that working with me stirs up a storm of memories. If we can get to know each other as adults—"

"You were an adult fourteen years ago. I was a child—"

"I was a man and you were a woman," he corrected, "but we were both pretty immature about some things."

She couldn't believe what he was saying. "You weren't immature," she argued. "You were experienced and worldly. You'd lived far more than I ever had."

"There's living, and there's living. But that's not the point. The point is that we've both changed. We've grown up. If we spend a little time together now, we can replace those memories with new ones...." He stopped talking when he saw that she'd shrunk back into her seat. Was that dread in her eyes? He didn't want it to be. God, he didn't want that! He sat forward pleadingly. "Don't you see, Marni? You were shocked seeing me today because the last thing we shared involved pain for both of us. Sure, fourteen years have passed, but we haven't seen or spoken with each other in all that time. It's only natural that seeing each other would bring back all those other things.

But it doesn't have to be like that. Not if we put something between those memories and us."

"I'm not sure I know what you're suggesting," she said in a tone that suggested she did.

"All I want," he went on with a sigh, "is to put the past aside for the time being. Hell, maybe it's a matter of pride for me. Maybe I want to show you what I've become. Is that so bad? Fourteen years ago, I was nothing. I wandered, I played. I never had more than a hundred bucks to my name at a given time. You had so much, at least in my eyes, and I'm not talking money now. You had a fine home, a family and social status."

Marni listened to his words, but it was his tone and his expression that reached her. He was sincere, almost beseechful. There was pain in his eyes, and an intense need. He'd never been quite that way with her fourteen years before, but she suddenly couldn't seem to separate the feelings she'd had for him then from the ache in her heart now. It occurred to her that the ache had begun when she'd first set eyes on him that morning. She'd attributed it to the pain of memory, and it was probably ninety-nine percent that, but there was something more, and she couldn't ignore it. Fourteen years ago she'd loved him. She didn't love him now, but there was still that…feeling. And those blue, blue eyes shimmering into her, captivating her, magnetizing her.

"I want to show you my world, Marni. I'm proud of it, and I want you to be proud, too. You may have thought differently, but my life was deeply affected by that summer in Camden." For a minute the blue eyes grew moist, but they cleared so quickly that Marni wondered if she'd imagined it. "Give me a chance, Marni. We'll start with dinner tonight. I won't pressure you for anything. I never did, did I?"

She didn't have to ponder that one. If anyone had done the pressuring—at least on the sexual level—it had been her. "No," she answered softly.

"And I won't do it now. You have my word on it. You also have my word that if anything gets too tough for you, I'll bring you back here and leave you alone. You *also* have my word that if, in the end, you decide you really can't do that cover, I'll abide by your decision. Fair?"

Fair? He was being so reasonable that she couldn't possibly argue. What wasn't fair was that he wore his suit so well, that his hair looked so thick and vibrant, that his features had matured with such dignity. But that wasn't his fault. Beauty was in the eye of the beholder.

She gave a rueful half smile and slowly nodded. "Fair."

He held her gaze a moment longer, as though he almost couldn't believe that she'd agreed, but his inner relief was such that he suddenly felt a hundred pounds lighter. He pushed back his cuff and glanced at the thin gold watch on his wrist.

"We've got reservations for five minutes ago. If I can use your phone, I'll let the maître d' know we're on our way."

She nodded and glanced toward the kitchen. When he rose and headed that way, she moved toward the small half bath off the living room. She suddenly wished she'd showered, done over her hair and makeup and changed into something fresher. Web was so obviously newly showered and shaved. She should have done more. But it was too late for that now, so the best she could do was to powder the faint shine from her nose and forehead, add a smidgen more blusher to her cheeks and touch up her lipstick.

Web was waiting when she emerged. He'd already put on his topcoat and was holding the coat she'd left ready and waiting nearby. It, too, was the same she'd worn that morning, but that decision she didn't regret. To wear silver fox with Web, even in spite of his own debonair appearance, seemed a little heavy-handed.

He helped her on with the coat, waited while she got her purse, then lightly took her elbow and escorted her to the door. They rode the elevator in a silence that was broken at last by Marni's self-conscious laugh. "You're very tall. I never wore high heels in Camden, but they don't seem to make a difference." She darted him a shy glance, but quickly returned her gaze to the patterned carpet.

He felt vaguely self-conscious, too. "I never wore shoes with laces in Camden. They add a little."

She nodded and said nothing more. The elevator door purred open. Web guided her through the plush lobby, then the enclosed foyer and finally to the street. He discreetly pressed a bill into the doorman's hand in exchange for the keys to his car, then showed Marni to the small black BMW parked at the curb. Before she could reach for it, he opened the door. "Buckle up," was all he said before he locked her in and circled the car to the driver's side.

The restaurant he'd chosen was a quiet but elegant one. The maître d' seemed not in the least piqued by their tardiness, greeting Web with a warm handshake and offering a similarly warm welcome to Marni when Web introduced them, before showing them to their table.

Web deftly ordered a wine. Then, when Marni had decided what she wanted to eat, he gave both her choice and his own to the waiter. Watching him handle himself, she decided he was as smooth in this urban setting as he'd been by the sea. He had always exuded a kind of confidence, and she assumed it would extend to whatever activity he was involved in. But seeing him here, comfortable in a milieu that should have been hers more than his, took some getting used to. It forced her to see him in a different light. She struggled to do that.

"Have you been here before?" he asked softly.

"For a business dinner once or twice. The food's excellent, don't you think?"

"I'm counting on it," he said with a grin. "So...tell me about Marni Lange and the Lange Corporation."

She shook her head. Somewhere along the line, she realized he was right. They'd been...friends once, and she *was* curious as to what he'd done in the past years. "You first. Tell me about Brian Webster the photographer."

"What would you like to know?"

"How you got started. I never knew you had an interest in photography."

"I didn't. At least, not when I knew you. But the year after that was a difficult one for me." His brow furrowed. "I took a good look at myself and didn't like what I saw."

She found herself defending him instinctively. "But you were an adventurer. You did lots of different things, and did them well."

"I was young, without roots or a future," he contradicted her gently. "For the first time I stopped to think about what I'd be like, what I'd be doing five, ten, fifteen years down the road, and I came up with a big fat zip."

"So you decided to be a photographer, just like that?" She was skeptical, though if that had been the case it would be a remarkable success story.

"Actually, I decided to write about what I'd been doing. There's always a market for adventure books. I envisioned myself traveling the world, doing all kinds of interesting things—reenacting ancient voyages across oceans, scaling previously unscaled mountain peaks, crossing the Sahara with two camels and canteens of water..."

"Did you do any of those things?"

"Nope."

"Then...you wrote about things you'd already done?"

"Nope." When she frowned, he explained. "I couldn't write for beans. I tried, Lord how I tried. I sat for hours and hours with blank paper in front of me, finally scribbling something down, then crossing it out and crumbling the sheet into a ball." He arched a brow in self-mockery. "I got pretty good at hitting the wastebasket on the first try."

A small smile touched her lips. "Oh."

"But—" he held up a finger "—it wasn't a total waste. Y'see, I'd pictured my articles in something like *National Geographic*, and of course there were going to be gorgeous photographs accompanying the text, and who better to take them than me, since I was there—actually I was in New Mexico at the time, on an archaeological dig."

"Had you ever used a camera before?"

"No, but that didn't stop me. It was an adventure in and of itself. I bought a used camera, got a few books, read up on what I had to do, and...click. Literally and figuratively."

He stopped talking and sat back. Marni felt as though she'd been left dangling. "And...?"

"And what?"

"What happened? Did you sell those first pictures?"

"Not to *National Geographic*."

"But you did sell them?"

"Uh-huh."

Again she waited. He was smiling, but he made no attempt to go on. She remembered that he'd been that way fourteen years ago, too. When she'd asked him about the things he'd done, there'd been a quiet smugness to him. He'd held things back until she'd specifically asked, and when his stories came out they were like a well-earned prize. In his way he'd manipulated her, forcing her to show her cards. Perhaps he was manipulating her now. But she didn't care. Hadn't he been the one to say that they should get to know each other?

"Okay," she said. "You photographed a dig in New Mexico and sold the pictures to a magazine. But photographing a dig is a far cry from photographing some of the world's most famous personalities. How did it happen? How did you switch from photographing arrowheads, or whatever, to photographing *head* heads?"

He chuckled. "Poetically put, if I don't say so myself. You should be the writer, Marni. You could write. I could photograph."

"I've already got a full-time job, thank you. Come on, Web. When did you get your first break?"

Just then the wine steward arrived with an ice bucket. He uncorked the wine, poured a taste for Web, then at Web's nod filled both of their glasses.

Web's thoughts weren't on the wine, but on the fact that he was thoroughly enjoying himself. The Marni sitting across from him now was so like the Marni he'd known fourteen years before that he couldn't help but smile in wonder. She was curious. She'd always been curious. She couldn't help herself, and he'd been counting on that. Personalities didn't change. Time and circumstances modified them, perhaps, but they never fully changed.

"Web...?" she prodded. "How did it happen?"

"Actually it was on that same trip. The dig I was working at was being used as the backdrop for a movie. Given the way I always had with people—" he winked, and she should have been angry but instead felt a delicious curling in her stomach "—I got myself into the middle of the movie set and started snapping away."

"Don't tell me that those first shots sold?"

"I won't. They were awful. I mean, they had potential. I liked the expressions I caught, the emotions, and I found photographing people much more exciting than photographing arrowheads or whatever. Technically I had a lot to learn, though, so I signed on with a photographer in L.A. After six months, I went out on my own."

"Six months? That's all? It takes years for most photographers to develop sufficient skill to do what you do and do it right."

"I didn't have years. I felt I'd already wasted too many, and I needed to earn money. There's that small matter of having a roof over your head and food enough to keep your body going, not to mention the larger matter of equipment and a studio. I started modestly, shooting outside mostly, working my buns off, turning every cent I could back into better equipment. I used what I'd learned apprenticing as a base, and picked up more as I went along. I read. I talked with other photographers. I studied the work of the masters and pored through magazine after magazine to see what the market wanted and needed. I did portfolios for models and actors and actresses, and things seemed to mushroom from there."

"Did you have a long-range goal?"

"New York. Cover work. Independence, within limits."

"Then you've made it," she declared, unaware of the pride that lit her eyes. Web wasn't unaware of it though, and it gave him unbelievable pleasure.

"I suppose you could say that," he returned softly. "There's always more I want to do, and the field keeps pace with changes in fashion. The real challenge is in making my work different from the others. I want my pictures to have a unique look and feel. I guess I need that more than anything—knowing I'll have left an indelible mark behind."

"Are you going somewhere?" she teased.

There was sadness in his smile. "We're all mortal. I

think about that a lot. At the rate I'm going, my work will be just about all I do leave behind."

"You never married." It was a statement, offered softly, with a hint of timidness.

"I've been too busy.... What about you?"

"The same."

The waiter chose that moment to appear with their food, and they lapsed into silence for a time as they ate.

"Funny," Web said at last, "I'd really pictured you with a husband and kids and a big, beautiful home in the country."

She gave a sad laugh. "So had I."

"Dreams gone awry, or simply deferred?"

She pondered that for a minute. "I really don't know. I've been so caught up with running the business that it seems there isn't time for much else."

"You must do things for fun."

"I do...now and again." She stopped pushing the Parisienne potatoes around her plate and put down her fork. "What about you? Are you still working as hard as you did at first?"

"I'm working as hard, but the focus is different. I can concentrate on the creative end and leave the rest to assistants. I have specialists for my finish work, and even though I'm more often than not at their shoulders, approving everything before it leaves the studio, I do have more free time. I try to take weekends completely off."

"What do you do then?"

He shrugged. "Mostly I go to Vermont. I have a small place there. In the winter I ski. In the summer I swim."

"Sounds heavenly," she said, meaning it.

"Don't you still go to Camden?"

She straightened, and the look of pleasure faded from her face. "My parents still do. It's an institution with them. Me, well, I don't enjoy it the way I used to. Sometimes staying here in New York for the summer is a vacation in itself." She gave a dry laugh. "Everyone else is gone. It's quieter."

"You always did like peace and quiet," he said, remembering that day so long ago when they'd gone mountain climbing.

Marni remembered, too. Her gaze grew momentarily lost in his, lost in the memory of that happy, carefree time. It was with great effort that she finally looked away. She took a deep breath. "Anyway, I try to take an extra day or two when I'm off somewhere on business—you know, relax in a different place to shake off the tension."

"Alone?"

"Usually."

"Then there's no special man?"

"No."

"You must date?"

"Not unless I'm inspired, and I'm rarely inspired." Just then her eye was caught by a couple very clearly approaching their table. Following her gaze, Web turned around. He pushed his chair back, stood and extended his hand to the man.

"How are you, Frank?"

The newcomer added a gentle shoulder slap to the handshake. "Not bad."

Web enclosed the woman's hand in his, then leaned forward and kissed her cheek. "Maggie, you're looking wonderful. Frank, Maggie, I'd like you to meet Marni Lange. Marni, these are the Kozols."

Marni barely had time to shake hands with each before Frank was studying her, tapping his lip. "Marni Lange... of the Lange Corporation?"

She cast a skittish glance at Web, then nodded.

"I knew your father once upon a time," Frank went on. "Gee, I haven't seen him in years."

"He's retired now," she offered gracefully, though mention of her father in Web's presence made her uneasy.

"Is he well? And your mother?"

"They're both fine, thank you."

Maggie had come around the table to more easily chat with her. "Frank was with Eastern Engineering then, though he went out on his own ten years ago." She looked over to find her husband engrossed in an animated discussion with Web, and she smiled indulgently. "You'll have to excuse him. I know it's rude for us to barge in on your dinner this way, but he's so fond of Brian that he simply had to stop in and say hello."

Marni smiled. "It's perfectly all right. Have you known... Brian long?"

"Several years. Our daughter is—was—a model. When she first went to Brian to be photographed, she was pretty confused. He was wonderful. I really think that if it hadn't been for him, she would have ended up in a sorry state. She's married now and just had her first child." Maggie beamed. "The baby's a jewel."

"Boy...girl?" Out of the corner of her eye, Marni saw Web standing with one hand in his trousers pocket. He looked thoroughly in command, totally at ease and very handsome. She realized that she was proud to be with him.

"A boy. Christopher James. He's absolutely precious."

Marni retrained her focus on Maggie. "And you're enjoying him. Do they live close by?"

"In Washington. We've been down several times—"

"Come on, sweetheart," Frank cut in. "The car's waiting, and these folks don't need us taking any more of their time."

Maggie turned briefly back to Marni. "It was lovely

meeting you." Then she gave Web a kiss and let her husband guide her off.

"Sorry about that," Web murmured, sitting down again. He pulled his chair closer to the table.

"Don't apologize." It was the first time she'd ever met any friends of Web's. "They seemed lovely. Maggie was mentioning her daughter. They're both in your debt, I take it."

He shrugged. "She was a sweet kid who was lost in the rat race of modeling. Maggie and Frank say that she was 'confused,' and she was, but she was also on drugs and she was practically anorexic."

"Isn't that true of lots of models?"

"Mmm, but it was particularly sad with Sara. She had a good home. Her folks are loaded. I'm not sure she even wanted to model in the first place, but she had the looks and the style, and she somehow got snagged. If she hadn't gotten out when she did, she'd probably be dead by now."

Marni winced. "What did you do for her?"

He grew more thoughtful. "Talked, mostly. I took the pictures and made sure they were stupendous. Then I tried to convince her that she'd hit the top and ought to retire."

"And just like that she did?"

"Not…exactly. I showed her my morgue book."

"Morgue book?"

"Mmm. I keep files on everyone I've photographed, with a follow-up on each. I have a special folder—pictures of people who made it big, then plummeted. When I'm feeling sorry for myself about one thing or another, I take it out, and it makes me grateful for what I've got. I don't show it to many people, but it gave Sara something to think about. She came back to see me often after that, and I finally convinced her to see a psychiatrist. Maggie and Frank are terrific, but Sara was their daughter, and the thought that she'd actually need a psychiatrist disturbed them."

"But it worked."

"It helped. Mostly what helped was meeting her husband. He's a rock, a lawyer with the Justice Department, and he's crazy about her. He supported her completely when she decided to go back to school to get the degree she missed out on when she began modeling." He cleared his throat meaningfully. "I think the baby has interrupted that now, but Sara knows she can go back whenever she's ready."

"That's a lovely story," Marni said with a smile. "I'll bet you have lots of others about people you've photographed." She propped her elbow on the table and set her chin in her palm. "Tell me some."

For the next hour, he did just that. There was a modesty to him, and she had to coax him on from time to time, but when he got going his tales fascinated her every bit as much as those he'd told fourteen years before had done. The years evaporated. She listened, enthralled, thinking how exciting his life was and how he was fully in control of it.

By the time they'd finished their second cup of coffee, they'd fallen silent and were simply looking at each other. Their communication continued, but on a different level, one in which Marni was too engrossed to analyze.

"Just like old times," Web said quietly.

She nodded and smiled almost shyly. "I could sit listening to you for hours. You were always so different from other people. You had such a wealth of experience to draw on. You still do."

"You've got experience of your own—"

"But not as exciting. Or maybe I just take it for granted. Do you ever do that?"

"I wish I could. If I start taking things for granted, I'll stop growing, and if that happens I'll never make it the way I want to."

"That means a lot to you…making it." So different from how he'd been, she mused. Then again, perhaps he'd only defined success differently fourteen years ago.

"Everyone wants success. Don't you? Isn't that why you pour so much of yourself into the business?"

She didn't answer him immediately. Her feelings were torn. Yes, she wanted to be successful as president of the Lange Corporation, but for reasons she didn't want to think about, much less discuss. "I guess," she said finally.

"You don't sound sure."

She forced herself to perk up. "I'm sure."

"But there was something else you were thinking about just now. What was it, Marni?"

She smiled and shook her head. "Nothing. It was really nothing. I think I'm just tired. It's been a long day."

"And a trying one."

"Yes," she whispered.

Not wanting to push her too far, Web didn't argue. He'd done most of the talking during dinner, and though there were still many things he wanted to know about Marni, many things he wanted to discuss with her, he felt relatively satisfied with what he'd accomplished. He'd wanted to tell her about his work, and he had. He'd wanted to give her a glimpse of the man he was now, and he had. He'd wanted to give her something to think about besides the past, and he had. He was determined to make her trust him again. Tonight had simply been the first down payment on that particular mortgage. There would be time enough in the future to make more headway, he mused as he dug into his pocket to settle the bill. There would be time. He'd make time. He wasn't sure what he wanted in the long run from Marni, but he did know that their relationship had been left suspended fourteen years ago, and that it needed to be settled one way or another.

They hit the cold night air the instant they left the restaurant. Marni bundled her coat around her more snugly, and when Web drew her back into the shelter of the doorway and threw his arm around her shoulder while they waited for the car, she didn't resist. He was large, warm and strong. He'd always been large, warm and strong.

For an instant she closed her eyes and pretended that that summer hadn't ended as it had. It was a sweet, sweet dream, and her senses filled to brimming with the taste, the touch, the smell of him. She loved Web. Her body tingled from his closeness. They were on their way to a secret rendezvous where he'd make the rest of the world disappear and lift her onto a plane of sheer bliss.

"Here we go," he murmured softly.

She began to tremble.

"Marni?"

Web was squeezing her shoulder. She snapped her eyes open and stared.

"The car. It's here."

Stunned, she let herself be guided into the front seat. By the time she realized what had happened, the neon lights of the city were flickering through the windshield as they passed, camouflaging her embarrassment.

Web said nothing. He drove skillfully and at a comfortable pace. When they arrived at her building, he left his keys with the doorman and rode the elevator with her to her door. There he took her own keys, released the lock, then stood back while she deactivated the burglar alarm.

With the door partially open, she raised her eyes to his. "Thank you, Web. I've...this was nice."

"I thought so." He smiled so gently that her heart turned over. "You're really something to be with."

"I'm not. You carried most of the evening."

He winked. "I was inspired."

Her limbs turned to jelly and did nothing by way of solidifying when he put a light hand on her shoulder. His expression grew more serious, almost troubled.

"Marni, about that cover—"

"Shhhh." She put an impulsive finger on his lips to stem the words, then wished she hadn't because the texture of his mouth, its warmth, was like fire. She snatched her hand away and dropped her gaze to his tie. It was textured, too, but of silk, and its smooth-flowing stripes of navy, gray and mauve were serene, soothing. "Please," she whispered. "Let's not argue about that again."

"I still want to do it. Don't you think it would be easier for you now?"

"I...I don't know."

"Will you think about it at least? We couldn't try it again until early next week anyway. Maybe by then you'll be feeling more comfortable."

She dipped her head lower. "I don't know."

"Marni?"

She squeezed her eyes shut, knowing she should slip through her door and lock it tight, but was unable to move. When he curved one long forefinger under her chin and tipped it up, she resisted. He simply applied more pressure until at last she met his gaze.

"It's still there," he whispered. "You know that, don't you?"

Eyes large and frightened, she nodded.

"Do we have to fight it?"

"I'm not ready." She was whispering, too, not out of choice, but because she couldn't seem to produce any-

thing louder. Her heart was pounding, its beat reverber-
ating through her limbs. "I don't know if I'm...ready for
this. I suffered so...last time..."

He was stroking her cheek with the back of his hand,
a hand that had once known every inch of her in the most
intimate detail. His blue eyes were clouded. "I suffered,
too. You don't know. I suffered, too, Marni. Do you think
I want to go through that again?"

She swallowed hard, then shook her head.

"I wouldn't suggest something I felt would hurt either
of us."

"What *are* you suggesting?"

"Friday night. See me Friday night. There's a party I
have to go to, make a quick appearance at. I'd like you to
come with me, then we can take off and do something—
dinner, a movie, a ride through the park, I don't care what,
but I have to see you again."

"Something's screwed up here. I was always the one
to do the chasing."

"Because I was arrogant and cocksure, and so caught
up in playing the role of the carefree bachelor that I didn't
know any better." His thumb skated lightly over her lips.
"I'm tired of playing, Marni. I'm too old for that now. I
want to see you again. I *have* to see you again.... How
about it? Friday night?"

"I can't promise you anything about the picture."

"Friday night. No business, just fun. Please?"

If fourteen years ago anyone had told Marni that Web
would be pleading with her to see him, she would never
have believed it. If thirteen years ago, ten years ago, five
or even one year ago anyone had told Marni that she'd *be*
seeing him again, she would never have believed it.

"Yes," she said softly, knowing that there was no other
choice she could possibly make. Web did something to

her. He'd *always* done something to her. He made her feel
things she'd never felt with another man. Shock, pain,
shimmering physical awareness…she was alive. That, in
itself, was a precious gift.

CHAPTER FOUR

THE PARTY WAS unbelievably raucous. Pop music throbbed through the air at ear-splitting decibels, aided and abetted by the glare of brightly colored floodlights and the sea of bodies contorting every which way in a tempest of unleashed energy.

The host was a rock video producer whom Web had met several months before through a mutual subject of their respective lenses. The guest list ran the gamut from actors to singers to musicians to technicians.

Marni could barely distinguish one garishly lit face, one outrageously garbed body from another, and she would have felt lost had it not been for the umbilical cord of Web's arm. He introduced her to those he knew and joined her in greeting others he was meeting for the first time. Marni couldn't say that it was the most intellectually stimulating group she'd ever encountered, but then her own mind could barely function amid the pulsating hubbub of activity.

In hindsight, though, it was an educational hour that she spent with Web at the party. She learned that he was well-known, well-liked and held slightly in awe. She learned that he didn't play kissy-and-huggy-and-isn't-this-a-*super*-party, but maintained his dignity while appearing fully congenial and at ease. She learned that he disliked indiscriminate drinking and avoided the coke corner like the plague, that he hated Twisted Sister, abided Prince, admired Springsteen, and that he was not much more of a dancer than she was.

"I think I'm getting a migraine," he finally yelled at her over the din. "Come on. Let's get out of here." He tugged her by the hand, leading her first for their coats, then out the door. Once in the lobby, where the music was little more than a dull vibration, he leaned back against the wall. Their coats were slung over his shoulder. He hadn't released her hand once. "Sorry about that," he said, tipping his head sideways against the stucco wall to look at her. "I hadn't realized it'd be so wild. Well, maybe I had, but I promised Malcolm I'd come. Are you still with me?"

She, too, was braced against the wall, savoring their escape. She gave his hand a squeeze and smiled. "A little wilted, but I'm still here."

"I want you to know that these aren't really my friends. I mean, Malcolm is, and I know enough of the others, but I don't usually hang around with them in my free time. Even if I did it'd be one at a time and in a quieter setting, but I really do have other, more reputable friends.... What are you laughing at?"

"You. You were so confident back there, but all of a sudden you're like a little boy, all nervous and apologetic." She punctuated her words with a chiding headshake, but she was grinning. "I'm not your mother, Web. And I'm not here to stand in judgment on your friends and acquaintances."

"I know, but...why is it I suspect that your friends are a little more...dignified?"

She grimaced. "Maybe because I'm the staid president of a staid corporation."

"Hey, I'm not knocking it.... What *are* your friends like?"

"Oh...diverse. Quieter, I guess." She paused pensively. "It's strange. When I think back to being a teenager, to the group I was with then, I remember irreverent parties and a general law-unto-ourselves attitude."

"You were never really that way."

"No, but I was on the fringe of it. When I think of what those same people, even the most rebellious ones, are doing now, I have to laugh. They're conventional, establishment all the way. Oh, they like a good time, and by and large they've got plenty of money to spend on one, but they seem to have outgrown that wildness they so prided themselves on."

"You say 'they.' You don't identify with them?"

She plucked at the folds of the chic overblouse she'd worn with her stirrup pants. "It wasn't that I outgrew it. I was shocked into leaving it behind. Somehow I lost a taste for it after...after..."

"After Ethan died," he finished for her in a sober voice. When she didn't reply, he took her coat from his shoulder. "Come on," he said gently. "Let's take a walk."

Without raising her head, she slipped her arms into the sleeves of the coat and buttoned it up, then let Web take her hand and lead her into the February night. The party had been in SoHo at the lower end of Manhattan. They'd taxied there, but a slow walk back uptown was what they both needed.

"You still miss him, don't you?" Web asked.

The air was cold, numbing her just enough to enable her to talk of Ethan. "I adored him. There were eight years between us, and it wasn't as though we were close in the sense of baring our souls to each other. But we shared a special something. Yes, I miss him."

Web wrapped his arm around her shoulders and drew her close as they walked. "He would have been president of Lange, wouldn't he?"

"Yes."

"You took over in his place."

"My parents needed someone."

"What about your sister...Tanya?"

Marni's laugh was brittle. "Tanya is hopeless. She ran in the opposite direction when she thought she might have to do something with the business. Not that Dad would have asked her. Maybe it was because he *didn't* ask her that she was so negative about it. She never did get her degree. She flunked out of two different colleges and finally gave up on the whole thing."

"What is she doing now?"

"Oh, she's here in New York. She's been through two husbands and is looking around for a third. She's got alimony enough to keep her living in style, so she spends her days shopping and her nights partying."

"Not *your* cup of tea."

"Not...quite."

"Were you ever close, you and Tanya?"

"Not really. We fought all the time as kids, you know, bickered like all siblings do. When I read things about sibling placement, about how the middle child is supposed to be the mediator, I have to laugh. Tanya was the *instigator*. It's like she felt lost between Ethan and me, and had to go out of her way to exert herself. I was some kind of threat to her—don't ask me why. She's prettier, more outgoing. And she can dance." They both chuckled. "But she always seemed to think that I had something she didn't, or that I was going to get something better than what she did."

"She was two years older than you?"

"Mmmm."

"Maybe she resented your arrival. If Ethan was seven when she was born, and she was the first girl, she was probably pampered for those first two years of her life. Your birth upset the applecart."

Marni sighed. "Whatever, it didn't—doesn't—make for a comfortable relationship. We see each other at family events, and run into each other accidentally from time to time, but we rarely talk on the phone and we never go out of our way to spend time together. It's sad, when you think of it." She looked up at Web. "You must think it's pathetic…being an only child and all."

"I wasn't an only child."

Her eyes widened. "No? But I thought…you never mentioned any family, and I always assumed you didn't have any!"

His lips twitched. "Just hatched from a shell and took off, eh?"

"You know what I mean. What *do* you have, Web? Tell me."

"I have a brother. Actually a half brother. He's four years younger than me."

"Do you ever see him?"

"We work together. He's my business manager, or agent, or financial advisor, or whatever you want to call it. Lee Fitzgerald. He was there Tuesday morning…but you don't remember much of that, do you?"

She eyed him shamefacedly. "I wasn't exactly at my best Tuesday morning."

"You wouldn't have had any way of knowing he was my brother. We don't look at all alike. But he's a nice guy, and very capable."

Marni was remembering what Web had said that Tuesday morning, in a moment of anger, about his being a bastard. "The name Webster?"

"Was my mother's maiden name."

"Did you ever know your father?"

"Nope. It was a one-night stand. He was married."

"Do you ever…wonder about him?"

He caressed her shoulder through the thickness of her coat as though he needed that small reassurance of her presence. Though his tone was light, devoid of bitterness, almost factual, Marni suspected that he regretted the circumstances of his conception.

"I wouldn't be human if I didn't. I used to do it a lot when I was a kid—wonder who he was, what he looked like, where he lived, whether he'd like me. I can almost empathize with Tanya. I spent all those years wandering, traveling, never staying in one place long. Maybe I didn't want to learn that he wasn't looking for me. As long as I kept moving, I had that illusion that he might be looking but, of course, couldn't find me. Pretty dumb, huh? He doesn't even know I exist."

Marni's heart ached for him. "Your mother never told him?"

"My mother never *saw* him, not after that one night. She knew his name, but he was a salesman from somewhere or other. She didn't know where. And she knew he was married, so she didn't bother. She married my stepfather when I was two. He wasn't a bad sort as stepfathers go."

They turned onto Fifth Avenue, walking comfortably in step with each other. "Is your mother still living?"

"She died several years ago."

"I'm sorry, Web," Marni said, feeling all the more guilty about the times she'd resented her own parents. At least they were alive. If she had a problem, she had somewhere to run. "Do you still wonder about your father?"

"Nah. I reached a point when settling down meant more than running away from the fact that he didn't know about me. I decided I wanted to do something, be something. I'm proud of what I've become."

"You should be," she said softly, holding his gaze for

a minute, until the intensity of its soul-reach made her look away.

They walked silently for a few blocks, their way lit frequently by storefront lights or the headlights of cars whipping through the city night. The sound of motors, revving, slowing, filled the air, along with the occasional honk of a horn or the squeal of brakes or the whir of tires.

"What about you, Marni? I know what you've become, but what would you have done if…things had been different. I knew you wanted a college degree, but you hadn't said much more than that. Had you always wanted to join the corporation?"

"I hadn't thought that far. Business, a career—they were the last things on my mind—" her voice lowered "—until Ethan died. I grew up pretty fast then."

"Why? I mean, you were only seventeen."

"Ethan had already started working, and I knew he was being groomed to take over Dad's place one day. It wasn't like I wanted the presidency per se, but my father needed someone, and it seemed right that I should give it a try."

"Did you go to Wellesley after all?"

"Mmmm. I did pretty lousy my first term. I was still pretty upset. But after that I was able to settle down. I got my M.B.A. at Columbia, and joined the corporation from there."

"Are you sorry? Do you ever wish you were doing something else?"

"I wish Ethan were here to be president, but given that he's not, I really can't complain. I do have an aptitude for business. I think I'm good at what I do. There's challenge to the work, and a sense of power because the corporation is profitable and I'm free to venture into new things."

"Like *Class*."

"Like *Class*."

They turned from Fifth Avenue onto a side street that was darker and more deserted. Marni couldn't remember the last time she'd walked through the city like this at night. She'd always been too intent on getting from one place to another, via cab or car or limousine, to think of walking. Yet, now it was calming, therapeutic, really quite nice. Of course, it helped that Web was with her. Talking with him was easy. He made her think about things—like Ethan—and doing so brought less pain than she'd have expected. Ethan was gone; she couldn't bring him back. But Web was here.

He'd never take the place of her brother; for that matter, she couldn't even *think* of Web as a brother. It wasn't a brother she wanted anyway. She wasn't sure just what she did want from Web—she hadn't thought that far. But his presence had an odd kind of continuity to it. Tonight, even Tuesday night when he'd taken her to dinner, she'd felt an inner excitement she hadn't experienced since she'd been seventeen years old. She felt good being with him— proud of what he was, how he looked, how he looked at *her*—and she felt infinitely safe, protected with his arm around her and his sturdy body so close.

Just then, a muffled cry came from the dark alleyway they'd just passed. They stopped and looked at each other, and their eyes grew wider when the sound came again. Suddenly Web was moving, pressing Marni into the alcove of a storefront. "Play dead," he whispered, then turned and ran back toward the alley. He'd barely reached its mouth when a body barreled into him, sending him sprawling, but only for an instant. Acting reflexively, he was on his feet and after the man, who was surprisingly smaller and slower than he.

But smaller and slower was one thing. When he dragged the nameless fugitive to the ground nearly halfway down the block, he found that he was no match for the shiny switchblade that connected with his left hand. Shards of pain splintered through him, and he recoiled, clutching his hand. He had no aspirations to be a hero or a martyr. Letting the man go, he ran back to where he'd left Marni. She was gone.

"Maaaarni!" he yelled, terrified for the first time.

"In here, Web! The alley!"

He swore, then dashed into the alley, skidding to a halt and coming down on his haunches beside her. She was supporting a young woman who was gasping for air.

"It's all right," Marni was saying softly but tightly. "It's all right. He's gone."

"Did he rape her?" Web asked Marni. He could see that the woman's clothes were torn.

She shook her head. "Our passing must have scared him off. He took her wallet. That's about it."

Web put a hand on the woman's quivering arm. "I'm going to get the police. Stay with Marni until I get back."

Her answering nod was nearly imperceptible amid her trembling, but Marni doubted she could have moved if she'd wanted to.

Web dashed back to the street, wondering where the traffic was when he wanted it. He ran to the corner of Fifth Avenue, intent on hailing some help. Cars whizzed by without pausing. The cabs were all occupied, so they didn't bother to stop. And there wasn't a policeman or a cruiser in sight. Spotting a pay phone, he dug into his pocket for a quarter, quickly called in the alarm, then raced back to the alley.

Marni was where he'd left her, still cradling the woman. Frightened, she looked up at him. "He must have hurt her. She has blood on her sleeve, but I don't know where it's coming from."

"It's mine," Web said, crouching down again. He was feeling a little dizzy. Both of his hands were covered with blood, one from holding the other. Tugging the scarf from around his neck, he wound it tightly around his left hand.

"My God, Web!" Marni whispered. Her heart, racing already, began to slam against her ribs. "What *happened*?"

"He had a knife. Lucky he used it on me, not her."

"But your hand—"

"It'll be all right."

The woman in Marni's arms began to cry. "I'm sorry... it's my fault. I shouldn't have...been walking alone...."

Marni smoothed matted strands of hair from the young woman's cheeks. She couldn't have been more than twenty-two or twenty-three, was thin and not terribly attractive. Yes, she should have known better, but that was water over the dam. "Shhhh. It's all right. The police will be here soon." She raised questioning eyes to Web, who nodded. Then she worriedly eyed his hand.

"It's okay," he assured her softly. He turned to the woman who'd been assaulted. "What's your name, honey?"

"Denise...Denise LaVecque."

"You're going to be just fine, Denise. The police will be along shortly." As though on cue, a distant siren grew louder. "They're going to want to know everything you can remember about the man who attacked you."

"I...I can't remember much. It was dark. He just... jumped out..."

"Anything you can remember will be a help to them."

The siren neared. It hit Marni that Denise wasn't the only one in for a long night. "They'll want to know every-thing you remember, too," she told Web.

He closed his eyes for a minute, frowning. His hand was beginning to throb. He wasn't sure if his wool scarf had been the best thing to wrap around it, but he'd needed to hide its condition from Marni—and from himself, if the truth were told. "I know."

Marni's hand on his cheek brought his eyes back open. "Are you really okay?" she whispered tremulously.

He gave a wan smile and nodded.

The siren rounded the corner and died at the same time a glaring flash of blue and white intruded on the darkness of the alley. It was a welcome intrusion.

The next few minutes passed by in a whir for Marni. A second police car joined the first, with four of New York's finest offering their slightly belated aid, asking question after question, searching the alley for anything Denise's assailant may have dropped, finally bundling Denise off in one car, Web and Marni in another. Marni wasn't sure what their plans were for Denise, but she was vocal in her insistence that Web be taken to a hospital before he answered any further questions.

The drive there was a largely silent one. Marni held Web's good hand tightly, worriedly glancing at him from time to time.

"It's just a cut," he murmured when he intercepted one such glance, but his head was lying back against the seat and the night could hide neither his pallor nor the blood seeping through the thickness of his scarf.

"My hero," was her retort, but it was more gentle than chiding, more admiring than censorious. She suspected that he'd acted on sheer instinct in chasing after the man who'd attacked Denise, and in a city notorious for its avoidance of involvement in such situations she deeply respected what Web had done. Of course, tangling with a switchblade hadn't been too swift....

The nurse at the emergency room desk immediately took Web to a cubicle, but when she suggested that Marni might want to wait outside, Marni firmly shook her head.

She continued to hold Web's hand tightly, releasing it only to help him out of his coat and to roll up his sleeve. He sat on the examining table with his legs hanging down one side; she sat with her legs hanging down the other, her elbow hooked with his, her eyes over her shoulder focusing past him to his left hand, which a doctor was carefully unwrapping.

She didn't move from where she sat. Her arm tightened periodically around Web's as the doctor cleaned the knife wound, then examined it to see the extent of the damage. When Web winced, so did she. When he grunted at a particularly painful probe, she moaned.

"You okay?" he asked her at one point. The doctor had just announced that the tendon in his baby finger had been severed and that it would take a while to heal, what with stitches and all.

"I'm okay," she told Web. "You're the one who's sweating."

He grinned peakedly. "It hurts like hell."

Feeling utterly helpless, she turned on the doctor. "He's in pain. Can't you help—"

"Marni," Web interrupted, "it's only my hand."

"But the pain's probably shooting up your arm, and don't you tell me it isn't!" She felt it herself, through her hand, her arm, her entire body. Again she accosted the doctor. "Aren't you going to anesthetize him or something?"

The doctor gave her an understanding smile. "Just his hand. Right now." He took the needle that the nurse assisting him had suddenly produced, and Marni did look away then, but only until Web rubbed his cheek against her hair.

"You can open your eyes now," he said softly, a hint of amusement in his tone. "It's all done."

What was done was the anesthetizing. The gash, which

cut through his baby finger and continued across his palm, was as angry-looking as ever.

"You may think this is funny, Brian Webster," she scolded in a hoarse whisper, "but I don't. Who knows what filthy germs were on that knife, or how you're going to handle a camera with one hand immobilized."

"Do you think I'm not worried about those same things?" he asked gently.

"No need to worry, Mr. Webster," the doctor interjected. "I'll give you a shot to counter whatever may have been on the knife, and as for your work, it's just your pinkie that will be in a splint. Between your thumb and the first two fingers of that left hand, you should be able to manage your camera. Maybe a little awkwardly at first, but you'll adapt."

"See?" Web said to Marni. "I'll adapt."

Marni didn't reply. She felt guilty for having badgered him, but she was worried and upset, and she'd had to let off the tension somehow. Turning her gaze back to his wound, which the doctor was beginning to stitch, she slid her free arm over Web's shoulder. He reached up, grasped her hand and wove his fingers through hers.

"Does it hurt?" she whispered.

He, too, was closely following the doctor's work, but he managed to shake his head. "Don't feel a thing."

"I'm glad one of us doesn't," she quipped dryly, and he chuckled.

Millimeter by millimeter the doctor closed the gash. Once, riding a wave of momentary fatigue, Marni pressed her face to the crook of Web's neck. He tipped his head to hold her there, finding intense comfort in the closeness.

When the repair work was done, the doctor splinted the finger and bandaged the hand. He gave Web the shot he'd promised, plus a small envelope with painkillers that he claimed Web might need as soon as the local anesthetic wore off. Marni would have liked nothing more than to take him home at that point, but the police were waiting just beyond the cubicle to take them to the station.

"Can't this be done tomorrow?" Marni asked softly. "I think he should be resting."

Web squeezed her hand. "It's okay. If we go now, we'll get it over with. The sooner the better, before the numbness wears off. Besides, I'm not sure I want to spend my Saturday poring through mug shots."

She would have argued further, but she realized he had a point. "You'll tell me if you start feeling lousy?"

"I think you'll know," he returned, arching one dark brow. She hadn't let go of him for a minute, and he loved it. Barely five minutes had gone by when she hadn't looked at his face for signs of discomfort or asked how he felt, and he loved it. He'd never been the object of such concern in his life. And he loved it.

He didn't love wading through page after page of mug shots in search of the man he'd seen and chased, but the police were insistent, and he knew it was necessary. He particularly didn't love it when the wee hours of the morning approached and they were still at it, he and Marni. His hand was beginning to ache again, and as the minutes passed, his head was, too. He knew that Marni had to be totally exhausted, and while he wanted to send her home, he also needed her by his side.

"Nothing," he said wearily when the last of the books were closed. "I'm sorry, but I don't think the man I saw tonight is here."

The officer who had been working with them rose from his perch on the corner of the desk and took the book from Web. "Hit and run. They're the damnedest ones to catch. May have been wearing a wig, or have shaved off a mustache. May not have any previous record, if you can believe that."

Marni, for one, was ready to believe anything the man said, if only to secure her and Web's release. Not only was she tired, but the events of the night had begun to take an emotional toll. She was feeling distinctly shaky.

"Is there anything else we have to do now?" she asked fearfully.

"Nope. I've got your statements, and I know where to reach you if we come up with anything."

Web was slipping his coat on. He didn't bother to put his left arm into the sleeve. It wasn't worth the effort. "Do you think you will?"

"Nope."

Web sighed. "Well, if you need us..."

The officer nodded, then stood aside, and Web and Marni wound their way through the maze of desks, doorways and stairs to the clear, cold air outside. They headed straight for a waiting taxi.

"I'd better get you home," he murmured, opening the door for Marni. As she slid in, she leaned forward and gave the cabbie Web's address. Web didn't realize what she'd done until they pulled up outside his riverfront building, at which point he was dismayed. "I can't send you home alone in a cab," he protested. "Not after what happened tonight."

Some of her spunk had returned. "I have no intention of going home alone, *especially* after what happened tonight. Come on, big guy." She was shoving him out the door. "We could both use a drink."

He was paying the cabbie when she climbed out herself. She was the one to put her arm around his waist and urge him into the building. "This is not...what...I'd planned," he growled, disgusted when he looked back on an evening that was supposed to have been so pleasant. "I never should have taken you to that party. If we hadn't gone, we wouldn't have been walking down that street—"

"And that poor girl would have been raped." Marni pressed the elevator button. The door slid open instantly, and she tugged him inside. "What-ifs aren't any good—I learned that a long time ago. The facts are that we did go to the party, that we were walking down that street, that we managed to deter a vicious crime, that your hand is all cut up and that we're both bleary-eyed right about now." The elevator began its ascent. "I'm exhausted, but I'm afraid to close my eyes because I'll see either that dark alleyway, that girl, or your poor hand…. How is it?"

"It's there."

"You wouldn't take one of the painkillers while we were at the police station. Will you take one now?"

"A couple of aspirin'll do the trick."

He ferreted his keys from his pocket and had them waiting when the elevator opened. Moments later they'd passed through the studio, climbed the spiral staircase and were in his living room. He went straight to the bar, tipped a bottle into each of two glasses without thought to either ice or water, took a long drink from his glass, then handed the other to Marni.

"Come. Sit with me." He moved to the sofa, kicked off his loafers and sank down, stretching out his legs and leaning his head back.

"Where's the aspirin?" Marni asked softly.

"Medicine chest. Down the hall, through the bedroom to the bathroom."

She found her way easily, so intent on getting something into Web that she saw nothing of the rest of his apartment but the inside of the medicine chest above the sink. When she returned, he downed the aspirin with another drink from his glass. She sat facing him on the sofa, her elbow braced on the sofa back.

"You look awful," she whispered.

He didn't open his eyes. "I've felt better."

"Maybe you should lie down."

"I am." He was sprawled backward, his lean body molded to the cushions.

"In bed. Wouldn't you be more comfortable there?"

"Soon."

Very gently, she lifted his injured hand and put it in her lap. She wanted to soothe him, to do something to help, but she wasn't sure what would be best. She began to lightly stroke his forearm, and when he didn't complain she continued.

He smirked. "Some night."

"It certainly was an adventure. You were always into them. This is the first one I've taken part in."

"I think I'm getting too old for this. I'm getting too old for lots of things. I should be up in Vermont. It's quieter there."

"Why aren't you? I thought you went up every weekend."

He opened one eye and looked at her. "I wanted to be with you. I didn't think you'd go up there with me." When she said nothing, he closed his eye and returned his head to its original position. "Anyway, I often wait till Saturday morning to drive up. If there's something doing here on a Friday night."

"You can't drive tomorrow! Well, you can, I suppose, but your hand will be sore—"

"Forget my hand." He made a guttural sound. "The way I feel now, I don't think I'm going to be able to drag myself out of bed before noon, and by then it'd be pretty late to get going."

"You'll go next weekend. It'll still be there."

"Mmmm." He lay still for several minutes, then drained his drink in a single swallow.

Marni set her own glass firmly on the coffee table. She took his empty one, put it beside hers, then gently slid her hand under his neck. "Come on, Web," she urged softly. "Let me get you to bed."

Very slowly and with some effort he pushed himself up, then stood. His hand was hurting, his whole arm was hurting. For that matter, his entire body felt sore. The aftermath of tension, he told himself. He *was* getting old.

Marni led him directly to the bed. The king-sized mattress sat on a platform of dark wood that matched a modern highboy and a second, lower chest of drawers. A plush navy carpet covered the floor. Two chairs of the same contemporary style as those in the living room sat kitty-cornered on one side of the room, between them a low table covered with magazines. Large silk-screen prints hung on the walls, contemporary, almost abstract in style, carrying through the navy, brown and white scheme of the room.

Clear-cut and masculine, like Web, Marni mused as she unbuttoned his shirt and eased it from his shoulders. As soon as it was gone, he turned and whipped the quilt back with his good arm, then stretched out full-length on the bed and threw that same arm across his eyes.

Marni stood where she was with his shirt clutched in her hands and her eyes glued to his bare chest. He was every bit as beautiful as he'd been fourteen years ago, though different in a way that made her heart beat faster than it ever had then. His shoulders were fuller, his skin more weathered. The hair that covered his chest was thicker, more pervasive, even more virile, if that were possible.

Anything was possible, she thought, including the fact that she was as physically attracted to him now as she'd been fourteen years before. Biological magnetism was an amazing thing. Web had been her first, but there'd been others. None of them had turned her on in quite the same way, with quite the intensity Web did.

None of them had stirred feelings of tenderness and caring that Web did either, and he was hurting now, she reminded herself with a jolt. Pushing all other thought aside, she dropped his shirt onto the foot of the bed and came to sit beside him. She unsnapped his jeans and was about to lower the zipper when his arm left his eyes and his hand stilled hers.

"I was...just trying to make you more comfortable," she explained, feeling the sudden flare of those blue eyes on her. "Wouldn't it be better without the jeans?"

"No. I'm fine as I am." Most importantly, he didn't want her to see his leg. She'd had as rough a night as he had, and he didn't feel she was ready to view those particular scars. They were old and well-faded, true, but the memories they'd evoke would be harsh.

Trusting that she wouldn't undress him further, he returned his arm to his eyes and gave a rueful laugh. "Y'know, since I saw you last Tuesday morning, I've been dreaming of having you again. Making love to you...here in my bed. Now here you are and I feel so awful that I don't think I could do a thing even if you were willing."

His words hung in the air, unresolved. Marni couldn't get herself to give the answer she knew Web wanted to hear. There was no doubt in her mind that on the physical level she was willing. Emotionally, well, that was another story. Much as she'd opened up to him since their reunion, much as she'd been able to talk of Ethan more easily than she had in the past, there were still thoughts that she couldn't ignore, raw feelings going back to that summer. Illogical perhaps, but logical ones as well. She knew from experience that one time with Web wouldn't be enough. He'd been an addiction that summer in Maine. She wasn't sure that if she gave in to him, to herself, it would be any different now. And the question would be where they went from there.

"I don't think the time's right for either of us," she said in a near-whisper. "You're right. You're feeling awful. And I feel a little like I've been flattened by a steamroller." She reached for the second pillow and carefully worked it under his bandaged hand. Then she rose from the bed. "I'll just sit over here—"

He raised his arm and looked at her. "You won't leave, will you?"

"No, I won't leave."

"Then why don't you lie down, too. The bed's big enough for both of us."

She wasn't sure she trusted herself that far. "In a little bit," she said, but paused before she sank into the chair. "Can I get you anything?"

Eyes closed, he shook his head. "I think I'll just rest..."

When his voice trailed off, she settled into the chair, studying him for a long time until a reflexive twitch of his good hand told her he was asleep. Soon after, her own eyelids drooped, then shut.

Ninety minutes later she came to feeling disoriented and stiff. The first problem was solved when she blinked, looked around the room, then saw Web lying exactly as he had been. The second was solved when she switched off the light, stretched out on the empty half of the bed, drew the quilt over them both and promptly fell asleep.

She awoke several times during the night when Web shifted and groaned. Once she felt his head and found it cool, and when he didn't wake up she lay down again. Her deepest sleep came just before dawn. When next she opened her eyes, the skylit room was bright. The same disorientation possessed her for a minute, but it vanished the minute she turned her head and saw Web.

He was still sleeping. His hair was mussed, and his beard was a dark shadow on his face. But it was his brow, corrugated even in sleep, that drew her gaze. He'd had an uncomfortable night. Silently, she slipped from beneath the sheet and padded to the bathroom for aspirin and water.

He was stirring when she returned, so she sat close by his side, raised him enough to push the aspirin into his mouth and give him a drink, then very gently set his head back down.

"Thanks," he murmured, coming to full awareness. He hadn't been disoriented, since this was his home. Finding Marni sitting beside him, well, that was something else.

"You're welcome. How does it feel...or shouldn't I ask?"

"You shouldn't ask," he drawled, then stretched, twisting his torso. When he settled back, his eyes were on her. "Actually, it's not bad. The discomfort's localized now. It was worse when I was sleeping, because I couldn't pinpoint it and it seemed to be all over." He raised the hand in question and glared at the white gauze. "Helluva big bandage. I'll have to get rid of some of this stuff."

"Don't you dare! If it was put on, it was put on for a reason."

"How am I gonna shower?"

"Hold your hand up in the air out of the spray...or forget the shower and take a bath."

"I never take baths."

She shrugged. "Then take a shower with your hand in the air, and be grateful it's your left hand. If it had been your right, you'd be in *big* trouble."

He ran his palm over the stubble on his jaw. "You've

got a point there." His gaze skittered hesitantly to hers. "I must look like something the cat dragged in."

She couldn't have disagreed with him more. He looked a little rough, but all man, every sinewy, stubbly, hairy inch. "You look fine, no, wonderful, given the circumstances." Her voice softened even more. "I've never seen you in the morning this way. We...we never spent a full night together."

He smiled in regret, his voice as soft as hers. "So now we've done it, and we haven't even *done* it." He raised his good hand and skimmed a finger over her lips, back and forth, whisper-light. "Do you know, I haven't even kissed you? Lord, I've wanted to, but I didn't know if you wanted it, and it seemed more important to talk."

Marni felt her insides melting. "Fourteen years ago it was the other way around."

"We're older now. Maybe we've got our priorities straight.... But I still want to kiss you." He was stroking her cheek ever so gently, and she'd begun to tremble. "Will you let me?"

"You always had the bluest eyes," she whispered, mesmerized by them, drowning in them. "I could never deny you when you looked at me that way."

"What way?"

"Like you wanted me. Like you knew that maybe it wasn't the smartest thing, but you wanted me anyway. Like there was something about *me* that you wanted, just me."

"There is." He slid his fingers into her hair and urged her head down. "There is, Marni. You're...very...special...." The last was whispered against her lips, the sound vanishing into her mouth, which had opened, and waited, but was waiting no more.

It started gently, a tender reacquaintance, kisses whispered from one mouth to the other in a slow, renewing exchange. For Marni it was a homecoming; there was something about the taste of Web, the texture of his lips, the instinctive way he pleased her that erased the years that had passed. For Web the homecoming was no less true; there was something about the softness of Marni's lips, the way they clung to his, the way her honeyed freshness poured warmly into him that made him forget everything that had come between this and their last kiss.

Familiarly their lips touched and sipped and danced. As it had always done, though, desire soon began to clamor, and whispered kisses were no longer enough. Web's mouth grew more forceful, Marni's demanded in return, and it was fire, hot, sweet fire surging through their veins, singeing all threads of caution.

Eyes closed under the force of sensation, Marni took everything he offered and gave as much in return. His mouth slanted openly against hers, hungrily devouring it. Her mouth fought fiercely for his, possessing it in turn. He ran his tongue along the line of her teeth and beyond; she caressed it with her own, then drew it in deeper. And while his hand wound restlessly through her hair, her own spread feverishly across his chest.

"C'mcrc," he growled, and swiftly rolled her over him until she was on her back and he was above her. Her neck rested in the crook of his elbow, and it was that elbow that propped him up so he could touch her as she'd done him.

Even had their mouths not come together again, she wouldn't have said a word in protest, because the fire was too hot, the sweetness too sweet to deprive herself of this little bit of heaven. Web had always been this for her, a flame licking at her nerve ends, spreading a molten desire within her that water couldn't begin to quench.

He cupped her breast through the knit of her overblouse, molding it to his palm, kneading and circling until at last his fingers homed in on the tight nub at its crest. Her flesh swelled, and she arched up, seeking even closer contact with the instrument of such bliss. She'd been starving for years; now she couldn't get enough. It was sheer relief when he impatiently tugged the overblouse from her hips.

"Lift up, sweet...there...I need...to touch you, Marni!"

She helped him, because she needed the very same thing, and she was tossing the blouse aside even as Web unhooked her bra and tore it away. Then he was lying half over her again, his large hand greedily rediscovering her blossoming flesh, and she was moaning in delight, straining for more, bunching the damp skin of his back in hands that clenched and unclenched, shifted, then clenched again.

She was in a frenzy. The tight knot in her belly was growing, inflamed not only by his thorough exploration of her nakedness but by the hardness of his sex pressing boldly against her thigh. When he slid down, she dug her fingers into his hair, holding on for dear life as his mouth opened over her breast, his tongue bathed it, his teeth closed around one distended nipple and tugged a path to her womb.

"Web!" she cried. "Oh, God, I need...I need..."

He slid back up, and her hand lowered instinctively to him, cupping him, caressing him until even that wasn't enough. His hand tangled with hers then, clutching at the tab of his zipper, tugging it down. He took her fingers and led them inside his briefs. He was trembling as badly as she was, and his voice shook with urgency.

"Touch me...touch me, sunshine..."

This time the pet name was so perfectly placed, so very right that it was stimulation in and of itself. She touched him, stroked him, pleasured him until he gave a hoarse cry of even greater need. Then he was tugging at her pants, freeing her hips for his invasion.

What happened then was something neither Marni nor Web had expected. She felt his tumescence press against the nest of curls at the apex of her thighs, and it was so intense, so electric that she recoiled and, in a burst of emotion, began to cry.

"Web...oh..." she sobbed, tears streaking down her cheeks and into the hairs of his chest. "Web... I...I..."

She couldn't say anything else. Her crying prevented it. He held her head tightly to his chest with his left arm and ran his good hand over and around her naked back, knowing that he could easily be inside her but ignoring that fact because, at the moment, her emotional state was far more important.

"It's okay. Shhhhh. Shhhhh."

"I want," she gulped, "want you...so badly, but...but..."

"Shhhhh. It's okay."

She wiped the tears from her eyes, but they kept flowing. She felt frustrated and embarrassed and confused. So she simply gave herself up to the outpouring of whatever it was and waited until at last the tears slowed before trying to speak again.

"I'm sorry...I didn't mean to do that...I don't know what happened..."

"Something's bothering you," he said softly, patiently. "Something snapped."

"But it's awful...what I did. A woman has no right to do that to...to a man."

"I know you want me, so you're suffering, too."

She raised wide, tear-filled eyes to his. "Let me help you." Her hand started back down. "Let me do it, Web—"

He flattened her body against his, trapping her hand. "No. I don't want that."

"But you'll be uncomfortable—"

"The discomfort is more in my mind than my body."

Her tears had instantly cooled his ardor. He allowed a small space between them. "Feel. You'll see. Go on."

She did as he told her and discovered that he was no longer hard. Her eyes widened all the more, and she suddenly grappled with her pants, tugging them up. "You *don't* want me..."

He gave a short laugh and rolled his eyes to the ceiling. "I'm damned if I do and damned if I don't." His gaze fell to catch hers. "Of course I want you, sunshine. You are my sunshine, y'know. You're bright and warm, the source of an incredible energy, but only when you're sure of yourself, when you're happy. Something happened just now. I don't know exactly what it was, but it's pushed that physical drive into the background for the time being."

Marni wasn't sure what to think. She nervously matted the hair on his chest with the flat of her finger. "It used to be that nothing could push that physical drive into the background."

"We're older. Life is more complex than it used to be. When I was twenty-six, sex was a sheer necessity. It was a physical outlet, sure, but it was also a means of communicating things that either I didn't understand or didn't see or didn't want to say." His arm was beginning to throb. Shifting himself back against the pillow, he drew Marni against him, cradling her with his right arm, letting his left rest limply on the sheet.

"If I was still twenty-six, I'd have made love to you regardless of your tears just now. I wouldn't have had the strength to stop, the control. But I'm not twenty-six. I'm forty. I have the control now, and the strength." He paused for a minute, but there was more he wanted to say. "I haven't been a monk all these years, Marni. For a while I was with any and every woman who turned me on. Then I realized that the turn-on was purely physical, and it wasn't enough. Maybe I've mellowed. I've become picky. I think...I think that when we do make love, you and I, it'll be an incredibly new and wonderful experience."

To her horror, Marni began to cry again. "Why do you...do you *say* things like that, Web? Why are...are you so incredibly understanding?"

He hugged her tighter. "It hurts me when you cry, sunshine. Please, tell me what's bothering you. Tell me what happened back there."

"Oh, God," she cried, then sniffled, "I wish I knew. I was so high, so unbelievably high, and then it was like... like this door opened somewhere in the back of my mind, and in a lightning-quick instant I felt burned to a crisp, and frightened and nervous and guilty..."

He held her face back. "Guilty?"

She looked at him blankly, her lashes spiked with tears when she blinked. "Did I say that?" she whispered, puzzled.

"Very clearly. What did you mean?"

"I don't know. Maybe...maybe it's that we haven't been together long..."

"Maybe," he returned, but skeptically. "You've been with other men since that summer, haven't you?"

She nodded. "But it's been a long time for me and... maybe it was too easy and that bothered me."

"You've always been honest with me, Marni," he chided softly. "Tell me. These are modern times, and you're a fully grown, experienced woman. If you met a guy and felt something really unique with him, and if he felt the same, and the two of you wanted desperately to make love, would you hold out on principle?" When she didn't answer, he coaxed gently, "Would you?"

"No," she whispered.

"But you do feel guilty now. Why, sunshine? Why guilty?"

"Maybe it was too fast. And your hand…"

"My hand wasn't hurting just then. Loving you blotted everything out. I wasn't complaining, or moaning. Come on, Marni. Why guilty?"

Her gaze darted blindly about the room. She frowned, swallowed hard, then began to breathe raggedly. "I guess… I guess that…maybe I felt that…well, we'd made love so much during that summer, and it was so good and right, and then…and then…" Her eyes were wide when she raised them to his. Fresh tears pooled on her lower lids but refused to overflow. "And then the accident happened and Ethan was killed and you were in the hospital and my parents…forbade me to…see you…"

Web closed his eyes. An intense inner pain brought a soft moan to his lips, and he slipped both arms around her. "Lord, what they've done…what they've done…"

He held her for a long time without saying a word, because only then did he realize the enormity of the hurdle he faced.

CHAPTER FIVE

WEB HAD MUCH to consider. He understood now that there was a link in Marni's mind between their lovemaking of fourteen years ago and Ethan's death. He understood that, though she may not have been aware of it at the time, some small part of her had felt guilty about their affair, and Ethan's death must have seemed to her a form of punishment. And he understood that her parents had done nothing to convince her it wasn't so.

Much to consider…so much to consider. He held Marni tightly, wanting desperately to protect her, to take away the pain. She was such a strong woman, yet still fragile. He tried to decide what to do, what to say. In the end he wasn't any more ready to discuss this newly revealed legacy of that summer in Maine than she was.

"Marni?" he murmured against her hair. He ran his hand soothingly over her naked back, then kissed her forehead. "Sweetheart?"

Marni, too, had been stunned by what she'd said. But rather than think of it, she'd closed her eyes and let the solid warmth of Web's body calm her. She took a last, faintly erratic breath. "Hmmm?"

"Are you any good at brewing coffee?"

She knew what he was doing and was grateful. A faint smile formed against his chest, and she opened her eyes. "Not bad."

"Think you could do it while I use the bathroom? I'm feeling a little muzzy right about now."

His voice did sound muzzy, so she took pity on him. Reaching for her discarded blouse, she dragged it over her breasts as she sat up. "I think I could handle that."

He was looking at the blouse, then at the hands that clutched it to her. "Hey, what's this?" he asked very softly, gently. When he met her gaze, his blue eyes were infinitely tender. "You never used to cover up with me."

Embarrassed, she looked away. "That was fourteen years ago," she whispered.

"And you don't think that what we have now is as close?"

"It isn't that…"

He lightly curled his fingers over her slender shoulders. "What is it, sunshine? Please, tell me."

Her eyes remained downcast. "I…I'm older…I look different now."

"But I saw you a few minutes ago. I touched you and tasted you, and you were beautiful."

"That was in the heat of passion."

"And you're afraid I'll look at you now and see a thirty-one-year-old body and not be turned on?"

She shrugged. "Time does things."

"To me, too. Don't you think I'm aware that my body is older? I'm forty, not twenty-six. Do you think I'm not that little bit nervous that you'll see all the changes?"

Her gaze shot to him. "But I saw you last night, and not in passion, and you're body's better than ever!"

"So is yours, Marni," he whispered. Very slowly he eased the knit fabric from her hands and drew it away. His eyes took on a special light as they gently caressed her bare curves. "Your skin is beautiful. Your breasts are perfect."

"They're not as high as they used to be."

"They're fuller, more womanly." He didn't touch her, but his heart was thumping as he captured her gaze. "If I wanted a seventeen-year-old now, I'd have one. But I don't want that, Marni. I want a mature woman. I want you." Very gently he pulled her forward and pressed a warm kiss to each of her breasts in turn. She sucked in a sharp breath, and her nipples puckered instantly. "And if you don't get out of here this minute, mature woman," he growled only half in jest, "I'm going to have you." He shot a disparaging glance at the front of his jeans, then a more sheepish one back at her.

"Oh, Web," Marni breathed. She threw herself forward and gave him a final hug. "You always know the right thing to say."

He wanted to say that he didn't, but the words wouldn't come out because he'd closed his eyes and was caught up enjoying the silken feel of her against him. Only when the pressure in his loins increased uncomfortably did he force a hoarse warning. "Marni...that coffee?"

"Right away," she whispered, jumping up and running for the door, then returning, cheeks ablaze, for her bra and blouse before dashing for the kitchen.

Not only did she brew a pot of rich coffee, but by the time Web joined her she'd scrambled eggs, toasted English muffins and sliced fresh oranges for their breakfast.

"So you can cook," he teased. He remembered her telling him, during those days in Camden, that Cook had allowed no interference in the kitchen.

Marni put milk in his coffee, just as he'd had it that night when they'd been at the restaurant, and set the mug beside him. Then she joined him at the island counter. "I may not be a threat to Julia Child, but I've learned something. Post-graduate work, if you will."

He sipped the strong brew and smiled in appreciation.

"An A for coffee." He took a forkful of the eggs, chewed appreciatively, then smacked his lips together. "An A for scrambled eggs. Very moist and light."

She laughed. "Don't grade the muffins or the orange. I really can't take much credit for either."

"Still, you didn't burn the muffins."

"You have a good toaster."

"And the orange is sliced with precision."

"You have a sharp knife, and I have a tidy personality." Amused, she was watching him eat. "You'll choke if you don't slow down."

"I'm suddenly starved. You should be, too. We didn't get around to having dinner last night."

Marni ate half of her eggs, then offered the rest to Web, who devoured them and one of her muffins as though his last meal had been days ago. When he was done, he sat back and studied her. "What now?" he asked softly.

"You're still hungry?"

"What now...for us? Will you stay a while?"

She'd been debating that one the whole time she'd been making breakfast. "I...think I'd better head home. A lot has happened. Too quickly. I need a little time."

He nodded. More than anything he wished she'd stay, but he understood her need for time alone to think. He could only hope it would be to his benefit.

She began to clean up the kitchen. "Will you be okay... your hand, and all?"

"I'll be fine.... Marni, what say we try for that picture again on Tuesday? If you can manage it with your schedule, I can make all the other arrangements."

She finished rinsing the frying pan, then reached for the dish towel. "Do you really think you'll be up for it?"

"I've got another shoot set for Monday. It has to go on, no matter what. I'll be up for it.... But that's not the real question here." Not wanting to put undue pressure on her, he remained where he was at the island. "Are you willing to give it another try?"

Her head was bowed. "You really think it's the cover we need?"

"I do. But more than that, I *want* to do it. You have no idea how much it means to me to photograph you and put your face out there for the world to see. I'm proud of you, Marni. Some men might want to keep you all to themselves, and I do in a lot of respects, but I'm a photographer, and you happen to mean more to me than any other subject I've ever photographed. I want you to be on the premier cover of *Class* because I feel you belong there, and because I feel that I'm the only one who can see and capture on film the beauty you are, inside and out." When she simply stood with her back to him, saying nothing, he grew more beseechful. "I know that may sound arrogant, but it's the way I feel. Give me a chance, Marni. Don't deny me this one pleasure."

"It's not only your eyes that get to me, Brian Webster," she muttered under her breath, "it's your tone of voice. How can you prey on my *vulnerability* this way?"

He knew then that he'd won. Rising, he crossed to the sink and gave her waist a warm squeeze. "Because I know that it's right, Marni. It's right all the way."

MARNI STILL HAD her doubts. She left him soon after that and returned to her apartment. She had errands to run that afternoon—food shopping, a manicure, stockings to buy—and she would have put them all off in a minute if she'd felt it wise to stay longer with Web. But she did need to be alone, and she did need to think. At least, that was what she told herself. Then she did everything possible to avoid being alone, to avoid thinking.

She dallied in the supermarket, spent an extra hour talking with the woman whose manicure followed hers, and whom she'd come to know for that reason, then browsed through every department of Bloomingdale's before reaching the hosiery counter. When she finished her shopping, she returned home in time to put her purchases away, then shower and dress for the cocktail party she'd been invited to. It was a business-related affair, and when she got there she threw herself into it, so much so that when she finally got home she was exhausted and went right to bed.

When she woke up the next morning, though, Web was first and foremost on her mind. She thought back to the same hour the day before, remembering being on his bed, on the verge of making love with him. Her body throbbed at the memory. She took a long shower, but it didn't seem to help. Without considering the whys and wherefores, she picked up the phone and dialed his number.

"Webster, here," was the curt answer.

She hesitated, then ventured cautiously, "Web?"

He paused, then let out a smiling sigh. "Marni. How are you, sunshine?"

"I'm okay.... Am I disturbing you?"

"Not on your life."

"You sounded distracted."

"I was sitting here feeling sorry for myself. Just about to drag out the old morgue book."

"Why feeling sorry for yourself?"

"Because I'm here and you're there, and because my hand hurts and I'm wondering how in hell I'm going to manage tomorrow."

"It's still really bad?"

"Nah. It's a little sore, but self-pity always makes things seem worse."

She grinned. "Then, by all means, drag out the old morgue book."

"I won't have to, now that you've called…. I tried you last night."

She'd been wondering about that, worrying…hoping. "I had to go to a cocktail party. It was a business thing. Pretty dry." In hindsight that was exactly what it had been, though she'd convinced herself otherwise at the time. No, not really dry, but certainly not as exciting as it might have been had Web been there.

"I sat here alone all night thinking of you," he said without remorse.

"That's not fair."

"I'll say it's not. You're out there munching on scrumptious little hors d'oeuvres while I dig into the peanut butter jar—"

"It's not fair that you're making me feel guilty," she corrected him, but she was grinning. If he'd spent last night with a gorgeous model, she'd have been jealous as hell.

He feigned resignation with an exaggerated sigh. "No need to feel guilty. I'm used to peanut butter—"

"Web…" she warned teasingly.

"Okay. But I really did miss you. I do miss you. Yesterday at this time we were having breakfast together."

"I know." There was a wistfulness to her tone.

"Hey, I could pick you up in an hour and we could go for brunch."

"No, Web. I have work to do. I promised myself I'd stay in all day and get it done."

"Work? On the weekend?"

She knew he was mocking her, but she didn't mind. "I always bring a briefcase home with me. Things get so hectic at the office sometimes that I need quiet time to reread proposals and reports."

"I wouldn't keep you more than an hour, hour and a half at most."

"I...I'd better not."

"You still need time to think."

"Yes."

He spoke more softly. "That I can accept.... We're on for Tuesday, aren't we?"

"I'll have to work it out with my secretary when I go in tomorrow, but I don't think I have anything that can't be shifted around."

"I've already called Anne. She'll have Marjorie get some clothes ready, but I said that I wanted as few people there for the actual shoot as possible. That'll go for my staff, too, and you can leave Edgar and Steve behind at the office."

"I will. Thank you."

He paused, his tone lightening. "Can I call you tomorrow night, just to make sure you don't get cold feet and back out on me at the last minute?"

"I won't back out once all the arrangements are made."

"Can I call you anyway?"

She smiled softly. "I'd like that."

"Good." He hated to let her go. Her voice alone warmed him, not to mention the visual picture he'd formed of her auburn hair framing her face, her cheeks bright and pink, her lips soft, the tips of her breasts peaking through a nightgown, or a robe, or a blouse—it didn't matter which, the effect was the same. "Well," he began, then cleared his throat, "take care, Marni."

"I will." She hated to let him go. His voice alone thrilled her, not to mention the visual picture she'd formed of his dark hair brushing rakishly over his brow, his lean, shadowed cheeks, his firm lips, the raw musculature of his torso. She took an unsteady breath. "Are you sure you can manage everything with your hand?" If he'd said that he was having trouble, she would have rushed to his aid in a minute.

He was tempted to say he was having trouble, but he'd never been one to lie. "I'm sure…. Bye-bye, sweetheart."

"Bye, Web."

MARNI WOULD INDEED have tried to back out on the photo session had it not been for the arrangements that had been made. Through all of Sunday, while she tried to concentrate first on the Sunday Times, then on her work, she found herself thinking of her relationship with Web. She was no longer seventeen and in that limbo between high school, college and the real world. She was old enough to have serious thoughts about the future, and she knew that with each additional minute she spent with Web those thoughts would grow more and more serious.

Though she wasn't sure exactly what he wanted, she knew from what he'd said that he envisioned some kind of future relationship with her. But there were problems— actually just one, but it was awesome. Her family.

It was this that weighed heavily on her when she arrived at Web's studio Tuesday morning. As he'd promised, Web had called the evening before. He'd been gentle and encouraging, so that when she'd hung up the phone she'd felt surprisingly calm about posing again. Then her mother had called.

"Marni, darling, why didn't you tell me! I had no idea what had happened until Tanya called a little while ago!"

Icy fingers tripped up Marni's spine. What did her mother know? She hadn't sounded angry…. What could *Tanya* know…or was it Marni's own guilty conscience at work? "What is it, Mother? What are you talking about?"

"That little business you witnessed on Friday night.

Evidently there was a tiny notice in the paper yesterday. I missed it completely, and if it hadn't been for Tanya—"

Marni was momentarily stunned. She hadn't expected any of that episode to reach the press, much less with her name printed…and, she assumed, Web's. She moistened her lips, unsure as to how much more her mother knew. All she could say was a slightly cryptic, "Tanya reads the paper?"

"Actually it was Sue Beacham—you know, Tanya's friend whose husband is a state senator? They say he's planning to run for Congress, and he'll probably make it. He has more connections than God. Of course, Jim Heuer had the connections and it didn't help. He didn't get Ed Donahue's support, so he lost most of the liberal vote. I guess you can never tell about those things."

Marni took a breath for patience. Her mother tended to run on at the mouth, particularly when it came to name-dropping. "What was it that Sue saw?"

"There was a little article about how you and that photographer were instrumental in interrupting a rape."

"It wasn't a rape," Marni countered very quietly. "It was a mugging."

"But it could have been a rape if you hadn't come along, at least that was what the paper said. I'd already thrown it out, but Tanya had the article and read it to me."

Marni forced herself to relax. It appeared that Adele Lange hadn't made the connection between Brian Webster, the photographer, and the notorious Web. "It was really nothing, Mother. We happened to be walking down the street and heard the woman's cries. By the time we got to her, her assailant was already on his way."

"But this photographer you were with—it said he was injured."

"Just his hand. He's fine."

"Who is he, Marni? You never mentioned you were seeing a photographer, and such a renowned one, at least that's what Tanya says. She says that he's right up there with the best, and I'm sure I've seen his work but I've probably repressed the name. Webster." Her voice hardened. "I don't even like to say it."

Marni's momentary reprieve was snatched away. It didn't matter that her mother hadn't actually connected the two. What mattered was that the ill will lingered.

"Are you seeing him regularly?" Adele asked when Marni remained quiet.

"He's doing the cover work for the new magazine. There were some things we had to work out."

"Do you think you *will* be seeing him? Socially, that is? A photographer." Marni could picture her mother pursing her lips. "I think you should remember that a man in a field like his is involved with many, many women, and glamorous ones at that. You'll have to be careful."

The "many, many women" Marni's mother mentioned went along with the stereotype. Marni felt no threat on that score. Indeed, it was the least of her worries.

"Mother," she sighed, "you're getting a little ahead of yourself."

"It doesn't hurt to go into things with both eyes open."

"I've *got* both eyes open."

"All right, all right, darling. You needn't get riled up. I only called because I was concerned. I know incidents like that aren't uncommon, but witnessing it on the street can be a traumatic experience for a woman."

"It was traumatic for the victim. I'm okay."

"Are you sure? You sound tired."

"After a full day at the office, I am tired."

"Well, I guess you have a right to that. I'll let you rest, darling. Talk with you soon?"

"Uh-huh." Marni had hung up then, but she'd spent a good part of the night brooding, so she was tired and unsettled when Web came to greet her at the reception area of the studio. His smile was warm and pleasure-filled, relaxing her somewhat, but he was quick to see that something was amiss.

"Nervous?" he asked her as he guided her into the studio.

"A little."

"It'll be easier this time."

"I hope so."

"Is...everything all right?"

"Everything's fine."

"Why won't you look at me?"

She did then. "Better?"

He shook his head. "Smile for me."

She did then. "Better?"

He gestured noncommittally, but she was looking beyond him again, so he didn't speak. "See? It's almost quiet here."

Indeed it was. Anne, who appeared to be the only one present from *Class*, waved to her from the other side of the room, where she was in conference with the makeup artist. Marni recognized the hairstylist and, more vaguely, several of Web's assistants.

"Lee?" Web called out. A man turned from the group and, smiling, approached. "Lee, I'd like you to meet Marni. Formally. Marni, my brother, Lee."

Marni's smile was more genuine as she shook Lee's warm hand. He was pleasant-looking, though nowhere near as handsome or tall as Web. Wearing a suit, minus its tie, he was more conservatively dressed than the other men in the room, but his easy way made up for the difference. Marni liked him instantly.

"I'm pleased to meet you, Lee. Web's had only good things to say about you."

Lee shot Web a conspiratorial glance. "I'd have to say the same about you. I've heard about nothing else for the past week." He held up his hand. "Not that he's telling everyone, mind you, but—" he winked "—I think the old man needs an outlet."

Marni wondered just how much Lee knew, then realized that it didn't matter. He was Web's brother. The physical resemblance may have been negligible, but there was something deeper, an intangible quality the two men shared. She knew she'd trust Lee every bit as much as she trusted Web. Of course, trust wasn't really the problem….

"Enough," Web was saying with a smile. "We'd better get things rolling here."

Marni barely had time to squeeze Lee's arm before Web was steering her off toward the changing rooms. Once again she was "done over," this time more aware of what was happening. She asked questions—how the hairstylist managed such a smooth sweep from her crown, what the makeup artist had done for her eyes to make them seem so far apart—but she was simply making conversation, perhaps in her way apologizing for having spoiled these people's efforts the week before. And diverting her mind from the worry that set in each time she looked at Web.

If the villain of the previous Tuesday had been the shock and pain of memory, now it was guilt. Marni saw Web's face, so open and encouraging, then the horror-filled ones of her parents when they learned she was seeing him again. She heard his voice, so gentle in instruction, then the harsh, bitter words of her family when they knew she was associating with the enemy.

Web tried different poses from the week before, used softer background music. He tried different lights and different cameras—the latter mostly on his tripod, which he could more easily manage, but in the end holding the camera in his hand with his splinted pinkie sticking straight out.

Halfway through the session, he called a break, shooing everyone else away after Marni had been given a cool drink.

"What do you think?" she asked hesitantly. The face she made suggested that she had doubts of her own but needed the reassurance. "Any better than last week?"

"Better than that, but still not what I want. It's a little matter of…this…spot." With his forefinger, he lightly stroked the soft skin between her brows. "No amount of makeup is going to hide the creases when you frown."

"But I thought I was smiling, or doing whatever it was you asked me to do."

"You were. But those little creases creep in there anyway. When I ask for a tiny smile, the overall effect is one of pleading. When I ask for a broad smile, you look like you're in pain. When I ask you to wet your lips and leave them parted, you look like you're holding your breath."

"I am," she argued, throwing up a hand in frustration. "I'm no good at this. I told you, Web. This isn't my thing."

She was leaning against the arm of a director's chair. He stood close by, looking down at her. "It can't be the crowd, because there's no crowd today. It can't be the music, or the posing. And it can't be shock. Not anymore…. You're worried about something. That's what the creases tell me."

"I'm worried that I'll never be able to give you what you want, that you won't get your picture and you'll be disappointed and angry."

"Angry? Never. Disappointed? Definitely. But I'm not giving up yet. I'm going to get this picture, Marni. One way or another, I'm going to get it."

He spoke with such conviction, and went back to work with such determination, that Marni began to suspect he'd have her at it every day for a month, if that's what it took. She did her best to concentrate on relaxing her facial muscles, but found it nearly impossible. She'd get rid of the creases, but then her mouth would be wrong, or the angle of her head, or her shoulders.

The session ended not in a burst of tears as it had last time, but in sighs of fatigue from both her and Web. "Okay," he said resignedly as he handed his camera to one of his assistants, "we'll take a look at what we've got. There may be something." He ran his fingers through his hair. "God only knows I've exposed enough film."

Marni whirled around and stalked off toward the dressing room.

"Marni!" he called out, but she didn't stop. So he loped after her, enclosing them in the privacy of the small room. "What was that about? You walked out of there like I'd insulted you."

"You did." She removed the chunky beads from around her neck and put them on a nearby table. Two oversized bracelets soon followed. "You're disgusted with me. You never have to go through this with normal models. 'God only knows I've exposed enough film.' Did you have to say that, in that tone, for everyone in the room to hear?"

"It was a simple comment."

"It was an indictment."

"Then it was as much an indictment of me as it was of you. I'm the photographer! Half of my supposed skill is in drawing the mood and the look from a model!"

She was swiftly unbuttoning her blouse, heedless of Web's presence. "I'm the model. A rank amateur. You're the renowned photographer. If anyone's at fault, we both know who it is."

"Then you're angry at yourself, but don't lay that trip on me!"

"See? You agree!" She'd thrown the blouse aside and was fumbling with the waistband of her skirt. Her voice shook as she released the button and tugged down the zipper. "Well, I'm sorry if I've upset your normal pattern of success, but don't say I didn't warn you. Right from the beginning I knew this was a mad scheme. You need a *model,* an *experienced* model." She stumbled out of the skirt, threw it on top of the blouse, then grabbed for her own clothes and began to pull them on. "I can't be what you want, Web, no matter how much you want to think otherwise. I am what I am. I do what I do, and I do it well, and if there's baggage I carry—like little creases between my eyes—I can't help it." She'd stepped into her wool dress, but left it unbuttoned. Suddenly drained from her outburst, she lifted a hand to rub at those creases.

Web remained quiet. He'd reached the end of his own spurt of temper minutes ago and was simply waiting for her to calm down enough to listen to what he had to say. When she sighed and slumped into a nearby chair, he slowly approached and squatted beside her.

"Firstly, I'm not angry at you. If anything I'm angry at me, because there's something I'm missing and I don't know how to get at it. Secondly, I'm not really angry, just tired." He flexed his unbound fingers. "My left hand is stiff because I'm not used to working this way." He put his hand down on her knee. "Thirdly, and most importantly, it *is* you I want. I'm not looking for something you're not. I'm not trying to make you into someone else. You're such a unique and wonderful person Marni—it's *that* that I'm trying to capture on film…. Look at me," he said softly, drawing her hand from her face. "You're right. It is much easier photographing a 'normal model,' but only because there isn't half the depth, because I can put there what I want. Creating a mood, a look, is one thing. Bringing out feeling, *individual* feeling is another. Don't you see? That's what's going to make this issue of *Class* stand out on the shelves. Not only are you beautiful to look at, but you'll have all those other qualities shining out from you. The potential reader of *Class* will say to herself, 'Hmmm, this looks interesting.'"

Marni was eyeing him steadily. Her expression had softened, taking on a glimmer of helplessness. He brushed the backs of his fingers against her cheek, thinking how badly he wanted to reach her, to soothe her.

"But what happened this morning," he went on in a whisper-soft tone, "what we've been arguing about in here is really secondary. You've got something on your mind that you haven't been able to shake. Share it with me, Marni. If nothing more, talking about it will make you feel better. Maybe I can help."

She only wished it were so. How could she say that she was falling in love with him again, but that her parents would never accept it? That they hated him, that she'd spent the last fourteen years of her life trying to make up for Ethan's death by being what he might have been if he'd lived, and that she didn't know if she had the strength to shatter her parents' illusion?

"Oh, Web," she sighed, slipping her arms over his shoulders and leaning forward to rest her cheek against his. "Life is so complicated."

He stroked her hair. "It doesn't have to be."

"But it is. Sometimes I wish I could turn the clock back to when I was seventeen and stop it there. Ethan would be alive, and you and I would be carrying on without a care in the world."

"We had cares. There was the problem of where to go

so that we could be alone to love each other. And there was the problem of your parents, and what would happen if they found out about us."

Marni's arms tightened around him, and she rubbed her cheek against his jaw, welcoming the faint roughness that branded him man and so very different from her. She loved the smell of him, the feel of him. If only she could blot out the rest of the world...

"It's still a problem, isn't it, Marni?" She went very still, so he continued in the same gentle tone. "I'm no psychologist, but I've spent a lot of time thinking the past week, especially the past few days, about us and the future. Your parents despised me for what I was, and wasn't, and for what I'd done. They'd be a definite roadblock for us, wouldn't they?"

Just then a knock sounded at the door. Web twisted around and snapped, "Yes?"

The door opened, and a slightly timid Anne peered in. Uncomfortably, she looked from Web to Marni. "I'm sorry. I didn't mean to interrupt. I just wanted to know if there was anything I could do to help."

"No. Not just now," Marni said. "You can go back to the office. I'll be along later."

"I'll take a look at the contact sheets as soon as possible and let you know what I think," Web added quietly.

Anne nodded, then shut the door, at which point Web turned back to Marni.

She was gnawing on her lower lip. "Did you know that there was an article in the newspaper about the incident last Friday night?" she asked.

His jaw hardened. "Oh, yes. I got several calls from friends congratulating me on my heroism. Of all the things I'd like to be congratulated on, that isn't one. I could kick myself for not instructing the cops to leave our names off any report they might hand to the press. Neither of us needs that kind of publicity." He frowned. "You didn't mention the article when I spoke with you last night."

"I didn't know about it."

"Then...?"

"My mother called right after you did."

He blinked slowly, lifted his chin, then lowered it. He might have been saying, "Ahhhhhh, that explains it."

"If you can believe it, my sister Tanya brought it to her attention." Marni's voice took on a mildly hysterical note. "Neither of them made the connection, Web. Neither one of them associated Brian Webster, the photographer, with you."

"But you thought at first they might have," he surmised gently, "and it scared the living daylights out of you."

Apologetically Marni nodded, then slid forward in the chair and buried her face against his throat. Her thighs braced his waist, but there was nothing remotely sexual about the pose. "Hold me, Web. Just hold me...please?"

She sighed when he folded his arms around her, knowing in that instant that this would be all she needed in life if only the rest of humanity could fade away.

"Do you love me, Marni?" he asked hoarsely.

"I think I do," she whispered in dismay.

"And I love you. Don't you think that's a start?"

She raised her head. "You love me?"

"Uh-huh."

"When did you... You didn't before..."

He knew she was referring to that summer in Maine. "No, I didn't before. I was too young. You were too young. I didn't know where I was going, and the concept of love was beyond me."

"But when...?"

"Last weekend. After you left me, I realized that I didn't want anyone but you pushing aspirin down my throat."

She pinched his ribs, but she wasn't smiling. "Don't tease me."

"I'm not. No one's ever taken care of me before. I've always wanted to be strong and in command. But somehow being myself with you, being able to say that I'm tired or that I hurt, seemed right. Not that I want to do it all the time—I'm not a hypochondriac. But I want to be able to take care of you like you did me. TLC, and for the first time, the L means something."

Marni lowered her head and pressed closer to him, feeling the strong beat of his heart as though it and her own were all that existed. "I do love you, Web. The second time around it feels even stronger. If only…if only we could forget about everything else."

"We can."

"It's not possible."

"It is, for a little while, if we want."

She raised questioning eyes to his urgent ones.

"Come to Vermont with me this weekend. Just the two of us, alone and uninterrupted. We can talk everything out then and decide what to do, but most importantly we can be with each other. I think we need it. I think we deserve it…. What do you say?"

She sighed, feeling simultaneously hopeless and incredibly light-headed. "I say that it's crazy…. The whole thing's crazy, because the problems aren't going to go away…but how can I refuse?" A slow grin spread over her face, soon matched by his. He hugged her again, then kissed her. It was a sweet kiss, deep in emotion rather than physicality. When it ended, she clung to him for a long time. "I feel a little like I'm seventeen again and we've just arranged an illicit rendezvous. There's something exciting about stealing away, knowing my parents would be furious if they knew, but doing it all the same."

He took her face in his hands and spoke seriously. "We're adults now. Independent, consenting adults. In the end, it doesn't matter what your parents think, Marni."

Theoretically speaking, he was right, she knew. Idealistically she couldn't have agreed with him more. Practically speaking, though, it was a dream. But then, Web hadn't grown up in her house, with her parents. He hadn't gone into her family's business. He hadn't been in her shoes when Ethan had died, and he wasn't in her shoes now. "Later," she whispered. "We'll discuss it later. Right now, let's just be happy…"

MARNI WAS HAPPY. She blocked out all thoughts except one—that she loved Web and he loved her. And she was very happy. Business took her to Richmond on Wednesday morning, but she called Web that night, and he was at the airport to meet her when she returned on Thursday evening. Her suitcase had been emptied and repacked, and was waiting by her door when he came to pick her up late Friday afternoon.

"I hope you know I've shocked everyone at the office," she quipped, shrugging into her down jacket. "They've never known me to leave work so early."

He arched a brow. "Did you tell them where you were going?"

"Are you kidding? And spoil the sense of intrigue?"

Web was more practical. It wasn't that he wanted any interruptions during the weekend, but neither did he want the police out searching for her. "What if there's an emergency? What if someone needs to reach you and can't? Shouldn't you leave my number with someone?"

"Actually, I did. Just the number. With my administrative assistant. If anyone wants me that badly, they'll know to contact her. She'll be able to tell from the area code that I'm in Vermont, but that's about it."

Web was satisfied. He felt no fondness for her parents, but regardless of her age, they might worry if she seemed to have disappeared from the face of the earth. He knew that *he*'d be sick with worry if he tried to reach her and no one knew where she was.

"Good girl," was all he said before grabbing her suitcase and leading her to the waiting car.

The drive north was progressively relaxing. The tension of the day-to-day world, embodied by the congestion of traffic, thinned out and faded. Marni's excitement grew. Her eyes brightened, her cheeks took on a natural rosy glow. She had only to look to her left and see Web for her heart to feel lighter and lighter until she felt she was floating as weightlessly as those few snowflakes that drifted through the cold Vermont night air.

Web suggested that they stop for supplies at the village market near his house, so that they wouldn't have to go out again if the weather got bad. Marni was in full agreement.

"So where is your place?" she asked when they'd left the market behind. "I see houses and lots of condominium complexes—"

"They're sprouting up everywhere. Vacation resort areas, they're called. You buy your own place, then get the use of a central facility that usually includes a clubhouse, a restaurant or two, a pool, sometimes a lake or even a small ski slope. Not exactly my style, and I'm not thrilled with all the development. Pretty soon the place will be overrun with people. Fortunately where I am is off the beaten track."

"Where *are* you?"

He grinned and squeezed her knee. "Coming soon, sunshine. Be patient. Coming soon."

Not long after, he turned off the main road onto a smaller dirt one. The car jogged along, climbing steadily until at last they reached a clearing.

Marni caught her breath. "It's a log cabin," she cried in delight. "And you're on your own mountain!"

"Not completely on my own, but the nearest neighbor is a good twenty-minute trek through the trees." He pulled into the shelter of an oversized carport on the far side of the house.

"This is great! What a change from the city!"

"That's why I like it." He turned off the engine and opened his door. "Come on. It'll be cold inside, but the heat'll come up pretty quickly."

"Heat? That *has* to be from an old Franklin stove."

He chuckled. "I'm afraid I'm more pampered than that. It's baseboard heating. But I do have a huge stone fireplace…if that makes you feel better."

"Oh, yes," she breathed, then quickly climbed from the car and tugged her coat around her. The air was dry, with a sharp nip to it. Snow continued to fall, but it was light, enchanting rather than threatening. Marni wondered if anything could threaten her at that moment. She felt bold and excited and happy.

She looked at Web and beamed. She was in love, and in this place, so far from the city, she felt free.

CHAPTER SIX

To MARNI'S AMAZEMENT, what had appeared to be a log cabin was, from within, like no log cabin she'd ever imagined. Soon after Web had bought the place, he'd had it gutted and enlarged. Rich barnboard from ceiling to floor sealed in the insulation he'd added. The furniture was likewise of barnboard, but plushly cushioned in shades of hunter green and cocoa. Though there was a hall leading to the addition that housed Web's bedroom and a small den, all Marni saw at first was the large living area, with the kitchen and dining area at its far end. Oh, yes, there was a huge stone fireplace. But rather than being set into a wall as she'd pictured, it was a three-hundred-and-sixty-degree one with steel supports that would cast its warm glow over the entire room.

Like the apartment above Web's studio, there was a sparseness to the decor, a cleanness of line, though it was very clearly country rather than city, and decidedly cozy.

After Marni had admired everything with unbounded enthusiasm, she helped Web stow the food they'd bought. Then he opened a bottle of wine, poured them each a glass and led her to the living area, where he set to work building a fire. The kindling caught and burned, and the dried logs were beginning to flame when he came to sit beside her on the sofa, opening an arm in an invitation she accepted instantly.

"I'm so happy I'm here with you," she whispered, rubbing her cheek against the wool of his sweater as she snuggled close to him.

He tightened his arm and pressed a slow kiss to her forehead. "So am I. This has always been my private refuge. Now it's *our* private refuge, and nothing could seem righter."

She tipped her head back. "Righter? Is that a word?"

"It is now," he murmured, then lowered his head and took her lips in a slow, deep, savoring kiss that left Marni reeling. Dizzily she set her wine on the floor and shifted, with Web's eager help, onto his lap, coiling her arms around his neck, closing her eyes in delight as she brushed her cheek against his jaw.

"I love you," she whispered, "love you so much, Web."

He set his own wine down and framed her face with his hands. His mouth breezed over each of her features before renewing acquaintance with her mouth. A deep, moist kiss, a shift in the angle of his head, a second deep, moist kiss. The exchange of breath in pleasured sighs. The evocative play of tongues, tips touching, circling, sliding along each other's length.

Marni hadn't had more than a sip of her wine, but she was high on love, high on freedom. She was breathing shallowly, with her head resting on his shoulder, when he began to caress her. She held her breath, concentrating on the intensity of sensation radiating from his touch. He spread his large hands around her waist, moved them up over her ribs and around to her back in slow, sensitizing strokes.

"I love you, sunshine," he whispered hoarsely, deeply affected by her sweet scent, her softness and warmth, her pliance, her emotional commitment. He brought his hands forward and inched them upward, covering her breasts, kneading them gently as she sighed against his neck.

Everything was in slow motion, unreal but exquisitely

real. He caressed her breasts while she stroked the hair at his nape. He stroked her nipples while she caressed his back. They kissed again, and it was an exchange of silent vows, so deep and heartfelt that Marni nearly cried at its beauty.

"I was going to give you time," Web whispered roughly. His body was taut with a need he couldn't have hidden if he tried. "I was going to give you time…I hadn't intended an instant seduction."

"Neither had I," she breathed no less roughly. Her eyes held the urgency transmitted by the rest of her body. "I'm so pleased just to be here with you…but I want you…want to make love to you."

As much as her words inflamed him, he couldn't forget the last time they'd tried. "Are you sure? No doubts? Or guilt?"

She was shaking her head, very sure. "Not here. Not now." She pulled at his sweater. "Take this off. I want to touch you."

He whipped the sweater over his head, and she started working at the buttons of his shirt. When they were released, she spread the fabric wide, gave a soft sigh of relief and splayed her fingers over his hair-covered chest.

"You're so beautiful," she whispered in awe. Her hands moved slowly, exploring the sinewed swells of him, delving to the tight muscles of his middle before rising again and seeking the flat nipples nested amid whirls of soft, dark hair. She rubbed their tips until they stood hard, and didn't take her eyes from her work until Web forced her head up and hungrily captured her mouth.

His kiss left her breathless, and forehead to forehead they panted until at length he reached for the hem of her sweater and slowly drew it up and over her head. Slowly, too, he released one button, then the next, and in an instant's clear thought Marni reflected on the leisure of their approach. Fourteen years ago, when they'd come together for the first time, it had been in a fevered rush of arms and legs and bodies. Last Saturday the fever had been similar, as though they'd had to consummate their union before either of them had had time to think.

This time was different. They were in love. They were alone, in the cocoon of a cabin whose solid walls, whose surrounding forest warded off any and every enemy. This time there was a beauty in discovering and appreciating every inch of skin, every swell, every sensual conduit. This time it was heaven from the start.

Entranced, Marni watched as Web pushed her blouse aside. He unhooked her bra and gently peeled it from her breasts, then with a soft moan he very slowly traced her fullness, with first his fingertips, then the flat of his fingers, then his palm. She was swelling helplessly toward him, biting her lip to keep from crying out, when he finally took the full weight of her swollen flesh and molded his hands to it. His thumbs brushed over her nipples. Already taut, they puckered all the more, and she had to press her thighs together to still what was too quickly becoming a raging inferno.

Web didn't miss the movement. "Here…" He raised her for an instant, brought her leg around so that she straddled him, and settled her snugly against his crotch. With that momentary comfort, he returned his attention to her breasts.

"Web…Web…" she breathed. Her arms were looped loosely around his neck, her forehead hot against his shoulder. He was stroking her nipples again, and the action sent live currents through her body to her womb. Helplessly, reflexively, she began to slowly undulate her hips. "What you do to me—it's so…powerful…."

"It's what I feel for you, what you feel for me that makes it so good."

She was shaking her head in amazement. "I used to think it was good back then...because we do have this instant attraction...but I can't *believe* what...I'm feeling now."

"Then feel, sunshine." He slipped his hands to her shoulders and pushed her blouse completely off, then her bra. "I want you to feel this..." He cupped her breasts and brought them to his chest, rubbing nipple to nipple until she wasn't the only one to moan. "And this..." He sought her lips and kissed her hotly, while his fingers found the snap of her jeans, lowered the zipper and slid inside.

He was touching her then, opening her, stroking deeper and deeper until she was moving against his hand, taking tiny, gasping breaths, instinctively stretching her thighs apart in a need for more.

Her control was slipping, but she didn't want it to. She wanted the beauty to last forever, no, longer. Putting a shaky hand around Web's wrist, she begged him, "Please... I want to touch you, too...I need to..."

"But I want you to come," he said in a hushed whisper by her ear.

"This way, later. The first time—now—I want you inside. Please...take off your pants, Web..."

His fingers stopped their sweet torment and slowly, reluctantly, withdrew. He didn't move to take off his clothes until he'd kissed her so thoroughly that she thought she'd disintegrate there and then. But she didn't, and he shifted her from his lap, sat forward to rid himself of his shirt, then stood and peeled off the rest of his clothes. For a moment, just before lowering his jeans, he suddenly wished he hadn't been as adept at building that fire and that it was still pitch-black in the room. The last thing he wanted was to spoil the mood by having Marni see his scars. But they were there; he couldn't erase them, and if she loved him...

Marni sat watching, enthralled as more and more of his flesh was revealed. It was a long minute before she even saw his leg, so fascinated had she been with what else was now bare. But inevitably her gaze fastened on the multiple lines, some jagged, others straight, that formed a frightening pattern along the length of his right thigh

"Web?" She caught her breath and, eyes filling with tears, looked up at him. "You didn't tell me... I didn't know...."

Quickly he knelt by her side and took both of her hands tightly in his. "Forget them, sweetheart. They're part of the past, and the past has no place here and now."

"But so many—"

"And all healed. No pain. No limp. Forget them. They don't matter." When she remained doubtful, he began to whisper kisses over her face. "Forget them," he breathed against her eyelids, then her lips. "Just love me...I need that more than anything..."

More than anything, that was what Marni needed, too. So she forgot. She pushed all thought of his scars and what had caused them from her mind. He was right. The past had no place here and now, and she refused to let it infringe on her present happiness. There would be a time to discuss scars she assured herself dazedly, but that time wasn't now, when the tender kisses he was raining over her face and throat, when the intimate sweep of his hands on her breasts was making clear thought an impossibility.

Her already simmering blood began to boil when he stood and reached for her hands to draw her up. She resisted, instead flattening her palms on his abdomen, moving them around and down. Gently, wonderingly, she encircled him and began a rhythmic stroking.

If he'd had any qualms about her reaction to his forty-year-old body, or fears that the sight of his leg would dull her desire, they were put soundly to rest by her worshipful ministration. He was digging his fingers into her shoulders by the time she leaned and pressed soft, wet kisses to his navel. Her hands, holding him, were between her breasts. Tucking in her chin, she slid her lips lower.

He was suddenly forcing her chin up, a pained smile on his face. "You don't play fair," he managed tightly. "I'm not made of stone."

"But I want you to—"

"This way, later," he whispered, repeating her earlier words. "For now, though, you were right..." When he reached for her hands this time, she stood, then with his help took off the rest of her clothes. They looked at each other, drenched in the pale orange glow of the fire. Then they came together, bare bodies touching for the first time in fourteen years, and it was so strangely new yet familiar, so stunningly electric yet right, that once again tears filled Marni's eyes and this time trickled down her cheeks.

Web felt them against his chest, and his arms tightened convulsively around her. "Oh, no..."

"Just joy, Web," she said as she laughed, then sniffled. "Tears of joy." She had her arms wrapped around his neck and held on while he lowered them both to the woven rug before the fire. Bracing himself on his elbows, he traced the curve of her lips with the tip of his tongue. She tried to capture him, but he eluded her, so she raised her head and tried again. Soon he was thrusting his tongue into her welcoming mouth, thrusting and retreating only to thrust again when she whimpered in protest at the momentary loss.

She welcomed the feel of his large body over hers. She felt sheltered, protected, increasingly aroused by everything masculine about him. Her hands skated over the corded swells of his back, glided to his waist and spread over his firm buttocks. She arched up to the hand he'd slipped between their bodies and offered him her breasts, her belly, the smoldering spot between her legs.

They touched and caressed, whispered soft words of love, of pleasure, of urging as their mutual need grew. It was as if nothing in the world could touch them but each other, as if that touch was life-giving and life-sustaining to the extent that their beings were defined by it. Web's lips gave form and substance to each of Marni's features, as his hands did to her every feminine curve. Her mouth gave shape and purpose to his, as her hands did to his every masculine line.

Finally, locked in each other's gaze, they merged fully. Web filled her last empty place, bowed his back and pressed even more deeply until he touched the entrance to her womb.

"I love you," he mouthed, unable to produce further sound.

The best she could do was to brokenly mouth the words back. Her breath seemed caught in her throat, trapped by the intensity of the moment. She'd never felt as much of a person, as much of a woman as she did now, with Web's masculinity surrounding her, filling her, completing her. Fourteen years ago they'd made love, and it had been breathtaking, too, but so different. Now she was old enough to understand and appreciate the full value of what she and Web shared. The extraordinary pleasure was emotional as well as physical, a total commitment on both of their parts to that precious quality of togetherness.

Web felt it, too. As he held himself still, buried deep inside Marni, he knew that he'd never before felt the same pleasure, the same satisfaction with another woman. The pleasure, the satisfaction, encompassed not only his body but his mind and heart as well, and the look of wonder on Marni's face told him the feeling was shared.

Slowly he began to move, all the while watching her. Waves of bliss flowed over her features as he thrust gently, then with increasing speed and force as she moved in tempo beneath him. The act he'd carried through so many times before seemed to have taken on an entirely new and incredible intimacy that added fuel to the flame in his combustive body.

Harder and deeper he plunged, his ardor matched by her increasing abandon. Before long they were both lost in a world of glorious sensation, a world that grew suddenly brilliant, then blinding. Marni caught her breath, arched up and was suspended for a long moment before shattering into paroxysms of mindless delight. The air left her lungs in choked spurts, but she was beyond noticing, as was Web, whose own body tensed, then jerked, then shuddered.

Only when the spasms had ended and his limbs grew suddenly weak did he collapse over her with a drawn-out moan. "Marni...my God! I've never...*never*..." He buried his face in the damp tendrils of hair at her neck and whispered, "I love you...so much..."

Marni was as limp and weak, but nothing could have kept the broad smile from her face. Words seemed inadequate, so she simply draped her arms over his shoulders, closed her eyes...and smiled on.

It was some time later before either of them moved, and then it was Web, sliding to her side, bringing her along to face him. He brushed the wayward fall of hair from her cheeks and let his hand lightly caress her earlobe.

"You give so much, so much," he whispered. "I almost feel as though I don't deserve it."

She pressed her fingers to his lips, then stroked them gently. "I could say the same to you."

He smiled crookedly. "So why don't you?"

"Because you know how I feel."

"Tell me anyway. My ego needs boosting, since the rest of me is totally deflated."

She grinned, but the grin mellowed into a tender smile as she spoke. "You're warm and compassionate, incredibly intelligent and sensitive. And you're sexy as hell."

"Not right now."

"Yes, right now." She raked the hair from his brow and let her fingers tangle in its thickness. "Naked and sweaty and positively gorgeous, you'd bring out the animal in me—" she gave a rueful chuckle "—if I had the strength."

"S'okay," he murmured, rolling to his back and drawing her against him, "a soft, purring kitten is all I can handle right about now. You exhaust me, sunshine, inside and out."

"The feeling's mutual, Brian Webster," she sighed, but it was a happy sigh, in keeping with the moment.

They lay quietly for a time, listening to the beat of each other's heart, the lazy cadence of their breathing, the crackling of the fire behind them.

"It's funny, hearing you call me that," he mused, rubbing his chin against her hair. "Brian. It sounds so formal."

"Not formal, just…strange. I keep trying to picture your mother calling you that when you were a little boy. 'Brian! Come in the house this minute, Brian!' When did they start calling you Web?"

"My mother never did, or my stepfather, for that matter. But the kids in school—you know how kids are, trying to act tough calling each other by their last names, then when they're a little older finding nicknames that fit. Web just seemed to fit. By the time I'd graduated from high school, I really thought of myself as Web."

"Did you consciously decide to revert to Brian when you got into photography?"

"It was more a practical thing at that point. I had to sign my name to legal forms—model releases, magazine contracts, that kind of thing. People started calling me Brian." He gave a one-shouldered shrug. "So Brian I became. Again."

"We'll call our son Brian."

He jerked his head up and stared at her. "Our son?"

She put her fingers back on his lips. "Shhh. Don't say another word. This is a dream weekend, and I'm going to say whatever I feel like saying without even thinking of 'why' or 'if' or 'how.' I intend to give due consideration to every impulse that crosses my mind, and the impulse on my mind at this particular moment is what we'll name our son. Brian. I do like it."

Once over the initial shock of Marni's blithe reference to "our son," Web found that he liked her impulsiveness. He grinned. "You're a nut. Has anyone ever told you that?"

"No. No one. I'm not usually prone to nuttiness. You do something to my mind, Web. Or maybe log cabins do something to me. Or mountains."

He propped himself on an elbow and smiled down at her. "Tell me more. What other impulses would you like to give due consideration to?"

"Dinner. I'm starved. Maybe *that*'s why I'm momentarily prone to nuttiness. I didn't eat lunch so I could leave the office that much earlier, and I can't remember breakfast, it was that long ago. I think I'm running on fumes."

Web nuzzled her neck. "I love these fumes. Mmmm, do I love these fumes."

Light-headed and laughing, Marni clung to him until, with a final nip at her neck, he hauled himself to his feet and gave her a hand up. He cleared his throat. "Dinner. I think I could use it, too." He ran his eyes the length of her flushed and slender body. "Did you bring a robe?"

"Uh-huh."

"Think you could get it?"

"Uh-huh."

"…Well?"

She hadn't moved. Her eyes were on his leanly muscled frame. "Have *you* got one?"

"Uh-huh."

"Think you could get it?"

"Uh-huh."

"…Well?"

Their gazes met then, and they both began to smile. If they'd been back in New York, they'd probably have made love again there and then, lest they lose the opportunity. But they were in Vermont, with the luxury of an entire weekend before them. There was something to be said for patience, and anticipation.

With a decidedly male growl, Web dragged her to his side and started off toward the bedroom, where he'd left their bags. Moments later, dressed in terry velour robes that were coincidentally similar in every respect but color—Web's was wine, Marni's white—they set to the very pleasant task of making dinner together. When Web opted out of chores such as slicing tomatoes and mushrooms for a salad, claiming that he was hampered by his injured hand, Marni mischievously remarked that his injured hand hadn't hampered his amorous endeavors. When Marni opted out of putting a match to the pilot light of the stove, claiming that she didn't like to play with fire, Web simply arched a devilish brow in silent contradiction.

They ate by the fire, finishing the wine they'd barely sipped earlier. Then, leaving their dishes on the floor nearby, they made sweet, slow love again. This time each touched and tasted the spots that had been denied earlier; this time they both reached independent peaks before their bodies finally joined. The lack of urgency that resulted made the coming together and the leisurely climb and culmination all the more meaningful. Though their bodies would give out in time, they knew, their emotional desire was never-ending.

After talking, then listening to soft music for a while as they gazed into the fire, they finally retired to Web's big bed. When they fell asleep in each other's arms, they felt as satisfied as if they'd made love yet again.

Saturday was a sterling day, one to be remembered by them both for a long time to come. They slept late, awoke to make love, then devoured a hearty brunch in the kitchen. Though the snow had stopped sometime during the night, the fresh inch or two on top of the existing crust gave a crispness, a cleanness to the hilly woodlands surrounding the cabin.

Bundled warmly against the cold, they took a long walk in the early afternoon. It didn't matter that Marni couldn't begin to make out a path; Web knew the woods by heart, and she trusted him completely.

"So beautiful…" Her breath was a tiny cloud, evaporating in the dry air as she looked around her. Tall pines towered above, their limbs made all the more regal by the snowy epaulets they wore. Underfoot the white carpet was patterned, not only by the footprints behind them and the tracks of birds and other small forest creatures, but by the swish of low-hanging branches in the gentle breeze and the fall of powdery clumps from branches. The silence was so reverent across the mountainside that she felt intrusive even when she murmured in awe, "Don't you wish you had a camera?"

It had been a totally innocent question, an unpremeditated one. Realizing the joke in it, Marni grinned up at Web. "That was really dumb. You *do* have a camera... camera*s*. I'd have thought you'd be out here taking pictures of everything."

He smiled back at her, thoroughly relaxed. "It's too peaceful."

"But it's beautiful!"

"A large part of that beauty is being here with you."

She gave a playful tug at the arm hers was wrapped around. "Flattery, flattery—"

"But I'm serious. Look around you now and try to imagine that you were alone, that we didn't have each other, that you were here on the mountain running away from some horrible threat or personal crisis.... How would you feel?"

"Cold."

"Y'see? People see things differently depending on where they're coming from. Right now I'm exactly where I want to be. I don't think I've ever felt as happy or content in my life. So you're right, this scene is absolutely beautiful."

Standing on tiptoe, she kissed his cheek, then tightened her arm through his. "Do you ever photograph up here?"

He shrugged. "I don't have a camera up here."

"You're kidding."

"Nope. This is my getaway. I knew from the first that if I allowed myself to bring a camera here, it wouldn't be a true escape."

"But you love photography, don't you?"

"I love my work, but photography in and of itself has never become an obsession with me. I've met some colleagues, both men and women, whose cameras are like dog tags around their necks. It gives them their identity. I've never wanted that. The camera is the tool of my trade, much like a calculator or computer is for an accountant,

or a hammer is for a carpenter. Have you ever seen a carpenter go away for the weekend with his tool belt strapped
around his waist just in case he sees a nail sticking out
on someone's house or on the back wall of a restaurant?"

Marni grinned. "No, I guess I haven't…. Why are you
looking at me that way?"

"You just look so pretty, all bundled up and rosy-
cheeked. You look as happy and content as I feel. I almost
wish I did have a camera, but I'm not sure I could begin to
capture what you are. Some things are better left as very
special images in the mind." He grew even more pensive.

"What is it?" she asked softly.

"Impulse time. Can I do it, too?"

"Sure. What's your impulse?"

"To photograph you out here in the woods. In the summer. Stark naked."

She quivered in excitement. "That's a naughty impulse."

"But that's not all." His blue eyes were glowing. "I'd
like to photograph you in bed right after we've made love.
You're all rosy-cheeked then too, and naked, but bundled
up in love."

She draped her arms over his shoulders. "Mmmm. I
like that one."

"But that's not all."

"There's more?"

"Uh-huh." His arms circled her waist. "I'd like to photograph you in bed right after we've made love. You're naked
and rosy and wrapped in love. And you're pregnant. You're
breasts are fuller, with tiny veins running over them, and
your belly is round, the skin stretched tightly, protectively
over our child."

Marni sucked in her breath and buried her face against
the fleece lining of his collar. "That's…beautiful, Web."

"But that's not all."

She gave a plaintive moan. "I'm not sure I can take much more of this. My legs feel like water."

"Then I'll support you." True to his words, he tightened his arms around her. "I'd like to photograph you with our child at your breast. It could be a little Brian, or a little girl named Sunshine or Bliss or Liberty—"

She looked sharply up in mock rebuke. "You wouldn't."

"Wouldn't photograph you breast-feeding our child? You bet your sweet—"

"Wouldn't name the poor thing Sunshine or Bliss or Liberty. Do you have any idea what she'd go through, saddled with any one of those names?"

"Then you choose the name. Anything your heart desires."

Marni thought for a minute. "I kind of like Alana, or Arielle, or Amber—no, not Amber. It doesn't go well with Webster."

"You're partial to *A*'s?"

She tipped up her chin. "Nope. Just haven't gotten to the *B*'s yet."

She never did get to the *B*'s because he hugged her, and she was momentarily robbed of breath. When he released her long enough to loop his arm through hers again and start them along the path once more, he was thinking of things besides children. "We could keep your place if you'd like. Mine above the studio wouldn't be as appropriate for the entertaining you have to do."

"I don't know about that. It might spice things up. If we were really doing something big, we could use the studio itself, or rent space at a restaurant. I think I'd like the idea of knowing you'd be there whenever I came home from work."

"Would you have to travel much?"

"I could cut it down."

"I'd feel lonely when you were away."

"Maybe you could come." Her eyes lit up. "I mean, if I knew far enough in advance so that you could rearrange your schedule, we could take care of my business and have a vacation for ourselves."

"With Brian or Arielle or whoever?"

"By ourselves. Two adults doing adult things. We'd leave the baby with a sitter…. Uh-oh, that could be one drawback about living above your studio. You wouldn't get much work done with a squalling baby nearby."

"Are you kidding? I'd love it! I mean, we would hire someone to take care of the baby, and no baby of ours is going to be squalling all the time. I'd be able to see him or her during breaks or when the sitter was passing through the studio going out for walks. I'd be proud as punch to show off my child. And I'd be right there in case of any problem or emergency."

"But you shoot on location sometimes."

"Less and less in the last year or so, and I've reached the stage where I could cut it out entirely if I wanted to. Just think of it. It'd be an ideal situation." His cheeks were ruddy, and his blue eyes sparkled.

"You really mean that, don't you?"

"You bet. I never knew my own father. I want to know my children and have them know me."

"Child*ren?* Oh, boy, how many are we having?"

"Two, maybe three. More if you'd like, but I'd hate to think of your being torn between your work and a whole brood of kids. I'm told that working mothers suffer a certain amount of guilt even with one child."

He was right, but she couldn't resist teasing him. "Who told you that?"

He shrugged. "I read."

"What?"

"Oh…lots of things."

She couldn't contain a grin. His cheeks were a dead giveaway, suddenly redder in a way that couldn't be from the cold. "Women's magazines?"

"Hell, my photographs are in them. Okay, sometimes one article or another catches my eye."

"And how long have you been reading about working mothers?"

"One article, Marni, that's it. It was—I don't know—maybe six or seven months ago."

"Did you know then that you wanted to have kids?"

"I've known for a long time, and when I read the article it was simply to satisfy an abstract curiosity." Smoothly, and with good humor, he took the offensive. "And you should be grateful that I *do* read. I'm thinking of you, sweet. Anything I've learned will make things easier for you."

"I'm not worried," she hummed, with a smile on her face.

They continued to walk, neither of them bothered by the cold air, if even aware of it. They were wrapped up in their world of dreams, a warm world where the sun was shining brightly. They talked of what they'd do in their leisure time, where they'd travel for vacations, what their children might be when they grew up.

The mood continued when they returned to the cabin. Marni sat on a barrel in the carport watching Web split logs for the fire. He sat on a stool in the kitchen watching her prepare a chicken-and-broccoli casserole. They sat by the fire talking of politics, the economy and foreign affairs, dreaming on, kissing, making love. Arms and legs entwined, they slept deeply that night—a good thing, because Sunday morning they awoke with the knowledge that before the day was through they'd be back in the real world facing those problems neither of them had been willing to discuss before.

Web lay in bed, staring at the ceiling. Marni was in a nearly identical position by his side. They'd been awake for a while, though neither had spoken. A thick quilt covered them, suddenly more necessary than it had seemed all weekend, for now they were thinking of an aspect of the future that was chilling to them both.

"What are we going to do about your parents, Marni?" Web asked. He'd contemplated approaching the topic gradually, but now he saw no point in beating around the bush.

She didn't twist her head in surprise, or even blink. "I don't know."

"What will they say if you announce that we're getting married?"

"Married. Funny...we haven't used that word before."

He tipped his head to look at her. "It was taken for granted, wasn't it?"

She met his gaze and spoke softly. "Yes."

"And you want it, don't you?"

"Yes."

"So—" his gaze drifted away "—what will they say?"

"They'll hit the roof."

He nodded, then swallowed. "How will you feel about that?"

"Pretty sick."

"It bothers you what they think?"

"Of course it does. They're my parents."

"You're not a child. You're old enough to make your own decisions."

"I know that, and I do make my own decisions every day of the week. This, well, this is a little tougher."

"Many adults have differences with their parents."

"But there are emotional issues here, very strong emotional issues."

"They blame me for Ethan's death."

"They blame you for everything that happened that summer."

"But mostly for Ethan's death." He sat up abruptly and turned to her, feelings he'd held in for years suddenly splintering outward. "Don't they know it was an accident? Those two cars collided and began spinning all over the road. There was no possible way I could have steered clear. Hell, we were wearing helmets, but a motorcycle didn't have any more of a chance against either of those monsters than Ethan's neck had against that tree."

Marni was lying stiffly, determined to say it all now. "It was your motorcycle. They felt that if Ethan had been with anyone else he would have been in a car and survived."

Frustrated, Web thrust his fingers through his hair. "I didn't force Ethan to come with me. For that matter, I didn't force Ethan to become my friend."

"But you were friends. My parents blame that on you, too."

"They saw their son as wasting his time with a no-good bum like me. Well, they were wrong, damn it! They were wrong! My friendship with Ethan was good for *both* of us. Ethan got a helluva lot more from me than he was getting from those other guys he hung around with, and I got more from him than you could ever believe. My, God! He was my friend! Do you think I wasn't crushed by his death?"

Tears glistened on his lower lids. Marni saw them and couldn't look away. She wanted to hold him, to comfort him, but at the moment there was a strange distance between them. She was a Lange. She was one of *them*.

"Y'know, Marni," he began in a deep voice that shook, "I lay in that hospital room bleeding on the inside long

after they'd stitched me up on the outside. I hurt in ways
no drug could ease. Yes, I felt guilty. It was my motorcycle, and I was driving, and if I'd been going a little faster
or a little slower we would have missed that accident and
been safe…. I called your father from the hospital. Did
you know that?"

Eyes glued to his, she swallowed. "No."

"Well, I did. The day after the accident, when I'd been
out from under the anesthetic long enough to be able to lift
the phone. It was painful, lifting that phone. I had three
cracked ribs, and my thigh was shattered into so many
pieces that it had taken five hours of surgery to make some
order out of it—and that's not counting the two operations
that followed. But nothing, *nothing* I felt physically could
begin to compare with the pain your father inflicted on
me. He didn't ask how I was, didn't stop to think that I was
hurting or that I was torn up by the knowledge that Ethan
had died and I was alive. No, all he asked was whether I
was satisfied, whether I was pleased I'd destroyed a life
that would have been so much more meaningful, so much
more productive than mine had ever been or could be."

An anger rose in Marni, so great that she could no longer bear the thought of presenting her parents' side of the
story. She sat up and moved to Web, her own eyes flooding as she curled her hands around his neck. "He had no
right to say that! It *wasn't* your fault! I told him that over
and over again, but he wouldn't listen to me. I was an irresponsible seventeen-year-old who'd been stupid to have
been involved with you, he said. That showed how much
I knew."

Web dragged in a long, shaky breath. He was looking
at her, but not actually seeing her. His vision was on the
past. "I cried. I lay there holding the phone and cried. The
nurse finally came in and took it out of my hand, but I kept

on crying until I was so tired and in so much pain that I just couldn't cry anymore."

She brushed at the moisture in the corners of his eyes, though his face was blurred to her gaze. "I'm so sorry, Web," she whispered. "So sorry. He was wrong, and cruel. There was nothing you could have done to prevent that accident. It wasn't your fault!"

"But I felt guilty. I still do."

"What about me?" she cried. "If it hadn't been for me—for my pestering the two of you to take me along—you would have been in Ethan's car as you'd originally planned. Don't you think that's haunted me all these years? I tried to tell that to my father, too, because it hurt so much when he put the full blame on you, but he wouldn't listen. All he could think of was that Ethan, his only son and primary heir, was gone. And my mother seconded everything he said, especially when he forbade me to see you again."

"What about Tanya? Didn't she come to your defense?"

"Tanya, who'd been itching for you from the first moment she knew we were involved with each other? No, Tanya didn't come to my defense. She told my mother everything she knew, about the times I'd said I was out with friends but was actually out with you. She was legitimately upset about Ethan, I have to say that much for her. But she did nothing to help me through what was a double devastation. She sided with my parents all the way."

Marni hung her head. Tears stained her cheeks, and her hands clutched Web's shoulders for the solace that his muscled strength could offer. "I wanted to go to you, Web." Her voice was small and riddled with pain. "I kept thinking of you in that hospital, even when we returned to Long Island for the funeral. I wanted to go back to Maine to see you, because I needed to know you were okay and I needed your comfort. You'd meant so much to me that summer.

I'd been in love with you, and I felt that you might be the only one to help me get over Ethan's death."

"But they wouldn't let you come."

"They said that if I made any move to contact you, they'd disinherit me. That if I tried to see you, they'd know that they'd failed as parents."

He smoothed her hair back around her ears, then said softly, "I waited. I was hoping you'd come, or call, because I thought maybe you could make me feel a little better about what had happened. I was in that godforsaken small-town hospital for two months—"

"How could I go against them?" she cried, trying desperately to justify what she'd done. "Regardless of how wrong they were about you, they were grief-stricken over Ethan. It wasn't the threat of being disinherited that bothered me. It wasn't a matter of money. But they'd given me everything for seventeen years. You'd given me other things, but for barely two months." She took a quick breath. "You said that you thought I was headstrong in my way even then, but I wasn't really, Web. I couldn't stand up for something I wanted. I'd already disappointed my parents. I couldn't do it again. They were going through too rough a time. Dad was never the same after the accident."

Web's expression had softened, and his voice was tinged with regret. "None of us were. That accident was the turning point in my life." His words hung, heavy and profound, in the air for a minute. Then he turned, propped the pillows against the headboard and settled Marni against him as he leaned back. "My leg kept getting infected and wouldn't heal, so I was transferred to a place in Boston. The specialist my stepfather found opened the whole thing up and practically started from scratch again, and between that and a second, less extensive operation, I was hospitalized for another six weeks. I had lots of time to think. Lots of time.

"Ethan and I, I realized, each represented half of an ideal world. He had financial stability, but though many of the things he had told me about in those hours we spent together sounded wonderful, they didn't come free. I had freedom and a sense of adventure, but without roots or money I was limited as to what I could do in life. As I lay there, I thought a lot about my father and about why I'd been running, and it was then I realized I wanted something more in life. Your parents thought I was dirt, and I felt like it after the accident. But I didn't want to be dirt. I wanted to be *someone*, not just a jock moving from job to job and place to place." He stroked her arm as though needing to reassure himself that he'd found a measure of personal stability at last.

"What happened to Ethan made me think about my own mortality," he went on in a solemn voice. "If I'd died then and there, no one—well, other than my immediate family—would have missed me, and it was questionable as to whether they'd really miss me, since I'd never been around all that much." He took a deep breath. "So I hooked onto that dig in New Mexico. It was the first time I'd ever done something with an eye toward the future. By the time I realized I'd never make it as a writer, my pictures were selling. I was on my way. I don't think anything could have stopped me from pushing ahead full steam at that point."

Marni, who'd been listening quietly, raised her face to his. "You've done Ethan proud. He gave you the motivation, and you worked your way up from scratch to become very successful."

Web was studying her tenderly. "And what about you? You've done much of what you have for him, too, haven't you?"

"For him...and my parents." She rushed on before he could argue. "I grieved so long after the accident, for both Ethan and you, and the sadness and guilt I felt were getting me nowhere. I decided that the only way I could redeem myself was to make my parents proud of me. Yes, I've tried to fill Ethan's shoes. I'm sure I haven't done it in the same way he would have, but I do think I've filled a certain void for my parents. After Ethan's death, Dad began to lose interest in the business. My decision to enter it was like a shot in the arm for him. Of course shots wear off after a while, and he eased away from the corporation earlier than he might have, but by then I was trained and ready to take over."

"You felt you were making up to your parents for having played a small part in Ethan's death."

Her whispered "Yes" was barely audible, but a shudder passed through Web, and he held her tightly to him.

"We've both suffered. We paid the fine for what we'd done, or thought we'd done, but the suffering isn't over if your parents are going to stand between us." They'd come full stride. "What are we going to do about them, Marni?"

"I don't know," she murmured, teeth gritted against the helplessness that assailed her. "I don't know."

"We'll have to tell them. We'll have to present ourselves and our best arguments to them—"

"Not 'we.' It'd never work that way, Web. They'd never listen. Worse, they'd kick you out of the house. It'd be better if I spoke with them first. I could break it to them gently."

"God, it's like we've committed some kind of crime."

"In their minds we have. What I've done will be tantamount to treason in their minds."

"They'll just have to change their way of thinking."

"That's easier said than done."

"What other choice will they have? They can't very well kick their own grown-up daughter out of the house. And then there's the matter of the corporation presidency. Your father may be chairman of the board, but no board worth its salt is going to evict its president simply because she falls in love with someone her father doesn't like. You've done a good job, Marni. You're invaluable to the corporation."

"Not invaluable. Certainly not indispensable. But I'm not really worried about anything happening at work. Dad wouldn't go *that* far. What I fear most is what will happen at home. Ethan's death left a gaping hole. Every time the family got together, we were aware of his absence. If Mom and Dad push us away because of my relationship with you, the unit will be that much weaker. If they could only reconcile themselves to gaining a son, rather than losing a daughter…"

"Reconcile. A powerful word."

Marni was deep in thought. "Mmmm…. What if I break it to them gently? Mother hasn't made the connection between you and that other Web. Apparently neither has Dad, since he didn't make a peep over the plans to use you as cover photographer for *Class*. What if I were to tell them that we were dating, that I was seeing the photographer and that we were pretty serious about each other?"

"They'd want to meet me. One look and they'd know."

"We could stall them. After all, I'm busy, and so are you, which would make it hard to arrange a meeting. In the meantime I could tell them all about Brian Webster, show them examples of your work and snow them with lists of your credits. I could create a picture in their minds of everything you are and everything you mean to me."

"And they won't ask about my background?" He knew very well they would.

"I could fudge it, be as vague as I like. Then, when

they've got this super image in their minds, when they're as favorably inclined as possible, I could tell them the rest."

He raised her chin with his forefinger. "A super image can shatter with a few short words. What if, in spite of the advance hype, they go off the deep end?"

His eyes were a mirror of hers. Marni saw there the same trepidation, the same worry that was making her insides knot. "Then I'll have to make a choice," she said at last.

The trepidation, the worry were transferred to his voice, which came out in a tremulous whisper. Once before Marni had had a choice to make, and she'd made it in favor of her family. Web felt that his very life was on the line. "What will you choose?" he asked in a raw whisper.

Neither her eyes, lost in his, nor her voice faltered. "You're my future, Web. I'm grateful for everything they've given me, and I do love them, but you're my future. The love I feel for you is so strong that there's really no choice at all."

Web closed his eyes. His sigh fanned her brow, and his arms tightened convulsively around her. "Oh, baby..." He said nothing more but held her, rocking her, savoring the moment, the joy, the intense relief he felt.

Inevitably, though, the ramifications of what she'd said loomed before him. "It's going to be hard. You'll be upset."

"Yes. It's sad that I have to risk alienating them by telling them that I'm—"

"—marrying the guy who killed their son."

Her head shot up, eyes flashing in anger. "You *didn't* kill Ethan. Don't ever say that again!"

He felt compelled to prepare her. "They'll say it."

"And they'll be wrong again. They may have used you for a scapegoat that summer, they may be doing it still, and I suppose it's only natural that parents try to find someone to blame, some reason to explain a tragedy like that. But, damn it, you've been their scapegoat long enough!"

"You're apt to take over that role, if it comes down to an estrangement."

"Oh, Web, Web, let's not assume the worst until we come to it...please?"

THEY LEFT THE discussion on that pleading note, but the rest of the day was nowhere near as carefree as the day before had been. They breakfasted, walked again through the woods, packed their bags and closed up the house, all the while struggling to elude the dark cloud hovering overhead.

An atmosphere of apprehension filled the car during the drive back to the city. Web clutched her hand during most of the trip, knowing the dread she was feeling and in turn being swamped by helplessness and frustration. At the door of her apartment, he hugged her with a kind of desperation.

"I'm so afraid of losing you, sunshine...so afraid. I was a fool fourteen years ago for not realizing what I had, but I'm not a fool anymore. I'm going to fight, Marni. I'm going to fight, if it's the last thing I do!"

Those words, and the love behind them, were to be a much-needed source of strength for Marni in the days to come.

CHAPTER SEVEN

MARNI HAD HAD every intention on Monday of calling her mother about the wonderful weekend she'd had with Brian Webster, but she didn't seem to find the time. When, as prearranged, Web came to take her to dinner that night, she explained that something had come up in the computer division, demanding her attention for most of the day. She'd had little more than a moment here or there to think of making the call.

On Tuesday it was a problem with the proposed deal in Richmond, one she thought she'd ironed out when she'd gone down there the week before. On Wednesday it was a lawsuit, filed against the corporation's publishing division by one of its authors.

"You're hedging," Web accused when he saw her that night.

"I'm not! These things came up, and I need a free mind when I call her."

"Things are always coming up. It's the nature of your work. You can put off that call forever, but it's not going to solve our problem."

"Speaking of problems, what are we going to do about the cover of *Class*?" She knew the second batch of pictures had been better than the first, but that Web was still not fully satisfied.

"You're changing the subject."

"Maybe, but it is a problem, and we both do have a deadline on that one."

"We've got a deadline on both, if you look at it one way. The longer you put off breaking the news about us to your parents, the longer it'll be before we can get married."

"I know," she whispered, looking down at the fingernail she was picking. "I know."

Web knew she was torn, that she loved him and wanted to marry him, but that she was terrified of what her parents' reaction was going to be. He sympathized, but only to a point.

"I'll make a deal with you," he sighed. "I'll study all the proofs and decide what to do about them, if you call your mother…. Sound fair?"

"Of course it's fair," she snapped. He was right. She was only prolonging the inevitable. "I'll call her tomorrow."

SHE DID BETTER than that. Fearful that she'd lose her nerve when the time came, she called her mother that night and invited her to lunch. It was over coffee and trifle, the latter barely touched on her plate, that Marni broached the subject.

"Mother, do you remember that photographer I was with that night we witnessed the assault?"

Adele Lange, a slender woman with a surprisingly sweet tooth, was relishing every small forkful of wine-soaked sponge cake, fruit, nuts and whipped cream that made up the trifle. She held her fork suspended. "Of course I remember." She smiled. "He's the famous one everyone knows about but me."

Marni forced her own smile as she launched into the speech she'd mentally rehearsed so many times. "Well, we've been dating. I think it's getting serious."

Adele stared at her, then set down her fork. "But I thought you said it was a business thing."

"It started out that way, but it's evolved into something more." So far, the truth. Marni kept her chin up.

"Marni! It's been—how long—a week since that incident? How many times could you have seen this man to know that it's getting serious?"

"I'm thirty-one, Mom. I know."

"Does he? Remember what I told you about photographers?"

"You're hung up on the stereotype. You've never met Brian."

"Then tell me. What's he like?" Slowly Adele returned to her trifle, but she was clearly distracted.

"He's tall, dark and handsome, for starters."

"Aren't they all?"

"No. Some are squat and wiry-haired—"

"And wear heavy gold jewelry, have their eyes on every attractive woman in sight and can't make it through a sentence without a 'darling' or 'sweetie' or 'babe.'"

Marni grinned. "Brian doesn't use any of those words. He doesn't wear any jewelry except a watch, which is slim and unobtrusive, and he may have the same appreciation that any other man his age has for a beautiful woman, but he's never looked at another woman the way he looks at me." Nicely put, Marni thought, almost poetic. She'd have to remember that one.

"How old is he?"

"Forty."

"And he's never married?"

"No."

"That's something strange to think about. Why hasn't he married? A man who's got looks and a name for himself...maybe he's queer."

If Marni had had a mouthful of coffee, she would have choked on it. It was all she could do to keep a straight face. "Would he be interested in me if he was?"

Adele's lips twitched downward in disdain. "Maybe he goes both ways."

"He doesn't. Take my word for it."

"And you take his word that he doesn't have an ex-wife or two to support?"

"He's never been married," Marni stated unequivocably, then took a sip of her coffee. She knew her mother. The questions were just beginning. She only wished they would all be as amusing.

"Where does he come from?"

"Pennsylvania, originally."

Adele took another tiny forkful of trifle. "What about his parents?"

"His mother is dead. His father is an insurance broker." She'd anticipated the question and had thought about the answer she'd give. To say "stepfather" would only be to invite questions. Web had never known his biological father, hence Marni felt justified in responding as she did.

Adele was chewing and swallowing each bit of information along with the trifle. "How long has he been a photographer?"

"He's been at it since his mid-twenties."

"I assume, given the reputation Tanya claims he has, that he earns a good living."

"What kind of a question is that, Mother?"

"It's a mother's kind of question."

"I'm an independent adult. I earn a more than comfortable salary for myself. Why should it matter what W-what Brian earns?" The sudden skip of her heart hadn't been caused by her indignation. She'd nearly slipped. Brian was a safe name; Web was not. She'd have to be more careful.

Adele scolded her gently. "Don't get upset, darling. For the first time in your adult life, you've told me that you're serious about a man. Your father and I have waited a long time for this. It's only natural that we be concerned about whether he's right for you. Realistically speaking, you're a wealthy woman. We wouldn't want to think that some man was interested in you for your money."

Farcical. That was what it was, and Marni couldn't help but laugh. "No, Brian is *not* interested in my money. Not that it matters, but he's far from being a pauper. He has an extremely lucrative career, he owns the building that houses his studio and his apartment and he's got a weekend home on acres of woodland in Vermont." She hesitated, wondering just how much to say, then decided to throw caution aside. "We were there last weekend. It's beautiful."

Adele's eyes widened fractionally, and she pursed her lips, but said nothing about Marni's having spent the weekend with her photographer. Marni was, after all, thirty-one, and these were modern times. It was too much to expect that her daughter was still a virgin. "Vermont. A little... backwoodsy, isn't it?"

Marni rolled her eyes. "Vermont has become the vacation place of most of New York, or hadn't you noticed? Some of the finest and wealthiest have second homes there. Times have changed, Mother. It doesn't have to be Camden, or South Hampton, or Newport anymore."

"I know that, darling," Adele said gruffly. She scowled at what was left of her dessert, then abandoned it in favor of her coffee.

"I want you to be *pleased*," Marni said softly. "Brian is a wonderful man. He's interesting and fun to be with, he's serious about his work and he respects mine, and he treats me like I'm the best thing that's ever happened to him."

"I am pleased. I just want to make sure you know what you're doing before you get in over your head."

Marni might have said that she was already in over her head, but it wouldn't have served her purpose. "I know what I'm doing," she said with quiet conviction. "I'm happy. That's the most important thing…don't you think?"

"Of course, dear. Of course…. So, when will we be able to meet this photographer of yours?"

"Soon."

"When?"

"When I get up the courage to bring him out."

"Courage? Why would you need courage?"

"Because you and Dad can be intimidating in the best of circumstances. I'm not sure I'm ready to inflict you on Brian yet." Her words had been offered in a teasing tone and accompanied by a gentle smile. Adele was totally unaware of the deeper sentiment behind them.

"Very funny, Marni. We don't bite you know."

"You could send Brian running if you grill him the way you've grilled me. No man likes to have his background, his social standing and his financial status probed."

"Social standing. We haven't even gotten into that."

"No need. He's well-liked and respected, he's the good friend of many well-placed people and he chews with his mouth closed."

"That's a relief," was Adele's sardonic retort. "I wouldn't want to think you were going with some crude oaf."

"Brian can hold his own with any crowd. He'll charm your friends to tears."

"Well, *your father and I* would like to meet him before we introduce him to our friends. Why don't you bring him out to the house on Sunday?"

Marni shook her head. "We're not up to a showing just yet."

"If you're so afraid that we'll scare the man off, maybe you're not so sure about him yourself."

"Oh, I'm sure. But it's still a little early for introductions," she explained with impeccable nonchalance. "When the time's right, I'll let you know."

"You WOULD HAVE BEEN proud of me, Web," Marni declared when she arrived at the studio that night. Web had kissed her thoroughly. She was feeling heavenly. "I was cool and relaxed, I followed the script perfectly and I didn't lie once."

"How did she take it?"

"Hesitantly, at first. She asked questions, just as I'd expected." She told him some of them, and they shared a chuckle over the one about money. "I planted the bug in her ear. If I know my mother, she's already on the phone trying to find out whatever she can about you." A sudden frown crossed her brow. Web picked up on it instantly.

"Don't worry. There's nothing she could learn that will connect me with who I was fourteen years ago. Lee is about the only one who knows anything about what I did during those years, and even if someone called him, which they wouldn't, he'd be tight-lipped as hell."

"He must think my parents are awful."

"Not awful. Just...prejudiced."

"Mmmm. I guess that says it." Her eyes clouded. "It remains to be seen whether they're vengeful as well."

"Don't even think it," Web soothed. "Not yet. We've got more pressing things to consider."

"More pressing?" she asked, worried. But Web was grinning, drawing her snugly against him. "Ahhh. More pressing..."

His lips closed over hers then, and soon he was leading her to the bedroom, where he proceeded to set her priorities straight. It was what she needed, what they both needed—a reaffirmation of all they meant to each other. Passion was a ready spark between them, had always been a ready spark between them, but it was love that dominated the interplay of mouths and hands and bodies, and it was love that transported them to an exquisite corner of paradise.

MARNI'S FATHER DROPPED BY her office on Friday morning. She was surprised to see him, because there wasn't a board meeting scheduled and he rarely came in for anything else. But deep down inside she'd been awaiting some form of contact.

They talked of incidental things relating to the corporation, and Marni indulged him patiently. In his own good time, Jonathan Lange broached the topic that had brought him by. His thick brows were low over his eyes.

"Your mother tells me that you have a special man... this photographer...Brian Webster?"

"Uh-huh." Her pulse rate had sped up, but she kept her eyes and her voice steady and forcefully relaxed her hands in her lap.

"I know your mother has some reservations," he went on in his most businesslike tone, "and I hope you take them seriously. People today get married, then divorced, married, then divorced. Your sister is a perfect example."

"I'm not Tanya," Marni stated quietly.

"Exactly. You're the president of this corporation. I hope you keep that in mind when you go about choosing a husband."

She had to struggle to contain a surge of irritation. "I know who I am, Dad, and I think I have a pretty good grasp of what's expected of me."

"Just so you do. This fellow's a photographer, and big-name photographers often live in the fast lane. I wouldn't want you—or him—to do anything to embarrass us."

Embarrassment had never been among Marni's many worries. "I think you're jumping the gun," she said slowly. "In the first place, you've adopted the same stereotype Mom has. There's nothing fast about Brian. He lives quietly, and his face hasn't been plastered all over the papers, with or without women." Web had assured her of that. All she'd needed was for her mother or Tanya to do a little sleuthing and come up with a picture that would identify Web instantly. "Furthermore, I don't believe I said anything to Mom about marriage."

Jonathan's frown was one of reproof. "Then you'd move in with the man, without a thought to your image?"

"Come on, Dad. These are enlightened times. No one cares if two adults choose to live together."

"Is that what *you* choose?"

"No! I've never even considered it."

"But you haven't talked marriage with this photographer?"

That one was harder to fudge. She bought a minute's time. "His name is Brian. You can call him Brian."

"All right. Brian. Have you talked marriage with Brian?"

She held his gaze. "I think we'd both be amenable to the idea."

"Then it *is* serious."

"Yes."

"We'll have to meet him. That's all there is to it."

Marni bit her lower lip, then let it slide from beneath her teeth. "You know, Dad, I am a big girl. Technically, I don't need your approval. You may hate him, but that wouldn't change my feelings for him."

Jonathan's gaze sharpened. "If he's as wonderful as you say, why would we hate him?"

"Different people see things differently. You and Mom aren't keen on his profession to begin with."

"That's true. But we'd still like to meet him, and soon, if you're as serious as you say about him."

"Okay, soon. You will meet him soon."

THERE WAS SOON, and there was soon. Marni had no intention of running out to Long Island that Sunday as her mother had originally suggested. Not only did she have more subtle PR to do, but she and Web were going back to Vermont for the weekend, and not for the world would she have altered their plans.

They had a relaxed, quiet, loving weekend and returned to New York refreshed and anticipating the next step in Marni's plan. On Monday she sent her parents tear sheets of the best of Web's work. Each piece was identified as to where it had appeared; it was an impressive collection of credits. She also sent along copies of blurbs and articles praising Web's work.

On Monday night she and Web took in a movie. On Tuesday they went out to dinner. On Wednesday morning she called her mother as a follow-up to the package she'd sent. Yes, Adele had received it, and, yes, it was an impressive lot. Yes, Marni was planning to bring him out to the house, but, no, it couldn't be this week because they were both swamped with work.

Marni and Web spent a quiet Wednesday night at her place, then a similarly quiet Thursday night at his. After the full days they put in at their respective jobs, they found these private times to be most precious.

Friday night, though, they had a party to attend. It was given by the most recently named vice president at Lange,

Heather Connolly, whom Marni had personally recruited from another company four years before.

Had the party been an official corporate function, Marni might have thought twice about bringing Web along. She felt she was progressing well with her parents and wouldn't have done anything to jeopardize her plan. But the party was a personal one, a gathering of the Connollys' friends. Marni was looking forward to it; it was the first time she would be introducing Web to any of her own friends.

They had fun dressing up, Web in a dark, well-tailored suit, Marni in a black sequined cocktail dress. It was a miracle they noticed anyone else at the party, so captivated were they by each other's appearance. But they did manage to circulate, talking easily with Heather and Fred's friends, their spouses and dates.

At ten o'clock, though, the unthinkable happened. A couple arrived: the man a tennis partner of Fred's, the woman none other than Marni's sister, Tanya.

Marni was the first to see them. She and Web were chatting with another couple when they entered the room. Her heart began to pound, and she stiffened instantly. Instinctively she reached for Web's arm and dug in her fingers. He took one look at her ashen face, followed her gaze and stared.

"Tanya?" he whispered in disbelief. It had been fourteen years, but he would have recognized her even had Marni's reaction not been a solid clue. Clearing his throat, he turned smoothly back to the couple. "Would you excuse us? Marni's sister has just come. We hadn't expected to see her." Without awaiting more than nods from the two, he guided Marni toward the back of the room, ostensibly to circle the crowd toward Tanya.

Marni's whisper was as frantic as she felt. "What are we

going to do? She'll recognize you! She's *sure* to recognize you, and she's trouble! Oh, God, Web, what do we do?"

He positioned himself so that his large body was a buffer between Marni and the rest of the crowd, then curved his fingers around her arms. "Take it easy. Just relax. There's not much we can do, Marni. If we try to slip out without being seen, our disappearance will cause an even greater stir. Tanya's not dumb. She'll put two and two together, and if she's the troublemaker you say, she'll run right back to your parents. The damage will be done anyway." He paused. "The best thing, the *only* thing we can do is to walk confidently up and say hello."

Marni's eyes were wide with dismay. "But she'll *recognize* you."

"Probably."

"But...that'll be awful!"

"It'll just bring things to a head a little sooner."

"Web, I don't want this...I don't want this!"

He slipped to her side, put his arm around her shoulder and spoke very gently. "Let's get it over with. The sooner the better. Take a deep breath...atta girl...now smile."

She tried, but the best she could muster was a feeble twist of her lips.

Web gave a tight smile of his own. "That'll have to do." He took his own deep breath. "Let's go."

Tanya and her date were talking with Heather and Fred when they approached. "Marni," Heather exclaimed, "look who's here! I never dreamed Tony would be bringing Tanya. Do you and Brian know Tony? Tony Holt, Marni Lange and Brian Webster."

Marni forced a smile in Tanya's direction. "Hi, Tanya." She clutched Web's arm. "I don't think you know Brian."

Tanya hadn't taken her eyes from Web since she'd turned at their approach. Her face, too, had paled, and there was a hint of shock in her eyes, but otherwise her expression was socially perfect. She extended a formal hand. "Brian...Webster, is it?"

If she'd put special emphasis on his last name, only Marni and Web were aware of it. Two things were instantly clear—first, that she did *indeed* know Brian and, second, that she was momentarily going along with the game.

Web took her hand in his own firm one. "It's a pleasure to meet you, Tanya."

"My pleasure entirely," was Tanya's silky response. The underlying innuendo was, again, obvious only to Web and Marni.

Web shook hands with Tony Holt, who, it turned out, was a plastic surgeon very familiar with his photographic work. Reluctantly, since he'd rather have been helping Marni, Web was drawn into conversation with the man. Heather and Fred moved off. Tanya seized Marni's arm. "We'll be in the powder room, Tony." She winked at her date. "Be right back."

Before Marni could think of a plausible excuse, she was being firmly led around the crowd and up the stairs to the second floor of the town house. Tanya said nothing until she'd found a bathroom and closed its door firmly behind them. Then she turned on Marni, hands on hips, eyes wide in fury.

"How could you! How could you *think* to do something like this to us! When I talked with Mom the other day, she told me you were serious about this Brian Webster. She didn't make the connection. *None* of us made the connection."

Marni refused to be intimidated. "The connection's unimportant."

"Unimportant? Have you lost your marbles?" Tanya raised a rigid finger and pointed to the door. "That man killed our brother, and you don't think the connection's important?"

"Brian did not...kill...Ethan," Marni stated through gritted teeth, her own fury quickly rising to match her sister's. "That accident was carefully documented by the police. Brian was in no way at fault."

Tanya sliced the air with her hand. "It doesn't matter what the police said. He was a bad influence on Ethan. If he hadn't come along that summer, Ethan would still be alive. Your *own brother*. How could you insult his memory by doing this?"

"Ethan liked and respected Web," Marni countered angrily. Quite unconsciously she'd reverted to calling Brian Web, but even if she'd thought about it, she'd have realized that there was no longer any need for pretense. "If he'd survived the accident, he'd have been the first one to say that Web wasn't at fault. And given the age that I am now, he'd have been the first to bless my relationship with Web."

"So you're desperate, is that it? You're thirty-one and single, and *that* man is your only hope?"

"Yes, that man is my only hope, but not because I'm thirty-one. I happen to love him. He fills needs I never realized I had."

"Very touching. Is that what you're going to say to Mom and Dad when they finally learn the truth? And when were you planning to tell them anyway? They're going to be thrilled, absolutely thrilled."

"Do you think I don't know that? Do you think I've been evasive simply to amuse myself? I'm finding no pleasure in this, Tanya, and the worst of it is that you people are making me feel guilty when I've got nothing to feel guilty about. I'd planned to tell Mom and Dad when the time was right. I was hoping that they'd form an image of what Brian Webster is like today, to somehow counter the image they've held of him all these years."

"You're dreaming, little sister—"

"Don't call me little sister," Marni said in a warning tone. "We're both adults now. It doesn't seem to me…." She closed her mouth abruptly. She'd been about to say that Tanya hadn't done anything with her life that would give her the right, or authority, to look down on Marni, but she realized that insults would get her nowhere. Yes, Tanya would go to their parents with what she'd learned, and maybe Marni *was* dreaming, but there was always that chance, that slim chance Tanya could be an ally.

Marni took a deep breath and raised both hands in a truce. "What I could use, Tanya, is your help. It's going to be very difficult for Mom and Dad, because I know they share your feelings that Web was responsible for Ethan's death. They're older, and Ethan was their child. I was hoping you could see things more objectively."

Tanya's eyes flashed. "You are *not* going to marry that man."

"And it matters that much to you who I marry?" Marni asked softly.

"You can marry anyone you please as long as it's not him."

Marni looked down at her hands and chose her words with care. "Fourteen years ago, you wanted Web for yourself. Could that be coloring your opinion?"

"Of course not. I didn't want him for myself. I knew what kind of a person he was from the start."

Marni bit back a retort concerning both Tanya's erstwhile interest in Web and the character of her two ex-husbands. "Do you know what kind of a person he is now?" she asked quietly.

"It doesn't matter. When I look at him I can only re-

member what he did. Mom and Dad are going to do the
same."

"But think. He has a good career. He's successful and
well-liked. He doesn't have the slightest blemish on his
record. Can you still stand there and claim he's a killer?"

Before Tanya could answer, a light knock came at the
door, then Web's voice calling, "Marni?" Marni quickly
opened the door. Web looked from one sister to the other,
finally settling a more gentle gaze on Marni. "Is everything okay here?"

"No, it's not," Tanya answered in a huff. "If you had any
sense, you'd get out of my sister's life once and for all."

Marni turned to her with a final plea. "Tanya, I could
really use your help—"

"When hell freezes over. I wouldn't—"

"That's enough," Web interrupted with quiet determination. His voice softened, and he reached for Marni's
hand. "We've got to run, Marni. I've already explained
to Heather that I have to be up early tomorrow. She un-
derstands."

With all hope that Tanya might aid her dashed, Marni
didn't look at her sister again. She took Web's hand and let
him lead her down the stairs and quietly out of the town
house. She leaned heavily against him as they began to
walk. Yes, Web had to be up early tomorrow. So did she.
They were heading for Vermont, where she wouldn't be
able to hear her phone when it began to jangle angrily.

CHAPTER EIGHT

MARNI'S PARENTS WEREN'T put off by the fact that she wasn't home to answer her phone. They quickly called her administrative assistant, who gave them Web's Vermont number.

It was shortly after two in the afternoon. Marni and Web had left New York early, had stopped at their usual market for food and were just finishing lunch. When the phone rang, they looked up in surprise, then at each other in alarm. In all the time they'd spent at the cabin, the phone hadn't rung once.

"Don't answer it," Marni warned. Neither of them had moved yet.

"It may not be them."

The phone rang a second time. "It is. We both know it is."

"It may be a legitimate emergency. What if one of them is sick?" He began to rise from his seat. The only phone was in the den.

Marni clutched his wrist, her eyes filled with trepidation. "Let it ring," she begged.

"They'll only keep trying. I won't have the weekend spoiled. If we let it ring, we'll keep wondering. But if we answer it, at least we'll know one way or another."

"The weekend will be spoiled anyway.... Web!"

He was on his way toward the den. She ran after him. He lifted the receiver and spoke calmly. "Hello?"

A slightly gruff voice came from the other end of the line. "Marni Lange, please."

"Who's calling?"

"...Her father."

As if Web hadn't known. He would have recognized that voice in any timbre. He'd last heard it when he'd been lying, distraught, in a hospital room.

"Mr. Lange—" Web began, not knowing what he was going to say, only knowing that he wanted to deflect from Marni the brunt of what was very obviously anger. He was curtly interrupted.

"My daughter, please."

Marni was at Web's elbow, trying to take the phone from him, but he resisted. "If this is something that concerns—"

"I'd like to *speak to my daughter!*"

Hearing her father's shout, Marni tugged harder on the phone. "Web, please..."

He held up his free hand to her, even as he spoke calmly into the receiver. "If you're angry, Mr. Lange, you're angry at me. Perhaps you ought to tell me what's on your mind."

"Are you going to put my daughter on the line?"

"Not yet."

Jonathan Lange hung up the phone.

Web heard the definitive click and took the phone from his ear, whereupon Marni snatched it to hers. "Dad? Hello? Dad?" She scowled at the receiver, then slammed it down. "Damn it, Web. You should have let me talk! What good does it do if he's hung up? Now nothing's accomplished!"

"Something is. Your father knows that I have no intention of letting you face this alone. You faced it alone fourteen years ago. I like to think I'm more of a man now."

"Then it's a macho thing?" she cried. "You're trying to show him who wears the pants around here?"

"Don't be absurd, Marni! Our relationship has been one of equals from the start. I simply want your father to know that we're standing together, that if he thinks he can browbeat you, he'll be browbeating both of us. And I don't take to being browbeaten."

"Then you'll shut every door as soon as it's opened. He *called*. *You* were the one who insisted on answering the phone. Now you've hung up on him—"

"He hung up on me!"

"Same difference—"

"No, it's not," Web argued angrily. "*He* shut the door. I was perfectly willing to talk."

"But he wouldn't talk with you, so now he's not talking with either of us."

"He'll call back. If he went to the effort of getting this number, he won't give up so easily."

"Then I'll answer it next time."

"And he'll bully you mercilessly. You've got to be firm with him, Marni! You've got to let him know that you're not a child who can be pushed around!"

"I'm *not* a child, and I don't like your suggestion that I am."

"I didn't suggest—"

"You don't trust me! You think I'm going to crumble. You think that I'll submit to every demand he makes. I told you I wouldn't, Web! I *told* you that my choice was made!"

"But you're torn, because you don't want to hurt them. Well, what about me? Don't I have a right to stand in my own defense? If he's going to call me a killer, it's my *right* to tell him where to get off!"

"But that won't accomplish anything!" she screamed, then caught her breath and held it. The silence was deafening, coming on the heels of their heated exchange. "Oh, God," she whimpered at last. She clutched his shoulders, then threw her arms around his neck and clung to him tightly. "Oh, God, he's doing it already. He's putting a wedge between us. Do you see what's happening? Do you see it, Web?"

His own arms circled her slowly, then closed in. Eyes squeezed shut, he buried his face in her hair. "I see, sweetheart. I see, and it makes me sick. If we start fighting about this, we'll never make it. And if *we* don't, *I* won't."

"Me neither," she managed shakily. "I love you so much, Web. It tears me up that you have to go through this, when you've already paid such a high price for something that wasn't your fault."

He rubbed soothing circles over her back. "That's neither here nor there at this point. I'm more than willing to go through hell if it means I'll get you in the end." His voice grew hoarse. "I don't know how I could have yelled at you that way. You're not responsible for the situation any more than I am."

The phone rang again. A jolt passed from one body to the other. Marni raised her face and looked questioningly at Web, who held her gaze for a minute before stepping back and nodding toward the phone.

Marni lifted the receiver. "Hello?"

"Marni!" It was her mother. "Thank goodness it's you this time! Your father is ready to—"

Cutting her off, Jonathan came on the line. "What do you think you're doing, Marni?" he demanded harshly. "Do you know who that man is?"

She felt surprisingly calm. Anticipation had prepared her well. With the moment at hand, she was almost relieved. "I certainly do. He's the man I'm going to marry." She reached for Web's hand and held it to her middle.

"Over my dead body!" came the retort. "Do you have any idea what this has done to your mother and me? You

were very cagey, telling us everything about this Brian
Webster of yours but his real identity. If Tanya hadn't
called—"

"Everything I told you was the truth."

"Don't interrupt me, Marni. You may be the president
of the corporation, but in this house you're still the baby."

"I am not still in that house, and I am *not* still the baby!
I'm a grown woman, Dad. Isn't it about time you accepted
that?"

"I had, until you pulled this little stunt. Are you out of
your mind? Do you have any *idea* how I feel about this?"

Marni took a deep breath in a bid for calm. She had to
be able to think clearly and project conviction. A glance
at Web gave her strength a boost. "Yes, I think I do. I also
think that you're wrong. But I won't be able to convince
you of it over the phone."

"Damned right you won't. I'd suggest you get *that* man
to drive you right back down here. He can drop you at the
door and then leave. I won't have him in this house."

"Listen to yourself, Dad. You sound irrational. The facts
are that Web and I are here in Vermont for the weekend,
and that when we do come by to see you, we'll be together.
Now, you can shut the door on us both, but that would be
very sad, because I am your daughter and I do love you."

"I'm beginning to doubt that, young lady."

It was a low blow, and one she didn't deserve after all
she'd done for her parents' sake in the past fourteen years.
Clenching her jaw against the anger that flared, she went
on slowly and clearly. "We'll be heading back to New York
tomorrow afternoon. We'll stop by at the house sometime
around seven. We can talk this all out then."

"Do *not* bring *him*."

"He'll be with me, and if you refuse to see me, we'll
be married by the end of the week. Think about it, Dad.

I'll see you tomorrow." Without awaiting his answer, she quietly put down the phone.

Web sucked in a deep breath, then let it out in a stunned whoosh. "You are quick, lady. I never would have dreamed up that particular threat, but you've practically guaranteed that he'll see us."

"Practically," she said without pride. Then she muttered, "He *is* a bastard."

Web drew her against him. "Shhhh. He's your father, and you love him."

"For that, yes, but as a person…"

"Shhhh. The door's open. Let's let it go at that."

THE DOOR WAS indeed open when Marni and Web arrived Sunday evening at the handsome estate where she'd grown up. Fourteen years before, Web would have been taken aback by the splendor of the long, tree-lined drive and the majesty of the huge Georgian colonial mansion. Now he could admire it without awe or envy.

They were greeted in the front hall by Duncan, Cook's husband, who'd served as handyman, chauffeur and butler for the Langes for as long as Marni could remember. "Miss Marni, it's good to see you. You're looking fine."

"Thank you, Duncan," she said quietly. "I'd like you to meet my fiancé, Mr. Webster."

"How are you, Duncan?" Web extended his hand. He, like Marni, was unpretentious when it came to hired help. He'd always treated the most lowly of his own assistants as important members of the crew. Whereas Marni was softhearted and compassionate, Web was understanding as only one who'd once been "hired help" himself could be.

Duncan pumped his hand, clearly pleased with the offering. "Just fine, Mr. Webster. And my congratulations to you both. I had no idea we'd be having a wedding coming up here soon."

Marni cleared her throat and threw what might have been an amused glance at Web had she not been utterly incapable of amusement at that moment. "We, uh, we haven't made final plans." She paused. "My parents are expecting me, I think."

"That's right," Duncan returned with the faintest hint of tension. "They're in the library. They suggested you join them there."

The library. Warm and intimate in some homes, formal and forbidding in this one. It had been the scene of many a reprimand in Marni's youth, and that knowledge did nothing to curb her anxiety now. There were differences of course. She was no longer in her youth, and Web was with her...

Head held high, she led the way through the large front hall and down a long hallway to the room at the very end. The door was open, but the symbolism was deceptive. Marni knew what she would find even before she entered the room and nodded to her parents.

Jonathan Lange was sitting in one corner of the studded leather sofa. His legs were crossed at the knees, and one arm was thrown over the back of the sofa while the other hand held his customary glass of Scotch. He was wearing a suit, customary as well; he always wore a suit when discussing serious business.

Adele Lange sat on the sofa not far from him. She wore a simple dress, nursed an aperitif and looked eminently poised.

"Thank you for seeing us," Marni began with what she hoped was corresponding poise. "I think you remember Brian."

Neither of the Langes looked at him. "Sit down," Jonathan said stiffly, tossing his head toward one of two leather chairs opposite the sofa. That particular symbolism did have meaning, Marni mused. The two chairs were well separated by a marble coffee table.

Marni took the seat near her father, leaving the one closer to her mother for Web. She sat back, folded her hands in her lap and spoke softly. "Brian and I are planning to get married. We'd like your support."

"Why?" Jonathan asked baldly.

"Because we feel that what we're doing is right and we'd like you to share our happiness."

"Why now? It's been fourteen years since you were first involved. Fourteen years is a long time for an engagement. Why the sudden rush to marry?"

Marni was confused. "We haven't been seeing each other all that time. I hadn't seen him since the day of the accident until three weeks ago when I went to his studio to be photographed."

"But you've carried a torch for him all these years."

"No! After the accident you forbade me to see him, so I didn't. I forced myself to forget about him, to put what we had down to a seventeen-year-old's infatuation, just as you said. It wasn't a matter of carrying a torch, and I never dreamed he'd be the photographer when I stepped foot in that studio—"

"I was wondering about that, too," Jonathan interrupted scornfully. "You were in favor of this magazine thing from the start—" his eyes narrowed "—and then to suddenly come up with the photographer who just happened to be the man you'd imagined yourself in love with—"

"It wasn't that way at all!"

Web, who'd been sitting quietly, spoke for the first time. "Marni's right. She had no idea I was—"

"I'm not talking to you," Jonathan cut in, his eyes still on Marni.

Web wasn't about to be bullied. "Well, I'm talking to you, and if you have *anything* to say to me, you can look me in the eye."

Marni put out a hand. "Web, please..." she whispered.

He softened his tone, but that was his only concession. His eyes were sharply focused on Marni's father. "I have pictures from that first photo session, one after the other showing the shock on Marni's face. She knew nothing of the past identity of Brian Webster the photographer. No one does except your family and mine."

Though Jonathan still refused to look at him, Adele did. Instinctively Web met her gaze. "Marni hadn't been pining away for me any more than I'd been pining away for her. In hindsight I can see that she was special even back then. But it's the woman I know today whom I've fallen in love with. And it's the man I am today whom I think you should try to understand."

"There's not much to understand," Adele returned. Her voice wasn't quite as cold as her husband's had been, but it was far from encouraging. "We firmly believe that had it not been for you our son would be alive today. Can you honestly expect us to let our daughter marry you, knowing that every time we look at you we'll remember what you did?"

Web sat back. "Okay, let's get into that. Exactly what *did* I do?"

"You were recklessly driving that motorcycle," Jonathan snapped, eyes flying to Web's for the first time.

Web felt a small victory in that he'd been acknowledged as a person at last. "Is that what the police said after the investigation?"

"Ethan would never have *been* on a motorcycle had it not been for you."

"I didn't force him to get on it. He wasn't some raw kid of fourteen. He was a man of twenty-five."

"You were a bad influence that entire summer!"

"That's what you assumed, since I was only an employee at the Inn. Did Ethan ever tell you what we did together? Did he tell you that we spent hours talking politics, or philosophy, or psychology? Or that we discussed books we'd both read, or that we played chess? I loved playing chess with Ethan. I beat him three times out of four, but he took it with a grin and came back for another game more determined than ever to win. There was nothing irresponsible about what we did, and I was probably a better influence on him than the spoiled and self-centered characters he would have been with otherwise. You really should have been proud of him. He chose to be with me because the time we spent together was intellectually productive."

Marni wanted to applaud, but her fingers were too tightly intertwined to move.

Jonathan wasn't about to applaud either. Choosing to ignore what Web had said, he turned his attention back to Marni. "What were you intending with the song and dance you've been doing for the past two weeks? Did you hope to pull the wool over our eyes? Did you think we were that foolish?"

"I had hoped that you'd see Brian as he is today. Aside from his profession, which you're unfairly biased against, he's everything I'd have thought you'd want in the man I decided to marry." She turned to her mother. "What did you find out? I'm sure you made calls."

"I did," Adele sniffed. "It appears he's fooled the rest of the world, but we know him as he is."

Marni scowled. "You don't know him at all. You may

have met him in passing once or twice that summer, but you never spent any time talking with him, and you certainly never invited him to the house. Don't you think it's about time you faced the fact that Ethan's death just *happened?*"

"You wouldn't say that if you were a mother, Marni. You'd be angry and grief-stricken, just like we were, like we are."

"For God's sake, it's been fourteen years!"

"Have *you* forgotten?" Adele cried.

Marni sagged in her seat. "Of course not. I adored Ethan. I'll never forget him. And I've never forgotten the sense of injustice, the anger I felt that those two cars had to collide right in Web's path. But you can't live your life feeding on anger and grief. Ethan would never have wanted it. Have you ever stopped to consider that? Web was his friend. Whether you like it or not, he was. He suffered in that accident, both physically and emotionally." She suddenly sat forward and rounded on her father. "Your response when Web called you from the hospital was *inexcusable!* How could you have done something like that? He's a human being, for God's sake, a human being!" She took a quick breath and sat straighter. "Web mourned Ethan just as we did, and he suffered through his share of guilt, though God only knows he had nothing to feel guilty for. But that's all in the past now. There's nothing any of us can do to bring Ethan back, and I refuse to live my life any longer trying to make up to you for his loss!"

"What are you talking about, girl?" Jonathan snarled.

"Marni," Web began, "you don't have to—"

"I do, Web. It's about time the entire truth came out." She faced her parents, looking from one to the other. "I felt guilty because I'd loved both Ethan and Web. Ethan was dead. Web was as good as dead to me because you never let up on the fact that he was to blame, and if he was to blame, *I* was to blame, too." She focused on her father. "Do you think I wasn't aware that you'd been grooming Ethan for the corporation presidency? And that you practically lost interest in the business after he died? Why do you think I buckled down and whipped through Wellesley, then Columbia? Didn't it ever occur to you that I was trying to be what Ethan would have been? That I felt I could somehow make things easier for you if I joined the corporation myself?" She tempered her tone, though her voice was shaky. "I'm not saying that I'd had my heart set on something else, or that I'm unhappy being where I am, but I think you should both know that what I did I did for you, even more than for me."

"Then you were a fool," was Jonathan's curt response.

"Maybe so, but I don't regret it for a minute. I did make things easier for you. You won't admit it, any more than you'll admit that I've done a good job. You never did that, Dad. Do you realize?" Her eyes had grown moist and her knuckles were white as she gripped the arms of the chair. "I tried so hard, and you promoted me and gave me more and more responsibility until finally I became president. But not once, *not once* did you tell me you were proud of me. Not once did you actually praise my work—"

Her voice cracked, and she stopped talking. She was unaware that Web had risen from his seat to stand behind hers until she felt his comforting touch on her shoulder. Her hands left the arms of the chair and found his instantly.

Jonathan's expression was as tight as ever, though his voice was quieter. "I assumed that actions spoke louder than words."

"Well, they don't! I beat my tail to the ground trying to win your approval, but I failed, I failed. And now I'm tired." Her voice reflected it. "I'm tried of trying to please someone else. I'm thirty-one years old, and it's about time I see to *my* best interests. I have every intention of continuing on as Lange's president, and I'll continue to do the best job I can, but for me now, and for Web. I'm going to marry him, and we're going to have children, and if you can't find it in your hearts to forgive, or at least forget, then I guess you'll miss out on the happiness. It's your choice. I've already made mine."

There was a moment's heavy silence in the room before Jonathan spoke in a grim voice. "I guess there's not much more to say, then, is there." It wasn't a question but a dismissal. Pushing himself from the sofa, he turned his back on them and walked toward the window.

Web addressed Adele. "There's one last thing I'd like to say," he ventured quietly. "I'd like you to consider what would have happened if Marni—or Tanya—had had Ethan for a passenger when her car crashed, killing him but only injuring her. Would you have ostracized one of your daughters from the family? Would you have held a permanent grudge? You know, that's happened in families, where two members were in an accident, one killed and the other survived. I don't know how those families reacted. Regardless of guilt or innocence, it's a tragic situation.

"Ethan and I were innocent victims of that accident fourteen years ago. Once those cars started spinning all over the road, the motorcycle didn't have a chance in hell of escaping them. If I had been the son of one of your oldest and dearest friends, would you still feel the way you do now?"

"You are *not* the son of one of our oldest and dearest friends," Jonathan said without turning. "And I thank God for it!"

MARNI AND WEB left then. They'd said what they'd come to say and had heard what they'd suspected they'd hear. They felt disappointed and saddened, hurt and angry.

"That's it, Web," Marni stated grimly as they began the drive into the city. "We know how they feel, and they're not going to change. I think we should get married, and as soon as possible."

Web kept his eyes on the road, his hands on the wheel. "Let's not do anything impulsively," he said quietly.

Her gaze flew to his face in dismay. "Impulsively? I thought marriage was what we both wanted! Weren't you the one who said that the longer we put off telling my parents the truth, the longer it would be before we got married? I thought *you* were the one who wanted to get married soon!"

"I do." His voice was even, and he didn't blink. "But we're both upset right now. It's not the ideal situation in which to be starting a marriage."

"Then what do we do? Wait forever in the hope that they'll do an about-face? They won't, Web!"

"I know. I know." He was trying to sort out his thoughts, to find some miraculous solution to their problem. "But if we rush into something, they'll be all the more perverse."

"I can't believe you're saying this! You were the one who felt so strongly that we were adults and didn't need their permission!"

He held the car steady in the right-hand lane. "We don't. And we are adults. But they're your parents, and you do love them. It'd still be nice if they came around. This all has to be a shock to them. Two days, Marni, that's all they've had."

"It wouldn't matter if it were two months!"

"It might. We presented our arguments tonight, and they were logical. I think your mother was listening, even if your father tried hard not to. Don't you think we owe them a little time to mull it over? They may never come fully around to our way of thinking, but it's possible they might decide to accept what they can't change."

Marni didn't know what to think, particularly about Web's sudden reluctance to get married. "Do you really think that could happen?" Her skepticism was nearly palpable.

"I don't know," he said with a sigh. "But I do think it's worth the wait. To rush and get married now will accomplish nothing more than throwing our relationship in their faces."

"It would accomplish much more. We'd be *married!* Or doesn't that mean as much to you as it does to me?"

"You're upset, Marni, or you wouldn't be saying that—"

"And why shouldn't we throw our relationship in their faces? We're in love. We want to get married. We asked for their support, and they refused it. They couldn't have been more blunt. I don't understand you, Web," she pleaded. "Why are you suddenly having reservations?"

He glanced at her then and saw the fear on her face. Reaching for her hand, he found it cold and stiff, so he enclosed it in his own, warmer hand and brought it to his thigh. "I'm not having reservations, sweetheart," he said gently. "Not about what I feel for you, or about getting married, or about doing all those things we've been dreaming about. If you know me at all, you know how much they mean to me. It's just that I'm trying to understand your parents, to think of what they must be feeling."

She would have tugged her hand away had he not held it firmly. "How can you be so generous after everything they've done to you?"

"Generosity has nothing to do with it," he barked. "It's selfishness from the word go."

"I don't understand."

Unable to concentrate on the road, he pulled over onto

its shoulder and killed the engine. Then he turned to her and pressed her hand to his heart. "It's for *us*, Marni," he stated forcefully. "You're right. They've done a hell of a lot to me—and to you, too—and for that they don't deserve an ounce of compassion. I'd like to ignore them, to pretend they don't exist, and in the end that may be just what we'll have to do. In the meantime, though, I refuse to let them dictate any of our actions, and that includes when we'll be getting married." His voice gentled, but it maintained its urgency, and his gaze pierced Marni's through the dark of night.

"Don't you see? Our rushing to get married just because of what happened tonight would be a kind of shotgun wedding in reverse. I won't have that! We'll plan our wedding, maybe for a month or two from now, and we'll do it right. I want you wearing a beautiful gown, and I want flowers all over the place, and I want our friends there to witness the day that means so much to us. I will *not* sneak off and elope behind someone's back. I won't have our marriage tainted in any way!"

Through her upset, Marni felt a glimmer of relief. She'd begun to think that Web would put off their marriage indefinitely. A month or two she could live with. And he did have a point; the only purpose of rushing to get married in three days would be to spite her parents. "In a month or two they'll still be resisting," she warned, but less caustically.

"True, but at least we'll know that we've given them every possible chance. If we've done our best, and still they refuse to open up their minds, we'll have nothing to regret in the future." He raised her hand to his lips and gently kissed her palm. "I want it to be as perfect as it can be, sweetheart. Everything open and aboveboard. We owe that to ourselves, don't you think?"

CHAPTER NINE

DURING THE DAY following the scene with Marni's parents, Web convinced himself that he'd been right in what he'd said to Marni. Deep in his heart he suspected that her parents would never accept their marriage, and he regretted it only in terms of Marni's happiness. He had cause to think of his own, though, when he received a call from a friend on Tuesday morning.

Cole Hammond wrote for New York's most notorious gossip sheet parading as a newspaper. The two men had met in a social context soon after Web had arrived in New York, and though Web had no love for Cole's publication, he'd come to respect the man himself. When Cole asked if he could meet with Web to discuss something important, Web promptly invited him over.

"I received an anonymous call today," Cole began soon after Web had tossed him a can of beer. They were in Web's living room. The studio was still being cleaned up from the morning's shoot. "It was from a woman. She claimed that she had a sensational story about you. Something to do with an accident in Maine fourteen years ago?"

Web had had an odd premonition from the moment he'd heard Cole's voice on the phone, which was the main reason he'd had him come right over. "Yes," he agreed warily. "There was an accident."

"This woman said that you were responsible for a man's death. Any truth to it?"

Curbing his anger against "this woman" and her allegations, Web looked his friend in the eye. "No."

"She gave me dates and facts. It was a rainy night, very late, and you were speeding along on a motorcycle with a fellow named Ethan Lange on the back."

"Not speeding. But go on."

"You skidded and collided with a car. Lange was thrown and killed."

"...Is that it?"

"She said you'd been drinking that night and that you had no business being on the road."

"What else?"

Cole shrugged. "That's it. I thought I'd run it by you before I did anything more with it."

"I'm glad you have, for your sake more than mine." Web's entire body was rigid with barely leashed fury. "If you're hoping to get a story out of this, I'd think twice. In the first place, she had the facts wrong. In the second place, the police report will bear that out. And in the third place, if you print something like this, you'll have a hefty lawsuit on your hands. I will not stand by and let you—"

"Hold on, pal," Cole interrupted gently, raising a hand, palm out. "I'd never print a thing without getting the facts straight, which is why I'm here. I know you don't trust the paper, but this is *me*. We've talked about situations like this many times. If the facts don't merit a story, there won't *be* a story." He sat back. "So. Why don't you tell me what happened that night?"

Web took a deep breath and forced himself to calm down. Very slowly and distinctly, he outlined the facts of the accident. By the time he was done, he was back on the edge of fury. "You're being used, Cole. I don't know who the caller was, but I've got a damned good idea.... Is this off the record now, just between us?"

"We're friends. Of course it is."

Web trusted him. He also knew that nothing he was about to say wouldn't come out eventually, and that if Cole chose to print it, friend or no, Web would have even greater grounds for a lawsuit. He knew that Cole knew it, too.

"I'm engaged to marry Marni Lange. It was her brother who died that night. Her parents have always blamed me for the accident, regardless of the facts or the police report. Needless to say, they're totally against our marriage. I suspect that it was her sister who called you, and that her major purpose was vengeance."

Cole ingested the possibility thoughtfully. "It's not a unique motive."

"You should be livid."

The other shrugged. "One out of four may be done for vengeance, but even then there's often a story that will sell."

"Well, there isn't one here. It's history. It may be tragic, but it's not spectacular. Hey, go ahead and check out my story. Get that police report. You can even interview the drivers of the other two cars. They were the first ones to say that there wasn't anything I could have done, that both of them had passed me on the road right before the accident, and that I wasn't weaving around or driving recklessly. The bartender at the tavern we'd been to said we'd been stone sober when we'd left. The first car skidded. The second one collided with it and started spinning. I braked, but the road was wet. I might even have been able to steer clear if one of those cars hadn't careened into me." He took a quick breath, then sagged. "It's all there in black and white. An old story. Not worth fiddling with."

"If you were a nobody, I'd agree with you." When Web bolted forward, he held up his hand again. "Listen, what you say makes sense. I'm just doing my job."

"Your job sucks. This isn't *news,* for God's sake!"

"I agree."

"Do you trust me?"

"I always have."

"Do you believe that what I've told you is the truth?"

Cole paused. "Yes, I believe you."

"Then...you'll forget you got that call?"

Another pause, then a nod. "I will." And a sly grin. "But will you?"

"Not on your life! Someone's going to answer for it!"

"Watch what you do," Cole teased. "You may give me a story yet. Though come to think of it, you've got my news editor wrapped around your little finger. I'm not sure she could bear to print anything adverse about you."

Web's answering grin was thin and dry. "If it'd sell, she'd do it.... Give her a kiss for me, will you?"

"My pleasure."

MARNI'S GUESS AS TO who the caller had been matched Web's, and her anger was as volatile as his had initially been. Fortunately he'd had time to calm down.

"Tanya! That bitch! How could she *dare* try to pull something like this?"

Web put his arm around her and spoke gently. "Maybe she's trying to score points with your parents."

"She's starting at zero, so it won't get her very far," Marni scoffed, then her voice rose. "Maybe my parents put her up to it!"

"Nah. I don't think so, and you shouldn't either, sweetheart. They wouldn't sink that low, would they? I mean, voicing their disapproval to us is one thing, dirty tricks another. And besides, if the whole story came out, particularly the part about our relationship, they'd be as embarrassed as anyone. They wouldn't knowingly hurt themselves."

"I'm not sure 'knowingly' has anything to do with it. They seem to be incapable of rational thought. That's the problem." She pulled away from Web and reached for the phone. "I'm calling Tanya."

His hand settled over hers, preventing further movement. "No. Don't do it."

"She may contact another paper. For that matter, how do we know she hasn't already?"

"Because Cole's is the sleaziest. It's the only one that would have considered touching the story. I'm sure she knew that."

Marni marveled at Web's composure. "Aren't you angry?"

"This morning I would have willingly rung Tanya's neck if I'd seen her. But that wouldn't accomplish anything. It's over, Marni. Cole won't write any story, and confronting Tanya will only make her more determined to do something else."

"What else could she do?" Marni asked with a hysterical laugh.

As IT HAPPENED, it wasn't Tanya, but Marni's father who had something else in mind. The first Marni got wind of it was in a phone call she received on Wednesday afternoon from one of the corporation's directors. He was an old family friend, which eased Marni's indignation somewhat when he suggested that her father was disturbed about her relationship with Brian Webster, and that he hoped she wasn't making a mistake. She calmly assured him that she wasn't, and that no possible harm could come to the corporation from her marriage to Web.

The second call, though, wasn't as excusable. It came

on Thursday morning and was from another of the directors. This one was not a family friend and therefore, theoretically, had no cause to question her private life. Livid, she hung up the phone after talking with him, then stewed at her desk for a time, trying to decide on the best course of action. Indeed, action was called for. If her father was planning to undermine her authority by individually calling each member of the board, she wasn't about to take it sitting down.

She promptly instructed her administrative assistant to summon the board members for a meeting the following morning.

"Your father, too?" Web asked incredulously when she called him to tell him what had happened.

"Yes, my father, too. You were right. Everything should be open and aboveboard. He can hear what I'm going to say along with everyone else."

"What *are* you going to say?"

Her voice dropped for the first time. "I'm not sure." With the next breath, her belligerency resurfaced. "But I'm taking the offensive. Dad's obviously been planting seeds of doubt about me. The only thing I can do is nip it in the bud." She paused, knowing that for all the conviction she might project, she'd called Web because she desperately needed his support.

He didn't let her down. "I agree, sweetheart. I think you've made the right decision. One thing I've learned from talking with you about the corporation is that you haven't gotten where you are by sitting back and waiting for things to happen. You're doing the right thing, Marni. I know it."

She sighed. "I hope so. If Dad has an argument with what I say, he can voice it before the board. Maybe *they* can talk some sense into him."

"Will they?" Web asked very softly. "Will they stand up for you instead of him? How strong is his hold over them?"

"I'll know soon enough, won't I?" she asked sadly.

MARNI STAYED LATE at the office, working with her administrative assistant and secretary to gather, copy and assemble for distribution an armada of facts, figures and reports.

She spent the night with Web at his place, but a pall hung over them, one they couldn't begin to shake. They both sensed that the outcome of Marni's meeting would be telling in terms of her future with the corporation. While on the one hand it was absurd to think that she'd be ousted simply because she married Web, on the other hand neither of them had dreamed Jonathan Lange would do what he already had.

"And if it happens, sweetheart?" Web asked. They were lying quietly curled against each other in bed. Sleep eluded them completely. "What if they side with your father? What will you do then?"

She'd thought about that. "My choice has been made, Web. I told you that. I love you. Our future together is the most important thing to me."

"But you love your work—"

"And I have no intention of giving it up. If the board goes against me, I'll submit my resignation and look for another position. Corporate executives often jump around. We keep the headhunters in business."

"Would you be happy anywhere else but at Lange?"

She smiled up at him, very sure about what she was going to say. "If it meant that I could have both you and my own peace of mind, I'd be happy. Yes, I'd be happy."

AT TEN O'CLOCK the following morning, Marni entered the boardroom. She'd chosen to wear a sedate white wool suit with a navy blouse and accessories. Her hair was perfect, as was her makeup. She knew that no one in the room could fault her appearance. She represented Lange well.

Twelve of the fourteen members of the board were present, talking quietly among themselves until she took her seat at one end of the long table. Her father was at the other. He stood stiffly, and the room was suddenly quiet.

"I will formally call this meeting to order, but since my daughter was the one who organized it, and since I am myself in the dark as to its purpose, I will turn it over to her."

Ignoring both his glower and his very obvious impatience, Marni stood. She rested her hands lightly on the alternating stacks of papers that had been set there for her by her assistant. "Thank you all for coming," she said with quiet confidence, looking from one face to the next, making eye contact wherever possible. "I appreciate the fact that many of you have had to cancel other appointments on such short notice, but I felt the urgency was called for." Pausing, she lifted the first pile of papers from the stack, divided it and sent one half down each side of the table. "Please help yourselves. These are advance copies of our latest production figures, division by division, subsidiary by subsidiary. I don't expect you to read through them now, but I think when you do you'll see that the last quarter was the most productive one Lange has had to date. We're growing, ladies and gentlemen, and we're healthy."

She went to the next pile of papers and passed them around in like fashion. "These are proposals for projects we hope to launch within the next few months. Again, read them at your leisure. I believe that you'll find them exciting, and that you'll see the potential profit in each." She waited until the last of the papers had been distributed, using the time to bolster herself for the tougher part to come. When she had the attention of all those present once more, she went on quietly.

"It is important to me that the board knows of everything that is happening at Lange, and since I'm its president, and as such more visible than our other employees, I want you to be informed and up-to-date on what is happening to me personally." As she spoke her gaze skipped from one member to the next, though she studiously avoided her father's face. He would either intimidate or infuriate her, she feared, and in any case would jeopardize her composure.

"At some point within the next two months, I'll be getting married. My fiancé's name is Brian Webster. Perhaps some of you have heard of him. If not, you'll read about him in the papers I've given you. He's been chosen as the cover photographer for *Class*, the new magazine our publishing division will be putting out. Let me say now that, although Mr. Webster and I knew each other many years ago, the decision to hire him was made first and foremost by the publishing division. At the time I didn't realize that the man I knew so long ago was the same photographer New York has gone wild for. We met, and I realized who he was only after the contracts had been signed and he'd begun to work for us."

There were several nods of understanding from various members of the group, so she went on. "The fact of my marriage will in no way interfere with the quality of work I do for Lange. I believe you all know of my dedication to the corporation. Mr. Webster certainly knows of it. My father built this business from scratch, and I take great pride in seeing that it grows and prospers." She dared a glance at her father then. He was sitting straight, his eyes hard, his lips compressed into a thin line. She quickly averted her gaze to more sympathetic members of the group.

"You may be asking yourself why I felt it so important to call you here simply to tell you of my engagement. I did it because I wanted to assure you that I intend to continue as president of Lange. But there was another reason as well. There is," she said slowly, "a very important matter concerning Brian Webster and my family that some of you may already know about, but which I wanted all of you to hear about first hand. There is apt to be speculation, and perhaps some ill will, but I'm counting on you all to keep that in perspective."

She lifted her hand from the last pile of papers and sent them around the table. "Fourteen years ago Brian Webster and my brother Ethan were good friends. Brian was the one driving the motorcycle on the night Ethan was killed."

Barely a murmur surfaced among those present, which more than anything told Marni that her father had been busier than she'd thought. The knowledge made her all the more determined to thwart his efforts to discredit both her and Web.

"What you have before you are copies of the police report from that night. You'll learn that Mr. Webster was found entirely without fault in the accident. I've also included excerpts from articles about Brian and his work. They were gathered by the publishing division when it cast its vote for him as the *Class* photographer. I don't think any of us can fault either his qualifications or his character."

She took a deep breath and squared her shoulders. "There are some who will claim that Brian was responsible for Ethan's death, and that I am therefore acting irresponsibly by thinking of marrying him. Once you've read what I've given you, I feel confident that you'll agree with me that this is not the case. In no way could Brian Webster embarrass this corporation, or me, and in no way could he adversely affect the job I plan to do as your continuing president."

She looked down, moistened her lips, then raised her chin high. "Are there any questions I might answer? If any of you have doubts as to my moral standing, I'd appreciate your airing them now." Her gaze passed from one director to another. There were shrugs, several headshakes, several frighteningly bland expressions. And then there was her father.

With both hands on the edge of the table, he pushed himself to his feet. "I have questions, and doubts, but you've already heard them."

"That's right. I have. I'd like to know if any of the other members of the board share your opinion. If a majority of the others agree with you, I'll submit my resignation as of now and seek a position elsewhere."

That statement did cause a minor stir, but it consisted of gasps and grunts, the swiveling of heads and a shifting in seats, so that in the end Marni wasn't sure whether the group was in her favor or against. Her gaze encompassed all those who would sit in judgment on her.

"I truly believe that what we have here is a difference of opinion between my father and myself." She purposely didn't include mention of her mother or Tanya. "It should have remained private, and would have, had it not been for calls that were made to several of you that I know of, perhaps all of you—which is why I've asked you here today. It's not your place to decide who I should or shouldn't marry, but since it is in your power to decide whether or not I remain as president of this corporation, I felt that my interests, and Brian's, should be represented.

"As it is, someone tried to plant a story in one of the local papers." She was staring at her father then and was oblivious to the other eyes that widened in dismay. "It would have been a scandal based on nothing but sleazy headlines. Fortunately, Brian is well enough respected in this community that the writer who received the anonymous tip very quickly dismissed it as soon as he heard the truth. Now—" her eyes circled the room again "—do any of you have questions I can answer before I leave?"

Emma Landry spoke up, smiling. "When's the wedding?"

Marni smiled in return. She knew she had one ally. "We haven't set the date yet."

"Will we all be invited?" asked Geoffrey Gould.

"Every one of you," she said, seeking out her father's gaze and holding it for a minute before returning her attention to the group. There were several stern faces among them, several more meek. All she could do was to pray she'd presented her case well.

"If there are no further questions," she said, taking a breath, "I'll leave you to vote on whether I'll be staying on as president. If you say 'yes,' I'll take it as a vote of confidence in what I've done at Lange during the past seven years. If you say 'no,' I'll accept it with regret and move on." Her voice lowered and was for the first time less steady as she looked at her father a final time. "I'll be at my mother's awaiting your decision."

That, too, had been a studied decision. Marni had felt that it would be a show, albeit false, of some support from her family. But she did want to tell Adele what she'd done. If she failed with this group, her mother would witness firsthand her pain. If she succeeded, it would be a perfect opportunity to try to swing Adele to her way of thinking.

Marni had no idea that Web was a full step ahead of her.

"I APPRECIATE YOUR seeing me, Mrs. Lange," Web said after he was shown into the solarium at the back of the house.

"I would have called beforehand, but I didn't want to be turned down on the phone. I know that your husband is in the city at a meeting of the board of directors."

"That's right," Adele said quietly. She was sitting in a high-backed wicker chair, with her elbows on its broad arms and her hands resting in her lap.

"You're probably wondering why I'm here, and, to tell you the truth—" he rubbed the tense muscles at the back of his neck "—part of me is, too. It was obvious at our last meeting that you agree with your husband in your opinion of me, and I'm not sure I could change it if I wanted to." He sighed and sat forward, propping his elbows on his thighs. He studied his hands, which hung between his knees, then frowned.

"Perhaps this is a sexist thing to say, but I thought I might appeal to your softer side. All women have a softer side. I know Marni does. Right about now it's not showing, because she's addressing the board of directors, and I'm sure she's making as businesslike a pitch as she can for their understanding. But the softer side's there, not very far from the surface. Marni loves me. She's aching because she loves you both, too, and it hurts her that she's had to make a choice between us."

"She chose you," Adele stated evenly. "I'd think you would be pleased."

He looked up. "Pleased, yes. I'm pleased, and relieved, because I don't think I could make it through a future without her. But I don't feel a sense of victory, if that's what you're suggesting. There's no victory when a family is torn apart, particularly one that has already suffered its share of loss."

Adele arched a brow. "Do *you* know about loss, Mr. Webster?"

"No. At least, not as you know it. One can't lose things

one has never had. I never had a father. Did you know that?"

"No. No, I didn't."

"There's a lot you don't know about me. I'd like to tell you, if I may."

Adele paused, then nodded. Though she maintained an outer semblance of arrogance, there was a hint of curiosity in her eyes. Web wasn't about to pass that up.

"I never knew my father. He and my mother didn't marry. When I was two my mother married another man, a good man, a hard worker. I'm afraid I didn't make things terribly easy for him. For reasons I didn't understand at the time, I was restless. I hated school, but I loved to learn. I spent my nights reading everything I could get my hands on, but during the days I felt compelled to move around. Instead of going to college, I took odd jobs where I could find them. I traveled the world, literally, working my way from one place to the next.

"Then I met Ethan. We shared a mutual respect. Through him, I realized I had to settle down, that I wouldn't get anywhere if I didn't focus in on one thing and try to be good at it. I was a jack of all trades, master of none. And I was tired of it."

He gazed at his thumbnail, pressed it with his other thumb. "Maybe I'd simply reached an age where it was time to grow up. After Ethan died, I did a lot of thinking. There were many unresolved feelings I had, about my father and about myself. I don't know who my father is, so those feelings will remain unresolved to a point. But fourteen years ago I realized that I couldn't let them affect my life, that I didn't really need to be running around to escape that lack of identity. That if I stayed in one place and built a life, a reputation for myself, I could make up for it."

He raised his eyes to Adele's intent ones and wondered

if she realized the extent of her involvement with his story. "I think I have. But there's more I want, and it involves Marni." He sat up in the chair. "I adore that woman, Mrs. Lange. You have no idea how much. I want to marry her, and we want children."

"You've already told us that," Adele pointed out, but the edge was gone from her voice.

"Yes, but I'm not sure if you realize how much Marni wants our family to encompass you and your husband. Do you want her to be happy, Mrs. Lange?"

"Of course. I'm her mother. What mother wouldn't want that for her daughter?"

"I don't know," he said slowly. "That's what I'm trying to understand."

"Are you accusing me of being blind to what Marni needs, when she sat here herself last Sunday night and announced that she'd go ahead with her plans regardless of what we said or did?"

He kept his tone gentle. "I'm not accusing you of anything. What I'm suggesting is that maybe you don't fully understand Marni's needs. I'm not sure I did myself until I heard what she said to you the other night. She badly wants your approval. You're right, she and I will go ahead and get married even if you continue to hold out. We'll have our home and our children, and we'll be happy. But there will always be a tiny part of Marni that will feel the loss of her parents, and it will be such a premature and unnecessary loss that it will be all the sadder." He paused. "How will *you* feel about such a loss? You lost your son through a tragedy none of us could control. This one would be a tragedy of your own making."

"Ethan would have been alive if it hadn't been—"

"Do you honestly believe that? *Honestly?* Am I a killer,

Mrs. Lange? Look at me and tell me if you think I am truly a killer."

Scowling, she shifted in her seat. "Well, not in the sense of a hardened criminal..."

"Not in any sense. I think in your heart you agree. Otherwise you never would have let me talk with you today."

"My husband's out. That's why I'm talking with you today."

"Then he's the one who dictates your opinion?"

"We've been married for nearly forty years, Mr. Webster. I respect what my husband feels strongly about."

"Even when he's wrong?"

"I...I owe him my loyalty."

"But what about the loyalty you owe your children? You had a choice when it came to picking your husband. Your children had no choice about being born. You gave them life and brought them into this world. They had no say in the matter. Marni didn't *choose* you to be her mother, any more than she chose to be Ethan's sister. And she didn't choose to have him killed in that accident, yet she's spent the past fourteen years trying to make up to you for it. Don't you owe her some kind of loyalty for that?"

"Now you're asking me to make a choice between my daughter and my husband."

"No. I'm simply asking you to decide for yourself whether Marni's marrying me would be so terrible, and if you decide that it wouldn't be, that you try to convince your husband of it. We're not asking for an open-armed welcome. We'll very happily settle for peaceful coexistence. You don't have to love me, Mrs. Lange, but if you love your daughter you'll respect the fact that *she* loves me."

"Web!"

Both heads in the room riveted toward its door, where

Marni was standing in a state of utter confusion. Web came instantly to his feet.

"What are you doing here?" she asked, her brows knitting as she looked from him to her mother and back.

"We were just talking." He approached her quickly, ran his hands along her arms and spoke very softly. "How did it go?"

"I don't know. I left before they took a vote. Then I needed a little time to myself, so I took the roundabout way getting here." Apprehension was written all over her face. "There's been no word?"

Web hesitated, then shook his head.

Adele frowned. "A vote? What vote?"

"As to whether I should remain as president. I tendered my resignation, pending the board's decision."

Adele, too, was on her feet then. "You didn't! What a foolish thing to do, Marni! You've been a fine president! You can't be replaced!"

"Oh, I can. No one's indispensable."

"But we always intended that the presidency should remain in the family!"

"Maybe Tanya should give it a try," Marni suggested dryly, only to be answered by an atypical and distinctly unladylike snort from her mother.

"Tanya! That's quite amusing." Her head shot up. "Jonathan! When did *you* get here?"

Web had seen the man approach, but Marni, with her back to the door, had had no such warning. Turning abruptly, her heart in her throat, she faced the tired and stern face of her father.

CHAPTER TEN

AT ONE TIME Marni might have run to Jonathan Lange. Too much had passed between them in recent days, though, and she grew rigid as he approached. Web dropped his hands to his sides but stayed close, offering his silent support as they both waited to hear what her father had to say.

The older man ran a hand through his thinning gray hair, then glanced at his wife. "I could use a drink."

"Duncan? Duncan!" Adele's voice rang out, and the butler promptly appeared. "Mr. Lange will have his usual. I'll have mine with water." She turned to Marni and Web, her brows raised. When they both shook their heads, she nodded to Duncan. "That will be all."

Jonathan walked past them, deeper into the solarium. He stopped before one glass expanse, thrust his hands in his pockets and, stiff-backed, stood with his feet apart as he gazed at the late March landscape.

Marni stared after him. She knew he had news, but whether it was good or bad she had no idea. In that instant she realized how very much she did want to stay on as president of Lange.

Adele looked from Marni to her husband, then back.

Web, standing close behind Marni, put his hands lightly at her waist. "Do you want to sit down?" he asked softly.

She shook her head, but her eyes didn't leave her father's rigid back. "Dad? What happened?"

Jonathan didn't answer immediately. He raised a hand

and scratched his neck, then returned the hand to his pocket. Duncan entered the solarium, offered Adele her drink from a small silver tray, then crossed the room to offer Jonathan his. Only when the butler had left did Jonathan turn. He held the drink in both hands, watching his thumbs as they brushed against the condensation beginning to form on the side of the glass.

"I didn't know she'd done that, Marni," he began solemnly. "I had no idea Tanya had called that reporter—"

"What reporter?" Adele interrupted fearfully. "What has Tanya done?"

There was sadness, almost defeat in the expression Jonathan turned on his wife. "Tanya tried to plant a story in the newspaper about the accident and Webster's role in it."

Adele clutched her glass to her chest. "Tanya did *that?*"

Jonathan's gaze met Marni's. "I have no proof that it was Tanya, but no one else would have had cause except perhaps your mother and I. But I never would have condoned something like that. I'll have a thing or two to say to your sister when I call her later."

Marni couldn't move. Her heart was pounding as she waited, waited. "It's not important. What happened at the meeting? Was a vote taken?"

He took a drink. The ice rattled as he lowered his glass. "Yes."

"And...?"

Jonathan studied the ice, but it was Marni who felt its chill. "You'll be staying on as president of Lange. There was an easy majority in your favor."

Marni closed her eyes in a moment's prayerful thanks. Web's hands tightened on her waist when she swayed. It was his support, and the warmth of his body reaching out to her, that gave her the strength to open her eyes and address her father again.

"And you, Dad? How did you vote?"

Jonathan cleared his throat. "I exercised my right to abstain."

It was better than a flat-out "no," but it left major questions unanswered. "May I ask why?"

He tipped his head fractionally in a gesture of acquiescence. "I felt that I was too emotionally involved to make a rational decision."

"Then you do question my ability as president?"

He cleared his throat again. As before, it brought him an extra few seconds to formulate his response. "No. I simply question my own ability to see the truth one way or the other."

Such a simple statement, Marni mused, yet it was a powerful concession. Up to that point, Jonathan had refused to see anything but what he wanted to see. The fact that he could admit his view might be jaded was a major victory.

Web felt the release of tension in Marni's body. He, too, had immediately understood the significance of Jonathan's statement, and he shared her relief and that small sense of triumph, even hope. Lowering his head, he murmured, "Perhaps we should leave your parents alone now. I think both you and your father have been through enough today."

She knew he was right. It was a matter of quitting while she was ahead. If she stayed and forced her father to say more, she might well push him into a corner. He was a proud man. For the present it was enough to leave with the hope that one day he might actually join her in *her* corner.

Mutely she nodded. Under Web's guiding hand, she left the solarium and walked back through the house to the front door. Only when she reached it did she realize that her mother had come along.

"Darling…" Adele began. Her hand clutched the doorknob, and she seemed unsure of herself. Marni had turned, surprised and slightly wary. "I…I'm pleased things worked out for you with the board."

"So am I," Marni answered quietly. "I never really wanted to leave Lange."

Adele's voice was a whisper. "I know that." She gave an awkward smile, reached up as if to stroke Marni's hair, but drew her hand back short of physical contact. "Perhaps… perhaps we can get together for lunch one day next week?"

Marni wasn't about to look a gift horse in the mouth. She was pleased, and touched. "I'd like that, Mom. Will you call?"

Adele nodded, her eyes suspiciously moist. She did touch Marni then, wrapping an arm around her waist and pressing a cheek to hers in a quick hug. "You'd better leave now," she whispered. "Drive safely."

Marni, too, felt the emotion of the moment. She nodded and smiled through her own mist of tears, then let Web guide her out the door and down the front steps to their cars.

"I DON'T BELIEVE THESE!" Marni exclaimed in delight. She was sitting cross-legged on Web's bed, wearing nothing but the stack of photographs he'd so nonchalantly tossed into her lap moments before. "They're incredible!"

He came to sit behind her, fitting his larger body to hers so that he could look over her shoulder at the pictures he'd taken three days before. "They're *you*. Exactly what I wanted for the premier cover of *Class*."

Astonished, Marni flipped from one shot to the next. "They're all so good, Web! How are you ever going to decide which one to use? For that matter, how did you ever get so many perfect ones?"

He nipped at her bare shoulder, then soothed the spot with his chin. "I had a super model. That's all there is to it. As for which one to use, I've got my personal preference, but your people will have some say in that." He curled one long arm around hers and extracted a print from the pile. "I sent a duplicate of this one to your parents yesterday."

She met his gaze at her shoulder. "You didn't."

"I did. It's beautiful, don't you think? Every parent should have a picture like this of his daughter."

"But...isn't that a little heavy-handed? I mean, Mom and I have just begun to talk things through." Two weeks had passed since the board meeting, and she'd met with her mother as many times during that stretch.

"You said yourself that she's softening up. And if anything will speed up the process, this will. Look at it, Marni. Look at your expression here. It's so...*you*. The determined set of chin, the little bit of mischief at the mouth, the tilt of the eyebrows with just a hint of indignation, and the eyes, ah, the eyes..."

"Filled with love," she whispered, but she wasn't looking at the picture. Her own eyes were reflected in Web's, and the love flowing between them was awesome.

Web caught his breath, then haphazardly scattered the pictures from Marni's lap and turned her so she was straddling his legs. His fingers delved into her hair, and he held her face steady. "I love you, sunshine. Ohhh, do I love you." When she smiled, he ran his tongue over the curve. Then he caught her lower lip between his own lips and sipped at it.

Marni was floating wild and free, with Web as her anchor, the only one she'd ever truly need. She slipped her arms around his neck and tangled her fingers in the hair at his nape, fighting for his lips, then his tongue, then the very air he breathed.

"Where did you ever...get that passion?" he gasped. His hands had begun a questing journey over the planes and swells of her soft body.

"From you, my dear man," she breathed, greedily bunching her fingers over the twisting muscles of his back. "You taught me…fourteen years ago…and I haven't been the same since…ahhh, Web…" He'd found her breasts and was taunting them mercilessly. "Will it always…be this way?"

"Always." He rolled her nipples between his thumb and forefinger and was rewarded by her gasp.

"Promise?" She spread her hand over his flat middle and let it follow the tapering line of dark hair to that point where it flared.

"Sunshine…mmmmmmm…ah, yesss…" What little thought her artful stroking left him was centered in his fingers, which found the tiny nub of pleasure between her legs and began to caress it as artfully. "Ahhhh, sweet… so moist, soft…"

They were both breathing shallowly, and Marni's body had begun to quiver in tune with his.

"C'mere," he ordered. Cupping her bottom, he drew her forward, capturing her mouth and swallowing her rapturous moan as he entered her.

Knees braced on either side of his hips, she moved in rhythm with him. Her breasts rubbed against his with each forward surge, and their mouths mated hungrily. They rose together on passion's ladder, reaching the very highest rung before Web held her back.

"Watch," he whispered. He lowered his gaze to the point of their joining, then, when her head too was bowed, he slowly withdrew, as slowly filled her again, then repeated the movement.

It was too much for Marni. She cried his name once, then threw back her head and closed her eyes tight upon the waves of pulsing sensation that poured through her.

Web held himself buried deep inside her, hoping to savor each one of her spasms, but their very strength was his undoing. Without so much as another thrust, he gave a throaty moan and exploded. Arms trembling, he clutched her tightly to him. She was his anchor in far more than the storm of passion. He could only thank God that she was his.

ON A BRIGHT, sunny morning in early June, Marni and Web were married. The ceremony was held beneath the trees in the backyard of the Langes' Long Island estate and was followed by a lavish lawn luncheon for the two hundred invited guests.

Marni's mother was radiant, exuding the air of confidence that was her social trademark. Marni's father was gracious, if stoical, accepting congratulations with the formality that was his professional trademark.

Marni was in seventh heaven. Her mother had been the one to insist that the wedding be held there, and she'd personally orchestrated every step of the affair. While her father hadn't once vocally blessed the marriage, Marni had seen the tears in his eyes in those poignant moments when he'd led her down the rose-strewn aisle and to the altar, then given her away. She'd whispered a soft "I love you" to him as she'd kissed him, but after that her eyes had been only for Web.

"I now pronounce you man and wife," the minister had said, and she'd gone into Web's arms with a sense of joy, of fulfillment and promise that had once only been a dream.

In the years to come, they'd have their home, their careers and their children. Most important, though, they'd have each other. Their ties went back to when they'd both been young. They'd weathered personal storms along the way, but they'd emerged as better people, and their love was supreme.

* * * * *

A SINGLE ROSE

CHAPTER ONE

VICTORIA LESSER TOOK a break from the conversation to sit back and silently enjoy the two couples with her. They were a striking foursome. Neil Hersey, with his dark hair and close-cropped beard, was a perfect foil for his fair and petite wife, Deirdre, but the perfection of the match didn't stop at their looks. Deirdre's quick spirit complimented Neil's more studied approach to life. In the nineteen months of their marriage, they'd both grown personally and professionally.

As had the Rodenhisers. Though married a mere six months, they'd been together for nearly fifteen. Leah, with her glossy raven pageboy and bangs and the large round glasses perched on her nose, had found the ideal mate in Garrick, who gave her the confidence to live out her dreams. Garrick, sandy-haired, tall, and bearded like Neil, had finally tasted the richness of life that he'd previously assumed existed only in a scriptwriter's happy ending.

Glancing from one face to the next as the conversation flowed around her, Victoria congratulated herself on bringing the four together. It had been less of a brainstorm, of course, than her original matchmaking endeavors, but it was making for a lively and lovely evening.

Feeling momentarily superfluous, she let her gaze meander among the elegantly dressed patrons of the restaurant. She spotted several familiar faces on the far side of the room, and when her attention returned to her own party, she met Deirdre's eye. "Recognize them, Dee?"

Deirdre nodded and spoke in a hushed voice to her husband. "The Fitzpatricks and the Grants. They were at the lawn party Mother gave last fall."

Neil's wry grin was a flash of white cutting through his beard. His voice was low and smooth. "I'm not sure I remember the Fitzpatricks or the Grants, but I do remember that party. We were leaving Benji with a baby-sitter, and almost didn't get away. He was three months old and in one hell of a mood." He sent a lopsided grin across the table. "He takes after his mother in that respect."

Deirdre rolled her eyes. "Don't believe a word he says."

"Just tell me it gets better," Leah Rodenhiser begged. "You heard what Amanda gave us tonight."

Victoria, who had never had a child of her own and adored even the baby's wail, answered with the gentle voice of authority. "Of course it gets better. Amanda was just frightened. My apartment is strange and new to her. So is the baby-sitter. I left this number, but we haven't gotten a frantic call yet, have we?"

"I think you're about to get a frantic call from across the room," came a gravelly warning from Garrick. "They've spotted you, Victoria."

"Oh dear."

"Go on over," Deirdre urged softly. "If you don't, they'll come here. Spare us that joy. We'll talk babies until you get back."

Victoria, who knew all too well Deirdre's aversion to many of her mother's friends, shot her a chiding glance. But the glance quickly mellowed, and touched each of her guests in turn. "You don't mind?"

Leah grinned and answered for them all. "Go. We're traveling sub rosa."

"Sub rosa?"

"Incognito." Beneath the table she felt Garrick squeeze her hand. Once a well-known television star, he cherished his privacy. Basically shy herself, Leah protected it well.

"Are you sure you can manage without me?" Victoria quipped, standing when Neil drew out her chair. "Talk babies. I dare you." Her mischievous tone faded away as she headed off to greet her friends.

Four pairs of eyes watched her go, each pair as affectionate as the next. Victoria held a special place in their hearts, and they weren't about to talk babies when there were more immediate things to be said.

"She is a wonder," Leah sighed. "Little did I know what a gem I'd encountered when I ran into her that day in the library."

Neil was more facetious. "We didn't think she was such a gem when she stranded us on her island up in Maine. I don't think I've ever been as furious with anyone before."

"You were pretty furious with me before that day was out," Deirdre reminded him.

His grin grew devilish. "You asked for it. Lord, I wasn't prepared for you." He shifted his gaze to Leah and Garrick. "She was unbelievably bitchy. Had her leg in a cast and a mouth—"

Deirdre hissed him into silence, but couldn't resist reminiscing on her own. "It was just as well there weren't any neighbors. We'd have driven them crazy. We yelled at each other for days."

"While Leah and I were silent," Garrick said. "We were isolated in my cabin together, barely talking. I'm not sure which way is worse."

"Amazing how both worked out," Leah mused.

Deirdre nodded. "I'll second that."

"We owe Victoria one," Neil said.

"Two," Garrick amended.

Deirdre twirled the swizzle stick in her spritzer. "It's a tall order. The woman has just about everything she wants and needs."

Leah frowned. "There has to be something we can do in return for all she's given us."

"She needs a man."

Deirdre was quick to refute her husband's contention. "Come on, Neil. She has all the men she wants. And you know she'll never remarry. Arthur was the one and only love of her life."

Garrick exchanged a glance with Neil. "That doesn't mean we can't treat her to some fun."

Leah studied her husband. "I'm not sure I care for that mischievous gleam in your eye. Victoria is my friend. I won't have you—"

"She's my friend, too," he interrupted innocently. "Would I do anything to harm her?"

Neil was on Garrick's wavelength all the way. "The idea is to do something for her that she wouldn't dream up by herself."

"But she does just about everything she wants to," Deirdre pointed out. "She lives in luxury, dabbles in ballet, ceramics, the cello. She travels. She has the house in Southampton...." Her eyes brightened. "We could rent a yacht, hire a crew and put them at her disposal for a week. She'd be able to go off alone or invite friends along."

Garrick absently chafed his mustache with a finger. "Too conventional."

"How about a stint with Outward Bound?" Leah suggested. "There are groups formed specifically for women over forty."

Neil shot Garrick a look. "Not quite what I had in mind."

Deirdre had caught and correctly interpreted the look.

"You have a one-track mind. Believe me, we'd be hard put to find a man with enough spunk for Victoria. Can you think of anyone suitable at Joyce?" Joyce Enterprises was Deirdre's family's corporation. Upon their marriage, Neil had taken it over and brought it from stagnation to productivity to expansion. Of the many new people he'd hired—or clients and associates of the company—Deirdre couldn't think of a single male who would be challenge enough for Victoria.

Neil's silence was ample show of agreement.

"It would be fun," Leah declared, "to turn the tables on Victoria."

"Someone good-looking," Deirdre said, warming to the idea.

Leah nodded. "And bright. We want a match here."

Neil rubbed his bearded jaw. "He'll have to be financially comfortable if he can afford to go in for adventure."

"Adventure," Garrick murmured. "That's the key."

Deirdre's brows lifted toward Neil. "Flash?" Flash Jensen was a neighbor of theirs in the central Connecticut suburb where they lived. A venture capitalist and a divorcé, he was always on the lookout for novel ways to spend his time.

Neil shook his head. "Flash is a little too much."

Leah chuckled. "We could always fix her up with one of Garrick's trapper friends. She'd die."

Garrick nodded, but he was considering another possibility. "There's a fellow I've met. One of my professors." Earlier he'd explained to the Herseys that he was working toward a Latin degree at Dartmouth. "Samson may well…fit the bill."

"Samson?" Leah echoed in mild puzzlement. She knew who he was, but nothing of what Garrick had told her in the past put the man forward as a viable candidate.

"He's a widower, and he's the right age."

Deirdre sat straighter. "Samson. From the name alone, I love him."

"That's because you've always had this thing about full heads of hair," Neil muttered in her ear. He'd never quite forgotten their earliest days together, when, among other things, she'd made fun of his widow's peak.

Deirdre hadn't forgotten either. As self-confident as Neil was, he had his sensitivities, and his hairline was one of them. "Forget hair," she whispered back. "Think strength. You have it even without the hair."

"You're putting your foot in deeper," he grumbled.

"I think you're right." Hastily she turned to Garrick, who'd been having a quiet discussion with Leah during the Herseys' private sparring. "Tell us about Samson."

Garrick was more than willing. "His name is Samson VanBaar. Leah thinks he's too conservative, but that's because she doesn't know him the way I do."

"He smokes a pipe," Leah informed them dryly.

"But that's all part of the image, love. Tweed jacket, pipe, tattered briefcase—he does it for effect. Tongue-in-cheek. A private joke."

"Weird private joke," was Leah's retort, but her tone had softened. "Do you really think he'd be right for Victoria?"

"If we're talking adventure, yes. He's good-looking and bright. He's independently wealthy. And he loves doing the unconventional." When Leah remained skeptical, he elaborated. "He's a private person, shy in some ways. He takes his little trips for his own pleasure, and they have nothing to do with the university. I had to coax him to talk, but once he got going, his stories were fascinating."

Deirdre sat forward, propping her chin in her hand. "We're listening."

"How does dogsledding across the Yukon sound?"

"Challenging."

"How about a stint as a snake charmer in Bombay?"

"Not bad, if you're into snakes."

"Try living with the Wabians in Papua New Guinea."

"That does sound a little like Victoria," Leah had to admit. "When I first met her, she was boning up on the Maori of New Zealand."

Neil rubbed his hands together. "Okay. Let's see what we've got. A, the guy is okay in terms of age and marital status. B, he's good-looking and reasonably well-off. C, he's a respected member of the academic community." At the slight question in his voice, Garrick nodded. "And D, he's an adventurer." He took a slow breath. "So how do we go about arranging an adventure that Victoria could join him in?"

"I believe," Garrick said with a smug gleam in his eye, "it's already arranged. Samson VanBaar will be leaving next month for Colombia, from which point he'll sail across the Caribbean to Costa Rica in search of buried treasure."

"Buried treasure!"

"Gold?"

"He has a map," Garrick went on, his voice lower, almost secretive. "It's old and faded—"

"You've seen it?"

"You bet, and it looked authentic enough to me. Samson is convinced that it leads to a cache on the Costa Rican coast."

"It's so absurd, it's exciting!"

"Could be a wild-goose chase. On the other hand—"

"Victoria would love it!"

"She very well might," Garrick concluded.

Neil was weighing the pros and cons. "Even if nothing comes of it in terms of a treasure, it'd certainly be a fun—how long?"

"I think he's allowed himself two weeks."

"Two weeks." Deirdre mulled it over. "Could be disastrous if they can't stand each other."

"She threw us together for two weeks, and we couldn't stand each other."

"It wasn't that we couldn't stand each other, Neil. We just had other things on our minds."

"We couldn't stand each other."

"Well, maybe at the beginning, but even then we couldn't keep our hands off each other."

Garrick coughed.

Leah rushed in to fill the momentary silence. "She threw us together for an indefinite period of time."

"Not that she planned it that way. She didn't count on mud season."

"That's beside the point. She sat by while I gave up my loft and put my furniture into storage. Then she sent me off to live in a cabin that had burned to the ground three months before. She knew I wouldn't have anywhere to go but your place, and those first few days were pretty tense...." Her words trailed off. Remembering the nights, she shot Garrick a shy glance and blushed.

Deirdre came to her aid. "There's one significant difference here, I believe. Victoria got us together in Maine; she got you two together in New Hampshire. Costa Rica—that's a little farther afield, and definitely foreign soil."

"It's a democratic country," Garrick pointed out, "and a peaceful one."

"Right next door to Nicaragua?" Leah asked in dismay, pushing her glasses higher on her nose as she turned to Neil. "Do you know anything about Costa Rica?"

"She is peaceful. Garrick's right about that. She's managed to stay out of her neighbors' turmoil. And she happens to be the wealthiest country in Central America."

"Then Victoria would be relatively safe?"

Garrick nodded.

"From Samson?" Deirdre asked. "Is he an honest sort of man?"

"Completely."

"Gentle?"

"Infinitely."

"Law abiding?"

"A Latin professor on tenure at one of the Ivies?" was Garrick's answer-by-way-of-a-question.

Neil stopped chewing on the inside of his cheek. "Is he, in any way, shape or manner, a lecher?"

"I've never heard any complaints," Garrick said. "Victoria can handle him. She's one together lady."

Having no argument there, Neil put the matter to an impromptu vote. "Are we in agreement that two weeks with Samson VanBaar won't kill her?"

Three heads nodded in unison.

"I'll speak with Samson and make the arrangements," Garrick offered. "I can't see that he'd have any objection to bringing one more person along on the trip, but we'd better not say anything to Victoria until I've checked it out."

"It'll be a surprise."

"She won't be able to refuse."

"She'll never know what hit her."

Garrick's lips twitched. "That'd be poetic justice, don't you think? After what she did to us—" His voice rose and he broke into his best show-stopping smile as the object of their discussion returned. "Hel-lo, Victoria!"

FIVE DAYS AFTER that dinner in New York, Victoria received a bulky registered letter from New Hampshire. Opening it, she unfolded the first piece of paper she encountered.

"Dear Victoria," she read in Garrick's classic scrawl.

"A simple thank you couldn't possibly convey our gratitude for all you've done. Hence, the enclosures. You'll find a round-trip ticket to Colombia, plus detailed instruction on where to go once you're there. You'll be taking part in a hunt for buried treasure led by one of my professors, a fascinating gentleman named Samson VanBaar. We happen to know you have no other plans for the last two weeks in July, and if you try to call us to weasel your way out, we won't be in. Samson is expecting you on the fourteenth. Have a wonderful time! All our love, Garrick and Leah and Deirdre and Neil."

Bemused, Victoria sank into the Louis XVI chair just inside the living-room arch. A treasure hunt? She set aside the plane tickets and read through the instructions and itinerary Garrick had seen fit to send.

New York to Miami to Barranquilla by plane. Accommodations in Barranquilla at El Prado, where Samson Van-Baar would make contact. Brief drive from Barranquilla to Puerto Colombia. Puerto Colombia to Costa Rica—Costa Rica—by sail. Exploration of the Caribbean coast of Costa Rica as designated by Samson VanBaar's treasure map. Return by sail to Colombia and by plane to New York. Expect much sun, occasional rain. Dress accordingly.

The instructions joined the letter and tickets on her lap. She couldn't believe it! She'd known they had something up their sleeves when she'd returned to the table that night and seen smugness in their eyes.

They'd been sly; she had to hand it to them. They'd waited until the arrangements were made before presenting her with the fait accompli. Oh, yes, she could graciously refuse, but they knew she wouldn't. She knew she wouldn't. She'd never gone in search of buried treasure before, and though she certainly had no need for treasure, the prospect of the search was too much to resist!

Other things had been swirling around in those scheming minds of theirs as well. She knew because she'd been there herself. And because she'd been there, she knew it had something to do with Samson VanBaar. Were they actually fixing her up?

She'd sent Deirdre and Neil to the island in Maine after receiving separate, desperate calls begging for a place of solitude. She'd sent Leah to New Hampshire, to a cabin that didn't exist, knowing Leah would have no recourse but to seek out Garrick, her nearest neighbor on the mountain. What would Victoria find when she arrived in Colombia?

If Samson VanBaar was one of Garrick's professors, he had to be responsible. He might be wonderful. Or he might be forty years old and too young for her, or old and stuffy and too dry for her. One of Garrick's professors. A Latin professor. Definitely old and stuffy and dry. Perhaps simply the organizer of the expedition. In which case the Herseys and the Rodenhisers had someone else in mind. Someone else in the group?

There were many questions and far too few answers, but Victoria did know one thing. She had already blocked out the last two weeks in July for a treasure hunt. It was an opportunity, a challenge, an adventure. Regardless of her friends' wily intentions, she knew she could handle herself.

As THAT DAY zipped by and the next began, Victoria couldn't help but think more and more about the trip. She had to admit that there was something irresistibly romantic about a sail through the Caribbean and a treasure hunt. Perhaps this Samson VanBaar would turn out to be a pirate at heart. Or perhaps one of the other group members would be the pirate.

That night, unable to shake a particularly whimsical thought, she settled in the chintz-covered chaise in the sitting area of her bedroom and put through a call to her niece.

"Hi there, Shaye!"

"Victoria?" Shaye Burke hadn't called Victoria "aunt" in years. Victoria was a dear friend with whom she'd weathered many a storm. "It's so good to hear your voice!"

"Yours, sweetheart, is sounding foreign. Do you have something against dialing the phone?"

Duly chastised, Shaye sank onto the tall stool by the kitchen phone and spoke with a fair amount of contrition. "I'm sorry, Victoria. Work's been hectic. By the time I get home my mind is addled."

"Did you just get in?"

"Mmm. We're in the process of installing a new system. It's time consuming, not to mention energy consuming." Shaye headed the computer department of a law firm in Philadelphia that specialized in corporate work. Victoria was familiar enough with such firms to know that computerization had become critical to their productivity.

"And the bulk of the responsibility is on your shoulders, I'd guess."

Shaye nodded, too tired to realize that Victoria couldn't see the gesture. "Not that I'm complaining. The new machines are incredible. Once we're fully on-line, we'll be able to do that much more that much more quickly."

"When will that be?"

"Hopefully by the end of next week. I'll have to work this weekend, but that's nothing new."

"Ahh, Shaye, where's your private life?"

"What's a private life?" Shaye returned with mock innocence.

Victoria saw nothing remotely amusing in the matter.

"Private life is that time you spend away from work. It's critical, sweetheart. If you're not careful, you'll burn out before you're thirty."

"Then I'd better get on the stick. Four more months and I'll be there."

"I'm serious, Shaye. You work too hard and play too little."

Suddenly Shaye was serious, too. "I've played, Victoria. You know that better than anyone. I had six years of playing and the results were dreadful."

"You were a child then."

"I was twenty-three when I finally woke up. It was a pretty prolonged childhood, if you ask me."

"I'm not asking you, I'm telling you. What you did then was an irresponsible kind of playing. We've discussed this before, so I'm not breaking any new ground. When I use the word 'playing' now, I'm talking about something quite different. I'm talking about reading a good book, or going shopping just for the fun of it, or watching a fluff movie. I'm talking about spending time with friends."

Shaye knew what she was getting at. "I date."

"Oh yes. You've told me about those exciting times. Three hours talking shop with a lawyer from another firm. Another firm—that is daring. Of course, the fellow was nearly my age and probably arthritic."

Shaye chuckled. "We can't all reach fifty-three and be as agile as you."

"But you can. It's all in the mind. That lawyer's mind was no doubt ready for retirement five years ago. And your stockbroker friend doesn't sound much better. Does he give you good leads, at least?"

"It'd be illegal for me to act on an inside tip. You know that."

Victoria did know it. She also knew that her niece gave wide berth to anything vaguely questionable, let alone illegal. Shaye Burke had become a disgustingly respectable pillar of society. "Okay. Forget about stock tips. Let's talk fun. Do you have fun with him?"

"He's pleasant."

"So is the dentist. Have you been with anyone lately who's fun?"

"Uh-huh. Shannon."

"Shannon's your sister!" Victoria knew how close the two were; they'd always been so. Shaye, the elder by four years, felt personally responsible for Shannon. "She doesn't count. Who else?"

"Judy."

Victoria gave an inward groan. Judy Webber was a lawyer in Shaye's firm. The two women had become friends. If occasional weekend barbecues with Judy, her husband and their two teenaged daughters comprised Shaye's attempts at relaxation, she was in pretty bad shape.

"How is Judy?" Victoria asked politely.

"Fine. She and Bob are heading for Nova Scotia next week. She's looking forward to it."

"That does sound nice. In fact, that's one of the reasons I called."

"To hear about Judy and Bob and Nova Scotia?"

"To talk to you about your vacation plans. I need two weeks of your time, sweetheart. The last two weeks in July."

"Two weeks? Victoria, I can't take off in July."

"Why not?"

"Because I'm scheduled for vacation in August."

"Schedules can be changed."

"But I've already made reservations."

"Where?"

"In the Berkshires. I've rented a cottage."

"Alone?"

"Of course alone. How else will I manage to do the reading and shopping and whatever else you claim I've been missing?"

"Knowing the way you've worked yourself to the bone, you'll probably spend the two weeks sleeping."

"And what more peaceful a place to sleep than in the country?"

"Sleeping is boring. You don't accomplish anything when you sleep."

"We're not all like you," Shaye pointed out gently. "You may be able to get by on five hours of sleep a night, but I need eight."

"And you don't usually get them because you work every night, then get up with the sun the next day to return to the office."

Shaye didn't even try to refute her aunt's claim. All she could do was rationalize. "I have six people under me—six people I'm responsible for. The hours are worth it because the results are good. I take pride in my work. And I'm paid well for my time."

"You must be building up quite some kitty in the bank, because I don't see you spending much of that money on yourself."

"I do. I live well."

"You're about to live better," Victoria stated firmly. "Two weeks in July. As my companion."

Shaye laughed. "Your companion? That's a new one."

"This trip is."

"What trip?"

"We're going to Colombia, you and I, and then on to Costa Rica."

"You aren't serious."

"Very. We're going on a treasure hunt."

Shaye stared at the receiver before returning it to her ear. "Want to run that by me again?"

"A treasure hunt, Shaye. We'll fly to Barranquilla, spend the night in a luxury hotel, drive to Puerto Colombia and then sail in style across the Caribbean. You can do all the sleeping you want on the boat. By the time we reach Costa Rica you'll be refreshed and ready to dig for pirates' gold."

Shaye made no attempt to muffle her moan. "Oh, Victoria, where did you dream this one up?"

"I didn't dream it up. It was handed to me on a silver platter. The expedition is being led by a friend of a friend, a professor from Dartmouth who even has a map."

"Pirates' gold?" Shaye echoed skeptically.

Victoria waved a negligent hand in the air. "Well, I don't actually know what the treasure consists of, but it sounds like a fun time, don't you think?"

"I think it sounds—"

"Absurd. I knew you would, but believe me, sweetheart, this is a guaranteed adventure."

"For you. But why me?"

"Because I need you along for protection."

"Come again?"

"I need you for protection."

Shaye's laugh was even fuller this time. "The day you need protection will be the day they put you in the ground, and even then, I suspect they'll be preparing for outrageous happenings at the pearly gates. Try another one."

Anticipating resistance, Victoria had thought of every possible argument. This one was her most powerful, so she repeated it a third time, adding a note of desperation to her voice. "I need your protection, Shaye. This trip was arranged for me by some friends, and I'm sure they have mischief in mind."

"And you'd drag me along to suffer their mischief? No way, Victoria. I'm not in the market for mischief."

"They're trying to fix me up. I know they are. Their hearts are in the right place, but I don't need fixing up. I don't want it." She lowered her voice. "You, of all people, ought to understand."

Shaye understood all too well. Closing her eyes, she tried to recall the many times people had tried—the many times Victoria herself had tried—to fix her up with men who were sure to be the answer to her prayers. What they failed to realize was that Shaye's prayers were different from most other people's.

"All I'm asking," Victoria went on in the same deliberately urgent tone, "is that you act as a buffer. If I have you with me, I won't be quite so available to some aging lothario."

"What if they're fixing you up with a younger guy? It's done all the time."

Then he's all yours, sweetheart. "No. My friends wouldn't do that. At least," she added after sincere pause, "I don't think they would."

Shaye began, one by one, to remove the pins that had held her thick auburn hair in a twist since dawn. "I can't believe you're asking this of me," she said.

Victoria wasn't about to be touched by the weariness in her voice. "Have I ever asked much else?"

"No."

"And think of what you'll be getting out of the trip yourself. A luxurious sail through the Caribbean. Plenty of sun and clean air. We can spend a couple of extra days in Barranquilla if you want."

"Victoria, I don't even know if I can arrange for those two weeks, let alone a couple of extra days."

"You can arrange it. I have faith."

"You always have faith. That's the trouble. Now your faith is directed at some pirate stash. For years and years people have been digging for pirate treasure. Do you honestly believe anything's left to be found?"

"The point of the trip isn't the treasure, it's the hunt. And for you it will be the rest and the sun and—"

"The clean air. I know."

"Then you'll come?"

"I don't know if I can."

"You have to. I've already made the arrangements." It was a little white lie, but Victoria felt it was justified. She'd simply call Samson VanBaar and tell him one more person would be joining them. What was another person? Shaye ate like a bird, and if there was a shortage of sleeping space, Victoria herself would scrunch up on the floor.

"You're forcing me into this," Shaye accused, but her voice held an inkling of surrender.

"That's right."

"If I say no, you'll probably call the senior partner of my firm first thing tomorrow."

"I hadn't thought of that, but it's not a bad idea."

Shaye screwed up her face. "Isn't there anyone else you can bring along in my place?"

"No one I'd rather be with."

"That's emotional blackmail."

"So be it."

"Oh, Victoria…."

"Is that a yes?"

For several minutes, Shaye said nothing. She didn't want to traipse off in search of treasure. She didn't want to take two weeks in July, rather than the two weeks she'd planned on in August. She didn't want to have to spend her vacation acting as a buffer, when so much of her time at work was spent doing that.

But Victoria was near and dear to her. Victoria had stood by her, compassionate and forgiving when she'd nearly made a mess of her life. Victoria understood her, as precious few others did.

"Are we on?" came the gentle voice from New York.

From Philadelphia came a sigh, then a soft-spoken, if resigned, "We're on."

Later that night, as Shaye worked a brush through the thick fall of her hair, she realized that she'd given in for two basic reasons. The first was the she adored Victoria. Time spent with her never failed to be uplifting.

The second was that, in spite of all she might say to the contrary, the thought of spending two weeks in a rented cottage in the Berkshires had a vague air of loneliness to it.

VICTORIA, MEANWHILE, BASKED in her triumph without the slightest twinge of guilt. Shaye needed rest, and she'd get it. She needed a change of scenery, and she'd get that too. Adventure was built into the itinerary, and along the way if a man materialized who could make her niece laugh the way she'd done once upon a time, so much the better.

A spunky doctoral candidate would do the trick. Or a fun-loving assistant professor. Samson VanBaar had to be bringing a few interesting people along on the trip, didn't he?

She glanced at the temple clock atop a nearby chest. Was ten too late to call? Definitely not. One could learn a lot about a man by phoning him at night.

Without another thought, she contacted information for Hanover, New Hampshire, then punched out his home number. The phone rang twice before a rather bland, not terribly young female voice came on the line. "Hello," it said. "You have reached the residence of Samson VanBaar. The professor is not in at the moment. If you'd care to leave a message, he will be glad to return your call. Please wait for the sound of the tone."

Victoria thought quickly as she waited. Nothing learned here; the man could be asleep or he could be out. But perhaps it was for the best that she was dealing with a machine. She could leave her message without giving him a chance to refuse her request on the spot.

The tone sounded.

"This is Victoria Lesser calling from New York. Garrick Rodenhiser has arranged for me to join your expedition to Costa Rica, but there has been a minor change in my plans. My niece, Shaye Burke, will be accompanying me. She is twenty-nine, attractive, intelligent and hardworking. I'll personally arrange for her flight to and from Colombia, and, of course, I'll pay all additional costs. Assuming you have no problem with this plan, Shaye and I will see you in Barranquilla on the fourteenth of July."

Pleased with herself, she hung up the phone.

Four days later, she received a cryptic note typed on a plain postcard. The postmark read, "Hanover, NH," and the note read, very simply, "Received your message and have made appropriate arrangements. Until the fourteenth—VanBaar."

Though it held no clue to the man himself, at least he hadn't banned Shaye from the trip, and for that she was grateful. Shaye had called the night before to say she'd managed to clear the two weeks with her firm, and Victoria had already contacted both the Costa Rican Embassy in New York regarding visas and her travel agent regarding a second set of airline tickets.

They were going on a treasure hunt. No matter what resulted in the realm of romance, Victoria was sure of one thing: come hell or high water, she and Shaye were going to have a time to remember.

CHAPTER TWO

THE FOURTEENTH OF JULY was not one of Shaye's better days. Having worked late at the office the night before to clear her desk, then rushing home to pack for the trip, she'd gotten only four hours' sleep before rising to shower, dress and catch an early train into New York to meet Victoria. Their plane was forty-five minutes late leaving Kennedy and the flight was a turbulent one, though Shaye suspected that a certain amount of the turbulence she experienced was internal. She had a headache and her stomach wouldn't settle. It didn't help that they nearly missed their transfer in Miami, and when they finally landed in Barranquilla, their luggage took forever to appear. She was cursing the Colombian heat by the time they reached their hotel, and after waiting an additional uncomfortable hour for their room to be ready, she discovered that she'd gotten her period.

"Why me?" she moaned softly as she curled into a chair.

Victoria came to the rescue with aspirin and water. "Here, sweetheart. Swallow these down, then take a nap. You'll feel better after you've had some sleep."

Not about to argue, when all she wanted was an escape from her misery, Shaye dutifully swallowed the aspirin, then undressed, sponged off the heat of the trip, drew back the covers of one of the two double beds in the room and slid between the sheets. She was asleep within minutes.

It was evening when a gentle touch on her shoulder

awakened her. Momentarily disoriented, she peered around the room, then up at Victoria.

"You missed the zoo."

"Huh?"

"And you didn't even know I'd gone. Shame on you. But I'm back, and I thought I'd get a bite to eat. Want anything?"

Shaye began to struggle up, but Victoria easily pressed her back to the bed.

"No, no, sweetheart. I'll bring it here. You need rest far more than you need to sit in a restaurant."

Shaye was finally getting her bearings. "But...your professor. Aren't we supposed to meet him?"

Settling on the edge of the bed, Victoria shook her head. "He sent a message saying he'll be tied up stocking the boat for a good part of the night. We're to meet him there tomorrow morning at nine."

"Where's there?"

"A small marina in Puerto Colombia, about fifteen miles east of here. The boat is called the *Golden Echo*."

"The *Golden Echo*. Appropriate."

Victoria gave an impish grin. "I thought so, too. Pirates' gold. Echoes of the past. It's probably just a coincidence, since I assume the boat is rented."

"Don't assume it. If VanBaar does this sort of thing often, he could well own the boat." She hesitated, then ventured cautiously, "He does do this sort of thing often, doesn't he?"

"I really don't know."

"How large is the boat?"

"I don't know that either."

"How large is our group?"

Victoria raised both brows, pressed her lips together in a sheepish kind of way and shrugged.

"Victoria," Shaye wailed, fully awake now and wishing she weren't, "don't you ask questions before you jump into things?"

"What do I need to ask? I know that Samson VanBaar is Garrick's friend, and I trust Garrick."

"You dragged me along because you *didn't* trust him."

"I didn't trust that he wouldn't try to foist me off on some unsuspecting man, but that's a lesser issue here. The greater issue is the trip itself. Garrick would never pull any punches in the overall scheme of things."

Shaye tugged at a hairpin that was digging into her scalp. "Exactly what *do* you know about this trip?"

"Just what I've told you."

"Which is precious little."

"Come on, sweetheart. The details will come. They'll unfold like a lovely surprise."

"I hate surprises."

"Mmm. You like to know what's happening before it happens. That's the computerized you." Her gaze dropped briefly to the tiny mark at the top of Shaye's breast, a small shadow beneath the lace edging of her bra. "But there's another side, Shaye, and this trip's going to bring it out. You'll learn to accept it and control it. It's really not such a bad thing when taken in moderation."

"Victoria…"

"Look at it this way. You're with me. I'll be your protector, just as you'll be mine."

"How can you protect me from something you can't anticipate?"

"Oh, I can anticipate." She tipped up her head and fixed a dreamy gaze on the wall. "I'm anticipating that boat. It'll be a beauty. Long and sleek, with polished brass fittings and crisp white sails. We'll have a lovely stateroom to share. The food will be superb, the martinis nice and dry…"

"You hope."

"And why not? Look around. I wouldn't exactly call this room a hovel."

"No, but it could well be the equivalent of a last meal for the condemned."

Victoria clucked her tongue. "Such pessimism in one so young."

Shaye shifted onto her side. She was achy all over. "Right about now, I feel ninety years old."

"When you're ninety, you won't have to worry about monthly cramps. When you're fifty, for that matter." She grinned. "I rather like my age."

"What's not to like about sixteen?"

"Now, now, do I sound that irresponsible?"

"Carefree may be a better word, or starry-eyed, or naive. Victoria, for all you know the *Golden Echo* may be a leaky tub and Samson VanBaar a blundering idiot."

Victoria schooled her expression to one of total maturity. "I've thought a lot about that. Samson won't be an idiot. Maybe an absentminded professor, or a man bent on living out his childhood dreams." She took a quick breath. "He could be fun."

"He could be impossible."

"But there will be others aboard."

"Mmm. A bunch of his students, all around twenty and so full of themselves that they'll be obnoxious."

"You were pretty full of yourself at that age," she reminded her niece, smoothing a stray wisp of hair from Shaye's pale cheek.

"And obnoxious."

"You didn't think so at the time."

"Neither will they."

But Victoria's eyes had grown thoughtful again. "I don't think there'll be many students. Garrick wouldn't have signed me on as a dorm mother. No, I'd guess that we'll be encountering adults, people very much like us looking for a break from routine."

"Since when do you have a routine you need a break from?"

"Not me. You. You need the break. I don't need anything, but my friends wanted to give me a good time, and that's exactly what I intend to have." She pushed herself gracefully from the bed. "Starting now. I'm famished. What'll it be—a doggie bag from the restaurant or room service later?"

Shaye tucked up her knees and closed her eyes. "Sleep. Tomorrow will be soon enough for superb food and nice dry martinis."

THE TWO WOMEN had no trouble finding the *Golden Echo* the next morning. She was berthed at the end of the pier and very definitely stood apart from the other craft they'd passed.

"Oh Lord," Shaye muttered.

Victoria was as wide-eyed as her niece. "Maybe we have the wrong one."

"The name board says *Golden Echo*."

"Maybe I got the name wrong."

"Maybe you got the trip wrong."

They stood with their elbows linked and their heads close together as, eyes transfixed on the boat before them, they whispered back and forth.

"She isn't exactly a tub," Victoria offered meekly.

"She's a pirate ship—"

"In miniature."

"Looks like she's been through one too many battles. Or one too few. She should have sunk long ago."

"Maybe not," Victoria argued, desperately searching for something positive to say. "She looks sturdy enough."

"Like a white elephant."

"But she's clean."

"Mmm. The chipped paint's been neatly scraped away. Lord, I don't believe I've seen anything as boxy since the Tall Ships passed through during the Bicentennial."

"They were impressive."

"*They* were."

"So's this—"

"If you close your eyes and pretend you're living in the eighteenth century."

Victoria didn't close her eyes, but she was squinting hard. "You have to admit that she has a certain...character."

"Mmm. Decrepit."

"She takes three sails. That should be pretty."

Her enthusiasm was lost on Shaye, who was eyeing in dismay the ragged bundles of canvas lashed to the rigging. "Three crisp...white...sails."

"Okay, they may not be crisp and white. What does it matter, if they're strong?"

"Are they?"

"If Samson VanBaar is any kind of friend to Garrick— and if Garrick is any kind of friend to me—they are."

Shaye moaned. "And to think that I could have been in the Berkshires, lazing around without a care in the world."

"You'll be able to laze around here."

"I don't see any deck chairs."

"But it's a nice broad deck."

"It looks splintery."

"So we'll lie on towels."

"Did you bring some?"

"Of course not. They'll have towels aboard."

"Like they have polished brass fittings?" Shaye sighed. "Well, you were right in a way."

"What way was that?" Victoria asked, at a momentary loss.

"We are going in style. Of course, it's not exactly *our* style—for that matter, I'm not sure whose style it is." Her voice hardened. "You may be crazy enough to give it a try, but I'm not."

She started to pivot away, intending to take the first cab back to Barranquilla, but Victoria clamped her elbow tighter and dragged her forward. "Excuse me," she was calling, shading her eyes from the sun with her free hand. "We're looking for Samson VanBaar."

Keeping step with her aunt through no will of her own, Shaye forced herself to focus on the figure that had just emerged from the bowels of the boat. "It gets worse," she moaned, then whispered a hoarse, "What *is* he?"

"I'm VanBaar," came the returning call. "Mrs. Lesser, Miss Burke?" With a sweep of his arm, he motioned them forward. "We've been expecting you."

Nothing they'd imagined had prepared either Shaye or Victoria for Samson VanBaar. In his mid to late fifties, he was remarkably tall and solid. His well-trimmed salt-and-pepper hair, very possibly combed in a dignified manner short days before, tumbled carelessly around his head, forming a reckless frame for a face that was faintly sunburned, though inarguably sweet.

What was arguable was his costume, and it could only be called that. He wore a billowy white shirt tucked into a pair of narrow black pants, which were tucked into knee-high leather boots. A wide black belt slanted low across his hips, and if it lacked the scabbard for a dagger or a sword, the effect was the same.

"He forgot the eye patch," Shaye warbled hysterically.

"Shh! He's darling!" Victoria whispered under her breath. Smiling broadly—and never once releasing Shaye, who, she knew, would head in the opposite direction given the first opportunity—she started up the gangplank. At the top, she put her free hand in the one Samson offered and stepped onto the deck. "It's a delight to meet you at last, Professor VanBaar. I'm Victoria Lesser, and this is my niece, Shaye Burke."

Shaye was too busy silently cursing her relationship with Victoria to say much of anything, but she managed a feeble smile in return for the open one the professor gave her.

"Welcome to the *Golden Echo*," he said, quietly now that they were close. "I trust you had no problem finding us."

"No, no," Victoria answered brightly. "None at all." She made a grand visual sweep of the boat, trying to see as little as possible while still conveying her point. "This is charming!"

Shaye nearly choked. When Victoria gave a tight, warning squeeze to her elbow before abruptly releasing it, she tipped back her head, closed her eyes and drew in an exaggerated lungful of Caribbean air. It was certainly better than having to look at the boat, and though Samson VanBaar was attractive enough, the insides of her eyelids were more reassuring than his getup.

"I felt that the *Golden Echo* would be more in keeping with the spirit of this trip than a modern yacht would be," he explained. "She's a little on the aged side, but I've been told she's trusty."

Shaye opened one eye. "You haven't sailed her yet?"

Almost imperceptibly he ducked his head, but the tiny movement was enough to suggest guilt. "I've sailed ones like her, but I just flew in yesterday myself, and the bulk of my time between then and now had been spent buying supplies. I hope you understood why I couldn't properly welcome you in Barranquilla last night."

"Of course," Victoria reassured him gently. "It worked out just as well, actually. We were both tired after the flight."

"You slept well?"

"Very well."

"Good." He ran a forefinger along the corner of his mouth, as though unsure of what to say next. Then his eyes brightened. "Your bags." He quickly spotted them on the pier. "Let me bring them aboard, then I'll give you the Cook's tour."

He'd no sooner descended the gangplank when Shaye whirled on Victoria. "The Cook's tour?" she whispered wildly. "Is he the cook or are we?"

"Don't fret," Victoria whispered back with confidence, "there's a cook."

"Like there's a lovely stateroom for us to share? Do you have any idea what's down there?"

"Nope. That's what the Cook's tour is for."

"Aren't you worried?"

"Of course not. This is an adventure."

"The boat is a wreck!"

"She's trusty."

"So says the professor who's staging Halloween three months early."

Victoria's eyes followed Samson's progress. "And I thought he'd be stuffy. He's precious!"

"Good. Since you like him so well, you won't need my protection after all. I'll just take my bag and head back—"

"You will not! You're staying!"

"Victoria, there'll be lots of other people…" The words died on her lips. Her head remained still while her eyes moved from one end of the empty deck to the other. She listened. "Where are they? It's too quiet. We were ten minutes late, ourselves. Where are the others?"

Victoria was asking herself the same question. Her plan was contingent on there being other treasure seekers, specifically of the young and good-looking male variety. True, in terms of rest alone, the trip would be good for Shaye, and Victoria always enjoyed her niece's company. But matching her up with a man—it had worked so well with Deirdre, then Leah… Where *were* the men?

Concealing her concern behind a gracious smile, she turned to VanBaar, who had rejoined them with a suitcase in either hand. "We don't expect you wait on us. Please. Just tell us what to do." She reached for her bag, but Samson drew it out of her reach.

"Chivalry is a dying art. You'll have plenty to do as time goes on, but for now, I think I can manage two bags."

Chivalry? Shaye thought, amused. *Plenty to do?* she thought, appalled.

Victoria was thinking about the good-looking young men she didn't see. "Is this standard service given to all the members of your group?" she ventured, half teasing, half chiding, and subtly fishing for information.

"No, ma'am. We men fend for ourselves. You and your niece are the only women along."

Swell, Shaye groused silently, *just swell*.

Victoria couldn't have been more delighted. "How many others are there, Professor VanBaar?"

He blushed. "Samson, please."

She smiled. "Samson, then. How many of us will there be in all?"

"Four."

"Four?" the women echoed in unison.

"That's right." Setting the bags by his booted feet, he scratched the back of his head. "Didn't Garrick explain the situation?"

Victoria gave a delicate little cough. "I'm afraid he didn't go quite that far."

"That was negligent of him," Samson said, but he didn't seem upset, and Victoria saw a tiny twinkle in his eye. "Let me explain. Originally there were to be just two of us, myself and an old college buddy with whom I often travel in the summer. When Garrick called me about your joining us, I saw no problem. Unfortunately, my friend had to cancel at the last minute, so I hoodwinked my nephew into taking up the slack." He stole a glance at Shaye's dismayed expression. "It takes two to comfortably man the boat, and since I didn't know whether either of you were sailors—"

"We're not," Shaye burst out. "I don't know about my aunt, but I get seasick."

"Ignore her, Samson. She's only teasing."

"*Violently* seasick."

"Not to worry," Samson assured her in the same kind tone that made it hard to hold a grudge. "I have medicine for seasickness, though I doubt you'll need it. We shouldn't run into heavy seas."

At that moment, Shaye would have paid a pirate's ransom to be by her lonesome in the Berkshires. A foursome—Victoria and Samson, Samson's nephew and her. It was too cozy, too convenient. Suddenly something smacked of a setup. Could Samson have done it? Or Garrick? Or... She skewered her aunt with an accusatory glare.

Victoria had her eyes glued to Samson. "I'm sure we'll be fine." She took a deep breath and straightened her shoulders. "Now then, I believe you said something about a tour?"

NOAH VANBAAR WAS nearly as disgusted as Shaye. Arms crossed over his chest and one knee bent up as he lounged on a hardwood bench within earshot of the three above, he struggled in vain to contain his frustration. He'd had other plans for his summer vacation, but when his uncle had called, claiming that Barney was sick and there was no one else who could help him sail, he'd been indulgent.

Samson and he were the only two surviving members of the VanBaar family, but even if sentimentality hadn't been a factor, Noah was fond enough of his uncle to take pity. He knew how much Samson looked forward to his little jaunts. He also knew that Samson was an expert sailor and more than capable of handling the boat himself, but that for safety's sake he needed another pair of hands along. If Noah's refusal meant that Samson had to cancel his trip, there was no real choice to be made.

Naturally, his uncle had waited until last night to inform him that they wouldn't be sailing alone. Naturally, he had waited until this morning to inform him that the pair joining them would be female.

Noah didn't want one woman along, much less two. Not that he had anything against women in general, but on this trip, they would be in the way. He'd planned to relax, to take a break from the tension that was part and parcel of his work. He'd planned to have one of the two cabins on the boat to himself, to sleep to his heart's content, to dress as he pleased, shave when and if he pleased, swim in the buff, and, in short, let it all hang out.

The presence of women didn't figure into his personal game plan. They were bound to screw things up. A widow and her niece. Charming. Samson was already carrying their bags. If they thought *he* was going to wait on them, they had another think coming!

Actually, he mused, the aunt didn't sound so bad. She

had a pleasant voice, sounded lively without being obnoxious, and to her further credit, had protested Samson's playing bellboy. He wondered what she looked like and whether Samson would be enthralled. He hoped not, because then he'd be stuck with the niece, who sounded far less lively and more obnoxious than her aunt.

It was obvious that the niece wasn't thrilled with the looks of the sloop. What had she expected? The *Brittania*? If so, he decided as his eyes skimmed the gloomy interior of the *Golden Echo*, she was in for an even ruder awakening than she'd already had.

Not that the boat bothered him; he'd sailed in far worse. This time around, though, he could have asked for more space. This time around he'd have preferred the *Brittania*, himself. At least then he'd have been able to steer clear of the women.

Though he didn't move an inch, he grew instinctively alert when he heard footsteps approaching the gangway. Samson was in the lead, his booted feet appearing several seconds before the two suitcases. "The *Golden Echo* was refurbished ten years ago," he was saying, his voice growing louder as his head came into view. "The galley is quite modern and the cabins comfortable—ah, Noah, right where I left you." Stepping aside, he set down the bags to give an assisting hand to each of the women in turn.

Noah didn't have to marvel at his uncle's style. Though a bit eccentric at times, Samson was a gentleman through and through, which was fine as long as he didn't expect the same standard from his nephew. Noah spent his working life straddling the lines between gentleman, diplomat and czar; he intended to spend his vacation answering to no one but himself.

"Noah, I'd like you to meet Victoria Lesser," Samson said. He knew better than to ask his nephew to rise. Noah was intimidating enough when seated; standing he was formidable. Given the dark mood he was in at the moment, intimidation was the lesser of the evils.

Noah nodded toward Victoria, careful to conceal the slight surprise he felt. Victoria had not only sounded lively, she looked lively. What had Samson said—that she was in her early fifties? She didn't look a day over forty. She wore a bright yellow, oversize shirt, a pair of white slacks with the cuffs rolled to mid-calf, and sneakers, and her features were every bit as youthful. Her hair was an attractive walnut shade and thick, loosely arranged into a high, short ponytail that left gentle wisps to frame the delicate structure of her face. Her skin was flawless, firm-toned and lightly made up, if at all. Her eyes twinkled, and her smile was genuine.

"It's a pleasure to meet you, Noah," she said every bit as sincerely. "Thank you for letting us join you on this trip. I've done many things in my day, but I've never been on a treasure hunt before. It sounds as though it'll be fun."

Lured by the subtle melody of her voice, Noah almost believed her. Then he shifted his gaze to the young woman who'd followed her down the steps and took back the thought.

"Shaye Burke," Samson was saying by way of introduction, "Noah VanBaar."

Again Noah nodded his head, this time a trifle more stiffly. Shaye Burke was a looker; he had to give her that. Slightly taller than her aunt, she was every bit as slender. Her white jeans were pencil thin, her blousy, peach-colored T-shirt rolled at the sleeves and knotted chicly at the waist. Her skin, too, was flawless, but it was pale; she'd skillfully applied makeup to cover shadows beneath her eyes and add faint color to her cheeks.

Any similarities to her aunt had already ended. Shaye's

deep auburn hair was anchored at the nape of her neck in a
sedate twist from which not a strand escaped. The younger
woman's lips were set, her nose marked with tension, and
the eyes that met his held a shadow of rebellion.

She didn't want to be here. It was written all over her
face. Adding that to the comments he'd overheard earlier,
he begrudged her presence more than ever. If Shaye Burke
did anything to spoil his uncle's adventure, he vowed, he
would personally even the score.

Samson, who'd sensed the instant animosity between
Noah and Shaye, spoke up quickly. "If you ladies will come
this way, I'll show you to your cabin. Once we've deposited your things there, we can walk around more freely."

Short of turning and fleeing, Shaye had no choice but to
follow Victoria, who followed Samson through the narrow
passageway. Her shoulders were ramrod straight, held that
way by the force of a certain man's gaze piercing her back.

Noah. Noah and Samson. The VanBaar family, she decided, had a thing about biblical names. But her image of
that Noah was one of kindness; *this* Noah struck her as
being quite different. Sitting in the shadows as he'd been,
she hadn't been able to see much beyond gloom and a
glower. She knew one thing, though: She hadn't expected
to have to protect her aunt, but if Noah VanBaar so much
as dared do anything to dampen Victoria's spirits, he'd
have to answer to her.

SAMSON LED VICTORIA and Shaye to the cabin they'd be
sharing, then backtracked to show them the salon, the galley and the captain's quarters in turn. Noah was nowhere
in sight during the backtracking, and Shaye was grateful
for that. There was precious little else to be grateful for.

"We do have our own bathroom," Victoria pointed out
when they'd returned to their cabin to unpack. She low-

ered herself to Shaye's side of the double bed that occupied three quarters of the small cabin's space. "I know that it's not quite what we expected, but if we clear our minds of those other expectations, we'll do fine."

Shaye's lips twisted wryly. "Grin and bear it?"

"Make the most of it." She jabbed at the bedding with a delicate fist. "The mattress feels solid enough." Her eye roamed the trapezoid-shaped room. "And we could have been stuck with a V-berth."

"This bed is bolted to the wall. I thought Samson said it'd be a calm trip."

"This one will be, but we have no idea what other waters the *Golden Echo* has sailed."

"If only she were somewhere else—without us."

"Shaye..."

"And where do we go to relax?"

"The salon."

"For privacy?" She was thinking of the dagger-edged gaze that had followed her earlier, and wasn't sure whether she'd be able to endure it as a constant.

Victoria's mind was still on the salon. "There are comfortable chairs, a sofa—"

"And a distinctly musty smell."

"That's the smell of the sea. It adds atmosphere."

Shaye snorted. "That kind of atmosphere I can do without." She knew she was being unfair; after all, the cottage she'd booked in the Berkshires very probably had its own musty smell, and she normally wasn't that fussy. But her bad mood seemed to feed on itself and on every tiny fault she could find with the boat.

"Come on, sweetheart," Victoria coaxed as she rose to open her suitcase. "We'll have fun. I promise."

Shaye's discouraged gaze wandered around the cabin, finally alighting on the row of evenly spaced, slit-like windows. "At least there are portholes. Clever, actually. They're built into the carving of the hull. I didn't notice them from the dock."

"And they're open. The air's circulating. And it's relatively bright."

"All the better to see the simplicity of the decor," Shaye added tongue-in-cheek. She watched her aunt unpack in silence for several minutes before tipping her head to the side and venturing a wary, "Victoria?"

"Uh-huh?"

"How much did you really know about all this?"

Victoria stacked several pairs of shorts in a pile, then straightened. "About all what?"

"This trip."

"Haven't we discussed this before?"

"But something's beginning to smell."

"I told you," Victoria responded innocently. "It's the sea."

"Not smell as in brine. Smell as in rat. Did you have any idea at all that there'd be just four of us?"

"Of course not."

"It never occurred to you that Samson would be 'precious' and that I'd be left with his nephew?"

Victoria gave a negligent shrug and set the shorts in the nearby locker. "You heard what Samson said. Noah's joining us was a last-minute decision. I mentioned this trip to you nearly a month ago."

But Shaye remained skeptical. "Samson didn't say exactly how 'last-minute' the decision was. Are you sure you're not trying to pair me up with Noah?"

"Would I do that—"

"She asks a little too innocently. You did it with Deirdre Joyce."

"I thought you approved."

"In that case I did—do. Neil Hersey is a wonderful man." Shaye had never forgotten that it was Neil, with his legal ability and compassion, who had come to the rescue when Shannon had been arrested.

Victoria was grateful that Shaye knew nothing of her role in bringing Garrick and Leah together. The less credence given the word *matchmaker,* the better, she decided. "Noah VanBaar may be every bit as wonderful."

Shaye coughed comically. "Try again."

"He may be!"

"Then you did do it on purpose?"

Victoria felt only a smidgen of guilt as she propped her hands on her hips in a stance of exasperation. "Really, Shaye. How could I have done it on purpose when I had no idea Noah would be along?"

"Then you intended to fix me up with Samson's old-fart friend?"

"I did not! I truly, truly expected that we'd be only two more members of a larger group."

Sensing a certain truth to that part of Victoria's story at least, Shaye sighed. "If only there *were* a larger group—"

"So you could fade into the woodwork? I wouldn't have let you do that even if there were fifty others on board this boat." She lifted a pair of slacks and nonchalantly shook them out. "What did you think of Noah, by the way?"

"I thought he was rude, by the way. He could have stood up when we were introduced. He could have said something. Do you realize the man didn't utter a single word?"

"Neither did you at that point."

"That's because I chose silence over saying something unpleasant."

"Maybe that's what he was doing. Maybe he's as tired as you are. Maybe he, too, had other plans before Samson called him."

"I wish he'd stuck to his guns."

"Like you did?"

Bowing her head, Shaye pressed the throbbing spot between her eyes. "I gave in because you're my aunt and my friend and because I love you."

Draping an arm around Shaye's shoulders, Victoria hugged her close. "You know how much that means to me, sweetheart. And it may be that Noah feels the same about Samson. Cheer up. He won't be so bad. How can he be, with an uncle like that?"

WHEN VICTORIA LEFT to go on deck, Shaye stayed behind to unpack. But there was only so much unpacking to do, and only so much to look at within the close cabin walls. She realized she was stalling, and that annoyed her, then hardened her. If Noah VanBaar thought he could cower her with his dark and brooding looks, he was in for a surprise.

Emboldened, she made her way topside to find Samson drawing up the gangplank. A powerboat hovered at the bow of the *Golden Echo*, prepared to tow her clear of the pier. At Samson's call, Noah cast off the lines, the powerboat accelerated and they were off.

When the other three gathered at the bow, Shaye took refuge at the stern. Mounting the few steps to the ancient version of a cockpit, she bypassed the large wooden wheel to rest against the transom and watch the shore slowly but steadily recede.

It was actually a fine day for a sail, she had to admit. The breeze feathered her face, cooling what might otherwise have been heated rays of the sun. But she felt a wistfulness as her gaze encompassed more and more of the Colombian shore. Given her druthers, she'd have stayed in Barranquilla and waited for Victoria's return. No, she insisted, given her druthers, she'd be working in Philadelphia, patiently waiting for her August break.

But that was neither here nor there. She was on the *Golden Echo*, soon to be well into the Caribbean, and there was no point bemoaning her fate. She had to see the bright side, as Victoria was doing. She'd brought books along, and she'd spotted cushions in the salon that could be used as padding in lieu of a deck chair. And if she worked to keep her presence as inconspicuous as possible, she knew she'd do all right.

"Having second thoughts?"

The low, taunting baritone came from behind her. She didn't have the slightest doubt as to whose voice it was.

"What's to have second thoughts about?" she asked quietly. "This is my vacation. I'm looking forward to it."

"Are you always uptight when you're looking forward to something?"

"I'm not uptight."

He moved forward until he, too, leaned against the wood. "No?"

Shaye was peripherally aware of his largeness and did her best to ignore it. "No."

"Then why are your knuckles white on that rail?"

"Because if the boat lurches, I don't want to be thrown."

"She's called a sloop, and she doesn't lurch."

"Sway, tilt, heel—whatever the term is."

"Not a sailor, I take it?"

"I've sailed."

"Sunfish? Catboat?"

"Actually, I've spent time on twelve-meters, but as a guest, not a student of nautical terminology."

"A twelve-meter is a far cry from the *Golden Echo*."

"Do tell."

"You're not pleased with her?"

"She's fine," Shaye answered diplomatically.

"But not up to your usual standards?"

"I didn't say that."

"You're thinking it. Tell me, if you're used to something faster and sleeker, what are you doing here?"

Shaye bit off the sharp retort that was on the tip of her tongue and instead answered calmly, "As I said, I'm on vacation."

"Why here?"

"Because my aunt invited me to join her."

"And you were thrilled to accept?"

She did turn to him then and immediately wished she hadn't. He towered over her, a good six-four to her own five-six, and there was an air of menace about him. She took a deep breath to regain her poise, then spoke slowly and as evenly as possible.

"No, I was not thrilled to accept. Sailing off in the facsimile of a pirate ship on a wild-goose chase for a treasure that probably doesn't exist is not high on my list of ways I'd like to spend my vacation."

Noah's gaze was hard as he studied her face. She was a beauty, but cool, very cool. Her features were set in rigid lines, her hazel eyes cutting. Had he seen any warmth, any softening, he would have eased off. But he was annoyed as hell that she was along, and to have her match his stare with such boldness was just what he needed to goad him on.

"That was what I figured." His eyes narrowed. "Now listen here, and listen good. If you repeat any of those pithy comments within earshot of my uncle, you'll regret it."

The blatant threat took Shaye by surprise. She'd assumed Noah to be rude; she hadn't expected him to be openly hostile. "Excuse me?"

"You heard."

"Heard, but don't believe. What makes you think I'd say anything to your uncle?"

"I know your type."

"How could you possibly—"

"You expected a luxury yacht, not a wreck of a boat. You expected a lovely stateroom, not a small, plain cabin. You expected a captain and a cook, not a professor who's staging Halloween three months early."

Shaye's blood began a slow boil. "You were eavesdropping!"

His eyes remained steady, a chilling gray, and the dark spikes of hair that fell over his brow, seeming to defy the wind, added to the aura of threat that was belied by the complacency of his voice. "I was sitting below while you and your aunt chatted on deck."

"So you listened."

"The temptation was too great. In case you haven't realized it yet, we'll be practically on top of each other for the next two weeks. I wanted to know what I was in for." His gaze dropped to her hands. "I'd ease up if I were you. Those nails of yours will leave marks on the wood."

Shaye's fingernails weren't overly long, though they were neatly filed and wore a coat of clear polish. Instead of arguing, she took yet another deep breath and squared her shoulders. "Thank you for making your feelings clear."

"Just issuing a friendly little warning."

"Friendly?"

"We-e-e-ll, maybe that is stretching it a little. You're too stiff-backed and fussy for my tastes."

Shaye's temper flared. "You have to be one of the most arrogant individuals I've ever had the misfortune to meet. You don't know me at all. You have no idea what I do, what I like or what I want. But I'll tell you one thing, I don't take to little warnings the likes of which you just issued."

"Consider it offered nonetheless."

"And you can consider it rejected." Eyes blazing, she made a slow and deliberate sweep from his thick, dark hair over his faded black T-shirt and worn khaki shorts, down long, hair-roughened legs to his solid bare feet. "I don't need you telling me what to do. I can handle myself and in good taste, which is a sight more than I can say for you." Every bit as deliberately as she'd raked his form, and with as much indifference to his presence as she could muster, she returned her gaze to the shrinking port.

"I'd watch it, if I were you. I'm not in the mood to be crossed."

"Another threat?" she asked, keeping her eyes fixed on the shore. "And what will you do if I choose to ignore it?"

"I'll be your shadow for the next two weeks. I could make things unpleasant, you know."

"I have the distinct feeling you'll do that anyway." Turning, she set off smoothly for the bow.

CHAPTER THREE

VICTORIA SQUINTED UP at Samson. "How much farther will we be towed?"

"Not much. We're nearly clear of the smaller boats, and the wind is picking up nicely."

Shaye joined them in time to catch his answer. "What happens if it dies once we're free?"

Samson grinned. "Then we'll lie on the deck and bask in the sun until it decides to come back to life."

She had visions of lying in the sun and basking for days, and the visions weren't enticing. Still smarting from her set-to with Noah, she feared that if they were becalmed she'd go stark, raving mad. "Given a reasonable wind, how long will it take to reach Costa Rica?"

"Given a reasonable wind, four days. The *Golden Echo* wasn't built for speed."

"What was she built for?" Shaye asked, her curiosity offset by a hint of aspersion.

"Effect," came Noah's tight reply as he took up a position beside her.

Her shadow. Was it starting already? Tipping up her head, she challenged him with a stare. "Explain, please."

Noah directed raised brows toward his uncle, who in his own shy way was a storyteller. But Samson shook his head, pivoted on his heel and headed aft, calling over his shoulder, "It's all yours. I have to see to the sails."

Noah would have offered his assistance if it hadn't been

for two things. First, Samson would have refused: he took pride in his sailing skill and preferred, whenever possible, to do things himself. Second, Noah wanted to stay by Shaye. He knew that he annoyed her, and he intended to take advantage of that fact. It was some solace, albeit perverse, to have her aboard.

"The *Golden Echo* was modeled after an early eighteenth century Colonial sloop," he began, broadening his gaze to include Victoria in the tale. "She was built in the 1920s by a man named Horgan, a sailor and a patriot, who saw in her lines a classic beauty that was being lost in the sleeker, more modern craft. Horgan wanted to enjoy her, but he also wanted to make a statement."

"He did that," Shaye retorted, then asked on impulse, "Where did he sail her?"

"Up and down the East Coast at first."

"For pleasure?"

Noah's eyes bore into her. "Some people do it that way."

Victoria, who'd been watching the two as she leaned back against the rail, asked gently, "Did he parade her?"

"I'm sure he did," Noah answered, softening faintly with the shift of his gaze, "though I doubt there was as much general interest in a vessel like this then as there is today. From what Samson learned, Horgan made several Atlantic crossings before he finally berthed the *Golden Echo* in Bermuda. When his own family lost interest and he grew too ill to sail her alone, he began renting her out. She was sold as part of his estate in the mid-sixties."

"That leaves twenty years unaccounted for," Shaye prompted.

"I'm getting there." But he took his time, leisurely looking amidship to check on his uncle's progress. By the time he resumed, Shaye was glaring out to sea. "The new owners, a couple by the name of Payne, expanded on the charter business. For a time, they worked summers out of Boston, where the *Golden Echo* was in demand for private parties and small charity functions. Eventually they decided that the season was too limited, so they moved south."

"Why aren't they with us now?" Shaye asked without turning her head.

"Because there isn't room. Besides, they have a number of other boats to manage. The business is headquartered in Jamaica."

"Why are we in Colombia?"

"Because that's where the last charter ended. It's a little like Hertz—"

"Noah!" came Samson's buoyant shout. "Set us free!"

With a steadying hand on the bowsprit, Noah folded himself over the prow, reaching low to release the heavy steel clip that had held the powerboat's line to the *Golden Echo*.

The powerboat instantly surged ahead, then swung into a broad U-turn. Its driver, a Colombian with swarthy skin and a mile-wide white grin, saluted as he passed. A grinning Victoria waved back, moving aft to maintain the contact.

Shaye was unaware of her departure. She hadn't even seen the Colombian. Rather, her eyes were glued to the spot where Noah had released the clip. The large, rusty ring spoke for itself, but what evoked an odd blend of astonishment and amusement was the fact that it protruded from the navel of a scantily clad lady. That the lady was time-worn and peeling served only to accentuate her partial nudity.

"That's the figurehead," Noah informed her, crossing his arms over his chest.

"I know what it is," she answered, instantly losing grasp

of whatever amusement she'd felt. "I just hadn't seen her earlier."

"Does her state of undress embarrass you?"

"I've seen breasts before."

Insolent eyes scanned the front of her T-shirt. "I should hope so."

Shaye kept her arms at her sides when they desperately wanted to cover her chest. She was far from the prude that Noah had apparently decided she was, but while she'd learned to control her desires, there was something about the way he was looking at her that set off little sparks inside. She felt nearly as bare-breasted as the lady on the bow and not nearly as wooden—which was something she sought to remedy by turning the tables on Noah.

"Does she excite you?"

"Who?"

Shaye tossed her head toward the bow, then watched as he bent sideways.

"She's not bad," he decided, straightening. "A little stern-faced for my tastes. Like you."

"Your tastes are probably as pathetic as old Horgan's. If he were building a boat like this today and dared to put a thing like that at the bow, he'd have women's groups picketing the pier."

Noah drew himself to his full height and glared down at her. "If there's one thing I can't stand it's a militant feminist."

She glared right back. "And if there's one thing *I* can't stand, it's a presumptuous male. You're just itching for a fight, aren't you?"

"Damn right."

"Why?"

"Why not?"

"The way I see it," she said, taking a deep breath for

patience, "either you're annoyed that I've come along or you didn't want to be here in the first place."

His hair was blowing freely now. "Oh, I would have been happy enough sailing off with Samson. He's undemanding. I'd have gotten the R and R I need."

"Then it's me. Why do I annoy you?"

"You're a woman, and you're prissy."

Unable to help herself, Shaye laughed. *Prissy?* Then some vague instinct told her that prissy was precisely the way to be with this man. "Prissy." She cleared her throat. "Yes, well, I do believe in exercising a certain decorum."

"I'm sure you give new meaning to the word."

Shaye was about to say that Noah probably didn't know the *first* meaning of the word when the sound of unfurling canvas caught her ear. She looked up in time to see the mainsail fill with wind, then down to see Samson securing the lines.

"Shouldn't you give him a hand?"

"He doesn't need it."

"Then why are you here at all?"

Noah's smile might have held humor but didn't. "To give you a hard time. Why else?" With that, he sauntered off.

Aware that he'd had the last word this time around, Shaye watched him until he disappeared into the companionway. Then she turned back to the bow and closed her eyes. His image remained, a vivid echo in her mind of tousled dark hair, a broad chest, lean hips and endless legs. He was attractive; she had to give him that. But the attraction ended with the physical. He was unremittingly disagreeable.

And exhausting. It had been a long time since she'd sparred with anyone as she was sparring with him. Not that she didn't have occasional differences with people at work, but that was something else, something professional.

In her private life she'd grown to love peace. She avoided abrasive people and chose friends who were conventional and comfortable. She dated the least threatening of men, indulging their occasional need to assert themselves over choice of restaurants or theaters because, through it all, she was in control. Not even her parents, with their parochial views, could rile her.

But Noah VanBaar had done just that. She wasn't sure how they'd become enemies so quickly. Was it his fault? Hers? Had she really seemed prissy?

A helpless smile broke across her face. Prissy. Wouldn't André and the guys from the garret—wherever they were today—die laughing if they heard that! Her parents, on the other hand, wouldn't die laughing. They'd choke a little, then breathe sighs of relief, then launch into a discourse on her age and the merits of marriage.

Prissy. It wasn't such a bad thing to be around Noah. If he hated prissiness so much, he'd leave her alone, which was all she really wanted, wasn't it?

Buoyed by her private pep talk, she sought out Victoria, who was chatting with Samson as he hauled up the first of two jibs. Indeed, it was Samson she addressed. "Would you like any help?"

Deftly lashing the line to its cleat, he stood back to watch the sail catch the wind. "Nope. All's under control." He darted them a quick glance. "Have you ladies had breakfast yet?"

"Victoria, has, but I, uh, slept a little later."

"You'll find fresh eggs and bacon in the icebox. Better eat and enjoy before they spoil."

Fresh eggs and bacon sounded just fine to Shaye, even if the word *icebox* was a little antiquated. Somehow, though, coming from Samson it didn't seem strange. Without pausing to reflect on the improvement in her attitude toward him, she asked, "How about you? Can I bring you something?"

"Ah no," he sighed, patting his belt. "I had a full breakfast earlier."

"How about coffee?"

"Now that's a thought. If you make it strong and add cream and two sugars, I could be sorely tempted."

Shaye smiled and turned to her aunt. "Anything for you?"

"Thanks, sweetheart, but I'm fine."

"See you in a bit, then." Still smiling, she entered the companionway, trotted down the steps and turned into the galley. There her smile faded. Noah was sprawled on the built-in settee that formed a shallow U behind the small table. He'd been alerted by the pad of her sneakers and was waiting, fork in hand, chewing thoughtfully.

"Well, well," he drawled as soon as he'd swallowed, "if it isn't the iron maiden."

"I though you'd already eaten."

"Samson has, but I don't make a habit of getting up at dawn like he does."

She was looking at his plate, which still held healthy portions of scrambled eggs and bacon, plus a muffin and a half, and a huge wedge of melon. "Think you have enough?"

"I hope so. I'm going to need all the strength I can get."

"To sit back and watch Samson sail?"

"To fight with you."

Determined not to let him irk her—or to let him interfere with her breakfast—she went to the refrigerator. "It's not really worth the effort, you know."

"I'll be the judge of that."

She shrugged and reached for two eggs and the packet

of bacon. After setting them on the stove, she opened one cabinet, then the second in search of a pan.

"In the sink," Noah informed her.

She took in the contents of the sink at a disdainful glance. "And filthy. Thanks."

"You're welcome."

Automatically she reached for the tap, only to find there was none.

"Try the foot pump. You won't get water any other way. Not that you really need it. Why not just wipe out the pan with a paper towel and use it again?"

"That's disgusting."

"Not really. You're having the same thing I had."

"But there's an inch of bacon fat in this pan."

"Drain it."

There was a subtle command in his voice that drew her head around. "I take it we're conserving water."

"You take it right."

She pressed her lips together, then nodded slowly as she considered her options. She could pump up the water in a show of defiance, but if water was indeed in short supply, she'd be biting off her nose to spite her face. Bathing was going to be enough of a challenge; a little water spared now would make her feel less guilty for any she used later.

Very carefully she drained the pan, then swabbed it out with a paper towel and set it on the stove to heat.

"Need any help?" he taunted.

"I can crack an egg."

"Better put on the bacon first. It takes longer."

"I know that."

"Then you'd better start separating the bacon. The pan will be hot and you'll be wasting propane."

"Are you always a tightwad?"

"Only when I'm with a spendthrift."

"You don't know what you're talking about."

"So educate me."

But Shaye wasn't about to do any such thing. It suited her purpose to keep Noah in the dark, just as it suited her purpose to leisurely place one rasher of bacon, then another in the pan. While they cooked, she rummaged through the supplies until she located the coffee, then set a pot on to perk.

"I'm impressed," Noah said around a mouthful of food. "I didn't think you had it in you."

She'd been acutely aware of his eyes at her back, and despite good intentions, her temper was rising. "Shows how much you know," she snapped.

"Then you don't have a cook back in wherever?"

"I don't have a cook."

"How about a husband?"

Without turning, she raised her left hand, fingers rigidly splayed and decidedly bare.

"The absence of a ring doesn't mean anything. Militant feminists often—"

"I am not a militant feminist!" Gripping the handle of the frying pan, she forked the bacon onto its uncooked side. Slowly and silently she counted to ten. With measured movements, she reached for an egg.

It came down hard on the edge of the pan. The yoke broke. The white spilled over the rim.

Repairing the damage as best she could, she more carefully cracked the second egg, then stood, spatula in hand, waiting for both to cook.

"I thought you said you could crack an egg."

She didn't respond to the jibe.

"Got anything planned for an encore?"

She clamped her lips together.

"You could always flip an egg onto the floor."

"Why don't you shut up and eat?"

"I'm done."

Eyes wide, she turned to see that his plate, piled high short moments before, was now empty. "You're incredible."

He grinned broadly. "I know."

Her gaze climbed to his face, lured there by a strange force, one that refused to release her. Even after the slash of white teeth had disappeared, she stared, seeing a boy-ishness that was totally at odds with the man.

Unable to rationalize the discrepancy, she tore herself away and whirled back to the stove. The tiny whispers deep in her stomach could be put down to hunger, and the faint tremor in her hands as she transferred the eggs and bacon to a dish could be fatigue. But *boyishness*, in *Noah*?

A warning rang in her mind at the same moment she felt a pervasive warmth stretch from the crown of her head to her heels.

"Like I said," Noah murmured in her ear, "I'll need all my strength."

One arm reached to her left and deposited his dish, uten-sils clattering, in the sink. The other reached to her right and shifted the frying pan to the cold burner. The overall effect was one of imprisonment.

"Do you mind?" she muttered as she held herself stiffly against the stove.

He didn't move. Only his nose shifted, brushing the upper curve of her ear. "You smell good. Don't you sweat like the rest of us?"

Shaye felt a paradoxical dampness in the palms of her hands, at the backs of her knees, in the gentle hollow between her breasts, and was infinitely grateful that he couldn't possibly know. "Would you please move back?" she asked as evenly as she could.

"Have you ever been married?"

"I'd like to eat my eggs before they dry up."

"Got a boyfriend?"

"If you're looking for something to do, you could take a cup of coffee to your uncle."

"You never get those sweet little urges the rest of us get?"

Swinging back her elbow, she made sharp contact with his ribs. In the next instant she was free.

"That was dirty," he accused, rubbing the injured spot as she spun around.

"That was just for starters." Her hands were balled at her sides, and she was shaking. "I don't like to be crowded. Do you think you can get that simple fact through your skull, or is it too much to take in on a full stomach?"

Noah's hand stilled against his lean middle, and he studied her for a long minute. "I think I make you nervous."

"Angry. You make me angry."

"And nervous." He was back to taunting. "You're flushed."

"Anger."

Silkily he lowered his eyes to her left breast. "That, too?"

She refused to believe that he could see the quick quiver of her heart, though she couldn't deny the rapidity of her breathing. Even more adamantly she refused to believe that the tiny ripples of heat surging through her represented anything but fury. "That, too."

His gaze dropped lower, charting her midriff, caressing the bunching of jersey at her waist, arriving at last at her hips. His brow furrowed. He seemed confused yet oddly spellbound. Then, as though suddenly regaining the direction he'd lost, he snapped his eyes back to her face. "Too bad," he said, his lips hardening. "You've got the goods. It's a shame you can't put them to better use."

Shaye opened her mouth to protest his insolence, but he had already turned and was stalking away. "You left your dirty things in the sink!" she yelled.

He didn't answer. His tall frame blended with the shadow of the companionway, then disappeared into the blinding light above.

SOME TIME LATER, bearing cups of coffee for Samson and herself, Shaye returned to the deck. Samson stood at the helm, looking utterly content. He accepted the coffee with a smile, but Shaye didn't stay to talk. He was in his own world. He didn't need company.

Besides, Noah sat nearby. His long legs formed an open circle around a coil of rope and, while his hands were busily occupied, he watched her every move.

So she proceeded on toward the bow, where Victoria leaned against the bulwark gazing out to sea.

"Pretty, isn't it?"

Shaye nodded. The Colombian coast was a dark ridge on the horizon behind. Ahead was open sea. Far in the distance a cargo ship headed for Barranquilla or Cartagena. Less far a trawler chugged along, no doubt from one of the fishing villages along the coast.

Her fancy was caught, though, by a third, smaller craft, a yacht winging through the waters like a slender white dove. Peaceful, Shaye thought. Ahh, what she'd give for a little of that peace.

"Everything okay?" Victoria asked.

"Just fine."

"You look a little piqued."

"I'm tired."

"Not feeling seasick?"

Shaye shot her the wry twist of a grin. "Not quite."

"Have you ever been seasick?"

"Nope."

"Mmm." Victoria shook back her head and tipped it up to the sky. "In spite of everything, you have to admit that this is nice." When Shaye didn't respond, she went on. "It doesn't really matter what boat you're on, the air is the same, the sky, the waves." She slitted one eye toward Shaye. "Still want to go back?"

"It's a little late for that, don't you think?"

"But if you could, would you?"

Shaye dragged in a long, deep breath, then released it in a sigh. "No, Victoria, I wouldn't go back. But that doesn't mean this is going to be easy."

"What happened in the galley?"

Shaye took a deliberately lengthy sip of her coffee. "Nothing."

"Are you sure?"

"I'm sure."

"You sound a little tense."

"Blame that on fatigue, too." Or on anger. Or on frustration. Or, in a nutshell, on Noah VanBaar.

"But it's not even noon."

"It feels like midnight to me. I may go to bed pretty soon."

"But we've just begun to sail!"

"And we'll be sailing for the next four days straight, so there'll be plenty of time for me to take it all in."

"Oh, Shaye..."

"If I were in the Berkshires, I'd still be in bed."

"Bo-ring."

"Maybe so, but this is my vacation, isn't it? If I don't catch up on my sleep now, I never will. Weren't you the one who said I could do it on the boat?"

Victoria yielded with grace. "Okay. Sleep. Why don't you drag some cushions up here and do it in the sun?"

Because Noah is on deck and there's no way *I could sleep knowing that*. "That much sun I don't need."

"Then, the shade. You can sleep in the shade of the sails."

But Shaye was shaking her head. "No, I think I'll try that bed of ours." Her lips twisted. "Give it a test run." She took another swallow of coffee.

Victoria leaned closer. "Running away from him won't help, y'know. You have to let him know that he doesn't scare you."

"He doesn't scare me."

"He can't take his eyes off you."

"Uh-huh."

"It's true. He's been watching you since you came on deck."

"He's worried that I'm going to spoil Samson's trip by saying something ugly."

"He said that?"

"In no uncertain terms."

"What else did he say?" Victoria said, and Shaye realized she'd fallen into the trap. But it wasn't too late to extricate herself. She didn't want to discuss Noah with Victoria, who would, no doubt, play the devil's advocate. Shaye wasn't ready to believe *anything* good about Noah.

So she offered a cryptic, "Not much."

Victoria had turned around so that her back was to the bulwark. Quite conveniently, she had a view of the rest of the boat. "He's very good-looking."

"If you say so," Shaye answered indifferently.

"He appears to be good with his hands."

"I wouldn't know about that."

"Do you have any idea what he does for a living?"

"Nope."

"Aren't you curious?"

"Nope."

"Then you're hopeless," Victoria decided, tossing her hands in the air and walking away.

"Traitor," Shaye muttered under her breath. "I'm only here because of you, and are you grateful? Of course not. You won't be satisfied until I'm falling all over that man, but I can assure you that won't happen. He and I have nothing in common. Nothing at all."

THEY DID, AS IT turned out. Noah was as tired as Shaye. He'd flown in the day before from New York via Atlanta, where he'd had a brief business meeting, and rather than going to a hotel in Barranquilla, he'd come directly to the *Golden Echo* to help Samson prepare for the trip.

Though he'd never have admitted it aloud, Shaye hadn't been far off the mark when she'd called the boat a wreck. Oh, she was seaworthy; he'd checked for signs of leakage when he'd first come aboard and had found none. The little things were what needed attention—lines to be spliced, water pumps to be primed, hurricane lamps to be cleaned—all of which should by rights have been done before the *Golden Echo* left Jamaica on her previous charter. But that was water over the dam. He didn't mind the work. What he needed now, though, was rest.

"I'm turning in for a while," he told Samson, who was quite happily guarding the helm. "If you need me for anything, give a yell."

The older man kept his eyes on the sea. "Do me a favor and check on Shaye? She went below a little while ago. I hope she's not sick."

Noah knew perfectly well that she'd gone below. He wouldn't have said that she'd looked particularly sick, since she'd seemed pale to him from the start.

"I'd ask Victoria to do it," Samson was saying, "but

I hate to disturb her." She was relaxing on the foredeck, taking obvious pleasure in both the sun and the breeze. "Since you're going below anyway..."

"I'll check."

But only because Samson had asked. Left to his own devices, Noah would have let Shaye suffer on her own. His encounter with her in the galley had left him feeling at odds with himself, and though that had been several hours before, he hadn't been able to completely shake the feeling. All he wanted was to strip down and go to sleep without thought of the woman. But Samson had asked...

She wasn't in the galley or the salon, and since she certainly wouldn't be in the captain's quarters, he made for her cabin. The door was shut. He stood for a minute, head bowed, hands on his hips. Then he knocked very lightly on the wood. When there was no answer, he eased open the door.

The sight before him took him totally by surprise. Shaye had pulled back the covers and was lying on her side on the bare sheets, sound asleep. She wore a huge white T-shirt that barely grazed her upper thighs. Her legs were slightly bent, long and slender. But what stunned him most was her hair. It fanned behind her on the pillow, a thick, wavy train of auburn that caught the light off the portholes and glowed.

Fascinated, he took one step closer, then another. She seemed like another woman entirely when she was relaxed. There was gentleness in her loosely resting fingers, softness in her curving body, vulnerability in the slight part of her lips and in the faint sheen of perspiration that made her skin gleam. And in her hair? Spirit. Oh, yes. There it was—promise of the same fire he'd caught from time to time in her eyes.

Unable to resist, he hunkered down by the side of the

bed. Her lashes were like dark flames above her cheek-bones. Free now of tension, her nose looked small and pert. Her cheeks were the lightest shade of a very natural pink that should have clashed with her hair but didn't. And that hair—he wondered if it were as soft as it looked, or as hot. His fingers curled into his palms, resisting the urge to touch, and he forced his eyes away.

It was a major mistake. The thin T-shirt, while gathered loosely in front, clung to her slender side and the gentle flare of her hip, leaving just enough to the imagination to make him ache. And edging beneath the hem of the shirt was a slash of the softest, sweetest apricot-colored silk. His gaze jumped convulsively to the far side of the bed, where she'd left the clothes she'd discarded. There, lying atop the slacks and T-shirt she'd been wearing earlier, was a lacy bra of the same apricot hue.

With a hard swallow, he flicked his gaze back to her face. Stern, stiff-backed and fussy—was that the image she chose to convey to the world? Her underthings told a different story, one that was enhanced by her sleeping form. It was interesting, he mused, interesting and puzzling.

Image making was his business. He enjoyed it, was good at it. Moreover, knowing precisely what went into the shaping of public images, he prided himself on being able to see through them. He hadn't managed to this time, though, and he wondered why. Was Shaye that good, or had his perceptiveness been muddled?

He suspected it was a little of both, and there was meager comfort in the thought. If Shaye was that good, she was far stronger and more complex than he'd imagined. If his perceptiveness had been muddled, it was either because he was tired...or because she did something to his mind.

He feared it was the latter. He'd been ornery because he hadn't wanted her along, but that orneriness had been out of proportion. He didn't normally goad people the way he had her. But Shaye—she brought out the rawest of his instincts.

In every respect. Looking at her now, all soft and enticing, he felt the heat rise in his body as it hadn't done in years. How could he possibly be attracted to as prickly a woman? Was it her softness his body sensed and responded to? Or her hidden fire?

His insides tensed in a different way when her lashes fluttered, then it was too late to escape. Not that he would have, he told himself. He'd never run from a woman, and he wasn't about to now. But he'd be damned if he'd let her know how she affected him. Retrieving his mask of insolence, he met her startled gaze.

Shaye didn't move a muscle. She simply stared at him. "What are you doing here?"

"Checking on you. Samson thought you might be sick."

"I'm not."

"Not *violently* seasick?"

"… No."

His gaze idly scored her body. "Did you lie about anything else?"

Why, she asked herself, did he sound as though he knew something he shouldn't? Victoria would never have betrayed her. And there was no way he could see through her T-shirt, though she almost imagined he had. She'd have given anything to reach for the sheet and cover herself, but she refused to give him the satisfaction of knowing that his wandering eye made her nervous. "No," she finally answered.

"Mmm."

"What is that supposed to mean?"

"That you're a contradiction," he said without hesitation. He'd obviously been thinking about her—or crouching here, watching her—for some time. The last thought made her doubly nervous, and the explanation he offered didn't help.

"Cactus-prickly when you're awake, sweet woman when you're asleep. It makes me wonder which is the real you."

"You'll never know," she informed him. Her poise was fragile; there was something debilitating about lying on a bed near Noah, wearing not much more than an old T-shirt.

His gray eyes glittered. "It'd be a challenge for me to find out. Mmm, maybe I'll make it my goal. I'll have two full weeks with not much else to do."

Shaye didn't like the sound of that at all. "And what about the treasure you're supposedly seeking?" she demanded.

"Samson's doing the seeking. As far as I'm concerned, there are many different kinds of treasure." He surveyed her body more lazily. "Could be that the one you're hiding is worth more than the one my uncle seeks."

"As though I could hide anything this way," she mumbled.

"Precisely."

"Look, I was sleeping. I happen to be exhausted. Do you think you could find a tiny bit of compassion within that stone-hard soul of yours to leave me be?"

He grinned, wondering what she'd have said if she'd known something else had been close to stone-hard moments before. No doubt she'd have used far more potent words to describe his character. Come to think of it, he wondered how many of those potent words she knew.

"You're really very appealing like this," he said softly. "Much more approachable than before. I like your hair."

"Go away."

"I hadn't realized it was so long. Or so thick. The color

comes alive when you let it down like that. Why do you
bother to tack it up?"

"To avoid comments like the ones you just made."

"I'd think you'd be flattered."

"I'm not."

"You don't like me," he said with a pout.

"Now you're getting there."

"Is it something I said, something I did?"

She squeezed her eyes shut for a minute, then, unable
to bear the feeling of exposure any longer, bolted up and
reached for the sheet.

Noah looked as though he'd lost his best friend. "What
did you do that for? I wouldn't have touched you."

There was touching and there was touching. He could
touch her with his hands, or with his eyes. Or he could
touch her with the innocent little expressions he sent her
way from time to time. She knew not to trust those little
expressions, but, still, they did something to her. Far better that he should be growling and scowling.

"It's your eyes," she accused as she pressed her back to
the wall. "I don't like them."

This time his innocence seemed more genuine. "What's
wrong with my eyes?"

"They creep."

"They explore," he corrected, "and when they find
something they like, they take a closer look." He shrugged.
"Can you blame them? Your legs are stunning."

She quickly tucked her legs under her. "Please. Just
leave and let me sleep."

Since the path had been cleared for him, he hopped up
and sat on the bed.

"Noah…" she warned.

"That's the first time you've called me by name. I like it
when you say it, though you could soften the tone a little."

"Leave this cabin now!"

He made himself more comfortable, extending an arm, propping his weight on his palm. "You never answered me when I asked about boyfriends. Do you have any back home? Where is home, by the way?"

"Philadelphia," she growled. "There, you've gotten some information. Now you can leave."

"A little more. I want a little more. Is there a boyfriend?"

In a bid for dignity, she drew herself up as straight as she could. Unfortunately he was sitting on the sheet, which ended up stretched taut. And even with the extra inches she felt dwarfed. Why did he have to be so *big*? Why couldn't he be of average height like her lawyer friend, or the stock-broker? For that matter, why couldn't he be malleable, like they were? They'd have left the instant she'd asked *if* they ever made it to her room at all.

"Boyfriends?" he prompted.

"That's none of your business."

"I'll tell you about me if you tell me about you," he cajoled.

"I don't want to know about you."

Bemused, he tipped his dark head to the side. "Wouldn't it be easier if you knew what you faced?"

"I'm not facing anything," she argued, but there was a note of desperation in her voice.

"Two weeks, Shaye. We're going to be together for two long weeks."

"Miss Burke, to you."

For a split second he looked chastised, then spoiled it with a helpless spurt of laughter.

"All right," she grumbled quickly. "Call me Shaye."

"Shaye." He tempered his grin. "Do you have any boyfriends?"

She knew she'd lost a little ground on the Miss Burke

bit, which even to her own ears had sounded inane. But she was supposed to be prissy. And as far as boyfriends were concerned, a few white lies wouldn't hurt.

"I don't date."

His eyes widened. "You've got to be kidding."

"No."

"With a body like yours?"

"For your information, there's more to life than sex." She wondered if she was sounding *too* prissy. She didn't want to overdo it.

"Really?"

"I'm too busy to date. I have a very demanding job, and I love it. My life is complete."

He shook his head. "Whew! You're something else." He didn't believe her for a minute, but if she wanted to play games, he could match her. "I have a demanding job myself, but I couldn't make it through life without steady helpings of sex. Women's liberation has its up side, in that sense."

"Then what are you doing on this trip?" she asked through gritted teeth. "How could you drag yourself away from all those warm beds and passionate arms?"

"And legs," he added quickly. "Don't forget legs. I'm a leg man, remember?"

She was getting nowhere, she realized. He looked as though he had no intention of budging, and she didn't think she had the physical strength to make him. "Please," she said, deliberately wilting a little, "I really am tired. I don't want to fight you, and I don't want to be on guard every minute of this trip. If you just leave me alone, I'll stay out of your way."

"Please, Noah."

"Please, Noah."

Her meekness was too much, he decided. When she was

meek, there was no fire in her eyes, and he rather liked that fire. "Well, I have learned something new about you."

"What's that?"

His eyes slid over the moistness of her skin. "You sweat."

"Of course I sweat! It's damn hot in here!"

He grinned. So much for meekness. "The question," he ventured in a deep, smooth voice, "is whether you smell as good like this as you did before." He leaned closer.

Shaye put up here hands to hold him off, losing her grip on the sheet in the process. But she'd been right; she was no match for his strength. Her palms were ineffective levers against his chest, and despite her efforts, she felt his face against her neck.

His nose nuzzled her. His lips slid to the underside of her jaw. He opened his mouth and dragged it across her cheek to her ear.

And all the while, Shaye was dying a thousand little deaths because she liked the feel of his mouth on her, she liked it!

"Even...better," he whispered hoarsely. His lips nipped at her earlobe, and the hoarse whisper came again. "You smell...even better."

Her eyes were shut and her breathing had grown erratic. "Please, stop," she gasped brokenly. "Please, Noah..."

He was dizzy with pleasure at the contact, and would have gone on nuzzling her forever had he not caught the trace of fear in her voice. He hadn't heard that before, not fear, and he knew instinctively that there was nothing put on about it. Slowly and with a certain amount of puzzlement, he drew back and searched her eyes. They were wide with fear, yes, but with other things as well. And he knew then, without a doubt, what he was going to do.

He'd leave her now, but he'd be true to his word. He'd

spend the next two weeks shadowing her, learning what made her tick. She might in fact be the prissy lady she wanted him to believe she was. Or she might be the woman of passion he suspected she was. In either case, he stirred her. That was what he read in her eyes, and though he wasn't sure why, it was what he wanted.

"Go back to sleep," he said gently as he rose from the bed. He was halfway to the door when he heard her snort.

"Fat chance of that! Can I really believe you won't invade my privacy again? And if I were to fall asleep, I'd have nightmares. Hmph. So much for a lovely vacation. Stuck on a stinking pirate ship with a man who thinks he's God's gift to women—"

Noah closed the door on the last of her tirade and, smiling, sauntered off through the salon.

CHAPTER FOUR

"*Ahh, mes belles aimes. Notre dîner nous attend sur le pont. Suivez-moi, s'il vous plaît.*"

Shaye, who'd been curled in an easy chair in the salon, darted a disbelieving glance at Victoria before refocusing her eyes on Samson. She'd known he'd been busily working in the galley and that he'd refused their offers of help. But she hadn't expected to be called to the table in flawless French —he was a professor of *Latin*, wasn't he?—much less by a man sporting a bright red, side-knotted silk scarf and a cockily set black beret.

Victoria thought he was precious; eccentric was the word Shaye would choose. But he was harmless, certainly more so than his nephew, she mused, and at the moment she was in need of a little comic relief.

It had been a long afternoon. She hadn't been able to fall back to sleep after Noah had left her cabin, though she'd tried her best. After cursing the sheets, the mattress, the heat and everything else in the room, she'd dressed, re-knotted her hair and gone on deck.

Noah hadn't been there—he was sleeping, Samson told her, which had irritated her no end. *He* was sleeping, after he'd ruined her own! She'd seethed for a while, then been gently, gradually, helplessly lulled by the rocking of the boat into a better frame of mind.

And now Samson had called them to dinner. The table, it turned out, was a low, folding one covered by a check-

ered cloth, and the seats were cushions they carried up
from the salon. Noah had lowered the jibs and secured the
wheel, dashing Shaye's hope that he'd be too busy sailing
to join them. To make matters worse, he crossed his long
legs and fluidly lowered himself to the cushion immediately on her left.

The meal consisted of a hearty bouillabaisse, served
with a Muscadet wine, crusty French bread and, for dessert, a raspberry tart topped with thick whipped cream.
Other than complimenting the chef on his work, Shaye
mostly stayed out of the conversation, which involved
Samson and Victoria and the other unlikely trips each
had taken.

Noah, too, was quiet, but his eyes were like living things
reaching out, touching her, daring her to reveal something
of herself as Victoria and Samson were doing. Since she
had no intention of conforming, she remained quiet and
ignored his gaze as best she could.

Samson, bless him, was more than willing to accept
help with the cleanup, and Shaye was grateful for the escape. By the time she finished in the galley, she was feeling better.

Armed with a cup of coffee and a book, she settled
in the salon. Hurricane lamps provided the light, cast-
ing a warm golden glow that she had to admit was atmo-
spheric. In fact, she had to admit that the *Golden Echo*
wasn't all that bad. Sails unfurled and full once again, the
sloop sliced gently through the waves. A crosswind whispered from porthole to porthole, comfortably ventilating
the salon. The mustiness that had bothered Shaye earlier
seemed to have disappeared, though perhaps, she reflected,
she'd simply grown accustomed to it.

She was well fed. She was comfortable. She was peace-
fully reading her book. Would a vacation in the Berkshires

have been any different? *It's all in the mind, Shaye.* Isn't that what Victoria would say? *He can only be a threat if you allow it, whereas if you put him from mind, he doesn't exist.*

For a time it worked. She flew through the first hundred pages of her book, finally putting it down when her lids began to droop. Victoria was still on deck. Samson had turned in some time before, intending to sleep until two, when he would relieve Noah at the helm.

Intending to sleep far longer than that, Shaye went to bed herself. When she awoke, though, it wasn't ten in the morning as she'd planned. It was three and very dark, and she was feeling incredibly warm all over.

A fever? Not quite. She'd awakened from a dream of Noah. A nightmare? she asked herself, as she lay flat on her back taking slow, easy breaths to calm her quivering body. Only in hindsight. At the time, it had been an excitingly erotic dream. Even now her skin was damp in response.

It isn't fair, she railed, silently. She could push him from her thoughts when she was awake, but how could she control the demon inside while she slept? And what breed of demon was it that caused her to dream erotic dreams about *any* man? She'd lived wildly and passionately for a time, and the lifestyle left much to be desired. She'd sworn off it. She'd outgrown it. She was perfectly content with what she had now.

Could that demon be telling her something?

Uncomfortable with the direction of her thoughts, she carefully rose from the bed so as not to awaken Victoria, dragged a knee-length sweatshirt over her T-shirt and padded silently to the door.

All was quiet save the slap of the waves against the hull and the sough of the breeze. She passed through the salon and the narrow passageway, sending a disdainful glance toward the door of the captain's cabin, where Noah would no doubt be sleeping by now, and carefully climbed the companionway.

On deck she dropped her head back and let the breeze take her unfettered hair as it would. The sea air felt good against her skin, and the sweatshirt was just loose enough, just warm enough to keep her comfortable. Almost reluctantly she straightened her head and opened her eyes, intending to tell Samson that she would be standing at the bow for a bit.

Only it wasn't Samson at the helm. Though the transom's hanging lamp left his face in shadows, the large frame rakishly planted behind the wheel could belong to no one but Noah.

The image struck her, then, with devastating force. He didn't need a billowing shirt, tight pants, boots and a cross belt. He didn't need anything beyond gently clinging shorts and a windbreaker that was barely zipped. He had the rest—thick hair blowing, broad shoulders set, strong hands on the wheel, bare feet widespread and rooted to the deck. Looking more like a descendant of Fletcher Christian than the nephew of Samson VanBaar, he was a rebel if ever there was one. And his prize? Her peace of mind… for starters.

"Welcome," he said with unexpected civility. "You wouldn't by chance care to take the helm for a minute while I go get a cup of coffee?"

She certainly wouldn't have allowed herself to turn tail and run once he'd seen her, but she felt impelled to explain her presence. The last thing she wanted was for him to think she was seeking him out. "I thought this was Samson's shift."

"He's exhausted. I decided to let him sleep a while longer."

"You seem tired yourself," she heard herself say. He certainly didn't *sound* like a rebel just then.

He shrugged. "I'll sleep later."

Nodding, she looked away. Something had happened. It was as though the intimacy they'd shared in her dream had softened her. Or was it his fatigue, which softened *him*? Or the gently gusting night air? Or the hypnotic motion of the sloop? Or the fact that starlit nights in the Caribbean were made, in the broadest sense, for love, not war?

Whatever, she turned and started back down the companionway.

"Don't go," he said quickly.

"I'll bring up some coffee."

It was an easy task to reheat what was in the pot. When she returned a few minutes later carrying two mugs, Noah accepted his with a quiet, "Thank you."

Nodding, Shaye stepped back to lean against the transom. For a time, neither spoke. Noah's eyes were ahead, Shaye's were directed northward.

Philadelphia seemed very far away, and it occurred to her that she didn't miss it. Nor, she realized, did she regret the fact that she wasn't heading for the Berkshires. Come light of day, she might miss both, but right now, she felt peaceful. Sated. As though…as though her dream had filled some need that she'd repressed. She felt as though she'd just made love with Noah, as though they were now enjoying the companionable afterglow.

"Couldn't sleep?" he asked quietly.

"I, uh, it must have been the rest I had earlier."

"That'll do it sometimes."

They relapsed into silence. Shaye sipped her coffee. Noah did the same, then set the mug down and consulted his compass.

"I was wondering about that," she ventured. "I didn't

see any navigational equipment when Samson showed us around."

"I'm not sure what was available when Horgan built the sloop in the twenties, but I assume he felt—and the Paynes must have agreed—that fancy dials would have been sacrilegious." He made a slight adjustment to the wheel, then beckoned to her. "Hold it for a second?"

Setting the mug by her feet, she grasped the wooden wheel with both hands while he moved forward to adjust the sails. When he returned, though, it was to take the place she'd left at the transom, slightly behind her, slightly to the right.

"So you use a compass?"

"And a sextant. My uncle's the expert with that."

"Is there a specific point we're aiming at?"

Noah took a healthy swallow of his coffee. "He has coordinates, if that's what you mean."

"For the treasure?"

"Uh-huh."

She was looking ahead, holding the wheel steady, assuming that Noah would correct her if she did something wrong. "He hasn't said much about that."

"He's a great one for prioritizing. First, the sail. Then the treasure."

She felt a nudge at her elbow and turned to find him holding out her mug. She took it and lifted it, but rather than drinking, she brushed her lips back and forth against the rim. "It's strange…"

"What?"

"That Samson should be a Latin professor and yet have such a proclivity for adventure. Not that I'm being critical. I just find it…curious."

"Not really," Noah said. He paused for a minute, deciding how best to explain. "It's a matter of having balance in one's life. Samson has his teaching, which is stable, and his adventures, which are a little more risqué. But there's a link between the two. For example, he sees the same beauty in Latin that he sees in this sloop. They're both ancient—forefathers of other languages, other boats. They both have an innate beauty, a romanticism. Samson is a romantic."

"I hadn't noticed," Shaye teased.

Belatedly, Noah chuckled. "Mmm. He must seem a little bizarre to you."

"No. He's really very sweet."

"He stages Halloween year-round."

She wondered if she'd ever live down that particular comment, but since Noah didn't seem to be angry anymore, there was no point in defending herself. "So I gather," she said with a little grin.

Noah was content with that. "Samson has always believed in doing what he loves. He loves teaching." Reaching out, he rescued a blowing strand of her hair from her mouth and tucked it behind her ear. "He takes delight in making the language come alive for his students. And he docs it. I've sat in on some of his classes. In his own quiet way, he is hilarious."

Shaye could believe it. "His stories are something else."

"You were listening?"

She shot him a quick glance. "Tonight? Of course I was."

"I wasn't sure. You were very quiet."

She wasn't about to say that listening hard to Samson had kept her mind off *him*. "Why interrupt something good when you have nothing better to add? It's really a shame that Samson doesn't write about his adventures. They'd make wonderful reading."

"They do."

"Magazine articles?" she asked with some excitement,

immediately conjuring up images of a beautiful *National Geographic* spread.

"Books."

"No kidding!"

"How do you think he pays for these little adventures?"

"I really hadn't thought about it." She frowned. "He didn't say anything tonight about writing."

"He's an understated man. He downplays it."

"Can he do that? Isn't there a certain amount of notoriety that comes with being a published author?"

Noah leaned forward and lowered his voice to a conspiratorial level. "Not if you publish under another name." He leaned back again.

"Ahh. So that's how he does it."

"Mmm." He took another drink. "But don't tell him I told you."

She grinned. "Can I ask him where he learned to cook?"

"Cooking he'll discuss any day. It's one of his passions."

Passions. The word stuck in Shaye's mind, turning slowly, a many-faceted diamond with sides of brilliance, darkness, joy and grief.

She shook her hair back, freeing it for the caress of the wind. "You and he seem to be very close. Do you live in Hanover?"

It was a minute before Noah heard the question. He was fascinated by the little movement she'd made. It had been totally unaffected but beguiling. Bare-legged as she was, and with that gorgeous mane of hair—soft, oh yes, soft—blowing behind her, she didn't look anything like the prissy little lady he'd accused her of being.

He closed his eyes for a second and shook off both images, leaving in their place the same gentle ambiance that had existed before. Did he live near Samson in Hanover? "No. But we see each other regularly. There's just him and me. All the others are gone. We have a mutual-admiration society, so it works out well."

"All the others—you mean, your parents?"

"And Samson's wife. Samson and Gena never had children of their own, and since Samson and my father had no other siblings, I was pretty much shared between them."

She smiled. "That must have been fun."

"It was."

She thought about her own childhood, the time she'd spent with her parents. Fun wasn't a word she'd ever used to describe those days. "Was your father as much of a character as Samson?"

"No. He was more serious. Dividing my time between the two men gave a balance to my life, too."

It was the second time he'd spoken of balance, and she wondered if he'd done it deliberately. Her life was far from balanced. Work was her vocation, her avocation, the sole outlet for her energies. Victoria argued that there was more to life, and Shaye smiled and nodded and gave examples of the men she dated and the friends she saw. But apart from her friendship with her sister, the others were largely token friendships. And she knew why. To maintain a steady keel in her life, she chose to be with people who wouldn't rock the boat. Unfortunately, those people were uninspiring. They left her feeling alone and frustrated. Her only antidote was work.

But Noah couldn't possibly know all that, could he?

Feeling strangely empty, she took a large gulp of her coffee, then set the mug down and grasped the wheel more firmly. But neither the solidity of the hard wood nor the warm brew settling in her stomach could counter the chill she was feeling. Unconsciously, she rubbed one bare foot over the other.

In the next instant a third foot covered hers, a larger,

warmer one. And then a human shield slipped behind her, protecting her back, her hips, her legs from elements that came from far beyond the Caribbean.

Noah had surrounded her this way in the galley, but the sense of imprisonment was far different now. It was gentle, protective and welcome.

She closed her eyes when she felt his face in her hair, and whispered, "Why are you being so nice?"

His voice was muffled. "Maybe because I'm too tired to fight."

"Then the secret is keeping you tired?"

"The secret," he said as his lips touched her ear, "is keeping your hair down and your legs bare and your mouth sweet. I think something happens when you screw back your hair and cinch yourself into your clothes. Everything tightens up. Your features stiffen and your tongue goes tart."

"It does not!" she cried, but without conviction. She couldn't believe how wonderful she felt, and she wasn't about to deny it any more than she could think to end it. When his face slid to her neck, she relaxed her head against his shoulder.

"I won't argue," he murmured thickly. "Not now."

"You're too tired."

"Too content."

He was pressing openmouthed kisses to the side of her neck, inching his way lower to the spot where her sweatshirt began. She felt a trembling start at her toes and spread upward, and she grasped the wheel tighter, though she wasn't about to move.

He shifted behind her, spreading his legs to cradle her at the same time his hands fell to her thighs and began to work their way upward.

"Noah…" she whispered.

"So soft…" His fingers were splayed, thumbs dragging up along the crease where her thighs met her hips, tracing her pelvic bones, etching a path over her waist and ribs. Then his fingers came together to cup her breasts, and she went wild inside. She arched into his hands, while her head came around, mouth open, tongue trapped against his jaw.

She was melting. Every bone in her body, every muscle, every inch of flesh seemed to lose definition and gather into a single yearning mass. Had she missed this so, this wonderful sense of anticipatory fulfillment? Had she ever experienced it before?

He was roughly caressing her breasts, but it wasn't enough, and her mouth, with hungry nips at his chin, told him so. Then her mouth was being covered, eaten, devoured, and she was taking from him, taste for taste, bite for bite.

Totally oblivious to her role at the helm she wound her arms backward, around Noah. Her hands slid up and down the backs of his thighs, finally clasping his buttocks, urging his masculine heat closer to the spot that suddenly and vividly ached.

"Oh God," he gasped, dragging his mouth from hers. He wrapped quivering arms tightly around her waist and breathed raggedly as his pelvis moved against her. "Ahh…"

More hungry than ever, Shaye tried to turn. She wanted to wrap her arms around his neck, to feed again from his mouth, to drape her leg over his and feel his strength where she craved it so. But he wouldn't have it. He squeezed her hard to hold her still, and the movement was enough to restore the first fragments of reason. When he felt that she'd regained a modicum of control, he eased up his hold, but he didn't release her.

With several more gusts of wind, their breathing, their pulse rates, began to slow.

Shaye was stunned. It wasn't so much what had happened but the force with which it had happened that shocked her most. She didn't know what to say.

Noah did, speaking gently and low. "Has it been a long time?"

She'd returned a hand to the wheel, though her fingers were boneless. "Yes," she whispered.

"It took you by surprise?"

Another whispered, "Yes."

"Will you be sorry in the morning?"

"Probably."

He released her then, but without anger. When he reached for the wheel, she stepped aside. "Go below... please?" he asked gruffly.

She knew what he was doing, and she was grateful. He was alerting her to the fact that if she stayed she might have even more to be sorry for in the morning. She'd felt his arousal; she'd actively fed it. She had to accept her share of responsibility for what had happened, just as she had to respect the pleading note in his voice. He was human. He wanted her. And he was asking her not to want him back...at least, not tonight.

Without saying a word, she climbed down the companionway. At the bottom, she gasped, a helpless little cry.

"I frightened you," Samson said. "I'm sorry. You seemed very deep in thought."

She was, but her heart was pounding at thoughts that had taken a sudden turn. *What if Samson had awakened earlier and come up on deck during...during...*

"I should have been up a while ago," he was saying. "Noah must be exhausted. I'm glad he wasn't alone all that time."

Shaye wasn't sure whether to be glad or not. As she made her silent way to the cabin, then stole back into bed, she wasn't sure of much—other than that she'd be furious with herself later.

SHE WAS FURIOUS. She didn't sleep well, but kept waking up to recall what had happened, to toss and turn for a while, then bury her face in the pillow and plead for the escape of sleep. Mercifully, Victoria was gone from the cabin by seven, which meant that Shaye could do her agonizing in peace.

She slept. She awoke. She slept again, then awoke again. The cycle repeated itself until nearly noon, when she gave up one battle to face the next.

Noah was in the galley. All she wanted was a cup of coffee, but even that wasn't going to be easy.

"Sleep well?" he asked in a tone that gave nothing away.

"Not particularly."

"Bad dreams?"

"It was what was *between* the dreams that was bad," she muttered, pouring coffee into a cup with hands that shook.

"Are you always this cheerful in the morning?"

"Always."

"If you'd woken up in bed with me, it might have been different."

Bracing herself against the stove, she squeezed her eyes shut and made it to the count of eight before his next sally came.

"I'll bet you're dynamite in bed."

She went on counting.

"You were dynamite on the deck."

She cringed. "Don't remind me."

"Are you schizophrenic?"

At that, she turned and stared. "Excuse me?"

"Do you have two distinct personalities?"

"Of course not!"

"Then why are you so crabby this morning when you were so sweet last night?" He gave her a thorough once-over, then decided, "It *has* to be the clothes. You're wearing shorts, but they must be binding somewhere." Her T-shirt was big enough for *him* to swim in, so it couldn't be that. "And your hair. Safely secured once again. Does it make you *feel* secure when it's pinned back like that?"

She grabbed her coffee and made for the salon.

He was right behind her. "Careful. You're spilling."

She whirled on him, only to gasp when several drops of coffee hit his shirt.

He jumped back. "Damn it, that's hot!"

She hadn't intended to splatter him. Without thinking, she reached out to repair the damage.

He pushed her hand away. "It's all right."

"Are you burned?" she asked weakly.

"I'll live."

"The coffee will stain if you don't rinse it out."

"This shirt has seen a lot worse."

Eying the T-shirt, Shaye had to agree. She guessed that it had been navy once upon a time, but no longer. It was ragged at the hem and armholes, and it dipped tiredly at the neck, but damn if it didn't make him look roguish!

Sighing unsteadily, she moved more carefully into the salon and sank into a chair. Her head fell back and she closed her eyes. She felt Noah take the seat opposite her.

"Why are you doing this to me?" she whispered.

He didn't have to think about it, when he'd done nothing else for the past few hours. "You intrigue me."

It wasn't the answer she wanted. "I didn't think you were intrigued by cactus prickly women."

"Ahh, but are you really cactus prickly? That's the question."

"I'm prissy."

"Really?"

"You said it yourself."

"Maybe I was wrong."

"You weren't."

"Could've fooled me last night."

Eyes still closed, she scrunched up her face. "Do you think we could forget about last night?"

"Jeeez, I hope not. Last night was really something."

She moaned his name in protest, but he turned even that to his advantage.

"You did that last night and I liked it. You wanted me. Was that so terrible?"

Her eyes shot open and she met his gaze head-on. "I do not want you."

"You did then."

"I was too tired to know what I was doing."

He was sitting forward, fingers loosely linked between spread knees. "That's just the point. Your defenses were down. Maybe that's the real you."

"The real me," she stated as unequivocably as she could, "is what you see here and now." She had to make him believe it. She had to make *herself* believe it. "I live a very sane, very structured, very controlled existence."

"What fun's that?"

"It's what I choose. You may say its boring, but it's what *I* choose!"

"Is that why you burst into flames in my arms?"

She was getting nowhere. She'd known from the moment she'd left the deck so early this morning that she was in trouble, and Noah wasn't helping. But then, she hadn't really expected he would. So she closed her eyes again and tuned him out.

"You were hungry."

She said nothing.

He upped the pressure. "Sex starved."

Still silence.

He pursed his lips. "You can't seduce Samson because he has his eye on your aunt, so that leaves only me."

"I wouldn't know how to seduce a man if I tried," she mumbled. It fit in with the image of prissiness, but it was also the truth. She'd never had to seduce a man. Sex had been free and easy in the circles she'd run in. Perhaps that was why it had held so little meaning for her. Last night—this morning—had been different. She was still trying to understand how.

"I told you. All you have to do is bare those legs, shake out that hair and say something sweet." He shifted and grimaced. "Lord, you're only one-third of the way there, and I'm getting hard."

Her eyes flew open. "You're crude."

He considered that. "Crude connotes a raw condition. Mmm, that's pretty much the same thing as being hard."

She bolted from the chair and stormed toward her cabin.

"You can't hide there all day, y'know!" he called after her.

"I have no intention of hiding here," she yelled back. "I'm getting a book—" she snatched it from her suitcase, which, standing on end, served as a makeshift nightstand "—and I'm going on deck." She slammed past Noah back through the salon, then momentarily reversed direction to grab a cushion from the sofa.

"You can't escape me there," he warned.

"No," she snapped as she marched down the alley toward the companionway, "but with other people around, you might watch your tongue."

He was on her heels. "I'd rather watch yours. I liked what it did to me last night."

"This morning." She stomped up the steps. "It was this morning, and I can guarantee it won't happen again."

"Don't do that," he pleaded, once again the little boy with the man's mind and body. "You really turned me on—"

"Shh!" She whipped her head around to give him a final glare, then with poise emerged topside, smiled and said, "Good morning, Samson."

NOAH STOOD AT THE WHEEL, his legs braced apart, his fingers curled tightly around the handles. Steering the *Golden Echo* didn't take much effort, but it gave him a semblance of control. He needed that. He wasn't sure why, but he did.

Shifting his gaze from the ocean, he homed in on Shaye. She was propped on a cushion against the bulwark in the shade of the sails, reading. Her knees were bent, her eyes never left the page. Not a single, solitary strand of hair escaped its bonds to blow free in the breeze.

Prickly. God, was she prickly! She was the image of primness, but he knew there was another side. *He* knew it. She refused to admit it. And the more he goaded her, the more prickly she became.

He was no stranger to women. Granted, he wasn't quite the roué he'd told Shaye he was, but his work brought him into contact with women all the time. He'd known charming ones, spunky ones, aggressive and ambitious ones. Shaye was as beautiful as any of them—or, he amended, she was when she let go. She'd done it last night, but it had been dark then. He wanted to see her do it now. If she freed her hair from its knot, relaxed her body, tossed back her head and smiled, he knew he'd take her image to his grave.

But she wouldn't do that. She wouldn't give him the satisfaction. He recalled the times when they'd bickered, when she'd bitten back retorts, taken deep breaths, done everything in her power to ignore his taunts. Sometimes she'd lost control and had lashed back in turn, but even then she'd been quick to regain herself.

What had she said—that she lived a structured and controlled existence? Beyond that he didn't know much, other than that she was from Philadelphia and that she had neither a husband nor a cook. He did know that she was aware of him physically. She couldn't deny what had happened right here, on this very spot, less than twelve hours before.

Nor could he deny it. He knew he was asking for trouble tangling with a woman who clearly had a hang-up with sex. But sex wasn't all he wanted. She intrigued him; he hadn't lied about that. He felt a desperate need to understand her, and that meant getting to know her. And *that* meant breaking through the invisible wall she'd built.

As he saw it, there were two ways to go about it. The first, the more civil way, was to simply approach her and strike up conversation. Of course, it would take a while to build her trust, and if she resisted him he might run out of time.

The second, the more underhanded way, was to keep coming at her as he'd been doing. She wouldn't like it, but he might well be able to wear her down. Since she was vulnerable to him on a physical level, he could prey on that—even if it meant prying out one little bit of personal information at a time.

He had to get those bits of information. Without them, he couldn't form a composite of her, and without that, he wouldn't be able to figure out why in the hell he was interested in the first place!

"HOW'S IT GOING, LADIES?"

Shaye looked up from her book to see Noah approach. So he'd finally turned the sailing over to Samson. She had to admit, albeit begrudgingly, that he was doing his share.

"I should ask you the same question," Victoria said, smiling up in welcome. "Are we making good progress?"

Noah looked out over the bow toward the western horizon. "Not bad. If the trade winds keep smiling and we continue to make five knots an hour, we'll reach Costa Rica right on schedule."

Shaye was relieved to hear that.

Victoria wasn't so sure. "I'm enjoying the sail," she said, stretching lazily. "I could take this for another month."

Noah chuckled, then turned to Shaye. "How about you? Think you could take it for another month?"

Had it not been for that knowing little glint in his eye, Shaye might have smiled and nodded. Instead, she boldly returned his gaze and said, "Not on your life. I have to be back at work."

He hunkered down before her, balancing on the balls of his feet. "But if you were to stretch your imagination a little and pretend that work wasn't there, could you sail on and on?"

She crinkled her nose. "Nah. I'm a landlubber at heart. Give me a little cottage in the Berkshires and I'd be in heaven."

"Not heaven, sweetheart," Victoria scoffed. "You'd be in solitary confinement."

"Is that what she usually does for her vacations?" Noah asked.

"What I usually do—"

"That's what she would have been doing this year if I hadn't suggested she come with me."

"Suggested! That's—"

"I can understand what she sees in it," Noah interrupted blithely, ignoring both Shaye and her attempts to speak. "I have my own place in southern Vermont. I don't usually make it there for more than a few days at a stretch, but those few days are wonderful. There's nothing like time spent alone in a peaceful setting to replenish one's energies."

Victoria disagreed. "No, no. Time spent with someone special—that's different. But alone?"

"You spent time alone," Shaye argued hurriedly before someone cut her off.

"Naturally. I can't be with people all the time. But to choose to go off alone—just for the sake of being alone— for days at a time isn't healthy. It says something about your life, if you need that kind of escape."

"We all need escapes from habit," Noah reasoned, "don't we, Shaye?"

He'd tagged on the last in an intimate tone, leaving no doubt in Shaye's mind that he was referring to what had happened between them beneath the stars.

"Victoria is right. Certain kinds of escape are unhealthy."

"But, hot damn, they're fun," he countered in that same low tone.

Victoria looked from one to the other. "Am I missing something?"

"You missed it but good," Noah said with a grin. His eyes were fixed on Shaye. "We had quite a time of it last night—"

"Noah—"

"You did? Shaye, you didn't *tell* me."

Shaye couldn't believe what was happening. "What Noah means is that we had a little disagreement—"

"Only after the fact. It wasn't a disagreement at the time."

Turning to Victoria, Shaye affected a confident drawl. "He gets confused. Poor thing, he's so used to being ornery that it doesn't faze him."

"What happened last night?"

"Nothing hap—"

"You stole out while I was asleep, clever girl." She turned to Noah. "I hope she didn't shock you."

"As a matter of fact—"

"Please!" Shaye cried. "Stop it, both of you!" In her torment she shifted her legs, the better to brace herself.

Noah's gaze shifted too.

She snapped her knees together.

With an almost imperceptible sigh of regret, he dipped his head to the side. "Your niece has beautiful hair, Victoria. It's thick and rich like yours, but the color—where did she get the color?"

"Her father is a flaming redhead. When Shaye was a child—"

"That's enough, Victoria."

Victoria ignored her. "When she was a child, hers was nearly as red as his."

"Does she get her temper from him, too?"

"What do *you* think?"

"Victoria, if you—"

"I think she does," Noah decided with a grin that turned wry. "I'm not sure if I should thank him or curse him."

"You should leave him out of this," Shaye cried.

"Now, now, Shaye," Victoria soothed, "no need to get upset."

Noah added, "I want to know about him. You're much too closemouthed, Shaye. In all the talking we've done, you've barely said a word about yourself."

"Shame on you, Shaye," Victoria chided. "You act as though you have something to hide."

It was a challenge, well intended but a challenge nonetheless. If Shaye denied that she had anything to hide, she'd have to answer Noah's questions. If she came right out and said that she *did* have something to hide, he'd be all the more curious. For a long minute she glared at her aunt, then at Noah, but she still didn't know what to do.

At last Noah took pity. At least, he mused mischievously, he was willing to defer the discussion of her parents until later. But he wasn't about to miss out on another golden opportunity.

In a single fluid movement, he was sitting by her side against the bulwark. "What say we go for a swim later?"

She didn't answer at first. Her right side was tingling— her arm, her hip, everywhere his body touched. She cleared her throat and looked straight ahead. "Be my guest."

"I said 'we.'"

"Thanks, but I don't care to be left in the water while the boat sails on ahead." Implied was that she wouldn't mind if *he* was left behind.

He ruled out that possibility. "We'll lower the sails and drift. The *Golden Echo* won't go anywhere, and we can play." With one finger he blotted the dampness from her upper lip. "It'll be fun."

She was afraid to move. "I'll watch."

"But the water will feel great." He pried his back from the bulwark. "My shirt's sticking. You'd think the breeze would help."

"You're too hot for your own good."

"I don't know about that," he said in a sultry tone, "but I am hot." Without another word, he leaned forward and peeled off his shirt.

Shaye nearly died. She'd never seen a back as strong and as well formed, and when he relaxed against the bulwark again, the sight of his broad, leanly muscled chest was nearly more than she could bear. She swallowed down a moan.

"Did you say something?" he queried innocently.

"No, no."

"Your voice sounds strange. Higher than usual."

"It's the altitude. We must be climbing."

"We're at sea level."

"Oh. Mmm. That's right."

Without warning he stole her hand, linked their fingers together and placed them on his bare thigh. Then he looked at Victoria. "Maybe you'd like to join us for that swim."

Victoria grinned. "I'd like that."

"'Course, if you come, I'll have to behave."

Shaye grunted. "Like you're doing now?" She tried to pull her hand away but only succeeded in getting a better feel of his warm, hair-roughened thigh.

He feigned hurt. "I'm behaving."

"You're half-naked."

"I'm also half-dressed. Would you rather I'd left on my shirt and taken off my shorts?"

Victoria laughed. He was outrageous! And still he went on, this time turning injured eyes her way.

"I beg your pardon, Victoria. Are you suggesting that I have something to be ashamed of?"

Unable to help herself, she was laughing again. "Of course not. I—"

"This is no laughing matter! You wound my pride!"

"No, no, Noah," she managed to gasp. "I didn't intend—"

"But the damage is done," he said with such an aggrieved expression that she burst into another peal of laughter, which only made him square his chin more. "I can guarantee you that I'm fully equipped."

"I'm sure—"

"You don't believe me," he said in a flurry. He looked at Shaye. "You don't believe me either." He dropped his hand. "Well, I'll show you both!" He had the drawstring of his shorts undone and his thumbs tucked under the waistband before Shaye pressed a frantic hand to his belly.

"Don't," she whispered. "Please?"

Never in his life had Noah seen as beseeching a look. Her hand was burning a hole in him, but she seemed not to notice. She was near tears.

In that moment he lost his taste for the game. "I was only teasing," he said gently.

She looked at him for a minute longer, her eyes searching his face, moving from one feature to another. Her lower lip trembled.

Then she was up like a shot, running aft along the deck and disappearing down the companionway.

He started after her, but Victoria caught his hand. "Let her be for a while. She has to work some things out for herself."

"I don't want to hurt her."

"I know that. I trust you. Your uncle is a talker once he gets going. He's proud of you, and with good reason."

Noah frowned. "When did he do all this talking?" His eyes widened. "While we were on deck last night?"

"While *we* were on deck this *morning*," she answered, grinning mischievously. "You and Shaye sleep late. Samson and I wake up early."

"Ahh," Noah said, but his frown returned. "I'm trying to understand Shaye, but it's tough. She doesn't like to talk about herself."

"She's trained herself to be that way."

He wanted to ask why, just as he wanted to ask Victoria about all those other things Shaye wouldn't talk about. But it wasn't Victoria's place to talk. What was happening here was between Shaye and him. Sweet as she was, Victoria wasn't part of it, and he refused to put her in the position of betraying her niece.

"She'll tell you in time," Victoria said.

"How can you be sure?"

"I know, that's all. Be patient."

Thrusting a hand through his hair, he realized that he had no other choice. With a sigh, he scooped up his shirt and started off.

"Noah?"

He turned.

She dropped a deliberate glance to his shorts, which, without benefit of the drawstring, had fallen precariously low on his hips.

"Oh." He tied the string almost absently, then continued on.

So comfortable with his body, Victoria mused. *So comfortable with his sexuality. If only he could teach Shaye to be that way....*

CHAPTER FIVE

NOAH WAS RIGHT, Shaye knew. She couldn't hide in her cabin forever. It had been childish of her to run off that way, but at the time she'd been unable to cope with the feelings rushing through her. Noah had been so close, so bare, so provocative, and she was so drawn to him on a physical level that it frightened her to tears.

Brash and irreverent, impulsive and uninhibited, he was on the surface everything she tried to avoid. What was beneath the surface, though, was an enigma. She didn't know much about him—what he did for a living, whether he was attached in any manner to a woman, where his deepest needs and innermost values lay. She wanted to label him as all bad, but she couldn't. He was incredibly devoted to Samson and unfailingly kind to Victoria, and that had to account for something.

So. Here she sat—eyes moist, palms clammy, feeling perfectly juvenile. A reluctant smile played along her lips. Was this the adolescence she'd never had? She'd matured with such lightning speed that she'd never had time to feel growing pains—as good a term as any to describe what she was feeling now. She was being forced to reevaluate her wants and needs. And it was painful.

But nothing was accomplished sitting here. She wasn't an adolescent with the luxury of wallowing for hours in self-pity. Her wisest move, it seemed, would be to pull herself together, rejoin the others and try to regain a little of her self-esteem. She would sort things out in time.

Changing into a bathing suit, she unknotted her hair, brushed it out, then caught it up into a ponytail at her crown. After splashing her face with water, she belted on a short terry-cloth robe and left the cabin.

Noah was waiting in the salon, sitting in one of the chairs. She stopped on the threshold and eyed him uncertainly. He didn't comment on her outfit, or on her bare legs, or on her hair. In fact, he seemed almost as uncertain as she, which was just the slightest bit bolstering.

"You said something about going swimming," she reminded him softly.

He sat still for another minute, his face an amalgam of confusion, hesitation and hope. "You want to?" he cautiously asked.

She nodded.

With the blink of an eye, his grin returned, "You're on." He stood and headed for his cabin. "Stay put. I'll just change into trunks and we'll be ready."

"But the sails—"

"Tell Samson to take them in. He'll be game; he loves to swim. And tell Victoria to change, too. She wanted to come."

The door of the aft cabin closed. Shaye watched it for a minute, then walked quietly past and started up the companionway. She wondered about the way he'd been sitting in the salon, about the uncertainty she'd read on his face. That was a side of him she'd never seen, one she hadn't thought existed. It was a far cry from the smugness—or arrogance or annoyance—he usually granted her, and even his returning confidence was somehow different and more manageable. If only she knew what was going on in his head...

Noah hung a rope ladder off the port quarter and let Shaye climb down first. She went about halfway before jumping. In the very first instant submerged, she realized by contrast how hot and grubby she'd felt before. Her sense of exhilaration was nearly as great as her sense of refreshment.

Ducking under a second time, she came up with her head back and a smile on her face. She opened her eyes in time to see Noah balance on the transom for an instant before soaring up, out, then down, slicing neatly into the waves. Feeling incredibly light, she treaded water until he appeared by her side.

"Not bad," she said, complimenting his dive.

"Not bad, yourself," he said, complimenting her smile. Then he took off, stroking strongly around the *Golden Echo*'s stern, then along her starboard side. Shaye followed a bit more slowly, but he was waiting for her at the bow before starting down the port side.

Completing the lap, he turned to her with a grin. "You're a good swimmer. It must be that suit you're wearing. It covers up enough of your body. Is it covering up a flotation device, too?"

She rolled her eyes. "Fifteen minutes."

"Fifteen minutes, what?"

"That's how long you made it without a snippy comment. But now you've blown it, and by insulting my suit, no less! There is nothing wrong with this suit." It was, in fact, a designer maillot that she'd paid dearly for.

He sank beneath the surface for a minute, tossing his hair back with a flourish when he came up. "I was hoping to see more of your body. I was hoping for a bikini."

"Sorry," she said, then turned and swam off.

He'd caught up to her in a minute. "You are not sorry. You take perverse pleasure in teasing me."

"Look who's talking!"

"But you're so teasable," he argued, eyes twinkling. "You rise to my taunts."

"No more," she decided and propelled herself backward.

He negated the distance with a single stroke. "Wanna test that out?"

"Sure." She turned sideways and tipped up her nose in an attempt to look imperturbable. It was a little absurd given the steady movement of her arms and legs, but she did her best.

Noah went underwater.

She waited, eventually darting a sidelong glance to where he'd gone down, then waited again, certain that any minute she'd feel a tug at her leg. When she felt so such thing, she glanced to the other side.

No Noah. No bubbles. Nothing but gentle waves.

Vaguely concerned, she made a complete turn. When she saw no sign of him, she submerged for an underwater look.

Nothing!

"Noah?" she called, reaching the surface again. "Noah!"

Samson's head appeared over the side of the boat. "Problem, Shaye?"

Her heart was thudding. "It's Noah! He went under and I can't find him!"

Samson cocked his head toward the opposite side of the boat. "Try over here," he said and disappeared.

Performing a convulsive breaststroke, Shaye sped to the port side, to find Noah riding the waves on his back, eyes closed, basking in the sun.

"You bastard!" she screamed, furiously batting water his way. "You terrified me!"

His serenity ruined by her splashing, he advanced on her, turning his face one way then the other against her wet attack. Then he cinched an arm around her waist and drew her against him, effectively stopping the barrage.

"Y'see?" he gloated. "It worked."

"That was a totally stupid thing to do!" she cried, tightly clutching his shoulders. "And irresponsible! What if something really had happened to you? I'm not a trained lifesaver. I couldn't have helped! And think of *me*. I could have gone under looking for you and stayed there too long. You would never have known I was drowning, because you were out of sight, on the far side of the boat, playing your silly little game."

"Samson was keeping an eye on you."

"That's not the point!" She narrowed her eyes. "Next time I won't even bother to look. You know what happened to the little boy who cried wolf?"

"But I'm not a little boy."

She snorted.

His arm tightened. "Wrap your legs around my waist."

"Are you kidding?"

"I'll keep us afloat."

"I don't trust you."

"You don't trust yourself."

He was right. "You're wrong."

"Nuh-uh." His lips twitched. "You don't want to wrap your legs around me because that would put you flush against my—hey, stop that!"

She'd found that he was ticklish, and in the nick of time. Within seconds they were both underwater, but at least she was free, and when she resurfaced, Noah was waiting. What ensued then was a good, old-fashioned, rollicking water fight that was broken up at length by Samson's, "Children! Children!"

The water settled some around them as they looked up.

"Bath time," he called. He was lowering a small basket that contained soap and shampoo.

Shaye looked at Noah; Noah looked at Shaye.

"Do you think he's trying to tell us something?" he asked.

"Diplomatically," she answered.

He wrinkled his nose. "Was I that bad?"

"Was *I*?"

"Maybe we canceled each other out."

"So we didn't notice?"

"Yeah." He scowled. "Hell, it's only been three days."

"Three? That's disgusting!"

His eyes widened in accusation. "It has to have been just as long for you."

"Two. Only two, and I've been—"

"Are you going to wash or not?" came the call from above. "We're dying to swim, but we don't want to go in until you get out!"

Shaye looked at Noah in horror. "Is it that bad that they don't want to be near us even in water?"

He laughed and swam toward the basket. "For safety, Shaye. One of us should be on the boat at any given time, and since no one should swim alone, it makes sense to divide it up, two and two." He drew a bright yellow container from the basket and squirted liberal jets of its contents on his arms, hands and neck.

"Joy?" she asked, swimming closer.

He tossed her the plastic bottle. "It's one of the few detergents that bubbles in saltwater," he explained as he scrubbed his arms, offering proof. "Go on. It does the trick."

She followed his lead and, scissoring steadily with her legs, had soon lathered her arms, shoulders and neck. Noah took the bottle from the basket again and filled his palm, then set to work beneath the waterline. Shaye took her time rinsing her arms.

His eyes grew teasing. "I'm doing my chest. How about you?"

"I'm getting there," she managed, but she was feeling suddenly awkward. She darted a self-conscious glance upward and was relieved to see no sign of Samson.

"You'll need more soap." He tossed his head toward the basket.

She took the bottle, directed a stream of the thick liquid into her hand and replaced the bottle. Then she stared at her palm, wondering how to start.

"Don't turn around," he said. "I want to watch."

"I'm sure."

"Come on. We're in the shadow of the boat. The water's too dark to see anything."

It wasn't what he could see that she feared. It was what he could picture. She knew what *she* was picturing as his shoulders rotated, hands out of sight but very obviously on that broad and virile chest.

"You'd better hurry, Shaye. Samson won't wait forever."

"Okay, okay." With hurried movements, she rubbed her hands together, then thrust them under her suit.

"You could lower the suit. It'd help."

"This is fine." Eyes averted, she soaped her breasts as quickly as she could.

"Look at me while you do that," he commanded softly.

She shot him a glance that was supposed to be quelling, but when her eyes locked with his, she couldn't look away. There was nothing remotely quelling in her gaze then; it mirrored the desire in his. Sudden, startling, explosive. They were separated by a mere arm's length, which, given the expanse of the Caribbean, seemed positively intimate.

Her hands worked over and around her breasts while

his hands worked over and around his chest, but it was his fingers she seemed to feel on her sensitive skin, his harder flesh beneath her fingers. When he moved his hands to his lower back, she followed suit and the tingling increased, touching her vertebrae, sizzling down to the base of her spine.

Her lips were parted; her breath rushed past in shallow pants. Her legs continued to scissor, though hypnotically. She was in Noah's thrall, held there by the dark, smoldering charcoal of his eyes and by the force of her own vivid imagination.

The curve of his shoulders indicated that his hands had returned to his front and moved lower. She gulped in a short breath, but her shoulders were also curving, her hands moving forward, then lower.

His eyes held hers, neither mocking nor dropping in an attempt to breach the sea's modest veil. The waves rose and fell around and with them, like a mentor, teaching them the movement, rewarding them with gentle supplementary caresses.

But supplementary caresses were the last things they needed. Shaye felt as though she were vibrating from the inside out, and Noah's muscles were tense, straining for the release that he wouldn't allow himself.

When he closed his eyes for an instant, the spell broke. Two sets of arms joined trembling legs in treading water, and it was a minute more before either of them could speak.

Noah's lips twisted into a self-mocking grin. "You are one hell of a lady to make love with," he said gruffly. "Com'ere."

Shaye gave several rapid shakes of her head.

"I want to do your hair."

"My hair's okay."

He was fishing a bottle of shampoo from the basket

when Victoria's voice came over the side. "Aren't you two done *yet*?"

"Be right up," Shaye gasped. She turned to start for the ladder, but a gentle tug on her ponytail brought her right back to Noah. The water worked against her then, denying her the leverage to escape him. And his fingers were already in her hair, easing the thick elastic band from its place. "Please don't, Noah," she begged.

His voice was close to her ear. "Indulge me this, after what you denied me just now."

"Denied you? I didn't deny you a thing!"

"You didn't give me what I *really* wanted…."

She wasn't about to touch that one. So she faced him and held out a hand, palm up. "The shampoo?"

"Right here," he said, pressing his gloppy hand on the top of her head and instantly starting to scrub.

She squeezed her eyes shut. "I'll do it, Noah."

"Too late," he said with an audible grin, then paused. "I've never washed a woman's hair before. Am I doing it right?"

His fingers were everywhere, gathering even the longest strands into the cloud of lather, massaging her scalp, stimulating nerve ends she hadn't known about. Was he doing it right? Was he ever!

She tried to think of something to say, but it was as though his fingers had penetrated her skull and were impeding the workings of her brain. Her eyes were still closed, but in ecstasy now. Her head had fallen back a little as he worked his thumbs along her hairline. She was unaware that her breasts were pushing against his chest, or that her legs had floated around his hips and she was riding him gently in the waves, because those were but small eddies in the overall vortex of pleasure.

His fingers were suddenly still, cupping her head, and

his voice was gruff as he pressed his lips to her brow. "Maybe this wasn't such a good idea after all. Better rinse and let me do mine. If our time isn't up, my self-control is."

Shaye opened her eyes then. They widened when she realized how she was holding Noah. "Oh Lord," she whispered and quickly let go. With frantic little movements, she sculled away.

"You're a hussy, Shaye Burke!" Noah taunted. He poured shampoo directly from the bottle onto his head.

She sank underwater and shook her own. When she resurfaced, he was scrubbing his hair, but wore a grin that was naughty.

"A hussy and a tease!"

"You are a corrupter!" she cried back.

"Me? I was washing your hair! You were the one who tried to make something more of it!"

Tipping her head to the right to finger-comb water through her hair, she glared at him. "That's exactly how you're going to look in ten years, Noah—all white-haired and prune-faced." She tipped her head to the left and rinsed the long tresses further. "*No* woman's going to want to look at you then!"

"So I'd better catch someone now, hmm? Take out an insurance policy?" He submerged, raking the soap from his hair with his fingers.

"I dare say the premiums would be too high," she called the minute he'd resurfaced.

"Are you selling?"

"To you? No way!" She headed for the ladder. "You are a sneaky, no-good…seducer of innocent women."

Noah caught her on the second rung, encircling her hips with one strong arm. He said nothing until she looked down at him, then asked quietly and without jest, "Are you innocent?"

She could take the question different ways, she knew, but if she were honest the answer would be the same. No, she wasn't innocent in what had just happened, because no one had told her to wrap herself so snugly around him. No, she hadn't been innocent last night. He hadn't asked her to go wild in his arms. And she wasn't innocent in that broadest sense; she'd lost her virginity half a lifetime ago.

Sad eyes conveyed her answer, but she said nothing. Noah held a frightening power over her already. That power would surely increase if she confirmed how truly less than innocent she was.

His gaze dropped over her gleaming shoulders and down her bare back to the edge of her suit. His hand slid lower, over the flare of her bottom to her thigh. When he gave her a gentle boost, she climbed the ladder, then crossed the deck to the bow, knowing Noah would remain at the stern to serve as lifeguard to Samson and Victoria.

She needed to be alone. The past weighed too heavily on her to allow for even the most banal of conversation.

SHAYE HAD BEGUN to rebel at the age of thirteen, when her father's fierce temper and her mother's conventionalism first crowded in on her budding adolescence. Life to that point had been placid, a sedate cycle revolving around school and church. But she had suddenly developed from a redheaded little girl into an eye-catching teenager, and even if she hadn't seen the change in herself, it would have been impossible for her to mistake the admiring male looks that came her way.

Those looks promised excitement, something she'd never experienced, and she thrived on them, since they compensated for the more dismissing ones she'd received before. Her father was a factory hand, and though he worked hard, the socio-economic class in which the Burkes were trapped was on the lower end of the scale. Donald Burke had been proud to buy the small, two-bedroom cottage in which they lived, because it was on the right side of the tracks, if barely. Unfortunately, the tracks delineated the school districts, which put Shaye and Shannon in classes with far more privileged children.

Gaining the attention of some of the most attractive boys around was a heady experience for Shaye. For the first time she was able to compete with girls she'd envied, girls whose lives where less structured and more frivolous. For the first time she was able to partake in that frivolity— as the guest of the very boys those girls covetously eyed.

In theory, Anne Burke wouldn't have objected to the attention her daughter received. She idolized her husband and was perfectly comfortable with their life, which was not unlike the one she'd known herself as a child. But she'd seen how well her sister, Victoria, had done in marrying Arthur Lesser, and she had no objection to her daughter aiming high.

What she objected to was the fact that Shaye was only thirteen and that the boys of whom she was enamored were sixteen and seventeen. They were dangerous ages, ages of discovery, and Anne Burke didn't want her daughter used. So she set strict limits on Shaye's social life, and when Shaye argued, as any normal teenager would, Donald Burke was there to enforce the law.

Perhaps, Shaye had often mused later, if they'd been a little more flexible she'd have managed—or if she'd been more manageable, they'd have flexed. But by the time she was fifteen, she felt totally at odds with her parents' conventionality, and her response was to flaunt it in any way she could. She stole out to a party at Jimmy Danforth's house, when she was supposedly studying at the library. She cut classes to go joyriding with Brett Hagen in the Mustang his parents had given him for his eighteenth birthday. She told her parents she was baby-sitting, when the baby in question was a dog that belonged to Alexander Bigelow.

Three days before her sixteenth birthday, she made love with Ben Parker on the floor of his parents' wine cellar. She'd known precisely what she was doing and why. She'd given her innocence to Ben because it was fun and exciting and a little bit dangerous—and because it was the last thing her parents wanted her to do.

She was her own person, she'd decided. If her parents were happy with their lives, that was fine, but she resented the dogma of hard work and self-restraint that they imposed on her. Discovering that she could have a wonderful time—and get away with it—was self-perpetuating.

She played her way through high school. Reasonably bright, she maintained a B average without much effort—a good thing, since she didn't have much time to spare from her social life. Fights with her parents were long and drawn out, until true communication became almost nonexistent. That didn't bother Shaye. She knew what she wanted to do, and she did it. She applied to NYU, was accepted on scholarship, and finally escaped her parents' watchful eyes.

New York was as much fun as she'd hoped. She liked her classes, but she liked even more the freedom she had and the people she met. And she adored Victoria, whom she saw regularly. In hindsight, Shaye knew that keeping in such close touch with her aunt represented a need for family ties. At the time she only knew Victoria understood her as her parents never had.

Victoria was as different from her sister, Anne, as night from day. While Anne chose to take the more traveled highways through life, Victoria took the back roads that led to greater beauty and pleasure. The one thing they shared was their devotion to their husbands, but since each had married a man to suit her tastes, their differences had grown more marked as time went on.

Shaye identified with Victoria. It wasn't that she yearned to be wealthy; wealth, or the lack of it, had never played as prominently in her mind as had adventure. But Victoria *did* things. She acted on her impulses, rather than putting them off for a day far in the future. And if she subtly cautioned Shaye to exercise moderation, Shaye put it down to the loyalty Victoria felt toward Anne.

Despite Victoria's subtle words of caution, Shaye had a ball. In February of her freshman year she hitchhiked with Graham Hauk to New Orleans for Mardi Gras. That summer she took a house in Provincetown with five friends, all of whom were working, as she was, in local restaurants. Much of her sophomore year was spent at the off-campus apartment of Josh Milgram, her latest love and a graduate student of philosophy, who had a group of ever-present and fascinating, if bizarre, friends.

She spent the summer before her junior year selling computer equipment in Washington. She'd secured the job principally on her interview, during which she'd demonstrated both an aptitude for handling the equipment and an aptitude for selling herself. She loved Washington. Sharing an apartment with two friends from school, she had regular working hours, which left plenty of time for play.

It was during that summer that Shannon joined her, and Shaye couldn't have been more delighted. She'd always felt that Shannon was being stifled at home. More than once she'd urged her sister to break out, but it was only by dint of a summer-school program held at American University for high school students that Shannon made it.

Proud of her sister, Shaye introduced her to all her friends. At summer's end, she sent Shannon back home reasonably assured that she was awakened to the pleasures of life.

Shaye whizzed through her junior year seeing Tom, Peter and Gene, but the real fun came in her senior year when she met André. André—né Andrew, but he'd decided that that name was too plebeian—was a perpetual student of art. He had a small garret in Soho, where Shaye spent most of her time, and a revolving group of friends and followers who offered never-ending novelty. André and Shaye were a couple, but in the loosest sense of the word. André was far from possessive, and Shaye was far from committed. She adored André for his eccentricity; his painting was as eclectic as his lovemaking. But she adored Christopher's brashness and Jamal's wild imagination and Stefan's incredible irreverence.

She was treading a fine line in her personal life, though at the time she didn't see it. Graduating from college, she took a position in the computer department of an insurance company, and if her friends teased her about such a staid job, she merely laughed, took a puff of the nearest pipe and did something totally outrageous to show where her heart lay.

She was one year out of college and living at the garret with André and his friends when the folly of her lifestyle hit home.

"Fräulein?"

Shaye's head shot up, her thoughts boomeranging back to the present. Her eyes focused on Samson, who was wearing a black tuxedo jacket with tails and, beneath it, a white apron tied at the waist and falling to mid-calf.

"Darf ich Sie bitten, an unserem Dinner teilzunehmen? Wir sind bereit; bitte sagen Sie nicht nein."

It was a minute before comprehension came. She didn't speak German, but a pattern was emerging, reinforced by the sight of Victoria and Noah already settling at the table on the other end of the deck.

She didn't know how long she'd been sitting so lost in thought—an hour, perhaps two—but she was grateful for the rescue. Smiling, she took the hand Samson graciously offered, realizing only after she'd risen that she was still wearing her bathing suit.

"Let me change first," she said softly.

"You don't need to."

But she'd be asking for trouble from Noah if she appeared at dinner so minimally covered. "I'll be quick."

Hurrying below, she discarded the suit and drew on a one-piece shorts outfit. She'd reached the companionway before realizing that her hair was still down. Deciding that it was too late to pin it up, she finger-combed it back from her face and continued to the deck.

Dinner was sauerbraten, red cabbage and strudel. It was accompanied by a sturdy red Ingelheimer whose mildly sedative effect helped Shaye handle both the lingering shadow of her reminiscing and Noah's very large, very virile and observant presence.

Actually, he behaved himself admirably, or so he decided. He didn't make any comments about Shaye's free-flowing hair, though he was dying to. Even more, he was dying to touch it. Clean and shining, it seemed thicker than ever, as though its life had been released by the sea and the breeze. Nor did he comment on her smile, which was coming more frequently. He wondered if it was the wine, or whether the afternoon swim had eased a certain tension from her. Somehow he doubted the latter, after the words they'd exchanged in the water. But she'd spent a good long time since then at the bow, and he wondered if what she'd been thinking about was responsible for the softening of her mood.

He'd watched her but she hadn't known it. She'd been lost in a world of her own. Even now, sitting over the last of the wine, she faded in and out from time to time. During those "out" phases her expression was mellow, vaguely sad—as it had been on the rope ladder when he'd asked about her innocence.

He was more curious about her than ever, but he could bide his time. Sunset was upon them. Soon it would be dark. Perhaps if her mellow mood continued, he'd be able to pry some information from her without a fight.

After dinner Shaye returned to her perch at the bow. She took a cushion with her, and though she'd fetched a book, she didn't bother to open it. Instead, she propped herself comfortably and studied the sky.

To the west were the deepening orange colors of the waning day, above that the purples of early night. As she watched, the purples spread and darkened, until the last of the sun's rays had been swallowed up.

She took one deep breath, then another. Her body felt clean and relaxed, and if her mind wasn't in quite that perfect a state, it was close. There were things to be considered, but not now, not when the Caribbean night was so beautiful.

Victoria was with Samson at the helm. They clearly enjoyed each other, and, deep down inside, Shaye was pleased. Samson was an interesting man. He had the style and spirit to make Victoria's trip an adventure even without the treasure no one had spoken of yet.

Shifting herself and the cushion so that she was lying down, she crossed her ankles, folded her hands on her middle and closed her eyes. So different from home, she mused. She couldn't remember the last time she'd lain down like this and just…listened. What was there to listen to in her Philadelphia apartment? Traffic? The siren of a police car or an ambulance? Peals of laughter from a party at one of the other apartments?

None of that here. Just the rhythmic thrust of the waves against the hull and the periodic flap of a sail. There was something to be said for going on a treasure hunt after all.

Her brow creased lightly. Noah had said that there were different types of treasures to be sought, and he was right. He seemed to be right about a lot of things. She had to define the treasure *she* was seeking. Was it a job well done in Philadelphia? Career advancement? Perhaps movement to a broader, more prestigious position?

After all she'd thought about that afternoon, she had to smile. Her life now was the antithesis of what it had been seven, eight, nine years before. If someone had told her then what she'd be doing in subsequent years, she'd have thought him mad.

But even back then, without conscious planning, she'd made provisions for a more stable life. She'd completed her education and had established herself in a lucrative field. Had her subconscious known something?

The question was whether the life she now had would stand her in good stead for the next thirty years. If so, if she was as self-contained and complete a being as she'd thought, why did Noah VanBaar make her ache? Did her subconscious know something else?

Eyes still closed, she grew alert. He was here now. She hadn't heard him approach, but she knew he was near. There was something hovering, newly coagulating in her mind…a sense of familiarity, a scent. Noah. Smelling of the sun and the sea, of musk and man.

She opened her eyes and met his curious gaze. He was squatting an arm's length away, a dimly-glowing lantern hanging from his fingers.

"I wasn't sure if you were sleeping."

"I wasn't."

"You've been lying here a long time."

And still she didn't move; she felt too comfortable. "It's peaceful." Was that a hint that he should leave? She was trying to decide if she wanted him to when he reached up, hooked the lantern on the bowsprit, then sat down and stretched out his legs. She'd known he wouldn't ask to join her; that wasn't his style. In a way she was glad he hadn't. She'd been spared having to make the choice.

Resting his head back, he sighed. "We're almost halfway there. From the looks of the clouds in the east, we may get a push."

"Clouds?" She peered eastward. "I don't see a thing."

"Mmm. No moon, no stars."

"Oh, dear. A storm?"

He shrugged. "Who knows? Maybe rain, maybe wind, maybe nothing. Storm clouds can veer off. They can dissipate. Weather at sea is fickle."

Sliding an arm behind her head, she studied him. "You must sail a lot."

"Not so much now. I used to though. Samson got me hooked when I was a kid. I spent several summers crewing on windjammers off the coast of Maine."

"Sounds like fun."

"It was. I love the ocean, especially when it's wild. I could sit for hours and watch the waves thrash about."

"You should have a place on the coast, rather than in Vermont."

"Nah. Watching the ocean in a storm is inspirational, not restful. When I leave the city on weekends, I need rest."

"The city—New York?"

He nodded.

"What do you do?"

"Are you sure you want to know?"

"Why wouldn't I?"

"Because knowing about me will bring us closer, and I had the impression that you wanted to stay as far from me as possible."

"True. But tell me anyway."

"Why?"

"Because I'm curious."

He considered that. "I suppose it's as good a reason as any. Of course," he tilted his head and his voice turned whimsical, "it would be nicer if you'd said that you've changed your mind about staying away, or that you want to know about the man who's swept you off your feet, or—" his voice dropped "—that you're as interested in exploring my mind as you are in exploring my body."

Her skin tingled and she was grateful that the lantern was more a beacon to other ships than an illuminator of theirs. The dark was her protector, when she felt oddly exposed. "Just tell me," she grumbled, then added a taunting, "unless you have something to hide."

That was all Noah needed to hear. "I'm a political pollster."

"A political—"

"Pollster. When a guy decides to make a run for political office, he hires me to keep tabs on his status among the electorate."

"Interesting," she said and meant it.

"I think so. Actually, I started out doing only polling, but the business has evolved into something akin to public relations."

"In what sense?"

Encouraged that she wanted to hear more, Noah explained. "John Doe comes to me and says that he's running for office. I do my research, ferreting out his opponent's strengths and weaknesses, plus the characteristics of the constituency. Between us we determine the image we want to project, the kind of image that will go across with the voters—"

"But isn't that cheating? If you tailor-make the candidate to the voters, what about issues? Isn't John Doe compromising himself?"

"Not at all. He doesn't alter his stand; he merely alters the way that stand is put across. One or another of his positions may be more popular among the voters, so we focus on those and push the others into the background. The key is to get the man elected, at which point he can bring other issues forward."

"Clever, if a little devious."

"That's the way the game is played. His opponent does it; why shouldn't he? It's most useful on matters that have little to do with the issues."

"Such as…?"

"Age. Marital status. Religion, ethnic background, prior political experience. Again, it's a question of playing something up or down, depending on the bias of the voters."

Shaye frowned. "Sounds to me like there's a very fine line between your job and an ad agency's."

"Sure is, and that's who takes over from me. Ad agencies, media consultants—they're the ones who put together the specifics of the campaign itself."

"And your job is done at that point?"

He shook his head. "We keep polling right up to, sometimes beyond, the campaign. Obviously, some candidates have more money to pay for our services than others. By the same token, some political offices require more ongoing work than others."

She could easily guess which offices those would be and was duly impressed. "I suppose that's good for you. Otherwise you'd have a pretty seasonal job."

"Seasonal it isn't," he drawled. "I use the word 'political' in the broadest sense. We do polling for lobbyists, for public interest groups, for hospitals and real estate developers and educational institutions."

"When you say 'we,' who do you mean?"

"I have a full-time staff of ninety people, with several hundred part-timers on call."

"But you're the leader?"

"It's my baby, yes."

"You started it from scratch?"

"Planted the seed and nurtured it," he said with an inflection of intimacy that made her blush. He didn't follow up, though, but leaned forward and rubbed his back before returning to his original position.

"You must feel proud."

"I do."

"There must be a lot of pressure."

He nodded.

"But it's rewarding?"

"Very." He sat forward again and flexed his back muscles, then grumbled crossly, "This boat leaves much to be desired by way of comfort. I've never heard of a boat with a deck this size and no deck chairs."

She was hard put not to laugh, clearly recalling the discussion she'd had with Victoria when they'd first boarded the sloop, a discussion Noah had overheard and mocked. "You don't like the *Golden Echo*?" she asked sweetly.

He heard the jibe in her tone and couldn't let it go unanswered. In the blink of an eye, he'd closed the distance between them, displaced her from the cushion and drawn her to him so that her back was against his chest.

CHAPTER SIX

SHAYE TRIED TO wiggle away, but Noah hooked his legs around hers. When she continued to squirm, he made a low, sexy sound. "Ooh, that feels good. A little more pressure…there…lower."

Abruptly she went still. "This is not a good idea, Noah."

"My back sure feels a hell of a lot better."

"Mine doesn't."

"That's because you've got a rod up it—" He caught himself and backed off. "Uh, no, that came out the wrong way. What I meant was that you've stiffened up. If you relax and let me cushion you, you'll be as comfortable as you were before."

That was what Shaye feared, but the temptation was great. It was a peaceful night and she'd been interested in what he'd been saying. Would it hurt to relax a little?

"Better," he said with a sigh when he felt her body soften to his. Though his legs fell away, his arms remained loosely around her waist. He'd thrown on a shirt after dinner, but it was unbuttoned. Her hair formed a thick pillow on his chest, with wayward strands teasing his throat and chin.

Having made the decision to stay in his arms, Shaye was surprisingly content. "Have you ever been married?"

"Where did that come from?"

"I was thinking about your work. You said there was pressure, and I assume the hours are long. I was curious."

Curious, again. Okay. "No. I've never been married."

"Do you dislike women?"

"Where did *that* come from?"

"One of the first things you said you didn't like about me was that I was a woman."

"Ah. That was because I hadn't known there were going to be women along on this trip until a few minutes before you and your aunt arrived."

"And it bothered you?"

"At the time."

"Why?"

"Because I wanted to get away from it all. Before Samson drafted me I'd planned to spend two weeks alone in Normandy."

"Normandy." She slid her head sideways and looked up at him. "A château?"

"A small one."

She righted her head. "Small one, big one…it sounds lovely."

"It would have been, but this isn't so bad."

"Would you have done anything differently if Victoria and I hadn't been along?"

"A few things."

"Like…?"

"Shaving. I wouldn't have bothered."

"You don't have to shave for our sakes. Be my guest. Grow a beard."

He'd been hoping she'd thank him; after all, stubble looked grubby, and then there was the matter of kissing. But she wouldn't consider that. Not Shaye.

"I don't want to grow a beard," he grumbled. "I just didn't want to have to shave unless I felt like it."

"So don't." She paused. "What else would you have done if we weren't along?"

"Swam in the nude. Sunbathed in the nude. *Sailed* in the nude," he added just for spite.

Forgetting that she was supposed to be prissy, she grinned. "That would be a sight."

"Oh God, are we onto that again? Why is it that everyone's always insulting my manhood?"

She shaped her hands to his wrists and gave a squeeze. "I'm just teasing…though I don't believe I've ever seen a naked pirate before."

"This is not a pirate ship," was his arch response.

"Then, a naked patriot."

"Have you ever seen any man naked?"

Her grin was hidden. He should only know. "I saw *American Gigolo*. There were some pretty explicit scenes."

He tightened his arms in mock punishment. "A real man. In the flesh. Have you ever seen one up close and all over?"

"I walked in on my father once when I was little."

He sighed. "I'm not talking about—"

"I've learned to keep my eyes shut since then."

Which told him absolutely nothing. So he put that particular subject on hold and tried one he thought she'd find simpler to answer. "What kind of work do you do?"

She hesitated, then echoed his own earlier question. "Are you sure you want to know?"

"Why wouldn't I?"

"Because you won't like the answer."

"Why not?"

"Because it fits my personality to a tee."

"You're the headmistress of an all-girls school?"

"Nope."

"A warden at a penitentiary?"

She shook her head.

"I give up. What do you do?"

Again she hesitated, then confessed, "I work with computers."

"That figures."

"I told you you wouldn't like it."

"I didn't say I didn't like it, just that it figures. You work with machines. Very structured and controlled." He lowered his voice. "Do they turn you on?"

"Shows how much you know about computers. Noah, you have to turn *them* on or they don't do a thing."

She was teasing, and he loved it. He wasn't quite sure why she was in such good humor, but he wasn't about to upset the applecart by saying something lewd. "Once you turn them on, what do you do with them?"

"Same thing you do. Program them to store information and spit it back up on command."

"Your command?"

"Or one of my assistants'."

"Then you're the one in charge?"

"Of the department, yes."

"Where is the department?"

"In a law firm."

"A law firm in Philadelphia." Her head bobbed against his chest. He loved that, too—the undulating silk of her hair against his bare skin. "So—" he cleared his throat "—what kind of information are we dealing with here?"

"Client files, financial projections, accounts receivable, attorney profitability reports, balance sheets." She reeled them off, pausing only at the end for a breath. "Increasingly we're using the computers for the preparation of documents. And we're plugged into LEXIS."

"What's LEXIS?"

"A national computer program for research. By typing certain codes into the computer, our lawyers can find cases or law review articles that they need for briefs. It saves hours of work in the library."

"I'm impressed."

She swiveled and met his gaze. "By LEXIS?"

"By you. You really know what you're talking about."

"You didn't think I would?"

"It's not that," he said. "But you sound so...so on top of the whole thing."

"How do you think I got where I am?"

"I don't know. How did you?" His voice dropped to a teasing drawl. He couldn't resist; she was so damned sexy peering up at him that way. "Did you wow all those computer guys with your body?"

She stared at him for a minute, then faced forward. "Exactly."

"Come on," he soothed, brushing her ear with his mouth. "I know you wouldn't do that. Tell me how you got hooked up with computers."

"I took computer courses in college."

"And that was it? A few courses and, pow, you're the head of a department?"

"Of course not. I worked summers, then worked after graduation, and by the time the opening came at the law firm, I had the credentials and was there."

"How large is the firm?"

"Seventy-five lawyers."

"General practice?"

"Corporate."

"Ahh. Big money-getters."

"Lucky for me. If they weren't, they'd never be able to support a computer department the size of ours, and my job would be neither as interesting nor as challenging."

"Are they nice?"

"The lawyers? Some I like better than others."

"Do they treat you well?"

"I'm not complaining."

"But you do love your work."

"Yes."

"Any long-range ambitions?"

"I don't know. I'm thinking about that. I've risen pretty fast in a field that's steadily changing."

"Personnel-wise?"

"Equipment-wise. Personnel-wise, too, I guess. A lot of people jumped on the bandwagon when computers first got big, but time has weeded out the men from the boys."

"Or the women from the girls."

"Mmm."

He nudged her foot with his. "What about marriage? Or pregnancy? Does that weed out the women from the girls?"

"Not as much as it used to. The firm is generous when it comes to maternity leave. Many of the women, lawyers included, have taken time off, then returned. In my department, word processing is done round the clock. Women can choose their shifts to accommodate child-care arrangements."

"Is that what you'll do?"

"I hadn't thought I was pregnant," she remarked blithely.

"Do you want to be?"

"I like what I'm doing now."

"Cuddling?"

"Heading the computer department."

He bent his knees and brought his legs in closer. "But someday. Do you want to have kids?"

"I haven't really thought about it."

"Come on. Every woman thinks about it."

"I've been too busy."

"To do it?"

"To think about doing it."

He dipped his head, bringing his lips into warm intimacy with her cheek. "I'll give you a baby."

She shifted, turning onto her side so she could better see his expression. "You're crazy, do you know that?"

"Not really."

"Give me a baby—why in the world would you say something like that? In case you don't know it, a baby takes after both its parents. I've been bugging you since I stepped foot on this sloop. How would you like to have a baby that bugged you from the day it was born?"

He shrugged. "There's bugging, and there's bugging." Her hand was using his chest for leverage; he covered it with his own. "You have certain qualities that I'd want in a child of mine."

"Like what?"

It was a minute before he answered. "Beauty."

She shot a quick glance skyward. "Spare me."

"Intelligence."

"That's a given." She tipped up her chin. "What else?" When he was quiet, she gave him a lopsided grin. "Run out of things already?"

It wasn't that he'd run out, just that he was having trouble concentrating. She was so soft in his arms, her face so pert as it tilted toward his, her legs smooth as they tangled with his, her hip firm as it pressed his groin.

"There's...there's spunk."

"Spunk?"

"Sure. Seven times out of ten you have answers for my jibes."

"Only seven?"

Almost imperceptibly, he moved her hand on his chest. He closed his eyes for a minute and swallowed hard. "Maybe eight."

"But I'm stern-faced and prissy," she said, shifting slightly. "Is that what you want your children to inherit?"

He'd closed his eyes again, and when he opened them, he was smiling ever so gently, ever so wryly, and his warning came ever so softly. "You're playing with fire."

"I…what?"

"Your legs brush mine, your hair torments me." His voice began to sizzle. "You move those hips and I'm on fire, and your hand on my skin gives me such pleasure…. Can't you feel what's happening?"

Her stunned eyes dropped to her hand. It was partially covered by his, but her fingers were buried in the soft, curling hairs on his chest. As she watched, they began to tingle, then throb above the beat of his heart.

"A little to your right," he whispered huskily. "Move them."

She swallowed. Her fingers straightened and inched forward until a single digit came to rest atop a clearly erect nipple.

He moaned and moved his hips.

Her eyes flew to his face.

"Shocked?" he asked thickly. "Didn't you know? Am I the only one suffering?"

"I…we were talking…I was comfortable." The words seemed feeble, but they were the truth. She couldn't remember when she'd ever been with a man this way, just talking, enjoying the physical closeness for something other than sex. "I'm sorry…."

But she didn't move away. Her senses were awakening to him with incredible speed. All the little things that had hovered just beyond sexual awareness—the sole of his foot against her instep, the brush of his hair-spattered legs against her calves and thighs, the solidity of his flesh beneath her hand, his enveloping male scent, the cradle of his body, the swelling virility between his legs—all came into vivid focus. And his voice, his voice, honing her awareness like scintillating sand...

"I'd like to make love to you, Shaye. I'd like to open that little thing you're wearing and touch you all over, taste you all over. I think I could bury myself in your body and never miss the world again. Would you let me do that?"

The rising breeze cooled her face, but she could barely breathe, much less think. "I...we can't."

"We can." He had one arm across her back in support while his hand caressed her hip. The other hand tipped up her face. "Kiss me, Shaye. Now."

Say no. Push him away. Tell him you don't want this. She had the answers but no motivation, and when his mouth closed over hers, she could do nothing but savor its purposeful movement. Caressing, sucking, stroking—he was a man who kissed long and well. He was also a man who demanded a response.

"Open your mouth," he ordered in an uncompromising growl. "Do it the way I like it."

Shaye wasn't quite sure how he liked it, but the break in his kiss had left her hungry. This time when he seized them, her lips were parted. As they had the night before, they erupted into a fever against his, building the heat so high that she had to use her tongue as a coolant. But that didn't work, either, because Noah's own response increased the friction. Her breath came quickly, and her entire body was trembling by the time he dragged his lips away.

"Ahh, you do it right," he said on a groan.

Gasping softly, she pressed her forehead to his jaw. She felt his hand on her neck, but she was too weak to object, and in a second that hand was inside her blouse, taking the full weight of her breast. Her small cry was lifted and carried away by the wind.

"This is what I want," he whispered. His long fingers kneaded her, then drew a large arc on her engorged flesh. The top snap of her blouse released at the pressure of his wrist, but she barely heard it. His palm was passing over her nipple once, then again, and his fingers settled more broadly when his thumb took command.

"Look at me, Shaye."

Through passion-glazed eyes, she looked.

His voice was a rasping whisper. "This is what I'd do for starters." As he held her gaze, he dragged his thumb directly across her turgid nipple. He repeated the motion. "Do you feel it inside?"

"Oh yes," she whispered back. The thrumming still echoed in her core. Her legs stirred restlessly. "Do it again."

A tiny whimper came from the back of her throat when he did, but then he was whispering again. "I'd touch the other one like that, too. And then I'd take it in my mouth…." Another snap popped and he lowered his head. She took handfuls of his hair and held on when his thumb was replaced by the heat of his mouth, the wetness of his tongue, the gentle but volatile raking of his teeth.

Nothing had ever felt so exciting and so right. Shaye had spent the past six years of her life denying that the two—exciting and right—could be compatible, but she couldn't deny what she felt now. As his mouth drew her swelling breast deeper and deeper into its hot, wet hold, she knew both peace and yearning. She wanted him to tell her what he'd do next, and she wanted him to do it. She ached to do all kinds of wild things in return. And still there was that sense of rightness, and it confused her.

"Noah… Noah, Samson…"

"Can't see. Shh."

She wanted, but she didn't. The feel of Noah's mouth firmly latched to her burning flesh was a dangerous Eden.

She didn't trust herself and her judgement of rightness, and she couldn't trust Noah to understand what she felt. She was in deep water and sinking fast. If she didn't haul herself up soon, she'd be lost.

Tugging at his hair, she pulled him away with a moan. "We have to stop."

"Samson's way back at the stern," Noah argued hoarsely. "The sails are between us and him, and it's dark."

But Shaye was already sliding from his lap. He watched her scramble against the bow, clutching the lapels of her blouse with one hand, holding her middle with the other. His body was throbbing and his breathing unsteady. He hiked his knees up and wrapped his arms around them. "It's not just Samson," he stated.

"No."

"Is it me?"

"No."

"Then it's you."

She said nothing, just continued to look at him. The wind had picked up, blowing her hair around her face. She was almost grateful for the shield.

Her insides were in knots. She felt as though she'd been standing on the brink of either utter glory or total disaster—only she didn't know which. If he took her back in his arms, coaxed the least bit, pushed the least bit, she'd give in. Her nipple was still damp where he'd suckled; both breasts—her entire body—tingled. She'd never in her life felt as strong a craving for more, and she didn't understand why.

But common sense cried for self-control. Self-control! Was it so much to ask? Shaye wondered. When she'd been younger, she'd thought that by doing her own thing when and where she wanted, she was controlling her life. In fact, the opposite had been the case. For years she'd been out of control, acting irresponsibly with little thought for the consequences of her actions.

Now she was older and wiser. Responsibility had closed in on her, weighing her down at times, uplifting her at others. Perhaps it was an obsession, but self-control had been a passion in and of itself.

"What is it, Shaye?" Noah asked. "You're not an eighteen-year-old virgin."

She'd never been an eighteen-year-old virgin, and that was part of the problem. She'd given in too soon, too fast, too far.

"Have you been hurt...abused?"

"No!"

"But you're afraid."

"I just want to stop."

"You're afraid."

"Think what you will."

"But it doesn't make sense!" he burst out in frustration. "One minute you want me, the next you don't."

"I know."

"Well? Are you going to explain?" The demands of his body had died. He stretched out his legs in a show of indolence he was far from feeling. The wind was whipping at his shirt, but when he folded his arms over his chest, it was more because he felt exposed to Shaye's whims than to those of the weather. He wasn't used to the feeling of exposure and didn't like it.

"I can't explain. It's just...just me."

"Have you ever been involved with a man?"

"I've never been in love."

"That wasn't the question. Have you ever had a relationship with a man?"

"Certainly—just as you have."

"Sexually. Have you ever been involved sexually with a man?"

"You pointed out—" she began, then repeated herself in a voice loud enough to breach the wind "—you pointed out that I'm not an eighteen-year-old virgin."

He sighed, but the sound was instantly whisked away. "Shaye, you know what I'm getting at."

"I've been involved with many men, but never deeply," she blurted out, then wondered why she had. At the time she'd thought herself deeply involved with Josh... or André...or Christopher. But "deep" meant something very different now. It was almost...almost the way she was beginning to think herself involved with Noah, and that stunned her.

"Have you ever lived with a man?"

It was a minute before she could answer. "I, uh, lived in a kind of communal setup for a while," she hedged, and even that was pushing it a little. The garret had been André's; the others had simply crashed there for a time. She'd spent seven months with Josh, who'd eventually run off—with her blessing—to follow the Maharishi. She'd lived with other men for brief periods; she'd quickly gotten restless.

"Communal setups can mean either constant sex or no sex at all. Which was it?"

"I'm prissy. Which do you think?"

"I'm beginning to think this prissy bit is a cop-out. I'm beginning to think you're not one bit prissy. At least, that's what your fiery little body leads me to suspect."

She shrugged.

"Damn it, don't do that," he snapped. The sloop seemed to echo his frustration with a sudden roll. "I'm trying to get information. Shrugging tells me nothing."

"I don't like being the butt of your polling."

He rubbed the tight muscles at the back of his neck. "Was it that obvious?"

"Now that I know what you do for a living, yes."

The flapping of canvas high above suddenly grabbed their attention. Noah sprang to his feet. "It's about to rain. Do you have a slicker?"

Shaye, too, had risen. She'd snapped up her blouse and was holding her hair off her face with both hands. "A poncho." She swayed toward the bulwark when the boat took a lunge.

"Better get it," he said as he started toward the stern. She was right behind him. "Better still, get below. This deck in a storm is no place for a woman."

Shaye was about to make a derisive retort when Noah started shouting to Samson. And at the moment the first large drops of rain hit the deck. Having no desire to get drenched, she made straight for the companionway.

For several hours, she remained in the salon with Victoria while the *Golden Echo* bucked the waves with something less than grace. The men had run below in turns to get rain gear, and Shaye's repeated offers of help had been refused. She noticed that Victoria wasn't offering. In fact, Victoria was very quiet.

"Are you feeling all right?"

"I'm fine," Victoria said softly. "Or I will be once the wind dies down."

"That could be hours from now."

The expression on Victoria's face would have been priceless if she hadn't been so pale. "Don't remind me."

"Why don't you lie down in the cabin?"

"I'm afraid that might be worse." She scowled. "This tub isn't the best thing to be on in weather like this."

"So it's a tub now, is it?" Shaye said with a teasing smile. "You didn't think so before."

"Before I wasn't being jostled. And the portholes were open then." Victoria fanned herself. "It's hot as Hades here."

"Would you rather the waves poured in?"

"No, no. Not that."

"Are you scared?"

"Are you?"

Shaye was, a little. But the storm was a diversion. It gave her something to think about besides Noah and herself. Even now, with little effort, she could feel his arms around her and his tongue on her breast. She felt the same yearning she had then, the same confusion, the same fear. She'd come so close to giving in....

But she couldn't think about that. There was the storm to consider, one danger exchanged for another. She did trust that Samson and Noah knew what they were doing. She wondered if they were frightened—but didn't really want to know.

So she pasted a crooked grin on her face and said to Victoria, "I'm sure we'll pull through fine. Look at the experience as exciting. It's not everyone who gets tossed over the high seas in an ancient colonial sloop."

"Cute," Victoria said, then gingerly pushed herself from the sofa. "On second thought, I will lie down."

Concerned, Shaye started out of her chair. "Can I do anything to help?"

But Victoria pressed her shoulder down as she passed. "If death is imminent, I'll call."

SHAYE DIDN'T WAIT for the call. She checked on Victoria every few minutes, trying to talk her out of her preoccupation with her insides. But with each visit, Victoria felt less like talking. By the third visit, she'd lost the contents of her stomach and was looking like death warmed over.

"Let me get you something."

Victoria moaned. "Leave me be."

"But I feel helpless."

"It'll pass."

"My helplessness?"

"My seasickness."

"What about my guilt?" Shaye asked in a meek stab at humor. "I was the one who joked about getting violently seasick."

"Tss. You're making it worse."

"Samson said he had medicine."

"Don't bother Samson. He has enough on his hands."

Shaye rose from the bed. "I'm getting his medicine."

"They'll think I'm a sissy."

"God forbid."

"Shaye, I'm fine—"

"You will be," she said as she left the cabin. Shimmying into her poncho, she climbed the companionway. She paused only to raise her hood and duck her head in preparation for the rain before pushing open the hatch. The wind instantly whipped the hood back and her hair was soaked before she'd reached the helm, where Samson stood wearing bright yellow oilskins and a sou'wester, looking for all the world like a seasoned Gloucester fisherman.

"Whatcha doin' up heah, geul?" he yelled in an accent to match.

The rain was coming down in sheets while the wind whipped everything in sight, but still Shaye laughed. His role playing conveyed a confidence that was contagious. "You're too much, Samson!"

"Best enjoy ev'ry minute!" he declared in a voice that challenged the storm.

Shaye tugged up her hood to deflect the rain from her face while she looked around. The sea was a mass of whitecaps. The jibs were down, the mainsail reefed. In essence, Samson was doing little more than holding the keel steady while they rode out the storm.

"Has Noah gone overboard?" she yelled.

"Not likely!"

She was about to ask where he was when the boat heaved and veered to port. Steadying herself as best she could, she shouted, "Are we in danger?"

He straightened the wheel and shouted back, "Nope!"

"How long do you think it'll keep up?"

"Mebbe an hour. Mebbe five."

"Victoria won't be terribly pleased to hear that."

"She'll prob'ly be hopin' it las' ten," he roared with an appreciative smile.

"I don't think so, Samson. She's sick!"

While the storm didn't faze him, that bit of news did. For the first time, he seemed concerned. The accent vanished. "Her stomach's acting up?"

Shaye nodded vigorously. "You said something about medicine?"

"In the locker by the galley. Noah may have it, though."

"Where *is* Noah?"

"In bed."

"What's he doing in bed when—oh, no, he's sick?"

"And not pleased about it at all! He wanted to stay on deck, but when he started to reel on his feet, I ordered him down."

Shaye had no way of knowing that the same concern she'd seen on Samson's face moments before now registered on her own. Noah sick? He was so large, so strong. She couldn't picture him being brought down by anything, much less *mal de mer*.

Actually, though, the more she thought about it, the more she saw a touch of humor in it. Or poetic justice.

"I didn't see him come in," she said more to herself than to Samson. "It must have been while I was with Victoria."

At the reminder of her aunt, she turned quickly back to the hatch. Once below, she peeled off the soaking poncho and checked the locker for Samson's medicine. It was there. Either Noah wasn't all that sick or he was too proud to take anything.

Victoria wasn't too proud. When Shaye lifted her head and pressed the pill between her lips, she sipped enough water to get it down, then sank weakly back to the pillow. Pill bottle in hand, Shaye returned to the locker. She paused before opening it, though, eyes moving helplessly toward the captain's quarters. Then, without asking herself why or to what end, she took the few steps necessary and quietly opened the door.

A trail of sodden clothes led to the bed, and on that bed lay Noah. He was sprawled on his stomach atop the bare sheets, one arm thrown over his head. The faint glow from the lamp showed the sheen of sweat that covered his body. He was naked.

Feeling not humor but a well of compassion that she'd never have dreamed she'd feel for the man, she quietly approached and knelt down by the bed. "Noah?" she asked softly.

He moaned and turned his face away.

"Have you taken something?"

He grunted.

Compassion turned to tenderness. She reached out and stroked his hair. It was wet from the rain, but his neck was clammy. "Victoria's sick. I just gave her some of Samson's medicine. If I get water, will you take some, too?"

He groaned. "Let me die in peace."

"You're not going to die."

He made a throaty sound of agreement. "I won't be so lucky."

"If you die, who'll be left to give me a hard time?"

There was a short silence from Noah, then a terse, "Get the pill."

Shaye brought water and held his head while he managed to swallow the pill. Then she sponged his back with a damp cloth.

"It's not helping," he mumbled. Though his head was turned her way, his eyes remained closed.

"Give it time."

"I haven't got time. I'm already in hell."

"Serves you right for living the life of a sinner."

He moaned, then grumbled, "What would you know about the life of a sinner?"

"You'd be surprised," she answered lightly, continuing to bathe him.

At length he dragged open an eye. "Why aren't *you* sick?"

"I'm just not."

"Are you scared."

"No."

"You should be. We're about to be swallowed by a great white whale."

"Does delirium come with seasickness?"

He gave up the effort of keeping that one eye open, pulled the pillow between his chest and the sheet and moaned again.

"Does that help?" she asked.

"What?"

"Moaning."

"Yes." A minute later he turned onto his side and curled into a ball, with the pillow pressed to his stomach. "God, I feel awful."

He looked it. His face was an ashen contrast to his dark hair, and tight lines rimmed his nose and mouth.

"Are you going to be sick?" she said.

"I *am* sick."

"Are you going to throw up?"

"Already have. Twice."

"That should have helped."

He grunted.

"It's really a shame. After Samson went to such efforts with the sauerbraten—"

"Shut up, Shaye," he gasped, then gave another moan.

"The storm should be over sometime tomorrow."

"If you can't say something nice…"

"I thought the storm was pretty exciting. I've never seen waves quite like that."

This time his moan had more feeling. Shaye said nothing more as she smoothed the cloth over his skin a final time. Then, brushing the damp hair from his brow, she asked, "Will you be okay?"

"Fine."

"I should get back to Victoria."

"Go."

"Can I check on you later?"

"Only if you're into autopsies."

She smiled. He was the fallen warrior, but there was something endearing about him. "I'll steel myself," she said, then quietly rose from his bedside and left the cabin.

She didn't steel herself for an autopsy, of course. She checked on Victoria, who'd settled some, then went to sleep to dream dreams of a long-legged, lean-hipped man whose body had to be the most beautiful she'd ever seen in her life.

CHAPTER SEVEN

THE STORM HAD DIED by morning. Shaye awoke to find Victoria on deck with Noah, who'd sent Samson below for a well-earned rest.

"Well, well, if it isn't our own Florence Nightingale," Noah remarked as she approached the helm.

The last time he'd said something like that, Shaye mused, he'd called her an iron maiden. She didn't particularly care for either image, but at least she didn't hear sarcasm this time.

She had wondered how he'd greet her after the state she'd last seen him in. Some men would have been embarrassed. Others, particularly those with a macho bent—and Noah did have a touch of that—would have been defensive. But Noah seemed neither defensive nor embarrassed. He'd bounced right back to his confident self. She should have known he would.

"You're both looking chipper," she said.

Victoria smiled. "Thanks to you."

Noah seconded that. "She really is a marvel. Has an unturnable stomach and an unrivaled bedside manner."

"Mmmm. She does have a way of coaxing down medicine."

"And bathing sweaty bodies."

Victoria gaped at him. "She bathed you? I didn't get a bath!"

"I guess she can't resist a naked man."

"Naked?" She turned to Shaye, but the twinkle in her eyes took something from the horror of her expression. "Shaye, how could you?"

Before Shaye could utter a word, Noah was wailing, "There you go again—suggesting that my body's distasteful! What is it with you women?"

"I didn't suggest anything of the sort," Shaye said smoothly, and turned to Victoria. "He actually has a stunning body—a sweet little birthmark on his right hip and the cutest pair of buns you'd ever hope to see."

"I didn't think you noticed," Noah drawled to Shaye, then said to Victoria, "but don't worry. I kept the best parts hidden."

Shaye didn't answer that. She'd seen the "best parts" too, and they'd been as impressive as the rest. But she wasn't about to play the worldly woman so far that she totally cancelled out the prissy one. So she tipped back her head, to find the sky a brilliant blue. "No clouds in sight, and we're making headway again. Did we lose much ground during the storm?"

"A little," Noah answered, indulgently accepting the change in subject, "but we're back on course."

"Good." She rubbed her hands together. "Anyone want breakfast?"

Noah and Victoria exchanged a glance, then answered in unison, "Me."

"You're cooking for all of us?" Noah asked.

"I'm feeling benevolent."

He snagged her around the shoulders and drew her to his side. "Domestic instincts coming to the fore?"

"No. I'm just hungry."

"So am I."

She sent him a withering look.

He didn't wither. "Just think," he murmured for her

ears alone, "how nice it would be to have breakfast together in bed."

"I never eat breakfast in bed."

"If I were still sick, would you have brought it to me there?"

"If you were still sick, you wouldn't have wanted it."

"What if my stomach was fine but my knees were so weak that I couldn't get up?"

"That'd be the day."

"You were very gentle last night. No one's taken the time to bathe me like that since I was a child."

She knew he was playing on her soft side, but before she should could come up with suitably repressive words, he spoke again.

"So you liked what you saw?"

"Oh yes. The storm was breathtaking."

"*Me.* My *body.*"

"Oh, that. Well, it wasn't quite as exciting as the sea."

"Catch me tonight, and I'll show you exciting."

"Is another storm brewing?" she asked, being purposely obtuse.

Noah wasn't buying. "You bet," he said with a naughty grin.

Shaye quickly escaped from his clutches and went below to fix breakfast. Throughout the morning, though, she thought of Noah, of his body and its potential for excitement. The more she thought, the more agitated she grew.

She tried to understand what it was about him that turned her on. He was cocky and quick-tongued. He could be presumptuous and abrasive. He was, in his own way, a rebel. There were so many things not to like. Still, he turned her on.

Always before she'd been safe, and it wasn't merely

a question of dating bland men. She encountered men at work, men in the supermarket, men in the bookstore, the hardware store, the laundry. She'd never given any of them a second glance.

Granted, she'd had no choice with Noah. She was stuck on a boat with him, and in such close quarters second glances were hard to avoid, particularly when the man in question made his presence felt at every turn.

Not only was she looking twice, she was also fantasizing. With vivid clarity she recalled how he'd looked naked. She hadn't been thinking lascivious thoughts at the time, but since then her imagination had worked overtime. Everything about him was manly, with a capital *M*—the bunching muscles of his back, the prominent veins in his forearms, the tapering of his torso, his neat, firm bottom, the sprinkling of dark hair on the backs of his thighs. And in front—she could go on and on, starting with the day's growth of beard on his face and ending with the heaviness of his sex.

If the attraction were purely physical, she could probably hold him off. But increasingly she thought of other things—his sense of humor, his intelligence, his daring, his disregard for convention—and she felt deeply threatened. Last night hadn't helped. What she'd felt when he'd been sick, when he'd needed her and she'd been there for him, came dangerously close to affection. She'd never experienced the overwhelming urge to care for a man before.

So why was it wrong? In principle, she had nothing against involvement. She supposed that some day she'd like to fall in love, just as some day she'd like to have children. She hadn't planned on falling in love now, though, when her career was in full swing. And she hadn't planned on falling in love with a man like Noah.

Not that she was in love with him, she cautioned herself quickly. But still...

The problem was that Noah wasn't meek. He wasn't conservative or conventional. She couldn't control him—or herself when she was with him. He was wrong for her.

Had she been in Philadelphia, she'd have run in the opposite direction. But she wasn't in Philadelphia. She was stuck on a boat in the middle of the Caribbean with Noah, and she was vulnerable. In his arms, she was lost—and she fell into his arms easily!

She'd just have to be on her guard, she decided. That was all there was to it.

THE AFTERNOON BROUGHT a torment of its own. Where the night before the wind had picked up, gusted, then positively raged, today it faded, sputtered, then died.

Shaye was sitting on deck reading when the sails began to pucker. She looked up at the mast, then at Victoria, who was sitting in blissful ignorance nearby, then down at her book again. But the sails grew increasingly limp, and at the moment of total deflation, she didn't need the unusual calm of the sea to tell her what had happened.

Noah sauntered by, nonchalantly lowering and lashing the sails.

"How long?" she asked.

He shrugged. "Maybe an hour or two. We'll see."

An hour or two didn't sound so bad. The part she didn't like was the "maybe." If their idle drifting lasted for eight hours, or sixteen, or God forbid, twenty-four...

"You look alarmed," he commented, tossing her a glance as he worked.

"No, no. I'm fine."

"View it as a traffic jam. If you were in the city, chances are you'd be on your way somewhere. But you wouldn't be able to move, so you'd be frustrated, and you'd be sick from exhaust fumes. Here you have none of that." He took a long, loud breath that expanded his chest magnificently. "Fresh air. Bright sun. Clear water. What more could you ask?"

Shaye could have asked for the wind to fill the sails and set them on their way again. The sooner they reached Costa Rica, the sooner they'd return to Colombia and the sooner she'd go home. One virile man with a magnificent chest was pushing her resolve.

"I couldn't ask for anything more," she said.

"Sing it."

"Excuse me?"

"The song. You know—" Noah jumped into a wide-spread stance, leaned back, extended both arms and did his best Ethel Merman imitation: "I got rhythm, I got music..."

She covered her face with a hand. "We did that in junior high. I believe the last line is, '*Who* could ask for anything more?'"

"Close enough."

She peered through her fingers. "Were you in the glee club?"

"Through high school. Then I was in an *a cappella* group in college. We traveled all over the place. It was really fun." His face suddenly dropped.

"What?"

"Well, it was fun for a while."

"What happened?"

He hesitated, then shrugged. "I resigned."

"Why did you do that?"

"I, uh, actually there were three of us. We got into a little trouble."

"What kind of trouble?"

He returned to his work. "It was nothing."

"What kind of trouble?"

He secured the last fold of the mainsail to the boom, then mumbled, "We went on a drinking binge in Munich. The administrators decided we weren't suitable representatives of the school."

"You didn't resign. You were kicked out."

"No, we resigned."

"It was either that or be kicked out."

He ran a hand through his hair. "You don't have to put it so bluntly."

"But that was what it boiled down to, wasn't it? You should be ashamed of yourself, Noah."

Victoria, who'd remained on the periphery of the discussion to that point, felt impelled to join in. "Aren't you being a little hard on the man, Shaye? You were in college once. You know what college kids do. They're young and having fun. They outgrow it."

"Thank you, Victoria," Noah said.

Shaye echoed his very words, but with a different inflection. She picked up her book again.

Having nothing better to do, Noah stretched out on his back in the sun. Within thirty seconds, he bobbed up to remove his shirt. Then he lay back again, folding his arms beneath his head. "I'll bet Shaye never did anything wrong in school. The model student. Hmmmm?"

Shaye didn't answer.

Victoria pressed a single finger to her lips, holding in words that were aching to spill out. Shaye shot her a warning look. The finger stayed where it was, which was both a good sign and a bad sign.

"Did you study all the time?" Noah asked.

"I studied."

"What did you do for fun?"

"Oh, this and that." She glanced toward the stern. "Where's Samson?"

"I believe he's cooking," Victoria answered, dropping her finger at last.

"What's it going to be tonight?"

Noah smirked. "Now, if he told us, it wouldn't be a surprise, and that's half the fun."

"I hate surprises."

"You hate fun. What a boring person."

"Noah," Victoria chided.

But Shaye could stand up for herself. "It's okay. I have a strong back."

"Stiff," Noah corrected in an absent tone. His eyes were closed, his body relaxed. "Stiff back. But not all the time. When I take you in my arms—"

Shaye cut him off. "Does Samson always cook foreign?"

He grinned and answered only after a meaningful pause. "Not always. He does a wicked Southern-fried chicken."

"What does he wear then?"

"I'm not telling."

She glared at him for a minute, but his eyes were still closed so he didn't see. "You wouldn't," she muttered, and returned to her book. She couldn't concentrate, of course. Not with Noah stretched out nearby. The occasional glances she darted his way brought new things to her attention—the pattern of hair swirling over his chest, the bolder tufts beneath his arms, the small indentation of his navel.

She looked back at her book, turned one page, waited several minutes, turned another. Then she set the book down in disgust. "How long have we been sitting?"

"Half an hour."

"And still no wind."

"It'll come."

"Why doesn't this boat have an engine? Nowadays every boat has an engine."

"The *Golden Echo* wasn't built 'nowadays.'"

"But she was refurbished. She has a stove and a refrigerator. Why doesn't she have an engine?"

Noah shrugged. "The Paynes must be purists."

With a snort, she picked up her book, turned several more pages, then sighed and lifted her ponytail from her neck. "Is it ever hot!"

Noah opened a lazy eye and surveyed the shorts and T-shirt she wore. "Feel free to strip."

Sending him a scowl, she pushed herself up, stalked to the companionway and went below.

He looked innocently at Victoria. "Did I say something wrong?"

Victoria didn't know whether to scold or laugh. She compromised by slanting him a chiding grin before she, too, rose.

"Hey," he called as she started off, "don't you leave me, too!"

"I'm going to visit with your uncle. It can't be much hotter down there than it is up here, and at least there's some shade."

Noah lay where he was for several minutes, then sat up and studied the horizon. He gave a voluminous sigh and pasted a jaunty smile on his face. This was what he wanted, wasn't it? Peace and quiet. The deck all to himself. He could relax if he wanted, sing if he wanted, do somersaults if he wanted.

So why did he feel restless?

Because he was hot and bothered and the damn sun wasn't helping. Abruptly dropping the smile, he surged to his feet, reached for the rope ladder, hung it from the starboard quarter, kicked off his shorts and dove into the sea. He'd done two laps around the boat when he overtook Shaye. He was as startled as she was.

"What are you doing here?" she gasped. "I thought I was alone."

"Who do you think put the ladder out?" he snapped. "And if you thought you were alone, why in the hell were you swimming? You're not supposed to swim alone."

"You were."

"That's different."

"How so?"

"I'm a man and I'm stronger."

"What a chauvinistic thing to say!"

"But it's true."

"It's absurd, and, besides, it's a moot point. You don't exactly need strength in a bathtub like this. If there were waves, there'd be a wind, and if there were a wind, we wouldn't be stuck out here floating in the middle of nowhere!"

"Always the logical answer. Y'know, Shaye, you're too rational for your own good. Ease up, will ya?"

She gave him a dirty look and started to swim around him, but he caught her arm and held it. "Let go," she ordered. "I want to swim."

"Need the exercise?"

"Yes."

"Feeling as restless as I am?"

"Yes."

"How about reckless?" he asked, his eyes growing darker.

Shaye recognized that deepening gray. His eyes went like that when he was on the verge of either mischief or passion. She didn't know which it was now, but she did know that with his hair slicked back and his lashes wet,

nearly black and unfairly long, he looked positively de-
monic. Either that or sexy. Was she feeling reckless? "No,"
she stated firmly.

"Do you *ever* feel reckless?"

She shook her head.

"Not even when I take you in my arms?" He did it then,
and she knew better than to try to escape. After all, he was
stronger then she. "Why do I frighten you?"

"You don't."

He tipped his head to the side and gave her a reprov-
ing look.

"You don't," she repeated, but more quietly. As though
to prove it—to them both—she put her hands on his shoulders.

"Are you afraid of sex?"

"I'm not a virgin."

"I know. We've been over that one before. I'm not asking whether you've done it, just whether you're afraid of it."

She was afraid of *him*, at that moment, because his
mouth was so close, his lips firm and mobile. She couldn't
seem to take her eyes from them. The lower was slightly
fuller than its mate and distinctly sensual. Both were wet.

"Shaye?"

She wrenched her gaze to his eyes. "I'm not afraid of
sex."

"Are you afraid of commitment?"

"No."

"Then why haven't you married?"

"I thought that was clear. I've been busy."

"If the right man had come along, you'd have married."

"How do you know that?"

"You ooze certain values. There's a softness to you that
wouldn't be there if you were a hard-bitten career woman

all the way. I have to assume that the right man just hasn't come along."

"I said that I don't date."

"You also said that you'd been involved with many men."

"But not recently. And if I don't date now, how can I possibly meet the right man?"

You don't have to date to meet men, Noah thought. *You could meet one during a vacation in the Caribbean.* "With your looks—come on, baby, with your looks the right man would make sure you dated. Him. Exclusively."

Baby. It was a stereotypically offensive endearment, yet the way he said it made her tingle. "What are you trying to prove, Noah?"

"I'm working on the theory that you turn away from men who threaten your very sane, very structured, very controlled existence. Just like you turn away from me."

"And now that you have me analyzed, you can let me go."

His arms tightened. "Hit a raw cord, did I?"

She slid her hands to his elbows and tried to push. "Not raw, nonexistent." Her teeth were gritted. "Let me go, Noah."

"I can make your body hum, but still you fight me. Why won't you let me make love to you, Shaye?"

"Because—" she was still pushing "—I don't want to."

"It'd be so easy. We could do it right here. Right now."

Her limbs were shaking, but it wasn't from the effort of trying to free herself. His tone was tender, his words electric. The combination was devastating. "Don't do this to me," she begged.

"What would I be doing that's so wrong? Is it wrong to feel drawn to someone? I do feel drawn to you, Shaye, sour moods and all."

She didn't want to hear this. Closing her eyes, she gave a firm shake of her head. "Don't say another word."

"I respect your work and your dedication to it. I respect what you feel for your aunt. I respect and admire your independence, but I want to know more about where it comes from. At the slightest mention of your family or your past, you clam up."

"I have two parents with whom I don't get along and a sister with whom I do. There. Are you satisfied?" She tried to propel herself away from him, but he wasn't letting go. She only succeeded in tangling her legs with his, which were warm, strong and very bare.

"Why don't you get along with your parents?"

"Noah, I'm getting tired. I'd like to go back on the boat."

"I'm not tired. I'll hold you. You know how."

She turned her head to the side and let out an exasperated breath. "Will you let me go?"

"No."

"I'll scream."

"Go ahead. There's no one to hear but Samson and Victoria, and they trust me." He pressed a warm kiss to her cheek, then asked gently, "Why do you do this to yourself? Why do you fight?"

His gentleness was her undoing. Suddenly tired of the whole thing, she dropped her chin to his shoulder. "Oh Lord, sometimes I wonder." Her arms slipped around him, and she felt his hands on the backs of her thighs, spreading them. In as natural a movement as she'd ever made, she wrapped her legs around his waist. "You're not wearing a suit," she murmured. "Why not?"

"I was in a rush to get in the water and there was no one around."

"Oh Noah."

He was nuzzling her ear. "What is it, hon?"

"I really am tired. I'm not used to constant sparring. I'm not good at it."

"Could've fooled me."

"All I wanted was a peaceful vacation in the Berkshires."

"Things don't always work out the way we plan. Good sometimes comes from the unexpected."

The lazy frog kick he was doing kept them bobbing gently on the sea's surface. Beneath the surface the bobbing was more erotic—the tiniest glide of their bodies against one another, a teasing, a soft simulation. Her suit was thin. She clearly felt his sex. But while her body craved the contact, she felt too spent to carry though.

"I'm so tired," she murmured, tightening her arms around him simply for the comfort of his strength.

"Things are warring inside?"

"Yes."

"Maybe if we talk it out you'll feel better."

She sighed sadly against his neck. "I don't know. For so long I've drummed certain things into my head…." Her voice trailed off.

He was stroking her back. "I'm listening."

But she couldn't go on. There were too many thoughts, too much confusion, and as comfortable as she was with him just then, she was deathly afraid of saying something she'd later regret.

"Hey," he breathed. He took her head in his hands and raised it to find her eyes brimming with tears. "Ah-h-h, Shaye," he whispered hoarsely, "don't do that. Don't torment yourself so."

She could only shut her eyes and shake her head, then cling more tightly when he hugged her again.

"I guess I've come on pretty strong."

She nodded against his neck.

"That wasn't very nice of me."

She shook her head.

"I'm really not a bad guy when you get to know me."

She was coming to see that, and it was part of the problem. Brashness she could withstand, as she could irreverence and impulsiveness. But mix any of those with gentleness, and she was in trouble.

"Come on," he said softly. His hands left her back and broke into a broad breaststroke. "Let's go back on board."

She made no effort to help him swim, and when they reached the ladder she was almost sorry to let go of him. It had been so nice holding on and being held without other threats. But she did let go and climbed the ladder, then stood on the deck pressing a towel to her face.

She heard Noah's wet feet on the wood behind her. She heard the swish of material that told her he was pulling on his shorts. For a fleeting instant she wondered whether he ever bothered with underwear, then his voice came quietly.

"Why don't you stretch out in the sun to dry? It looks like we're not going anywhere yet."

Dragging the towel slowly down her face, she nodded. Moments later, she was lying on her stomach in the sun. She cleared her mind of all but her immediate surroundings—the warmth of the sun feeling good now on her wet skin, the utter silence of the air, the gentle sway of the boat as it drifted. Noah sat nearby, but he did nothing to disturb her other than to ask if she wanted a cool drink, then fetch it when she said yes.

She knew that there were other things he could have done and said, such as stretching out beside her, offering to spread lotion on her back, suggesting that she lower the straps of her suit to avoid getting marks. He could have prodded her, pried into her thoughts, forced her to think about those things she was trying so hard to avoid.

But he did none of those things. He seemed to respect the fact that she needed a break from the battle if she was to regain her strength for the skirmishes ahead.

Late in the afternoon, Victoria joined them on deck, followed a few minutes after that by Samson. Conversation was light and for the most part flowed around Shaye. When the others decided to swim, she took her turn and savored the coolness but remained subdued, and after climbing back on board she went below to change for dinner.

When all four had gathered back on deck, Samson declared, *"Nu, yesly vnyesyosh stol, Noah, ee vee pryekrasnie zhenshchina vnyes yote pagooshkee, prig at oveem yest."*

"Myehdlyeenyehyeh, pahzhahloostah," Victoria requested.

Straightening the red tunic over his shorts and shirt, Samson repeated his instructions, but more slowly this time. He accompanied them with hand motions, for which Victoria was grateful. Her course in conversational Russian had only gone so far, and she was rusty.

By the time she was ready to interpret, the others had gotten the drift of Samson's request. Noah set up the table, while Shaye and Victoria brought cushions from the salon. Samson then proceeded to serve a dinner of *kulebiaka* and salad, and with a free-flowing vodka punch, the meal was lively.

Still, Shaye was more quiet than usual. She listened to the others joke about experiences they'd had, following particularly closely when Noah spoke. She learned that he'd taken Spanish through college, that he'd spent a semester in Madrid, that he'd spent the year following graduation working on a cattle ranch in Argentina. She also learned that, while there, he'd been nicknamed the Playboy of the Pampas, and though he'd been annoyed when Samson had let that little jewel slip, he hadn't denied it.

They lingered for a long time over coffee. With no wind, there was nowhere to go and no work to do. At length Samson went below deck, reappearing moments later wearing a tricorne. Then, with one of the hurricane lamps supplementing the silver light of the moon, he produced his treasure map.

Not even Shaye could resist its lure. She sat forward with the others to study the weathered piece of paper-thin parchment. "Where did you get it?" she asked.

"I was on Montserrat last winter and befriended an old British chap, who'd found it in an old desk in the villa he'd bought there fifteen years before. We'd been discussing the lore of the pirates in these parts when he brought out the map."

Victoria leaned closer to peer at the markings. "When was it supposed to have been drawn?"

"In the mid eighteen hundreds. My friend—Fitzsimmons was his name—theorized that the crew of a pirate ship stashed its booty and left, planning to return at a later, safer time."

"Only they never made it?"

"We don't know that for sure, but it's doubtful, since the map was well hidden and intact. The desk in which Fitzsimmons found it was traced back to a man named Angus Cummins, and Englishman who settled on Montserrat in the 1860s. No one seems to have known much about Cummins other than that he was a shady character, usually drunk and alone. My own research showed him to have been quartermaster on an English vessel that was shadowed by trouble. In 1859, during one of its last voyages to the Caribbean, the captain died at sea. When the boat returned to England, there were rumors of piracy and murder, but the crew stood as one and nothing was ever proven."

Victoria expelled a breath. "Murder!"

Samson shrugged. "We'll never know, but given this," he tapped the map, "there's reason to suspect that the crew was involved in piracy."

"But if that's true, why didn't Cummins—or one of the others—ever return for the treasure?" Shaye asked.

"Cummins may have been the only one with the map. As quartermaster, he was in a position of power second only to the captain. My guess is that he left England under dubious circumstances, stationed himself on Montserrat in the hope of one day crossing the Caribbean to retrieve the treasure, but never quite found the wherewithal to do it."

Assuming the accuracy of Samson's research, Noah agreed with his guess. He was skeptical, though, about the treasure still existing. "People have been searching for gold along the Costa Rican coast since Columbus dubbed the country the 'rich coast,' but the only riches discovered were bananas. If there were anything else hidden there, wouldn't it have been long since plundered?"

Feeling an odd sense of vindication, Shaye glanced at Victoria. She'd expressed a similar sentiment when Victoria had first called her about the trip.

But Samson was undaunted. "They didn't have the map." He held up a hand. "Now, I'm not saying that the treasure's there. I've checked with the Costa Rican authorities and they have no record of anyone reporting a stash being found in the area where we're headed. But that doesn't mean the treasure hasn't been stolen. Cummins may have gone back for it, then lived out his life in frustration when he realized he couldn't return to England a wealthy man. It's possible, too, that only his small portion of the take was hidden. Then again, the map may have been a fraud from the start."

Shaye leaned closer. "It looks authentic enough."

"Oh, it's authentic. At least, it was drawn during the right time period. I had it examined by experts who attested to that."

"Then how could it be fraudulent?" Victoria asked.

"Cummins may have drawn the map on a whim. He may have drawn it to indicate the spot where he'd put a treasure if he ever had one."

"You mean, there may never have been any treasure to begin with?"

"There's always that possibility." He smiled. "For the sake of adventure, though—and until we prove otherwise— we'll assume the treasure's there."

Shaye was grateful that she'd had a few drinks with dinner. Though the coffee had lessened the vodka's effects, her senses were still numbed. Had they not been, she feared she'd have said something blunt, and she didn't want to dampen Samson's enthusiasm any more than she wanted to evoke Noah's ire. "Are we talking gold?" she asked carefully.

"Most likely. Artifacts would be found in an undersea wreckage. I doubt that a man who planted a treasure with the intention of retrieving it in his lifetime would want anything but gold."

Noah was studying the map. "This spot is between Parismina and Limón?"

Samson cleared his throat, pushed the tricorne back on his head and got down to business. "That's right." His finger traced the pen scratchings. "The Costa Rican coast is lowland. Between the Nicaraguan border at the north and Puerto Limón, which lies about midway to Panama at the south, much of that lowland is swampy."

"Swampy?" Shaye cried in dismay.

"Not to worry. We're heading for a sandy spot just north

of Puerto Limón, a small bay, almost a lagoon. It should be lovely."

She hoped he was right. "And once we get there...?"

"Once we get there, we look for the rose."

Shaye bit her lip. She shot a glance at Victoria, then lowered her eyes to her lap.

Victoria was as dismayed as Shaye but had the advantage of being the quintessential diplomat. "An orchid I could believe," she began softly. "Orchids are the national flower. Roses, though, are not indigenous to Central America. Is it possible that a rose Cummins planted would still be alive?"

Noah chuckled as he looked from Shaye's face to Victoria's. "Tell them, Samson. They're dying."

Samson, too, was smiling. "The rose is a rock, possibly a boulder. Cummins must have taken one look at it and associated its shape with the flowers he knew from home. The treasure, if it exists, will be found in a series of paces measured from the rock."

Dual sighs of relief came from the women, causing Noah to chuckle again. But while Samson elaborated on the specifics of those paces, Shaye's thoughts lingered on the rock.

The rose. Was it pure coincidence...or an omen? She had a rose of her own, and it symbolized all she'd once been and done. She hid it carefully; no more than a handful of people had ever seen it. It was her personal scarlet letter, and she was far from proud of its existence.

She'd never been a superstitious person, but at that moment, she wanted nothing at all to do with the Costa Rican rose.

CHAPTER EIGHT

NOAH AWOKE AT EIGHT on the fourth day of the trip and lay in bed for a long time. After spending most of the night on deck, manning the sails when the wind picked up shortly after one, he'd expected to sleep later. But Shaye had invaded his dream world as much as she was invading his thoughts now that he was awake.

A change had come over her in the water yesterday, and it hadn't been a momentary thing. She'd been distracted for most of the afternoon and thoughtful for much of the evening.

Was it surrender? Not quite. She hadn't come to him that night on deck to declare her devotion and beg him to make love to her. But she did seem to have conceded to an inner turmoil. She seemed to have realized that it wouldn't just go away, that it had to be faced.

He wished he knew what was at the root of that inner turmoil, but she guarded it closely. He wasn't dumb; he knew when to push a subject and when to back off. Not that he really thought of her as a "subject." He was too personally involved for that. But his feel for people had gotten him where he was professionally, and he was counting on it now.

She'd opened up a bit before she'd gone to bed. He'd produced a deck of cards and they'd played several games of gin, and during this she'd mentioned that she and her sister, Shannon, had played gin when they'd been kids. It was one of the few things her parents had thought harmless, she'd said wryly, and when he'd teased her, she'd admitted that her parents were strict. She obviously resented that, yet from what he could see she was nearly as strict with herself as they'd been with her.

Wouldn't she have rebelled? That was what often happened to the offspring of strict parents. Or perhaps she had rebelled and been subsequently swamped by guilt. Ingrained values were hard to shake.

She was a passionate woman. He didn't doubt that for a minute. The way she'd come alive to him on those few occasions when she'd stepped out of her self-imposed mold had been telling. She had a fire inside, all right. The question was whether she'd allow it to burn.

He wasn't about to let it go out, though he was biding his time just now. He'd found her weakness and knew that when he played it soft and gentle she was more vulnerable. Yes, he was impatient; soft and gentle hadn't traditionally been strong points in his character. But then, he'd never met a woman quite like Shaye—or felt quite as compulsively drawn to one before.

He had to admit, with some surprise, that behaving softly and gently toward Shaye wasn't as much of a hardship as he might have expected. She responded well to it. Of course, that didn't mean that his loins didn't ache. He felt an utterly primal urge to make her his. But he wanted far more than a meaningless roll in the hay—or on the deck, or in a cabin, as the case might be.

Hell, where could they do it? His cabin was Samson's, too, and Shaye shared hers with Victoria. The deck was neither comfortable nor private. There was always the water, but he wanted leverage, not to mention access to certain parts of her body without fear of drowning. On the other hand, a sandy beach on the Costa Rican coast...

Allowing for the time they'd lost during the storm and then being becalmed, they had two days' sailing ahead before they reached their destination. Two days in which to soften her up. He'd have to work on it, he decided as he sprang from the bed and reached for a pair of shorts. He'd have to work on it, starting with a soft and gentle morning talk.

He went on deck to find Victoria and Samson but no sign of Shaye. And since he was reserving all his softness and gentleness for her, his impatience found vent in the demand, "Where is she?"

Samson tried to conceal a grin and didn't quite make it. "I haven't seen her yet this morning."

"I think she's still sleeping," Victoria added innocently. "It was after two before she finally dozed off."

A scowling Noah left them and crossed to the bow.

"Now how would you know that?" Samson drawled softly. "You were asleep yourself by eleven."

Victoria didn't ask him how *he'd* known *that*. While Noah and Shaye had been playing cards on deck, Samson had walked her to her cabin, then sat talking with her until she'd fallen asleep. She was normally a night owl, but knowing Samson relieved Noah at the helm between three and four, she'd wanted to be up soon after. Watching the sunrise with him was a memorable experience.

"Actually," she whispered, "I don't know it for sure, but I could feel her tossing and turning. And it won't do any harm to let Noah know she's losing sleep over him."

"Is that what she's doing?"

"I believe so."

He narrowed one eye. "Are you matchmaking?"

She narrowed an eye right back at him. "No more than you."

He lowered his head in that same subtle gesture of guilt

that Victoria and Shaye had seen the first day. "I wasn't matchmaking, exactly," he hedged. "But when you called to say that your niece was coming along and that she was twenty-nine, attractive, intelligent and hardworking—well, I couldn't help but think of Noah."

"So you *did* get him to come after I called."

"Barney was ticked off."

"But other than what I said, you knew nothing about Shaye."

"I knew Noah. He needed a break, and not at an isolated château in Normandy. He needs a woman. He's the proverbial man who has everything...except that. Besides," he added with a roguish smile, "Garrick had told me about you, and I knew that if the niece took after the aunt in any small way..."

Victoria reached up to kiss him lightly. "You're a very sweet man. Have I told you that lately?"

"I don't mind hearing it again."

"You're a very sweet man. Thank you for the compliment...and for bringing Noah along. He and Shaye are right for each other. I just know it."

At that moment, Noah swung by en route to the companionway. "Enjoy yourselves, folks."

"Where are you off to?" Samson asked.

"Breakfast," was all Noah said before he disappeared.

It was a brainstorm, he mused as he quickly whipped up pancake batter. She was still in bed, and she hadn't eaten since dinner, and since he was hungry and she was bound to be hungry... Very innocent, he decided, it would all be very innocent. He'd simply carry in breakfast, wake her gently, and they'd eat.

As he spooned batter onto the griddle, he recalled his initial fear that she'd expect to be waited on. But he wasn't waiting on her, at least not in the sense of pandering to a woman who refused to do for herself. She'd proven more than willing to pitch in. She'd even made him breakfast yesterday. So now he was returning the favor. Only with a sightly different twist.

A short time later, balancing the tray that Samson always used to cart food to the deck, he went to her cabin. When a light knock at the door produced no response, he quietly opened it and slipped inside. Then he stood there for a minute, stunned as always by the sight of her in bed. She was on her stomach this time, dark red hair spilling around her head, more vivid than ever against the white linens. Where the sheet left off at mid-back, her T-shirt took over in covering her completely. Still she was alluring. All white and red, primness and fire. God, was she alluring!

He quietly set the tray down by the side of the bed and perched on its edge. "Shaye?" he whispered. His hand hovered over her shoulder for a minute before lowering and squeezing lightly. "Shaye?"

She stirred, turning her head his way. Her eyes were still closed. Lock by lock, he stroked her hair back from her face.

She barely opened her mouth, and the words were slurred. "Something smells good."

"Pancakes and apple butter. I thought maybe you'd join me."

She was quiet for such a long time that he wondered if she'd fallen back to sleep. Then she murmured, "I never eat breakfast in bed."

"Are you turning down room service?"

Again a pause. Her eyes remained closed. "No."

He swallowed down a tiny sigh of relief. "Would you rather sleep a little longer?"

She yawned and struggled to open one eye. "What time is it?"

"Nine-thirty."

With a moan, she turned away. "I didn't get to bed until two."

"Get to bed" versus "doze off." Two very different connotations. "Get to bed" meant she could have been reading; he'd been on deck, so he hadn't seen whether she'd stayed in the salon for a while. "Doze off," the phrase Victoria had used, suggested that she'd tried to sleep but that her thoughts had kept her awake. He hoped it was the latter, but he wasn't about to ask. For someone who usually woke up crabby, she was in a relatively civil mood.

"Are you falling asleep on me?" he whispered.

She shook her head against the pillow.

"Just taking it slow?"

She didn't move. At length she said, "I'm trying to decide whether or not to be angry. You woke me up."

The fact that she didn't sound at all angry gave Noah hope. "I'll leave if you want. I'm hungry enough to eat both helpings."

She turned over then, pushed herself up until she was sitting against the wall, straightened the sheet across her hips and patted her lap.

With a smile he reached for the tray.

Few words were exchanged as they ate. She glanced at him from time to time, thinking how considerate it had been of him to bring her breakfast, and how good he looked even before he'd shaved, and how well he wore an unbuttoned shirt. He glanced at her from time to time, thinking how the shadows beneath her eyes had faded, and how becoming her light tan was, and how disheveled and sexy she looked.

From time to time their glances meshed, held for a second or two, broke away.

When Shaye had finished the last of her pancakes she said, "You're nearly as good a cook as Samson."

"Breakfast is my specialty."

"Between you and your uncle, you could run a restaurant."

"I have enough to do already, thank you."

She sat very still for a minute. "We're moving."

"Have been since one this morning."

She hadn't realized that and wondered how she could have been so caught up in her thoughts that she hadn't noticed.

"Want to go on deck?" Noah asked.

"I'll have to get dressed first."

"You do that while I take care of these," he said, indicating the dishes. "I'll meet you up there in, say, ten minutes?"

"Okay," she agreed quietly and watched him leave.

Ten minutes later they were standing side by side at the bow. She raised her face and closed her eyes. "Mmm, that feels good."

Noah didn't comment on the fact that she'd left her hair down, or that it was positively dancing in the breeze, or that it was tempting him nearly beyond reason. Instead he took a deep breath and asked casually, "Where do you live in Philly? An apartment?"

"Condominium. It's in a renovated building not far from the historic area."

"Is your family in Philly, too?"

"Uh-uh. Connecticut."

He turned around to lean back against the bulwark. The sails were full. He studied them, wondering if he dared ask more. Before he had a chance to decide either way, she asked, "How about you? A condo in the city?"

"Yup."

"What's your place like in Vermont?"

"Contemporary rustic."

She laughed softly. "That's honest. Most people would pride themselves on saying rustic, when in fact they have every modern amenity imaginable."

A short time later, after they'd watched a school of fish swim by, she asked, "Do you ski?"

"Sure do. You?"

"I tried a few times in college, but I never really went at it seriously."

He wanted to say that she could use his place anytime, that he'd teach her how to ski, that the most fun was après-ski, with a warm fire, a hot toddy and a bear rug before the hearth. Instead he asked what she'd been reading the day before.

Eventually they brought cushions up and made themselves more comfortable. Their talk was sporadic, never touching on deep issues, but even the trivia that emerged was enlightening.

Shaye learned that Noah was an avid Mets fan, that he want to games whenever he could spare the time, which wasn't often enough, and that he'd even became friends with a few of the players. Once he'd been mistaken for a bona fide member of the team by a small-town reporter, who interviewed him outside the locker room after a game. She learned that when he watched television, it was usually a program of the public information or documentary type. He had certain favorite restaurants he returned to often, the most notable of which was a no-name dive on the Lower East Side that had filthy floors, grumpy waiters and the best guacamole north of Chihuahua. She learned that he hated shopping, loved dressing up on Halloween—which, he assured her, came only once a year at his office—and fantasized about buying a Harley and biking across the country.

Noah learned that Shaye talked to her plants and that she generally hated to cook but could do it well when inspired. He learned that she'd always loved to read and belonged to a book group, that she wanted to take up aerobics but didn't have the time, that she liked Foreigner, Survivor, and Chicago but never went to live rock concerts.

The day passed with surprising speed. Shaye wasn't quite sure whether the new Noah, the one who was companionable rather than seductive, was the real Noah. But since he'd offered her a respite from the torment he'd previously inflicted, she wasn't about to raise the issue aloud.

Her subconscious wasn't quite as obedient. No sooner had she gone to bed that night than the sensual Noah popped up in her dreams, only it was worse, now, because the man who excited her physically was the same one she'd begun to respect. She awoke in a frenzy, torn apart and sweaty, and immediately put the blame on the Vietnamese dinner Samson had prepared that night. By the next morning, though, that excuse had worn thin. One look at Noah, freshly shaved and wearing nothing but a low-slung pair of shorts, stirred her blood.

She fought it all day, but to no avail. They were together nearly constantly, and though he didn't fall back on either double entendres or provocative observations, his eyes held the dark sexuality that expressed her own deepest thoughts. She was acutely, viscerally, passionately aware of him.

While they ate breakfast, which he consumed in bulk and with enthusiasm, she was entranced by his mouth. It was mobile and firm, yet sensual. She couldn't help but recall how aggressively it had consumed her own, and when her eyes met his for a fleeting moment, she knew he was remembering the same.

Later she sat with him on deck while he cleaned the hurricane lamps, his long, lean fingers working the cloth over brass. She was mesmerized by those fingers and finally had to tear her eyes away, but the memory of them working her breasts with agile intimacy caused a rush of warmth to spread beneath her skin. Noah didn't comment on the blush or on the sudden shift of her gaze, but when she dared look back at him, she caught a starkly hungry expression.

Later still, when he relieved Samson at the helm, she relaxed against the transom—or she'd intended to relax, until Noah's bold stance commanded her attention. He had a beautiful body and he held it well, shoulders back, head up. Whether standing with his legs spread or with his ankles crossed or with his weight on one hip, he oozed self-confidence. And when he walked, as he did to occasionally adjust the sails, he oozed masculinity. She wondered what it was about tight-hipped men who moved with nothing more than the subtlest shift of their bottoms—whether it was the economy of movement that made a woman greedy, or the pelvic understatement that was overwhelmingly suggestive, or simply the fact that between waist and thigh men were built so differently from women.

Of course, she couldn't remember ever having taken much notice of men's bottoms before, not even in the old days. So it had to be Noah.

Self-confident, sexy, every move natural and spontaneous. He wasn't a preener. Not one of his motions seemed tutored. His body was simply...his body. And his very indifference to it made him all the more attractive to Shaye.

And all *that* was before she got down to the details. The roughened skin on his elbows...the compact lobes of his ears...the symmetry of his upper back, the gleam of sun-bronzed skin over flexing muscles...the shallow dip at his hipline just before his shorts cut off the view... So many things she wanted to touch, so many things that touched her even without actual physical contact.

Like his chest. Noah's chest inspired wanton behavior. She wanted to feel its varying textures, to touch her finger to a smooth spot, a hairy spot, a firm spot, a soft spot. His nipples were small in that male kind of way, but that didn't mean there was anything less intimate about them. The more she looked, the more intimately she was moved.

In the end, though, it was his eyes, always his eyes that touched her most deeply. To say that his eyes stripped her naked was too physical a description. They delved far deeper, burrowing beneath her skin and touching hidden quarters that no man, *no* man had ever touched. With each look she felt his thoughts, and she knew that he wanted her.

So the sexual tension built. What had rippled in the morning was simmering by noon and smoldering three hours later. The air between them grew positively charged, but they could no more have left each other's sides than they could have denied that the charge existed.

Then, shortly before five, a low shadow materialized on the distant horizon.

"Land, ho!" Noah shouted from the bow, grateful to relieve his tension with the hearty yell.

Shaye was at his elbow. "Costa Rica?"

"It had better be," he said, "or we're in trouble."

She knew he wasn't referring to an accidental landing in another country. They needed a diversion, and they needed one fast.

"What happens now?" Victoria asked, joining them.

Noah and Shaye exchanged a quick, hot look. "Now," he said, "we try to find out exactly where we are."

Samson was already doing that, working with binoculars, a compass, and the charts and notes he'd made. "We're pretty much on target," he finally announced to his waiting audience. "Assuming that the cargo ships we've seen are heading for either Limón or Moin, all we need to do is to sail a little north. Once we're in closer, I'll know more."

It took a while, for the wind lessened the closer they got, but they gradually worked their way in the right direction. Shaye, who'd begun the trip with a minimum of enthusiasm for Costa Rica, couldn't deny the country's tropical beauty. Spectral mountains provided a distant backdrop for the lush jungle growth that grew more delineated as they neared the shore. The graceful fronds of tall palms arched over small stretches of sandy beach. Thicker mangroves and vines populated swampier sections.

They approached a small bay, and three pairs of eyes sought Samson's. But he shook his head. "The configuration is wrong."

"Perhaps it's changed with time?" Shaye asked.

"Not that much," was his answer. So they sailed on.

After a time they neared another sandy area. Low outcroppings of rock lay at either end, curving out to give a lagoon effect. "Could be," Samson said. "It's broad enough in the middle, flat enough from front to back…. Could be," he repeated, this time with enthusiasm. "I won't know for sure until can take a reading with the sextant, and it looks like the stars will be elusive for a while."

Those three pairs of eyes joined him in scanning the cloud cover that was fast moving in.

Recalling how sick she'd been on the second night of the trip, Victoria asked with a touch of horror, "Another storm?"

"Probably nothing more than rain," Noah guessed, then asked Samson, "Should we go in and drop anchor?"

"That's our best bet."

By the time the *Golden Echo* was anchored about two

hundred yards from shore, night had fallen. The four gathered in the salon, with an air of great expectancy.

"This is frustrating," Victoria decided. "To be here and not really know whether we are, in fact, here…."

"Patience," Samson urged with a smile. "We'll know soon enough. We've made good time, and I've allowed five days to search for the treasure. That's far more than we should need once we reach the right lagoon. Even if this one isn't it, we can't be far."

Shaye's eyes met Noah's for a minute before slanting away.

Victoria's eyes were on Samson. "How does the Costa Rican government take to treasure hunts like ours?"

"I filed the proper papers and was granted a permit. The government has a right to half of anything we recover."

Victoria knew by this time that Samson had as little need of gold as she did. "What will you do with it?"

"The treasure? Of the half that's left, only a quarter will be mine." His gaze skipped meaningfully from one face to another.

"I don't want any treasure," Shaye said quickly. It had never occurred to her that she'd receive a thing, and picturing the rose-shaped rock, she felt vehement about it.

"Count me out, too," Noah said forcefully. He looked at Shaye, and his eyes grew smoky. *There are many different kinds of treasure….*

"I'm bequeathing my portion to you," Victoria informed Samson. "Lord only knows I pay enough in taxes now." She settled more comfortably onto the sofa. "What will you do with it?"

Samson gave a quick shrug. "Give it to charity—four times as much as I'd originally planned."

Victoria grinned. "I like that idea. What do you think, Shaye?"

Shaye's head popped up. She'd been studying her knotted hands, wishing that they could somehow take the tension from inside her and wring it away. "Excuse me?"

"Charity. Samson plans to give our treasure to charity."

"I like that idea."

Victoria laughed. "That was what I said."

"Oh."

"How about you, Noah?" Samson asked. "Any objections?"

Hearing his name, Noah tore his gaze from Shaye. "To you and Victoria splitting the treasure?"

Samson sighed. "To my giving the entire thing to charity."

"I like that idea," Noah said, then frowned when both Samson and Victoria laughed. He'd obviously missed something, but he didn't know what it was. He did know that he was the brunt of the joke. Then again, Shaye wasn't laughing.

Victoria took pity on him and turned to Samson with what she hoped was a suitably serious expression. "What's for dinner tonight?"

"Bologna sandwiches."

"Bologna sandwiches?"

"That's right."

Neither Noah nor Shaye showed the slightest reaction to his announcement. They were alternately looking at each other, looking at the floor, looking at Samson or Victoria for the sake of politeness. They saw little, heard even less.

"So you finally got tired of cooking," Victoria declared with relief. "You're human, after all."

Arching a brow her way, Samson grabbed her hand, pulled her from the sofa and made a beeline for the galley, muttering under his breath, "I could probably open a can of dog food and neither of them would notice."

He was right. Neither Noah nor Shaye commented on the artlessness of the menu, though both drank their share of the Chianti Samson decanted.

Shaye tried, really she did, to concentrate on the dinner conversation, but her thoughts and senses were too filled with Noah to allow space for much else.

Noah tried every bit as hard to interject a word here or there to suggest he was paying attention, but more often than not the word was inappropriate, several sentences too late or offered in a totally wrong inflection.

They roused a bit when it began to rain and everything had to be carried below deck in a rush, but the alternate arrangements had them sitting close together in the galley. Not only was sane thought all the harder, but the tension between them rose to a fevered pitch.

"Why don't we adjourn to the salon and finish the wine?" Samson suggested at last. "There's no reason why Chianti won't go with Ding Dongs."

"You didn't bring Ding Dongs," Victoria chided.

"I certainly did. Next to chocolate mousse, Ding Dongs are my favorite dessert."

Neither Noah nor Shaye had a word to say about Ding Dongs, but they came to when Samson and Victoria rose to leave. "I'll clean up," they offered in unison, then eyed each other.

Shaye said, "You go on into the salon with the others. I'll take care of this."

Noah said, "There isn't much. I don't mind. You go relax."

"I've been relaxing all day. I'd like to do something."

"And I feel guilty because my uncle has been the major cook. The least I can do is clean up."

"Noah, I'll do it." She started stacking dirty plates.

He had the four wineglasses gathered, a finger in each. "*I'll* do it."

"We wanted those glasses," Samson remarked.

Noah sent him a confused look. "I thought we were done."

"I had suggested that we finish the wine in the salon."

"Oh." He looked down at the glasses. "But they're mixed up now. I don't know whose is whose."

"Obviously," said Samson, whereupon Noah turned on Shaye.

"If you hadn't been so stubborn, this wouldn't have happened."

"Me, stubborn? You were the one who was being difficult."

"How can you say that someone offering to do the dirty work is being difficult?"

"*I* offered to do the dirty work *first*."

"Then *you* were the one who was difficult, when all I wanted was to relieve you of the chore."

"But I didn't *want* to be relieved—"

Victoria cut her off with a loud declaration. "We'll take clean glasses." She did just that and led Samson from the galley.

Shaye attacked the dishes with a vengeance.

"Take it easy on the water," Noah snapped. "There's no need to run more than you need."

"I need *some*, if you want the plates clean."

"Of course I want the plates clean, but you could be economical."

She thrust a dripping plate his way. "Dry this."

"You're very good at giving orders. Is that what you do all day at work?"

"At least I don't get any back talk there."

"I'm sure they wouldn't dare or you'd boot them out.

I assume," he drawled, "that you have the power to hire or fire."

"In my department, I certainly do. Lawyers know nothing about computers or the people who use them."

He held up the plate he'd been drying and asked with cloying sweetness, "Is this shiny enough for Her Highness?"

She simply glared at him and handed him another, then started on the next with a double dose of elbow grease.

"You're gonna break that plate if you're not careful."

She ignored him. "And you're a fine one to talk. You're the head of your own company—a power trip if there ever was one. I'll bet *you* run a tight ship. A regular Captain Bligh."

"I have high standards, as well I should. My name's on top. I get the blame when someone flubs up."

"And the same isn't true for me? Don't you think the lawyers get on *my* back when documents come out screwed up?"

"What I want to know," he snarled, "is if they ever get you *on* your back."

The glass she'd been scrubbing came close to breaking against the sink. "You have the filthiest mind I've ever been exposed to!"

"And who's been fueling it? Little looks here, darting glances there. I'm not made of stone, for Christ's sake!"

She'd rinsed off the glass she'd nearly broken and was onto another. "Could've fooled me. Your eyes are as lecherous as your mind. You sit there making me squirm, and what do you expect me to do—whistle 'Dixie'?"

"You couldn't whistle if you tried. Your lips are too stiff."

"It's a lucky thing they are. Anything but a stiff lip around you would result in a physical attack."

"I have never physically attacked a woman in my life! But I'm beginning to wonder about you and that past you try so hard to hide. It comes out, y'know. I can see it in your eyes. You've had sex, and you've had it but good. What was it—with a married guy? Or a highly visible guy you're determined to protect?"

"You're out in left field, Noah." She thrust a handful of forks and knives at him, then, having run out of things to wash, went at the sink itself.

"I think it was with a married guy. You fell in love, gave him everything and only after the fact learned that he wasn't yours for the taking."

"Dream on." She began to wipe down the table with a fury.

"Either that, or you're totally repressed. Your parents instilled the fear of God in you and you're afraid to do a damn thing. But the urges are there. You live them vicariously through sexy rock ballads, but you don't have the guts to recognize what you need."

"And you know what that is, I suppose?"

"Damn right I do. You need a man and lots of good, old-fashioned loving. You may like to think of yourself as a prim and proper old maid, but I've seen your true colors. They're hot and vibrant and dripping with passion."

She turned to him, hands on her hips, nostrils flaring. "What I need is none of your business. I sure don't need *you*."

"You need a man who's forceful. I fight you, and I'd wager that's a hell of a lot more than any other man has ever done."

"Power trip, ego trip—they're one and the same with you, aren't they?" Throwing the damp rag into the sink, she whirled around and stalked out of the galley. A second later she was back, glowering at Noah while she reached for a clean wineglass.

Snatching up his own, he followed her. He filled it as soon as she'd set down the bottle, then took his place in the same chair he'd had before dinner.

"We were talking about pirates," Victoria said. She and Samson sat on the sofa, hard-pressed to ignore the foul moods the newcomers were in. "Samson's done a lot of reading. He says that many of the stereotypes are wrong."

"In what way?" Shaye demanded.

Noah grunted. "They were frustrated men, stuck on a boat without a willing woman to ease their aches."

"Not every man is fixated on his libido," she snapped, then turned to Samson. "Tell me about pirates."

"Pirates turn you on, huh?"

"Keep quiet, Noah. You were saying, Samson…"

"I was saying that when one begins to study the age of piracy, one learns some interesting things. For example, pirates rarely flew the skull and crossbones. They rarely made anyone walk the plank. They rarely marooned a man."

Noah snorted. "And when they did, they left him a pistol so that he could put an end to his misery. That's compassion for you."

"I'm not trying to idealize the buccaneer, simply to point out that he was more than a blood-thirsty ruffian with no respect for life. Pirates had their own kind of code."

"Nonpolitical anarchy," was Noah's wry retort.

"It worked for them," Samson said. "They chose their captains at will and could dismiss them as easily."

"Dismiss or execute?"

"Noah, let the man talk."

Noah slid lower in his chair. His brows formed a dark shelf over his eyes, but he said nothing.

"They did execute their captains on occasion," Samson conceded, "but only when those captains mistreated them. You have to understand that most of the men who crewed on pirate ships had known the brunt of poverty, or religious or political persecution at home. Fair treatment was one of the few benefits of piracy."

"But what about the gold they captured?" Shaye asked. "Didn't they benefit from that?"

Noah looked her in the eye. "They blew it on women in the first port they hit. I hope to hell the doxies were worth it."

"You'll never know, will you?" she asked sweetly.

He glared at her. She glared right back. Then he bolted from his chair and stormed toward the companionway.

"Where are you going?"

"Out."

"But it's raining!"

"Good!"

Shaye dragged her gaze back to the salon. She looked first at Victoria, then at Samson. "He's impossible!"

Samson contemplated that for a minute, then went on in his customary gentle voice, "The popular image is that pirates were irreligious plunderers who had a wonderful time for themselves, but it wasn't so. They were unhappy men. With each voyage, their hopes of returning home dimmed. It didn't matter that home wasn't wonderful. Home was familiar. It had to have been frustrating."

Shaye dropped her gaze to her hands. Victoria took up the slack and continued talking with Samson, but it wasn't until Noah reappeared that Shaye raised her eyes.

He was soaking wet and impatient. "Come on," he said, grabbing her hand.

"What—"

"We'll be back," he called over his shoulder as he led her toward the companionway.

"Hold on a minute." She tugged back on her hand. "I'm not going up there."

But he refused to let go, and he wasn't stopping. "You won't melt." He pushed the hatch open and had pulled her through before she could do anything about it.

CHAPTER NINE

THE RAIN WAS a warm, steady shower, drenching Shaye within seconds. "Noah, this is crazy!"

He loomed over her, the outline of his face glistening in the light of the lamp that hung at the stern. "We're going ashore."

"But it's pouring!"

Plowing his fingers into her hair, he took her mouth in a kiss that was as fevered as the tension had been earlier, as hungry as he'd felt all day, as wild as he'd ever been at his boldest moments. By the time he raised his head, Shaye was reeling.

"We're going ashore," he repeated hoarsely.

The night was dark and stormy, but that meager light from the stern clearly illuminated the intent on his face and the desire in his eyes. At that moment, she knew precisely what he had in mind. And she knew at that moment that she wouldn't refuse him. The flame within her was too hot to be denied. It blotted out everything but a basic, driving need.

"How?" she whispered shakily.

"The dingy." Snatching up a huge flashlight, he aimed it over the side of the boat, where the small rubber lifeboat he'd just inflated bobbed in the rain. Then he swung onto the rope ladder and started down. Midway, he waited for Shaye. When she was just above him, he lowered himself into the raft. As soon as she was safely settled, he began to row quickly toward shore.

With a trembling hand, Shaye tossed back her dripping hair. She didn't know whether what she was doing was right, but she knew that she had no choice. The darkness abetted her primal need; it erased reality, leaving only the urgency of the moment. Her entire body shook in anticipation of the intimacy she was about to share with Noah. Her eyes were locked on his large dark form throughout the brief trip, receiving an unbroken message that sizzled through the rainy night.

The dingy touched shore with a quivering bump. Noah jumped out seconds before Shaye, made a brief survey of the beach with the light, then dropped it and, in a single flowing movement, whipped the boat onto the sand and reached for her.

She was made for his arms, fitting them perfectly. Her hands went into his wet hair as her open mouth met his. Tension, hunger, fierceness—the combined effect was galvanic. His tongue plunged deeply. She nipped it, sucked it, played it wildly with her own.

With a groan, Noah set frenzied fingers to work tugging the soaked T-shirt from her body. But he was unwilling to release her mouth for an instant, so he abandoned it at her shoulders and dug his fingers under the waistband of her shorts. She helped him in the tugging, her lips passionate beneath his all the while. As soon as the soggy cotton passed her knees, she kicked free of the shorts and turned her efforts to Noah's. They'd barely hit the sand when he dropped his hands to her thighs and lifted her onto his waiting heat.

At the bold impaling, Shaye cried out.

"It's okay, baby," he soothed, panting. "It's okay."

She gasped his name and clung to his neck. "I feel so full…"

"You're hot and tight around me. Ahh, you feel good!" His fingers dug into her bottom, holding her bonded to him as he sank to his knees. "Have I hurt you?" he asked between nips at her mouth.

"No. Oh, no."

"I was afraid you'd change your mind, and I couldn't last another minute without being inside." His hands had risen to cover her breasts, stroking her through silk, then hastily releasing the front catch of her bra and seeking out her naked flesh.

Again she cried out. His fingers were everywhere, circling her, kneading her, daubing her nipples with raindrops. She was in a lagoon. She couldn't see the lagoon or the jungle, but she knew it was paradise, she just knew it, and with less thought than Eve she gave in to temptation.

Her hands began a greedy exploration under his shirt, over his waist, across his buttocks, up and down his thighs. He wasn't moving inside her, but she could feel every inch of him against her moist sheath, and the solid stimulation was breathtaking. Whispering his name, she tried to move her hips. But he followed the movement with his own, preventing even the slightest withdrawal.

"You're mine now," he said with the tightness of self-restraint. "We'll take it slow."

She raked her teeth against his jaw. "I want to feel you move."

"Soon, baby. Soon."

His mouth plundered hers. His thumbs began a slow, sliding rotation of her nipples. Live currents snapped and sizzled so hotly inside her that she almost feared she'd be electrocuted in the rain. Noah was grounding her, she told herself, yet still she burned. She caught at his hair and kissed him more deeply. She drew her nails across his shoulders, then dug them in and tried to move again, but he wouldn't have it.

"Noah…"

He worked her T-shirt over her head and pushed the bra straps from her shoulders, leaving her naked in the night but hot, so hot against him. "Soon," he murmured thickly. "Soon." The last was breathed against her breast moments before he sucked her in.

For a minute all she could do was hold his head. Her own was thrown back, her eyes were closed, and the rain was as gentle, as persistent and seductive as his ever-moving tongue. With the visual deprivation imposed by the night, her senses grew that much sharper. She felt everything he did with vivid clarity, and the knot of need inside her grew tighter.

Shaye wondered where he got his self-control and vowed to break it. While her mouth grew more seductive, her hands taunted his chest. Short, wet hairs slid between her marauding fingers and his nipples grew hard. She undulated her middle, then, when he clutched her there to hold her still, her hips. She felt him quiver insider her, and, encouraged, repeated the motion.

But through it all there was something more. Instead of simply snapping his control, she wanted to give him a pleasure so hot and intense that he'd be branded every bit as deeply as she was. Bent on that, she reached low and stroked that part of him that hung so heavily between his thighs.

The bold caress was his undoing. Making a low, guttural sound, he tumbled her down to the sand. Bowing his back, he withdrew, then thrust upward with a force that thrilled her. She'd been right to want movement, for the friction, the sliding pressure was exquisite. But Noah had been right, too, for the wait had enhanced both her desire and appreciation.

He set a masterful rhythm that varied with their needs. Faster or slower, she met him and matched him, each arching stroke stretching the heavenly torment into an ever-tautening fine wire.

The tension snapped with a final, agonizingly deep thrust. Implosion and explosion, simultaneous and mind shattering, sent blind cries slicing through the beat of the rain. Soft gasps followed, an occasional whimper from Shaye, a moan from Noah. They clung tightly to each other until they were totally limp, and then the rain began to soothe their bodies, cleansing, cooling and replenishing.

When Noah had regained a modicum of strength, he maneuvered them both into the kneeling position from which they'd fallen. He wasn't ready to leave Shaye, and given the renewed strength of her hold, he suspected he'd have been unable to if he tried. It was gratifying, the perfect denouement to what had been a heartrending experience.

He spread his hands over her bare back, able to savor now the delight of her shape as he hadn't had the patience to do earlier. "I knew it would be like that," he murmured. "We're like tinder, Shaye. All it takes is a single match and we go up." He gave a throaty laugh. "I'm still up."

She could feel that. Oh, she could feel it, and she was astonished to find that corresponding parts of her were similarly alert. "You're a powerful lover," she whispered. It was an understatement, but she didn't think the words existed to adequately describe what she'd felt.

"I could say the same about you," he whispered back. He was thinking that he didn't care how many other lovers she'd had or who had first awakened her to the fiery art of passion, but he didn't say so. It wasn't that he didn't want to know, because that jealous male part of him did, but he didn't want to disturb the precious peace that existed between them. So he asked, "Do you mind the rain?"

"No. There's something erotic about it."

"There's something erotic about this whole setting. I wish to hell I could see it."

Resting her cheek on his shoulder, she chuckled. She knew what he meant. But then, she needed the darkness. She didn't want to see herself, and she didn't want Noah to see her. There was still the matter of the small mark on her breast; she had no idea how she would explain it, whether she wanted to, what the ramifications would be. Too much thought at too sensitive at time…she was still into feeling, rather than thinking.

"Take off your shirt," she whispered, then slid her hands to his waist to hold their bodies together while he complied. When he was as naked as she, she wrapped her arms around his neck, bringing her breasts into contact with his chest for the very first time.

The feeling was heavenly. She moved gently against him. He sucked in a shaky breath, and when she felt him swell inside her, her muscles automatically tightened.

"Ohh, baby…"

"You can feel that?" She smiled when his groan clearly indicated that he could, but then he was kissing her smile away and touching her in ways that reduced her to quivering jelly. She sighed when he released her mouth, only to gasp when he slid a hand between their bodies and began an ultra-sensitive stroking. It wasn't long before she reached a second fierce climax.

She was panting against his shoulder, her hands grasping his chest, thumbs on his nipples, when he went tense, uttered a strangled cry and pushed more deeply into her.

A SINGLE ROSE

She felt the spasms that shook him, felt his warmth flowing into her and knew an incredible joy.

"Ahh, Shaye," he whispered when he could finally speak, "you're amazing."

She basked in the glow of his words. She'd heard similar ones before, but never spoken with quite the same awe, and that meant the world to her. Pressing her face to his neck, she nestled into his arms. It was apparently the right thing to do, for he held her closely and seemed as satisfied as she with the silence.

At length, though, it occurred to her that a rainy Eden had its drawbacks. She wanted a bed. She wanted to lie down beside Noah in the darkness, to breathe in his undiluted scent, to hear the unaccompanied beat of his heart. She wanted to rest in his arms, just rest. She was suddenly very tired.

"I think we'd better go back," he murmured into her hair.

She wondered if he'd read her mind. His voice sounded as tired as she felt. More than that, it contained a note of sadness that she understood; no matter how they looked at it, there wasn't a bed for them to share.

She let him help her to her feet and together they retrieved their clothing. As though afraid of breaking the spell further, Noah didn't turn on the flashlight. He set the dingy in the water, helped Shaye inside, then climbed in and more slowly rowed back to the *Golden Echo*. As had been the case during the trip to shore, her eyes held him the entire way back. This time, though, rather than the heat of desire, she felt something even deeper and more tender. Shaye wasn't about to put a name to it any more than she was ready to face what it entailed. She simply wanted it to go on and on.

After securing the dingy to the stern of the sloop, they

climbed back on deck. Holding Shaye's hand firmly in his, Noah cast a despairing glance at the rain that continued to pour. Then he guided her down the companionway and closed the hatch.

"Want to change into dry things and sit in the salon for a little while?" he asked softly.

She nodded, but still she didn't move. Their fingers were interlaced; she tightened hers. She feared that even the briefest parting would allow for an unwelcome intrusion.

Noah raised her hand and gently kissed each of her fingers, then lowered his head and gently kissed her mouth. "Go," he whispered against her lips. "I'll be waiting for you."

Determined to change as quickly as possible, she whirled around and promptly stumbled. She'd have fallen to the floor had not Noah caught her. While he held her to his side, he frowned at the cause of her near-accident. A large bundle and one about half its size were stacked in the passageway by the aft cabin.

"My duffel bags?" he asked softly. His confused gaze shifted to Shaye before returning to the bundles. "Packed?" He stared at them a minute longer, then, with dawning awareness, broke into a lopsided grin. "I'll be damned...."

Shaye left his side long enough to check out the forward cabin. It was empty. "They must both be in your cabin," she whispered, draping an arm around his neck in delight.

"Looks that way."

"But...how did they know?"

"Maybe they had the dingy bugged."

"Impossible."

"Then they're simply very wise people."

"Or very selfish."

"Hell, they deserve pleasure, too. On the other hand,

maybe they meant this as punishment for the way I behaved earlier."

"You could be right."

He scowled. "That's not what you were supposed to say."

Her eyes turned innocent, while her heart positively brimmed. "What was I supposed to say?"

"That I was only being ornery out of frustration." His whisper grew softer. "Are you going to make me sleep on the couch?"

She gave a quick shake of her head.

"I can share your bed?"

She nodded as quickly.

"Because you feel sorry for me?"

"Because I want you with me."

His smile was so warm then, so filled with satisfaction that she knew a hundred-fold return on her honesty. He didn't make a smug comment on her primness, or lack thereof. He didn't accuse her of being wanton. He just smiled, and another bit of the retaining wall surrounding her defenses fell away.

Without a word, he scooped up his bags and followed her to the forward cabin. Once side, he dropped his things and took her in his arms. He didn't kiss her. He didn't caress her. He simply held her.

"Shall I light the lamp?" he asked quietly.

"No."

"I'd like to get out of these wet things."

"Me, too."

"Got a towel?"

She nodded, and when he released her, went to get it. He'd shed his shorts and shirt by the time she returned with the towel, and by the time she'd wrestled her way out of her own things, he was ready to dry her. There was nothing seductive in his touch; it was infinitely gentle and made her feel more special than she'd ever felt before. The feeling remained when they curled next to each other in bed, and it was so strong and gave her such confidence that she probably would have answered any question he'd asked just then.

He only asked one thing. "Comfortable?"

"Mmm."

He was quiet for a time before he spoke. "There is such pleasure in this. Just lying here. Close."

"I know," she whispered and softly kissed his chest.

"I just want to hold you."

"Me, too."

"I want you with me when I wake up."

"I will be."

"You can kick me if I snore."

She yawned. "Okay."

"If Samson wakes us at five to go digging for his damned treasure, I'll wring his neck."

"I'll help you."

"On the other hand," he added, his voice beginning to slur, "maybe they'll sleep late themselves."

"Or maybe they'll take pity on us."

"Fat chance…"

"Mmm…"

ALL THINGS WERE relative. The knock on the door didn't come until eight the next morning, but Shaye and Noah weren't ready for it even then. They'd been awake on and off during the night and were dragged out of a sound sleep by Samson's subsequent shout.

"We've been waiting for two hours! Can you give us an ETA?"

"That's Expected Time of Arising," Victoria called.

After bolting upright in alarm, Noah collapsed, burying his face in Shaye's hair. "Make them go away," he
whispered.

"Noon!" she shouted to the two beyond the door.

"Noon?" Victoria echoed. "That's obscene!"

Samson agreed. "If you think we're going to wait until
noon to go ashore, think again!"

"Go ashore," Shaye suggested, tugging the sheet higher.
"I'll just sleep a little longer."

"But I need Noah's help," Samson argued.

"He's on shore. I left him there last night."

"What do you mean, you left him there?"

"He was behaving like a jackass." She twisted over
Noah to muffle his snicker. "What choice did I have? And
it's a good thing I did leave him there. Exactly where did
you expect him to sleep?"

There was silence on the other side of the door, so she
went on. "That was a fine stunt you two pulled—behaving
like a pair of oversexed teenagers." Noah nuzzled her collarbone. She slid to her side again and wrapped her arms
around his neck. "What kind of an example is that to set?
I have to say that I was a little shocked—"

Her words were cut off by the abrupt opening of the
door. Victoria stood with one hand on the knob, the other
on her hip. Samson was close behind her. Their eyes went
from Shaye to the outline of bodies beneath the sheet.

"I am assuming," Victoria said drolly, "that Noah is
hidden somewhere under that mane of hair. Either that,
or you've grown an extra body, a pair of very long legs
and a dark beard."

"Tell her to go away," came Noah's muffled voice.

"Go away," Shaye said.

"ETA?" Samson prodded.

"Noon."

Victoria made a face. "Nine."

"Eleven."

"Ten," said Samson. "Ten, and not a minute later." He raised his voice. "Do you hear me, Noah?"

Noah groaned. "I hear."

"Good. Ten o'clock. Topside." His hand covered Victoria's as he pulled the door shut.

Closing her eyes, Shaye slid lower to lay her head on Noah's chest. He wrapped an arm around her back and murmured, "I'd like to stay here all day."

"Mmm."

"Sleep well?"

"Mmm."

"Shaye?" He began to toy with her hair.

"Mmm?"

"That little mark on your breast. What is it?"

Her eyes came open and for several seconds she barely breathed. "Nothing," she said at last.

"It isn't nothing. It looks like a tattoo."

She was silent.

"Let me see."

She held him tighter.

"Shaye, let me see." Taking her shoulders, he set her to the side. His eyes didn't immediately lower, though, but held hers. "You didn't really hope to hide it forever, did you?" he asked gently. "I've touched and tasted every part of you. There's pleasure to be had from looking, too."

She bit her lip, but she knew that she wouldn't deny him. If he'd sounded smug or lecherous, she'd have been able to put up a fight. But against gentleness she was helpless.

Very carefully he eased the sheet away. He sat up and pushed it lower, then leaned back on his elbow while his eyes began at her toes and worked their way upward. His hand followed, skimming her calves and her thighs, brushing lightly over auburn curls before tracing her hip bones and belly to her waist.

His hand was growing less steady. He swallowed once and took a deep breath. "Your body is lovely," he whispered as his eyes crept higher. He touched her ribs, then slowly, slowly outlined her breasts.

She'd been lying on her left side. Gently rolling her to her back, he brought a single forefinger to touch the small mark that lay just above her pounding heart.

"A rose," he breathed. It was less than half the size of his smallest fingernail, delicately etched in black and red. His gaze was riveted to it. "When did you get it?"

"A lifetime ago," she whispered brokenly.

"Why?"

"It...I...on a whim. A stupid whim."

"You don't like it?"

She shook her head, close to tears. "But I can't make it go away."

Lowering his head, he kissed it lightly, then dabbed it with the tip of his tongue. "It's you," he whispered.

"No!"

"Yes. Something hidden. A secret side."

She was clenching her fists. "Please cover it up," she begged.

He did, but with his mouth rather than with the sheet, and at the same time he covered the rest of her body with his. "You are beautiful, tattoo and all. You make me burn." Holding the brunt of his weight on his forearms, he moved sensuously over her.

Shaye, too, burned. She'd lost track of the number of times they'd made love during the night, but still she wanted him. There was something about the way she felt when he made love to her—a sense of richness and completion. When he possessed her, she felt whole. When she was with him, she felt alive.

It didn't make sense that she should feel that way, when what she'd found with Noah was a moment out of time, when he was everything she'd sworn she didn't want, when he was everything she feared. But it wasn't the time to try to make sense of things. Not with his lips closing over hers and his hand caressing her breast. Not with their legs tangling and their stomachs rubbing. Not with his sex growing larger by the minute against her thigh.

Raising her knees to better cradle him, she responded ardently to his kisses. She loved the firmness of his lips and their mobility, just as she loved the feel of his skin beneath her fingers. His back was a broad mass of ropy muscles, his hips more narrow and smooth. The heat his body exuded generated an answering heat. His natural male scent was enhanced by that of passion.

Slowly and carefully, he entered her. When their bodies were fully joined, his back arched, his weight on his palms, he looked down at her and searched her eyes. "I want to see this, too," he said hoarsely. His breathing was unsteady. The muscles of his arms trembled. He was working so hard to rein in the same desires that buzzed through her, and he was doing so much better a job of it than she, that she broke into a sheepish smile.

Carefully he brought her up onto his lap, then, hugging her to him, inched his way backward until he'd reached the edge of the bed. When he slid off to kneel on the floor, she tightened the twist of her ankles at the small of his back. Not once was the penetration broken.

Shaye couldn't believe what happened then. Where another man would have simply begun to move while he watched, Noah cupped her face and kissed her deeply. He worshipped her mouth, her cheeks, her chin. He plumped up her breasts with his hands and devoured them as adoringly. And only when she was thinking she'd die from the searing bliss did he lower his gaze. Hers followed.

He withdrew and slowly reentered. A long, low moan slipped from his throat. His head fell back, eyes momentarily closed against the enormity of sensation.

Needing grounding of her own, Shaye looped her arms around his neck and dropped her forehead to his shoulder. She was panting softly. Her insides were on fire. She was stunned by the depth of emotion she felt, the profoundness of what they were doing, the overwhelming sense of rightness.

His cheek came down next to hers. He pulled back his hips, slowly pushed forward, pulled back, pushed forward. Every movement was controlled and deeply, deeply arousing.

When Shaye began to fear that she'd reach her limit before him, she unlocked her ankles and moved her thighs against his hips. Unable to resist, Noah ran his palms the length of her legs. The feel of the smooth, firm silk was too much. He made a low, throaty sound and within seconds surged into a throbbing climax. Only then did she allow herself the same release.

He whispered her name over and over until their bodies had begun to quieten. Then he framed her face with his hands and tipped it up. "I love you, Shaye." He sealed the vow with a long, sweet kiss, and when he held her back again, there were tears in her eyes. "There are more secrets. I know that. But I do love you. Secrets and all. I don't care where you've been or what you've done. I love you."

She didn't return the words, but held him in tight, trembling arms. *Do I love him? Can I love him? Will I be ask-*

ing for trouble if I love him? I can't control him. I can't control myself when I'm with him. If love is forever, can it possibly work?

THE ACTIVITY THAT FOLLOWED offered Shaye a welcome escape from her thoughts. She and Noah dressed, ate a fast breakfast, then joined Victoria and Samson on deck. Though the rain had stopped, the sky remained heavily overcast. Ever the optimist, Samson said it was for the best, that without the sun, they'd be cooler.

Shaye wondered about that. It was hot and sticky anyway. One glance at Noah told her he felt the same, and she noted that Samson had even passed up his pirate outfit in favor of more practical shorts and T-shirt. He wore his tricorne, though. She couldn't begrudge him that.

Since there had, as yet, been no stars by which to measure their position, Samson was left with making a sight judgment. Having carefully studied the small bay from the deck of the sloop, he'd already decided that it compared favorably with the one on his map. When he questioned Noah and Shaye about what they'd seen when they'd been ashore the night before, they looked at each other sheepishly. He didn't pursue the issue.

Loading the dingy with shovels and a pick, they left the *Golden Echo* securely anchored and rowed to shore. As soon as they'd safely beached the raft, Samson pulled out his map.

"Okay, let's look for the rose."

Shaye winced. Noah sent her a wink that made her feel a little better. Then he, too, turned his attention to the map. "According to this, the rock should be near the center of the back of the lagoon and not too far from shore."

Samson nodded distractedly. His gaze alternated between the map and the beach before them. "That's what the map suggests, though I dare say it wasn't drawn to scale." He refolded and pocketed the fragile paper. "Let's take a look."

The spot where they were headed was a short distance along the beach. After allowing Samson and Victoria a comfortable lead, Noah took Shaye's hand and they set off.

"Excited?" he asked.

"Certainly."

He cast her a sidelong glance. "Is that a little dryness I detect in your tone?"

"Me? Dryness?"

"Mmm. Do you believe we'll find a treasure?"

"Of course we'll find a treasure," she said. Her eyes were on Samson's figure striding confidently ahead.

"Forget about my uncle. What do *you* think?"

"Honestly?" She paused. "I doubt it."

"Are you in a betting mood?"

"You think there is a treasure?"

"Honestly? I doubt it."

"Then why bet?"

"'Cause it's fun. You say no. I say yes. Whoever wins... whoever wins..."

She was smiling. "Go on. I want to know. What will you bet?"

"How about a pair of Mets tickets?"

"Boo-hiss."

"How about a weekend in the country?"

"Not bad." She pursed her lips. "What country?"

He chuckled. She'd deftly ruled out his place in Vermont. "Say Canada—the Gaspé Peninsula?"

"Getting warm."

"England—Cornwall?"

"Getting warmer."

"France?"

"A small château in Normandy?" At his nod, she grinned. "You're on."

He studied her upturned face. "You look happy. Feeling that confident you'll win?"

"No. But win or lose I get to visit Normandy."

He threw back his head with an exaggerated, "Ahh," and made no mention of the fact that according to the terms of the bet, win or lose, she'd be visiting Normandy with *him*. For a weekend? No way. It'd be a full week or two if he had his say.

Draping an arm around her shoulder, he held her to his side. Their hips bumped as they walked. She suspected he was purposely doing it and, in the spirit of fun, she bumped him right back. They were nearly into an all-out-kick-and-dodge match when Samson's applause cut into their play.

"Bravo! Nice footwork there, Shaye. Noah, your legs are too long. Better quit while you're ahead." Turning his back on them, he propped his hands on his hips and studied the shoreline. "This is our starting point."

"Quit while I'm ahead," Noah muttered under his breath as he looked around. There wasn't a rock in sight. He lowered his head toward Shaye's. "Seaweed, driftwood, sand and palm trees. That's it."

"Ahh, but beyond the palm trees—"

"More palm trees."

"And a wealth of other trees and shrubs—"

"And monkeys and parrots and alligators—"

"Alligators! Are you kidding?"

"Would I kid you about something like that?"

"Victoria," Shaye cried plaintively, "you didn't tell me there'd be alligators!"

"No problem, sweetheart," Victoria said breezily. "Just watch where you step."

Samson started toward the palms and gestured for them to follow. Within ten minutes it was clear that they were going to have to broaden the search. They'd seen quite a few rocks among the foliage, but nothing of significant size and nothing remotely resembling a rose.

"Let's fan out. Shaye, you and Noah head south. Victoria and I will head north. Don't go farther inland then we are now, and head back out to the beach in, say—" he checked his watch "—half an hour. Okay?"

"Okay," Shaye and Noah answered together. They stood watching as Samson and Victoria started off.

Noah raked damp spikes of hair from his forehead. "Man, it's warm in here."

"Do you want to take off your shirt?"

"And get bitten alive?" He swatted something by his ear. "Was there any insect repellent in the dingy?"

"I think Samson had some in his pocket."

"Lots of good it'll do us there," he grumbled, then did an about-face to study the area Samson had assigned them. "Wish we had a machete."

"It's not that dense." She took a quick breath. "Noah, wouldn't alligators prefer a wetter area?"

"There are marshes just a little bit inland." He was studying the jungle growth. "I think if we work back and forth diagonally we'll be able to cover the most space in the least time."

"Is it alligators that bite, or crocodiles?"

"Crocs, I think." He rubbed his hands together, clearly working up enthusiasm. "Okay. L-l-l-l-l-let's hit it!"

Shaye stayed slightly behind Noah on the assumption that he'd scare away anything crawling in their path. She kept a lookout on either side, more than once catching herself when her eyes skimmed right past a rock formation simply because it didn't have a scaly back, a long tail, four squat legs and an ominous snout.

They followed a zigzag pattern, working slowly from jungle to shore and back. Soon after the third shore turn, they stopped short.

"It is a large rock," Shaye said cautiously.

"Would you go so far as to call it a boulder?"

"Depends how you define boulder. But it does have odd markings. Do you think it resembles a rose?"

Noah tipped his head and, squinted. "With a stretch of the imagination."

"Mmm. Let's look around a little more."

They completed that zig and the next zag and found a number of rocks that could, by that same stretch of the imagination, be said to resemble a rose. None were as large, though, and none stood alone as the first had.

"That has to be it," Noah decided.

Against her better judgment, Shaye felt a glimmer of excitement. "Let's tell the others." They started back. When they cleared the palms, they saw Samson and Victoria heading their way.

"We found it!" Shaye cried.

Victoria stopped short. "*We* found it!"

"Oh boy," Noah murmured.

Samson beamed. It looked as though they had a double puzzle on their hands, which was going to make the adventure that much more exciting.

CHAPTER TEN

THE FOUR TREKKED from one rock to the other. "Either could be it," Victoria decided.

"Or neither," said Shaye.

Noah mopped his face on the sleeve of his T-shirt. "If you ask me, there are half a dozen other rocks here that could fit the bill." He received three dirty looks so quickly that he held up a hand. "Okay. Okay. I'll admit that these two are more distinctive than the others." He frowned at the rock. "What do you think, Samson—could the markings be man-made?"

"They could be, but I don't think they are. Even allowing for lousy artistry and the effects of time, something man-made would be more exact. These are just irregular enough to look authentic."

"Which leaves the major problem of choosing between the two rocks," Shaye reminded them. "Does the map give any clue?"

Samson removed the map from his shirt pocket and extended it to her. She unfolded it and studied it. Victoria peered in from her right side, Noah hung over her left shoulder.

After a short time, Shaye and Victoria looked at each other in dismay. "You were right before," Victoria told Noah. "According to the map, the rose is smack in the middle of the back stretch of beach. But there wasn't any rose-shaped rock there. It has to be one of these two."

"But which one?" Shaye asked.

"Which looks more like a rose?"

"I don't know, so we're back to square one."

Victoria held up a finger. "I want to look at the other rock." Grabbing Shaye's arm, she propelled her through the jungle to the second rock.

Samson and Noah didn't move. They waited until the women returned, then Noah asked, "Okay, ladies, which rock will it be?"

"This one—"

"That one—"

He dug into his shorts pocket. "I'll flip a coin."

"You can't flip a coin on something as crucial," Victoria cried.

Shaye agreed.

"I don't have a coin anyway," Noah said and turned to Samson. "Got a coin?"

Samson produced a jackknife. "We'll let it fall. The slant of the handle will determine which rock we go with."

"A jackknife—"

"Is worse than a coin!"

The women were overruled. Samson flipped the knife. They went with the southern rock, the one Shaye and Noah had found and, coincidentally, the one Shaye thought looked more like a rose.

Putting defeat behind her, Victoria read off instructions from the map. "Seventeen paces due west."

"How long is a 'pace'?" Shaye asked.

"An average stride. Noah, you walk it off."

"Noah's stride can't be average. Samson, you walk it off."

"Samson is nearly as tall as Noah," Victoria pointed out. "Shaye you do it. Just stretch your stride a little."

With the others supervising, Shaye accepted and consulted the compass, marked off fifteen paces due west, then stopped.

"You need two more," Noah said.

"Two more paces will take me into the middle of that bromeliad colony. What do the instructions say from there, Victoria?"

"Twenty paces due south."

"Twenty paces due south," Shaye murmured, making estimates as she positioned herself on the south side of the bromeliads. "Say we're two paces south now. Three... four...five..."

Her progress was broken from time to time by another bit of the forest that was impenetrable, but she finally managed to reach twenty. Victoria, Samson and Noah were by her side.

"What now?" she asked.

"Southeast twenty-one paces," Victoria read.

"This is really pretty inexact—"

"Twenty-one paces," Noah coaxed. "Walk 'em off."

Compass in hand, she started walking. Victoria counted, while Samson followed the progress with an indulgent smile on his face. In the same manner they worked their way through additional twists and turns.

"What next?" Shaye finally asked.

"Nothing," Victoria said. "That's it. A big X on the map. You're standing on the treasure."

Shaye looked at the hard-packed sand beneath her feet. "It could be here, or here." She pointed three feet to the right. "Or even over there. Now, if we had some kind of metal detector, we might be in business."

"No metal detector," Samson said. "That would be cheating."

"But treasure hunters always use metal detectors," Shaye argued.

"We don't have one," Noah said in a tone that settled the matter. If there was no metal detector, there was no metal detector.

Shaye pointed straight down and raised skeptical eyes to Noah, who gave a firm nod.

A quick trip to the dingy produced the digging equipment and a knapsack that Victoria had filled with sandwiches and cans of soda earlier that morning. The soda had gone a little warm, but none of them complained. It was thirst quenching. The sandwiches were energizing. The insect repellent was better late than never.

They started digging in pairs, trading off every few minutes. There were diversions—a trio of spider monkeys swinging through the nearby trees, the chatter of a distant parrot—and the occasional reward of a quick swim in the bay. But by three in the afternoon, they had a large, deep hole and no treasure.

They'd initially dug down three feet, then another, then had widened the hole until it was nearly five feet in diameter. Now Noah stood at its center with his arms propped on the shovel handle. He looked hot and tired.

Shaye, who'd stopped digging several minutes before, sat on the edge of the hole. Victoria was beside her, and Samson stood behind them with a pensive look on his face.

"How much deeper do we go before we give up?" Shaye asked softly. She felt every bit as hot and tired as Noah looked.

"It has to be here," Victoria said. "Maybe we marked it out wrong."

"It *doesn't* have to be here," Shaye reminded her. "We knew there was the possibility the map was a sham."

Noah leaned against their side of the pit. He pushed his hair back with his forearm, smudging grime with the sweat. "I've dug the pick in another foot and hit nothing.

I doubt a pirate would have buried anything deeper than this."

"If only we knew what we were looking for," Victoria mused. "Large box, small box, tiny leather pouch..."

Shaye sighed. "It's like trying to find a needle in a haystack, and you don't even know which haystack to look in."

"The other rock," said Noah. "It has to be that. We picked the wrong one to start pacing from." He hoisted himself from the hole. "Y'know, whoever drew up this map was either a jokester, a romantic or an imbecile."

Shaye was right beside him, followed by Victoria and Samson, as he strode quickly toward the other rock. "What do you mean?"

"The directions. They were given in paces west, south, southeast, etc., when we would have reached the same spot by one set of paces heading due south. When I first saw the map, I assumed there were natural barriers to go around, but we didn't find any." He'd reached the second rock and was studying the map. Then he closed his eyes and made some mathematical calculations.

"How many paces due south?" Samson asked.

"Let's try sixty-five."

He stood back while Shaye marked sixty-five paces due south. When she finished counting, she was standing directly before the first rock. She looked up at the others.

Victoria was the only one who seemed to share her surprise. "Let's walk it off the original way," she suggested.

So Shaye went back, walked through the directions again, and wound up in the same spot, directly before the second rock. "He was a jokester," she decided in dismay.

Samson scratched the back of his head. "He has made things interesting."

"Interesting?" Victoria echoed, then grinned. "Mmm, I

suppose he's done that." She shifted her gaze from Samson to Noah, who was striding off. "Where are you going?"

"To get the shovels."

"We're not going to do this now, are we?"

"Why not?"

Shaye ran after him, looping her elbow through his when she caught up. "Isn't it a little late in the day to start something new?"

"It's only four."

"But we've been digging all day."

"All afternoon," he corrected.

"The treasure's not going anywhere."

His eyes twinkled. "I'm curious to see if it's there."

"But wouldn't it be smarter to start again fresh tomorrow morning?"

Having arrived back at the first hole, he scooped up the pick and shovels. Then he leaned in close to Shaye and whispered, "But if we finish this up tonight, we can do whatever we want tomorrow."

She took in a shaky breath and whispered back, "But aren't you tired?"

"Are you?"

"Yes. And it looks like it might rain any minute."

"Then we'll have to work quickly," he said with a mischievous grin and started back toward the rock.

As it happened, Noah did most of the work. Shaye made a show of assisting, silently reasoning that she was young and strong. But the digging she'd done earlier had taken its toll. She was tired. She had blisters. To make matters worse, the hole was only three feet deep and wide when it started to drizzle.

"Leave it," Shaye urged.

Samson agreed. "She's right, Noah. We can finish in the morning."

"No way," he grunted, setting to work with greater determination. "Another eighteen inches either way." He hoisted a shovelful of wet sand and tossed it aside with another grunt. "That's all we need."

"We can do it tomorrow—"

"And have the rain wash the sand—" another toss, another grunt "—back into this hole during the night? Just a little more now—give me forty-five minutes." Another shovelful hit the pile. "If I haven't struck anything by then, I'll quit."

The rain grew heavier. When Shaye eased into the hole and started to shovel again, Noah set her bodily back up on the edge. Likewise, when Samson tried to give a hand, Noah insisted that he could work more freely on his own.

They were all soaked, but no one complained. The rain offered relief from the heat. Unfortunately, though, it made Noah's work harder. Each shovelful of sand was wetter and heavier than the one before, and, if anything, he seemed bent on making this hole bigger than the last. He was obviously tiring. And neither the shovel nor the pick, which he periodically used, were turning up anything remotely resembling hidden treasure.

Then it happened. Shaye was watching Noah work under the edge of the large rock, wondering what would happen if the rain lessened the stability of the sand, when suddenly that side of the hole began to crumble.

"Noah!" she cried, but the rock was already sliding. Through eyes wide with horror, she saw Noah twist to the side and try to scramble away without success. He gave a deep cry of pain as the lower half of his right leg was pinned beneath the rock. In a second, Shaye had shimmied down into the narrow space left and was pushing against the rock, as were Samson and Victoria from above.

It wouldn't budge.

"Oh God," Shaye whispered. She took a quick look at Noah's ashen face and pushed harder, but the rock had sunk snugly in the hole with precious little space for maneuvering.

Samson, too, was pale, but he kept calm. "Let me take your place, Shaye. You and Victoria scoot up against the side, put your feet flat against the rock and push as hard as you can when I say so."

They hurried into position. He gave the word. They pushed. Nothing happened.

"Again," he ordered. "Now!"

Nothing happened that time or, when they'd slightly altered position, the next. Even Noah tried then, though he wasn't at the best angle—or in the best condition—to help. Despite the varied attempts they made, the rock didn't move.

Samson shook his head. "We can't get leverage. If we could only raise it the tiniest bit, even for a few seconds, you could pull free. A broom handle would snap. We could try a palm—"

Noah gave a rough shake of his head and muttered, "Too thick."

"Not at the top, but it's too weak there. We need metal."

"We don't have metal," Noah said tightly. The lower part of his leg was numb, but pain was shooting through his thigh. In an attempt to ease the pressure, he turned and sank sideways on the sand.

Shaye's heart was pounding. She couldn't take her eyes off him. "There has to be something on the *Golden Echo* we can use," she said frantically, then tacked on an even more frantic, "isn't there?"

Noah groped for her hand, but it was Samson to whom he spoke. "There's nothing on the boat. You'll have to go for help."

Samson had reached the same conclusion and was already on his feet and motioning for Victoria. "We'll make a quick trip to the boat for supplies. You'll stay here, Shaye?"

"Yes!"

With a nod, he was gone.

Shaye turned back to Noah. He was resting his head against the side of the hole. She combed the wet hair from his forehead. "How do you feel?"

He was breathing heavily. "Not great."

"Think it's broken?"

"Yup."

"I should have seen it coming. I should have been able to warn you."

"My fault. I was careless. Too tired." The word broke into a gasp. "I usually do better—"

She put a finger to his lips. "Shh. Save your strength."

He grabbed her hand. "Stay close."

She slid into the narrow space facing him and tucked his hand beneath her chin. For a long time neither of them spoke. The rain continued to fall. Noah closed his eyes against the pain that he could feel more clearly now below his knee.

Shaye alternately watched him and the shore. "Where are they?" she demanded finally in a tight, panicky whisper.

Noah didn't answer. It was fast getting dark. The rain continued to fall.

Samson and Victoria returned at last with a replenished knapsack, rain ponchos and two lanterns. Then Samson knelt with a hand on Noah's shoulder. "We'll be back as soon as we can. There are painkillers in the sack. Don't be a hero, and whatever you do, don't try to tug that leg free now or you'll make the damage worse."

Noah, who'd already figured that out, simply nodded.

"Hurry," Shaye whispered, hugging both Victoria and Samson before they left. "Hurry." Moments later, she watched them push off in the dingy, then she sank down beside Noah and put her hand to his cheek. "Can I get you anything?"

He shook his head.

"Food?"

Again he shook his head.

"Drink?"

"Later."

She didn't bother to ask if he wanted the poncho. She knew that he wouldn't. In spite of the rain, the night was warm. It did occur to her, though, that they'd feel more comfortable if they were leaning against rubber rather than grit. Popping up, she spread the ponchos over the side of the hole. Noah shifted and helped, then sank back against them with his head tipped up to the rain. Very gently, she washed the lingering grime from his face with her fingers, then slid back to his side and watched him silently.

His facial muscles twitched, then rested. His brow furrowed, then relaxed. Then he swore under his breath.

"The leg?"

"God, it hurts."

"Damn the rose. I had a feeling. I knew it would be bad luck."

"No. My own stupid fault. I was so determined to dig, so determined to find that treasure."

"It was the bet—"

"Uh-uh. I just wanted to get it done. But I should have anticipated the problem. Take the ground out from under a rock and it's gonna fall."

"You didn't take much out. I had to have been the rain."

"I should have seen it coming."

"*I* should have. I was the one sitting there watching. If I'd been able to give you a few more seconds' warning…"

Noah curved his hand around the back of her neck and brought her face to his throat. "Not your fault." He kissed her temple and left his mouth there. "I'm glad you're with me."

She lifted her face and kissed him. "I just wish there were something I could do to make you more comfortable."

"How about…that drink…"

She quickly dug into the knapsack, extracted first a can of Coke, then, more satisfactorily, a bottle of wine. Tugging out the cork, she handed it to him. "Want a sandwich with it?"

He tipped the bottle and took several healthy swallows. "And dilute the effects? No way?"

"You want to get smashing drunk?"

He took another drink. "Not smashing. Just mildly." He closed his eyes again, and the expression of pain that crossed his face tore right through Shaye.

"Is it getting worse?" she whispered fearfully.

He said nothing for a minute, but seemed to be gritting his teeth. Then he took a shaky breath and opened his eyes. "Talk to me."

"About what?"

"You."

"Me? There's nothing much to say—"

"I want to hear about the past. I want to hear about all the things you've sidestepped before."

"I haven't—"

"You have."

She searched his eyes, seeing things that went beyond the physical pain he was experiencing. "Why does it matter?"

"Because I love you."

She put her fingertips to his mouth, caressing his lips moments before she leaned forward and kissed them. "I didn't expect you in my life, Noah," she breathed brokenly, then kissed him again.

"Tell me what you feel."

"Frightened. Confused." She sought out his lips again, craving their drugging effect.

He gave himself up to her kiss, but as soon as it ended, the pain was back. "Talk to me."

She carried his hand to her mouth and kissed his knuckles.

"My leg hurts like hell, Shaye. If you want to help, you can give me something to think about beside the fact that it's probably broken in at least three places."

"Don't say that—"

"Not to mention scraped raw."

"Noah—"

"I may well be lame for life."

"Don't even think that!"

"Tell me you wouldn't care."

"If you were lame? Of course, I'd care! The thought of your being in pain—"

"Tell me that you wouldn't care if I were lame, that you'd love me anyway."

"I'd love you if *both* legs were lame! What a stupid thing to ask."

"Not stupid," he said quietly, soberly, almost grimly. "Not stupid at all. Do you love me, Shaye?"

Shocked, she looked at him.

"Do you?" he prodded.

She bit her lip. "Yes."

"You haven't thought about it before now?"

"I've tried not to."

"But you do love me?"

She frowned. "If loving a person means that you like him even when you hate him, that you think about him all the time, that you hurt when he's hurt—" she took a tremulous breath "—the answer is yes."

"Ahh, baby," he said with a groan that held equal parts relief and pain. He drew her in close and held her as tightly as his awkward sideways position would allow.

"I love you," she whispered against his chest, "do love you."

His arms tightened. He winced, then groaned, then mumbled, "Talk to me. Talk to me, Shaye. Please?"

There seemed no point in holding back. With the confession he'd drawn from her, Noah had broken down the last of her defenses. He knew her. He knew what made her tick. He knew what pleased her, hurt her, drove her wild. Revealing the details of her past to him was little more than a formality.

Closing her eyes, Shaye began to talk. She told him about her childhood and the teenage years when she'd grown progressively wild. She told him about going off to college, about being free and irresponsible and believing that she had the world on a string. She told him about the boys and the men, the trips, the adventures, the apartments and the garret. Once started, she spilled it all. She wanted Noah to know everything.

For the most part, he listened quietly. Once or twice he made ceremony of wiping the rain from his face, but she suspected he was covering up a wince. At those times she stopped, offered him aspirin, and finally plied him with more wine, which was all the painkilling he'd accept. And she went on talking.

Only when she was near the end did she falter. She grew still, eyes downcast, hands tightly clenched.

"What happened then?" he prodded in a voice weakened by pain. "You were with André when you got a call from Shannon, and…?"

She raked her teeth over her lower lip.

"Shaye?"

She took a broken breath. "She was in trouble. She'd been hanging around a pal of André's named Geoff, and when he introduced her to another guy, a friend of his, she didn't think anything of it. The friend turned out to be from the vice squad. Poor Shannon. She was nineteen at the time, not nearly sophisticated enough to protect herself from the Geoffs of the world. He was picked up on a dozen charges. She was arrested for possession of cocaine. She never knew what hit her."

"And you blamed yourself."

"I was at fault. I'd introduced her to André, André had introduced her to Geoff. I should have checked Geoff out myself." She waved a hand impatiently. "But it was more than that. The whole *scene* was wrong. Rebellion for the sake of rebellion, adventure of the sake of adventure, sex for the sake of sex—very little that went deeper, and nothing at all that resulted in personal growth. For six years I did that." She was shaking all over. "Blame myself? Not only was I responsible for what happened to Shannon, by rights, I should have been the one arrested!"

"Shh," Noah whispered against her temple. "It's okay."

"It's not!"

"What finally happened to Shannon?"

Shaye took several quick breaths to calm herself. "Victoria came to the rescue. She introduced us to a lawyer friend who introduced us to another lawyer friend, and between the two of them, Shannon got off with a suspended sentence and probation. She went on for a degree in communications and has a terrific job now in Hartford."

He shifted, and swallowed down a moan. The pain in

his leg was excruciating. He had to keep his mind off it. "Sounds like she got off lighter than you did," he said tightly.

"Lighter?"

"You sentenced yourself to a lifetime of hard labor."

"No. I just decided to become very sane and sensible."

"Where do I fit into sane and sensible?"

She smoothed wet hair back from her forehead with the flat of her hand. "I don't know."

"Do you see me as being sane and sensible?"

"In some respects, yes. In others, no."

"And the 'no's' frighten you."

She nodded.

"Why?"

"Because I can't control them. Because you can be spontaneous and impulsive and irreverent, and that's everything I once was that nearly ended tragically!"

"But you like it when I'm that way. That's part of the attraction."

"I know," she wailed.

"And it's not bad. Look at it rationally, Shaye. You're nearly thirty now. Your entire outlook on life has matured since the days when you were wild." He caught in a breath, squeezed his eyes shut, finally went on in a raspy voice. "But you haven't found a man to love because the men you allow yourself to see don't excite you. You'd never have allowed yourself to see me if we'd met back in civilization, would you?"

"No."

"But there's nothing wrong with what we share! Okay, so we go nuts together in bed. Is that harmful? If it's just the two of us, and we're consenting adults, and we get up in the morning perfectly sane and sensible. Where's the harm?" His voice had risen steadily in pitch, and he was breathing raggedly by the time he finished.

"Oh God, Noah," she whispered. "What can I do—"

"Talk. Just talk."

She did, trying her best to tune out his pain. "I hear what you're saying. It makes perfect sense. But then I get to worrying and even the sensible seems precarious."

"You trust me?"

"I...yes."

"And love me?"

She nodded.

"Nothing is precarious. I'll protect you."

"But I have to be responsible, myself. That was one of the first things I learned from Shannon's fiasco."

"Ahh, Shaye, Shaye..." He tightened his arm around her shoulder and pressed his cheek to her wet hair. "You've gone to extremes. You don't have to be on guard every minute. There are times to let go and times not to." He stopped, garnering his strength. "Where's the lightness in your life, the sunshine, the frivolity? We all need that sometimes. Not all the time, just sometimes. There has to be a balance—don't you see?" His words had grown more and more strained. He loosened his hold on her and took a long drink of wine.

Shaye looked up, eyes wide. She stroked the side of his face with the backs of her fingers. "Don't talk so much, Noah. Please. It must be taking something out of you."

"It's the only thing that's helping. No, that's not true. The wine helps. And you. Your being here. Marry me, Shaye. I want you to marry me."

"I—"

"It looks like the trip is going to be cut short. We have to face the future."

"But—"

"I love you, Shaye. I didn't plan to fall in love. I've never really been in love before in my life. But I do love you."

"But these are such…bizarre circumstances. How can you possibly know what your feelings will be back in the real world?"

"I know my feelings," he said with a burst of strength. "I know what's been wrong with my life, what's been missing in the women I've known. You have everything I want. You're dignified and poised and intelligent. You're witty and gentle. You're compassionate and loyal. You're gorgeous. And you're spectacular in my arms. I meant it when I said I wanted you to mother my children. I do want that, Shaye. But I want you first and foremost for *me*." He punctuated the last with a loud, involuntary groan, followed by a pithy oath.

Shaye was on her knees in a minute, cradling his dripping face with both hands. "Let me get the codeine."

He shook his head. "Wine." He lifted the bottle and swallowed as much as he could.

"Where are they?" she cried, looking out to sea.

"They've just left. Won't be back until morning."

"Morning! Why morning?"

"It's a lee coast. We lucked out yesterday. It'll take them a while to reach Limón—"

"Isn't Moín closer?"

"No resources. Samson may try it, but by the time he locates a rescue team—"

"He has to do something before morning. You're in pain."

"Make that agony."

"This is no time for joking, Noah."

"I'm not."

"Oh. Oh God, isn't there anything I can do?"

"Say you'll marry me."

"I'll marry you."

"Ahh. Feels better already." He pried his head from the poncho. "Is there another bottle of wine?"

She reached for the bottle he held and saw that it was nearly empty. With relief, she found two more bottles in the knapsack. Opening one, she gave it to Noah in exchange for the first, the contents of which she proceeded to indulge in herself.

Had she just agreed to marry Noah?

She took another drink.

He drew her against his chest and encircled her with his arms, leaving the wine bottle to dangle against her side. "I need to hold on," he said, his voice husky with pain.

"Hold on," she whispered. "Hold on."

They sat like that for a while. Shaye heard the rain and the lap of the sea on the shore, but mostly she heard Noah's heart, beating erratically beneath her ear.

"I'm well-respected in the community," he muttered out of the blue. "I give to charity. I pay my taxes. Okay, so I do the unexpected from time to time, but I've never done anything illegal or immoral."

Gently, soothingly, she stroked his ribs, working at the tension in the surrounding muscles.

"I'll buy us a place midway between Manhattan and Philly, so you won't have to leave your job."

She kissed his collarbone.

"In fact," he rushed on, "you don't have to work at all if you don't want to. I'm loaded."

She laughed.

"I am," he protested.

"I believe you," she said, still smiling, thinking how incredibly much she did love him.

He took a shuddering breath, then another drink of

wine. "I want the whole thing—the house, the kids, the dog, the station wagon."

"You do?"

"Don't you?"

"Yes, but I didn't think you would."

"Too conventional?"

"No, no. Very stable."

He closed a fist around her ponytail, pressed her head to his throat and moaned, "This isn't how it was supposed to be. There's nothing romantic in this. It's *sick*. My damn leg's caught under a rock. I can't move. I can't sweep you off your feet and carry you to bed, or bend you back over my arm and kiss you senseless. I'm not sure I can even get it up—that's how much everything down there hurts!"

Shaye knew he was in severe pain. She knew he was feeling frustrated. She couldn't do anything about either, so she decided to use humor. "The Playboy of the Pampas—impotent?"

"Not impotent—temporarily sidelined. You'll still marry me, won't you?"

"I'll still marry you." She took a deep breath and looked around. "It is a waste, though. We did so well in the rain last night, just think of what we could have done tonight." She moved her lips against his jaw, her voice an intimate whisper. "I'd like to make love in the water. Not deep water—shallow, just a few feet out from shore. Do you remember how it was when we were swimming? Only this time neither of us would have suits on, and there'd be a sandy floor for maneuvering, but the tide would wash around us. I'd wrap my legs around you—"

Noah interrupted her with a feral growl. "Enough. You've made your point."

"I have?"

He tried to shift to a more comfortable position, which was nearly impossible, given the circumstances.

Shaye felt instantly contrite. "Can I help?" she whispered, dropping her hand to his swollen sex.

He covered it and pressed it close for a minute, then raised it to his chest. "I think I'll take a rain check."

He took another drink, then held the bottle to her lips while she did the same. The sounds of the rain and the sea and the jungle night surrounded them, and for a time they sat in silence. Then Shaye asked, "The lanterns will keep the alligators away, won't they?"

He nodded.

"Hungry?"

He shook his head.

"Is there any chance of this hole flooding?"

He shook his head again.

"Do you have Blue Cross-Blue Shield?"

"Through the nose." A little while later, he said, "Maybe you're pregnant."

"No."

"Are you taking the pill?"

"No. But my period just ended. Last night was about as safe a time as any could be."

He considered that, then said, "No wonder you felt so lousy at the start of the trip."

She snorted. "You should have seen me when we first got to the hotel in Barranquilla."

"Don't use anything."

"What?"

"When we make love. I like knowing that there's a chance..."

"You really do want children."

"Very much. If you want to wait, though. I'll understand."

But the more she thought about it, the more Shaye liked the idea of growing big with Noah's child. She smiled into the night.

"You are going to marry me, aren't you?" he asked.

"I've said I would."

"What if you change your mind?"

"I won't."

"What if you have second thoughts when we get back home?"

"I won't."

"Why not?"

"I can't answer that now. Ask me again later."

He did, several times during the course of the night, but it wasn't until a pair of helicopters closed noisily in on the beach the following morning that Shaye had an answer for him.

She'd been with Noah throughout the night, had suffered with him and worried for him, had done what little she could to make him comfortable. She'd forced him to eat half a sandwich for the sake of his strength and had limited her own intake of wine to leave more for him. She'd sponged him off when the rain stopped and the air grew thick and heavy. She'd batted mosquitoes from his skin and had held his hand tightly when he'd twisted in pain.

The night had been hell. She never wanted to live through another like it. But she knew she wouldn't have been anywhere else in the world that night, and that was what she told Noah when the sheer relief of his impending rescue loosened her thoughts.

"You have the ability to make me happy, sad, excited, frustrated, angry, aroused and confused—but through it all I feel incredibly alive."

She combed her fingers through his hair. "You have the spirit and the sense of adventure I had before, only you've channeled it right." Affectionately she brushed some sand off his neck. "I want you to help me do that. Make my life full. Be my friend and protector." She kissed his forehead. "And lover. I want all that and more." She shot a glance at the crew bounding from the chopper, then tacked on, "Think you can handle it?"

He was a mess—dirty, sweaty, with one leg crushed beneath a boulder— but the look he sent her was eloquent in promise and love. She knew that she'd never, never forget it.

EPILOGUE

"Two HELICOPTERS?" Deirdre asked.

Victoria nodded. "One for the medics, the other for the fellows who raised the rock."

Leah winced. "Noah must have been out of his mind with pain by that time."

"He was out of it with something—whether pain or wine, I'll never know. The doctors in Limón did a preliminary patch-up job while Samson arranged for our transportation home. Noah's had surgery twice in the six weeks we've been back. He's scheduled to go in for a final procedure next week."

"Is the prognosis good?"

"Excellent, thank God. But even if it weren't, Noah's a fighter." She sighed. "He's quite a man."

Deirdre curled her legs beneath her on the chaise. It was the last day in August, a rare cool, dry, sunny summer day in New York, and Victoria's rooftop garden was the place to be. "When did they get married?"

Victoria smiled. "Four days after we got back. It was beautiful. Very simple. A judge, their closest friends and relatives." Her eyes grew misty. "Shaye was radiant. I know they say that about all brides, but she was. She positively glowed. And when Noah...presented her with... that single rose..."

Leah handed her a tissue, which Victoria waved around, as though it didn't occur to her to wipe her tears.

"When he gave her the rose, he said…he said—" her voice dropped to a tremulous whisper "—so softly and gently that I wouldn't have heard if I hadn't been standing right there…"

Both women were waiting wide-eyed. Deirdre leaned forward and asked urgently, "What did he say?"

Victoria sniffled. "He said, 'One rose. Just one. Pure, fresh and new. And it's in our hands.'" She took in a shuddering breath. "It was so…beautiful…" She pressed the tissue to her trembling lip.

Leah didn't understand the deeper significance of Noah's words any more than Deirdre did, but the romance of it was still there. She sighed loudly, then burst into a helpless smile. "Victoria Lesser strikes again." She was delighted with Victoria's latest story. She'd had no idea what to expect when Victoria had invited her down for a visit, and now she couldn't wait to get back to tell Garrick. But there was still more she wanted to know. "What about you and Samson?"

Victoria took a minute to collect herself. "Yes?"

"I thought you liked him. You said that in spite of the accident the trip was wonderful."

"It was."

"Well?" Deirdre prompted. "Is that all you have to say—just that it was wonderful? Neil will spend the entire night cross-examining me if I don't have anything better to give him when I get home."

Gracefully pushing herself from her chair, Victoria breezed across the garden to pluck a dried petal from a hanging begonia. "It'd serve you right," she said airily, "after what the four of you did."

"It was poetic justice," Deirdre argued.

Leah agreed. "Just deserts."

"A taste of your own medicine."

"Lex talionis." When Victoria turned to arch a brow her way, Leah translated. "The law of retribution. But all with the best of intentions." She paused. "So. Were our good intentions in vain?"

Victoria hesitated for a long moment. Her gaze skipped from Leah's face to Deirdre's. Then she slanted them both a mischievous grin. "I won't remarry, you know."

"We know," Deirdre said.

"He was…very nice."

Leah held her breath. "And…?"

"And we've decided to make a return visit to Costa Rica next summer to find out for sure whether that treasure does exist. Noah and Shaye weren't thrilled with that thought; they're hung up on the idea of going to some château in Normandy. So we'll just have to put together another group. In the meantime, Samson thought he'd do a bicycle tour of the Rhineland and asked if I'd like to go along."

"Where does he get the time?" Deirdre asked. "I thought he taught."

"Vacations, sweetheart. Vacations." Her eyes twinkled and her cheeks grew pink. "And weekends. There are lovely things that can be done on weekends." Turning her back on the two younger women, she busied herself hand pruning a small dogwood. "I was thinking that I'd drive north next month. The foliage is beautiful when it turns. Samson has invited me to stay with him in Hanover, claims he makes a mean apple cider. Now, theoretically, making apple cider should be as boring as sin. But then, theoretically, Latin professors should be as boring as sin, too, and Samson isn't. I guess I'll have to give his apple cider a shot…."

* * * * *

Two timeless and endearing love stories from the
New York Times bestselling author

BARBARA DELINSKY

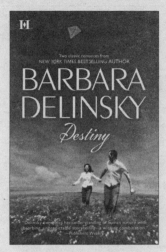

Destiny

Available in stores today!

"Delinsky combines her understanding of human nature
with absorbing, unpredictable storytelling—
a winning combination."
—*Publishers Weekly*

HARLEQUIN® HQN™
www.Harlequin.com

PHBD714

BARBARA DELINSKY

77726	ETERNITY	___ $7.99 U.S.	___ $9.99 CAN.
77714	DESTINY	___ $7.99 U.S.	___ $9.99 CAN.
77618	SANCTUARY	___ $7.99 U.S.	___ $9.99 CAN.
77494	FRIENDS & LOVERS	___ $7.99 U.S.	___ $9.99 CAN.
77425	DREAM MAN	___ $7.99 U.S.	___ $8.99 CAN.

(limited quantities available)

TOTAL AMOUNT	$_____
POSTAGE & HANDLING	$_____
($1.00 FOR 1 BOOK, 50¢ for each additional)	
APPLICABLE TAXES*	$_____
TOTAL PAYABLE	$_____

(check or money order—please do not send cash)

To order, complete this form and send it, along with a check or money order for the total above, payable to Harlequin HQN, to: **In the U.S.:** 3010 Walden Avenue, P.O. Box 9077, Buffalo, NY 14269-9077; **In Canada:** P.O. Box 636, Fort Erie, Ontario, L2A 5X3.

Name: _____
Address: _____ City: _____
State/Prov.: _____ Zip/Postal Code: _____
Account Number (if applicable): _____

075 CSAS

*New York residents remit applicable sales taxes.
*Canadian residents remit applicable GST and provincial taxes.

HARLEQUIN® HQN™
www.Harlequin.com

PHBD1113BL